Autumn's Return

LAUREN ECKHARDT

One

Unease claimed a home in my bones months ago—
irregular bodily twitching that seemed to be screaming premoni-
tions of *big life changes*. It didn't seem to be the move to Italy,
even though that was big—and problematic for reasons no one
else knew about. It didn't seem to be the fact that I was turning
thirty, even though that felt strangely monumental too. No, it was
only once I returned to the theoretical security of my hometown,
with my mom excitedly proclaiming that the entire world would
soon be celebrating me through a never-heard-of-before social
media experiment that I thought, *yep*, this is exactly what my
subconscious has been preparing for. It's like a part of me could
sense there was something brewing, long before I became aware
of it.

Reaching for my phone on the dresser, I check my messages.
Mark's text pops up first with a beautiful picture of Palermo, Italy
from his hotel room balcony.

Happy Birthday to the love of my life. Can't
wait until you're here with me. It'll be a great
birthday. Enjoy every second.

I shake my head. How is it that even after being married for four years, he doesn't understand how terrified an event like this makes me? My parents' strange way of publicly embarrassing me for my birthday since I was seven years old is one thing—I have come to expect it—but Mark has outdone anything they could ever do.

Several messages *ping* from family and friends, but I set the phone back down instead of reading them. Each one is converting into a siren screaming that a birthday party unlike any other is about to take place, and I am the guest of honor.

I unwrap myself from my messy entanglement with the sheets and stumble out of bed to sit in the bay of my bedroom window. Staring outside, I push the looming party out of my mind long enough to appreciate the beauty that surrounds my quaint cottage. Sparkles prance on the body of water, so vast that it looks like an ocean rather than a lake, as red pines wave from the shorelines, dancing in the perfect warmth of July's late morning sun.

This is why I so desperately needed to come back. My heart was molded here. In all my travels, I've found nothing that inspires my writing quite like this sight, framed by my arched window, providing a cosmic overlook of Lake Michigan, made ever magical by the continual changing colors of trees surrounding it as they sway through the seasons. Even the most brutally cold winters are turned lovely by this view, and since my heart has felt cold for much too long, this is the medicine I needed.

Honk, honk. Rose's horn wakes me from my daze. My partner in crime since I was six years old waves animatedly from her Civic, as she parks behind my Jeep Cherokee in the half-moon driveway. When she gets out, she holds up a finger to say, "Be right there," and pops open her trunk while a burgundy leather satchel dangles from her hand. She's filling the bag with things from her trunk that I can't see. I swear the trunk of that car is a real-life clown car, one that you can keep pulling out items and they never stop coming. Need a staple gun? Rose has it. Need a ladder? Rose has it. Need a six-inch sub? Rose has it. She's the most prepared and organized person I know, and that trunk containing the most random assortment of items I've ever seen is her lifeline.

"How cool is this?" Rose cries out the moment she bursts in the door. Her gymnast-toned legs have her standing in front of me in no time, as she drops her satchel and reaches for my hands. Her long brown hair is curled and swept to the side, while her eyelash extensions widen her doe-like brown eyes, complementing her flawless skin. With her low-cut, A-line dress accenting her recent spray tan, she looks ready for a big movie premiere. I let go of her hands and pat my hair down, tugging my wrinkly tank down further over my abdomen. I'm sure I look like roadkill from the restless sleep I had last night.

"You will die when you hear about the activities! Just think about it. Not only are you one of the first to try out a new social media platform that will change the world, but all these awesome people are coming from around the world, just to celebrate you!"

"Yeah, it's... great." Words are my forte, yet they have already escaped me, and the day has just begun.

"Great?! Oh, you just wait. We gotta get some coffee in you and wake you up! It's a big day!" Rose tugs on my hands until I'm standing up, and she embraces me in a big hug. "Happy birthday, Autumn! I love you." She kisses my cheek three times loudly. I'm pretty sure she's already ten cups of coffee in.

When we pull apart, I reach for her shoulder where I hold up a long red strand of hair. "See? I just turned thirty an hour ago, and I'm already losing my hair."

"Well, you may be losing hair on your head, but..." She leans in closely to my chin and touches it gently. "You may be growing some hair here to make up for it."

"What? No!" I cup my chin and run to the bathroom, slipping on the bedroom rug in my haste. I peer into the mirror, tilting my head every angle to locate the dreaded chin hair. Only three weeks ago, Rose sent me a link to a magazine article after she found a random, singular, black hair growing around her nipple. The article highlighted all the changes females may experience in various seasons of their life. Random hair growth was one they went into vast detail on, and every single interviewee said the first one appeared almost instantly when they turned thirty. *We're doomed*, her text had said. *But I'll take a breast hair over a chin hair.*

Rose's face appears in the mirror as she peers over my shoulder. Laughing, she says, "Made you look."

"Rose!" I turn around and playfully slap her arm. "That is not funny on this day, out of all days!"

"Hey, it got you to wake up! Besides, you have light-colored hair. They'd only see it if they zoomed in *really* close to you." She cups her hands as though she has a video camera and gets as close as she can to my chin.

I rub my face and groan, nudging her away. "How many cameras do you think will be on me?"

"From the way Mark talked about it, I would assume at least three for most of the night."

My mouth gapes. I want to say something about how ridiculous and pointless that is, but no words are coming out.

"Hey." She puts her hands on my shoulders, "Start with a shower and a clear head, okay? Baby steps. One foot in front of the other. I promise you, this will all be worth it. Besides, it's your birthday! And we're gonna make it a good one!"

Rose heads for the kitchen to make coffee as her voice drones on, but I only catch every few words. My brain is a scrambled mess. *Three* cameras on me at all times? What if they catch a reaction on my face that I don't want them to see? What if I look as uncomfortable as I feel the whole time? What if they can see the doubt in me?

I lean my head against the white wooden frame and sigh as I watch her, attempting to take breaths and lean into the peace that my house has always infused in me. This cottage was my first big purchase, my official paid entry into adulthood. Eight years saving, while serving meals and refilling drinks with blistered feet that didn't stop moving for sixty hours each week at three different diners in Door County, Wisconsin to keep the tourists well fed. All the fruit from my labor was poured into this cozy one-bedroom, one-bathroom cottage to fix it up and make it my own.

As much as I loved the crimson brick on the outside, the private moments inside this house were the most special. The tapping of my computer keyboard into the late night and early morning hours as my heart and soul were expressed through poetry and fiction. The pieces of hard clay still stuck between the crevices in counters and floorboards from many sleepovers with my nieces and nephews where we have spent hours creating medieval dynasties with clay, boxes, and Legos. The lingering smell of baked cookies clashing with the smell of burnt popcorn during movie nights with Rose and Jessi as we hurriedly baked and cooked whatever we could make with what was in my cupboards before the previews were finished, as though on our own episode of *Chopped*.

It was Rose who ran over with a pregnancy test when I couldn't stop throwing up years ago, and it was there on the floor next to the wood-burning fireplace that I found out I was fleetingly pregnant. It was on the Bohemian-style oval rug that my mom made where we danced with joy, because this was something I had wanted for so long, before I ran to the mint-colored toilet and got sick again. It was the same spot I returned to when I cried for a week straight because the pregnancy abruptly ended. Rose, Jessi, and my family took turns bringing me soup and tissues.

Some of the most important memories in my life happened here.

It's why selling my cottage is something I would have never agreed to do, and Mark out of all people should know that. Even when Mark and I got married and moved to Boston, I kept one foot here, coming back to write in my favorite spot when I needed the inspiration.

Six months of actively planning our move to Italy, yet it's only when Mark is running out the door to catch his plane, he chooses to inform me he's already started the process of selling my cottage, as though it didn't deserve a deeper discussion. He shrugged off my shocked anger, as though it wasn't a possibility to hold onto my house while we're overseas, and I was crazy to think otherwise. I was left alone to pack up the final belongings of our Boston penthouse, simmering in what felt like betrayal.

To add fuel to the fire, while he took the initiative to sell off what is essentially a piece of my soul, he was simultaneously planning the most extravagant surprise birthday celebration I've ever experienced. Neither of these two events would be how I'd choose to enter the next decade of my life, and until this point, I would have assumed my *husband* out of all people knew this.

I drag myself to the shower, discarding my tank and pajama pants to the floor, and let the hot water wash over my body, praying for a boldness to rise up in the steam that I can latch onto.

The calmness I normally feel standing under the oversized steam and rain shower head is washed away by the surge of my heartbeat. My body overheats as a wave of nausea passes through and I wonder briefly if I will be able to make it to the toilet in time. Today, I will connect with thirty strangers from around the globe to hear about the things that changed their lives, all while being filmed. Then I'll have to *do* those things and document my journey. I close my eyes and picture the blank stares of those strangers as they watch my every move, disappointed by their expectations of a great performance that I didn't sign up to give.

Quickly, I open my eyes to push away the scene, focusing on the eucalyptus stems hanging from the showerhead, and take a deep breath. The nausea slowly dissipates, so I take a few more for good measure. A party of this magnitude is the worst idea for someone with stage fright. Not to mention the added pressure of representing Mark's business investment on a day when I'd prefer to be reading a good book or getting massages with my girls—not in the spotlight.

I have to go back to Crimson Bay, honey. I have to. That's what I told Mark when he said it may take a few months of scouting office locations before even finding a house while we were in Italy. I told him that I needed this time to find my peace, knowing how hard it's going to be oceans away from my family, two best friends, and my favorite writing spot. He was reluctant at first since we've never spent that much time apart, but then he agreed. This was supposed to be three months of *me* time in seeking closure, to sort through the thoughts and emotions I hadn't truly faced in our years together, yet it got hijacked by *him*.

I turn off the water before the truth paralyzes me from moving at all. I have to focus on just getting to the end of this night. As I wrap myself in a towel and step over the tub, Rose returns to the bathroom with two steaming cups of coffee. I eagerly reach for my favorite green stoneware mug, given as a gift from Neigleman Tech when I worked there as a temp and soon met Mark. I take a sip, letting the liquid slide down my throat and temporarily calm my nerves.

"Thanks for being here."

"Of course," Rose smiles and hops up on the counter, the soles of her five-inch, glittery heels tapping the lower cabinets. We've spent many mornings throughout the years perched on each other's bathroom counters while one or both of us get ready, stealing each other's makeup and skincare items like sisters living in the same house. "Full disclosure, though. I also have handcuffs and a taser in the car, as we all assumed you may not come on your own will."

I stop rubbing lotion into my face long enough to glance up at her and ask, "Please tell me you're joking."

Stone-faced, Rose replies, "I swung by The Bridge and picked up the taser on the way here."

"You're not joking." The infamous taser left behind by some traveling police officer that Jessi, the third in our little trio, seduced one night. She spent a straight year carrying it around, threatening to use it on people when they got out of line with their drinking. "What else did you stuff in that bag?"

Rose reaches over and pulls her satchel up from the ground

with a grunt like she's reeling in a big fish. She unzips it and I peer inside. "Every curler I could find to get your hair just right and every hair product sample I've collected throughout time. We gotta find one that will make your hair appear as soft as a cloud when really, it's as stiff as plastic, so it doesn't move a centimeter."

"Well, that's one positive from today. I get a makeover from the best of the best."

"That's my girl," Rose says with a relieved smile as she hops down from the counter and takes the comb from my hand to finish getting the tangles from my hair. "You lost a little of your natural optimism last night that makes you so darn charming, so I was hoping it'd make a return today."

I defend myself, "It was a lot to take in last night! You all have known about this for months and I'm finding out barely a day before."

"It wouldn't be a surprise without the surprise! Do you feel like you've got a grip on what's happening? Did everything Mark shared yesterday make sense?"

I reach for an eyelash curler, ignoring the fluttering of my stomach. "I blacked out about part way through when I realized it wasn't a formal business presentation and was actually an event meant for me." Mark was on video conference from Italy as I sat in my parents' den listening to him explain that Neigleman Tech was supposed to invest in Bridging the Six Degrees, a startup company that focuses on party planning with an unusual social media twist. He wanted to test them out by using them for my— an introvert who loathes being the center of attention—thirtieth birthday celebration. *Great* idea.

Rose snorts. "I can only imagine that he comes to you with a Prezi presentation every time he wants to get it on."

I shift uncomfortably on my foot, a nagging feeling all too present. She isn't totally wrong. Mark is rarely out of businessman mode. I would have preferred a private conversation with him instead of him revealing the plans for my party through a presentation meant for everyone else's ears. My family was all crowded behind me, eager to see my reaction since they had all been scheming for months, while I stared at Mark on screen wondering if he could even truly see me. It's something I've wondered a lot recently.

"Okay, so... I'm considered the Target, is that right? That's what stood out the most because it's a terrible name. It's like I should expect water balloons thrown at me or paintballs aimed at me."

"I already gave Mark that feedback, it's too aggressive. Immediately, I knew a man was behind the company."

I giggled at that. Rose attracts men left and right, but her line of defense is strong. She will knock one down verbally, and physically, before they ever have a chance to get too close. "And the people I'm meeting are called..."

"Senders." Rose sets down the comb to unlock her phone and swipe at the screen, careful to not damage her pedicured nails as she scrolls. "Okay, found it. This is from the email Mark sent us to get us on board: registered and paid members of Bridging the Six Degrees, called Senders, share an activity that has changed their life so much, they want to encourage someone else to do it, too. The person the party is for, called the Target—" she clears her throat and exaggerates an eyeroll, "then has ninety days to complete the chosen Sender activities. The goal is to bring all the Senders and Target closer together in a meaningful way, as in Bridging the Six Degrees of Separation. Not only is it about connecting more people across the world so we don't feel so separated from each other, but it's about seeing how we're all connected at the core of who we are as well. It's a reminder that we're all in this human experience together."

"Hence the name," I mutter, rubbing my temple. "I just don't know why he didn't choose the basic package. Meeting these people online, listening to them share their activities, and then freely doing the activities sounds so much better."

"But what's the point of investing in a company if you can't test out their crème de la crème offering? The Celebrate Your Life

Package." Rose scans her hand across the air as though lighting up the letters on a billboard. "It's definitely not cheap to fly everyone out here. You get to do all these activities for free, and somehow, this company and Mark's still profit. Hefty investment."

"Why didn't he do this party for you? This is right up your alley."

"You married the man, not me."

I bite my tongue. I'm pretty sure Rose is more fitting for Mark's lifestyle than I am.

"Listen." Rose reaches for my hands, rubbing her thumb across them like some sort of Reiki trick she learned from YouTube. "The Senders are on their way; most are probably already here. Everything is in motion. It's only a few hours, okay? This will be more amazing than terrifying. I wouldn't let you do it if it wasn't guaranteed to be an adventure. I'm here."

"And I love you for that. But isn't it weird that Mark isn't here? In all of this, he didn't even talk to me about it in advance. I made it very clear two years ago that I never wanted to be a guinea pig for any of his acquisitions. Yet here I am. On my birthday, nonetheless, and my last trip here in Crimson Bay for who knows how long..." Tears fill my eyes with the last few words.

Rose throws her arms around me. "You know men have weird ways of expressing themselves. Mark is showing his love. You'll understand more tonight. Besides, when is the last time you were able to have an actual adventure without Mark? You two have been attached at the hip for five years now, save for your random writing escapes, of which you hardly even tell me you're back."

"That's true," I relent. A little thrill manages to stir in me at the idea of doing all these challenges and—for once—getting outside of my comfort zone without Mark by my side. "But... do you really think he's doing this for me? Or is it more for the success of Neigleman Tech?"

Rose takes a step back and eyes me carefully. "Are you really concerned about that?"

I look back at Rose, trying to decipher the look in her eyes, whether she's glad I'm questioning it or concerned that I am. Guilt rushes at me so fast that I get lightheaded. I'm sure there's been so much behind the scenes with him planning this and Rose and all of my family helping. It's probably the worst time in the world for me to be questioning Mark. Finally, I respond, "Just nervous about today."

She nods once, unconvinced, as she pulls the foldable stool from the closet and plops it in front of the mirror. "I'll blow dry your hair. We've got to get you there on time."

I sink into the stool feeling even more guilty as the loud hum of the blow dryer fills the silence. She can read me better than anyone, so I don't know why I hold things back. I haven't said the words out loud to anyone yet, even though they're screaming within, firing cannonballs at my ribs inside, dying to break free. *I don't think this life with Mark is one that I want.* It's the voice I haven't been able to silence, despite desperately trying. But the harder I tried to make his life work for me, the more I missed my own.

Our romance was such a whirlwind, starting from the minute I first shook his hand, blushing as we were introduced, that I hardly had time to catch my breath. We married sixteen months from the day we met. He has the height of a pro-basketball player with wavy brown hair and the chiseled cheeks of a BIC razor model. He naturally captures attention, yet he's quiet with soulful brown eyes and can equally blend into the wall of a crowded room. We connected over a love for helping people turn their dreams into reality; him through business ventures and me through philanthropic opportunities.

Mark's passion for this mission was so great that every minute of his days was dedicated to his role as Chief Operating Officer for Neigleman Tech, an investment and technology firm committed to supporting the success of impact-driven startups. From technology conferences and charity events, to networking dinners and ribbon cuttings, in places like Chicago, Dallas, Los Angeles, Miami, Paris, Amsterdam, and Dubai, we were always on the go.

When his promotion moved him to Boston, I followed without a second thought. We were regularly wined and dined on free trips paid entirely by the company. It was a classier version of the way I once dreamt I'd travel the world.

When Mark and I first met, anything seemed possible. The world was at our fingertips, a romance made for Hallmark movies. What more could I possibly want?

What I truly wanted became clear on the darkest day of my life, as I sat in the bathroom, bleeding from the loss of our little girl. I wanted to be surrounded by a close-knit family like mine. I wanted kids of my own.

The executive decisions in our life were made by Mark. Since his company was making an impact, it always took precedence. As much as I love changing the world, there's a part of my soul that craves something more. I wanted what I thought we were supposed to have because my dreams are as important as his.

I rub my eyes, sick to my stomach thinking about the next three months away from Mark. I know I still love him deep down, because at the core, he's an incredible man. He's so giving with his time and energy, always willing to help anyone out at the drop of a hat.

But I lost myself in his life years ago, and I'm ready to reclaim *me*. Perhaps I would have had the chance to do that during the three months here, and I could have joined him in Italy feeling renewed and more confident in our relationship and our future. Yet he's given me an agenda that will benefit his work, rather than allowing me the opportunity to find my peace.

Rose stops the dryer and brushes out my hair. "Ready for a refill?"

I nod once as I hold out my mug to her, my mouth too dry to speak. If I say anything right now, I fear I may shatter.

After one hour of Rose forcing me to repeat mantras like, "This will be good for me. I trust those who love me," Rose's makeover of me is complete. Walking to the standalone full-sized mirror in the corner of my bedroom, I take my reflection in. Rose curled my crimson strands, pinning one side back to give me an elegant, yet still casual and very much *me* look. My makeup remains natural but highlights the sun's speed in bringing forth my freckles after a recent weekend beach vacation with Mark. My sea green sundress turns my eyes into shimmering emeralds. The belt at my waist gives definition to my otherwise straight body, making it womanlier and curvier, while matching the cognac wedges that decorate my feet, displaying my cherry toenails from yesterday's pedicure.

Rose stands behind me, gripping the sides of my arms with her hands and resting her chin on my shoulder. "You look beautiful. You've got this."

I nod, noting the look of determination on my face and the encouragement on hers. *This is what you signed up for, Autumn,* I remind myself. *You chose Mark, so you chose this life.* It's the only thing I can chant to drown out the reoccurring thought of, *What if this isn't the life I want?*

I TRY TO HOLD MY NERVES TOGETHER AS ROSE DRIVES to my parents' house, but my knees are bouncing, giving me away. Rose has been firing questions at me since the moment I buckled in, clearly trying to distract me. Rose only feels anxious when other people she loves feel anxious, so I know her strategy is for her as much as it is for me. Otherwise, she's one of the calmest and most cool-headed people I've ever known.

"Any updates on your book?"

"I promised that I would have the polished first draft to her by October, and I'm about one chapter off from my timeline. My mind has just felt so burdened lately with all this packing; it's been hard to focus. But the deadline is real, and I was hoping to work on it while here, but now with all of this—"

"You'll reach your deadline. You always do," Rose encourages me, intentionally cutting off my complaint of the party. "When did you meet her anyway? It hasn't been that long, has it?"

My mind is so muddy. I can't even recall one of the most exciting moments of my life; when my literary agent requested my full manuscript, after the first three chapters we workshopped were deemed promising. I pull out my phone and search for the date. "The workshop was in February."

"That's a pretty quick turnaround for a full book."

"But worth it for the chance of a childhood dream to come true," I mutter, distracted as I quickly scroll through more happy birthday texts, my heart pounding with each one. Usually, I love reading sweet messages from everyone, but almost every single person seems to know about my "party," and it's making me wonder just how many people will be there today.

"How's my boyfriend?" Rose asks.

Yep, that's the kind of distraction I need. A smile crosses my face and I turn off my phone.

"Oh, Henry," we say in unison and bat our eyelashes at each other, resulting in giggles.

Henry. I miss him already. My Italian neighbor in Boston, who Mark and I instantly adopted as family when a brief, "nice to meet you, neighbor" introduction turned into a seven-hour conversation. He was well into the senior years of his life, always decked out with his plaid newsboy cap, strands of thin gray hair poking out of the sides, a suede jacket, and his beautiful antique mahogany cane—passed down through many generations. I wasn't surprised Rose fell in love with his charm and sweet personality about as quickly as Mark and I did. Henry has been the only man she's ever called a boyfriend in her entire life, and of course it would be a man that could be her grandfather and lives thousands of miles away—not to mention a man who, for once, has no romantic interest in her.

"Is he excited to get back home?"

"Yes, and nervous, I think. It's been over three decades since he and Lenora were last there. He's aware it's going to be different being back, but he says he'd rather die where he was born and he's taking Lenora's ashes with him."

"God, he's not going there to die, is he?"

"Rose! Sheesh, don't even put that out into the universe. Let's hope he's got many more years in him."

When Mark found out we were relocating to Italy, it only made sense to invite Henry to come with us. We are quite attached. I've taken many walks with Henry throughout the years, exploring Boston and listening to the historical facts he would spout off. We've spent many nights sipping wine with him while watching the city from our rooftop. One night, Henry admitted we are the kids he never had, and that he's grateful for finding us because he didn't know how to survive without Lenora.

Lenora passed six years earlier to ovarian cancer, and she was the last remaining person in his family. Lenora and Henry were both the only child of their respective families, disowned once they chased their dreams by leaving Montone and moving to America to start a new life. Henry in all his trials had the perseverance to become a successful business owner of Lenory, an upscale men's genuine leather shoes retailer, popular on the East Coast. He sold it fifteen years ago to spend the last years of Lenora's life holding her hand, never leaving her side.

I am confident that the Italy work opportunity was not by chance, rather a result of Mark's efforts to help Henry, but he wouldn't admit to it. I know Mark looks at Henry like a father figure, which he's needed ever since he lost his own dad in a car accident when he was only a teenager. They have quite a special bond and sometimes I'll sneak away just to leave them alone in their own conversations.

"You know I would visit Henry in Boston if he wasn't tagging along with you guys."

"Well, he won't be flying out for another month. You've got time to shoot your shot. You did always like the old ones."

"You mean men who have aged like a fine wine? Sure do." Rose tilts her sunglasses down and glances at me. "Speaking of my lover boy, what would Henry tell you in this moment?"

I smile. I know what she's doing, and I know exactly what he would say. "It'll be fine. Everything always turns out fine." I imagine we're sitting on our stoop in Boston and he's patting my hand while he says it. It was his signature phrase. As cliché as it was, he genuinely believed it, making it impossible to argue. I could use that pat of the hand from him right now.

"He's a wise man. Everything always turns out fine. This party isn't an exception to the rule."

"I know, but—"

"Shh, "Rose puts her finger to her mouth. "Your family and I wouldn't have let you go through with this if we didn't think it was truly something remarkable. Mark may have proposed the idea, but we all agreed to take part."

"That's the thing—*you* all agreed. I never did. It's not like this is only a three-hour endeavor. It's for three *months!* My whole stay in Crimson Bay."

"Listen, it's your party and you can cry if you want to." She pauses and gives me a snarky look. I roll my eyes at what I once deemed as the most annoying song of all time since she used to sing it nonstop for every single birthday I had from ages six to thirteen. She was forced to break the cycle when she had to get her jaw realigned for braces and couldn't speak for four weeks, which happened to fall during my thirteenth birthday. Thirteen became my favorite number from that year on. "But maybe, just maybe, this turns into the best thing that has ever happened to you."

Goosebumps line my arms. I'm not sure if it's from Rose's words or if it's the breeze, as we are greeted by the waterfront again and pull into my parent's driveway. I roll up the window just as the scene in front of me comes into view. My once serene, classic, lake-style childhood home is transformed, surrounded by large trucks, two local news crews, and people milling about in every direction carrying supplies, setting up tents, and putting up signs. A considerable portion of my parents' yard is marked off for parking with an attendant already present, prepared to take tickets from guests.

Rose yells out her window, "We've got the guest of honor in the car!"

The parking attendant, who is clearly the same kid who works the Ice Cream Hut every summer, unhooks a chain linked sign and waves us through. I stare at all the cars that are pooled in the yard.

"Toto, I don't think we're in Kansas anymore." I mutter as Rose parks in the driveway. We step out of the car, surveying the changed landscape that we once could walk with our eyes closed. If we tried that now, we'd stumble over strange people milling about and cords being strapped down to the ground.

"Aww, look. You're already recognizing the magic of Oz."

"Just please tell me there won't be giant flying monkeys," I say as I dodge two guys carrying a massive heating lamp out into the yard.

We weave our way through the workers and succeed in climbing the stairs to the white wrap-around porch. We don't even make it to the door before we hear my mom's voice.

"She's here, she's here!" My mom's excitement seeps through the walls as she tugs open the oak front door, hand-carved by my dad. "Autumn! You look beautiful!" My mom's eyes sparkle as she half-hops in the doorframe, her medium bobbed hair bouncing on her shoulders. Clearly mother and daughter, most of our physical features are the same from our 5'6" height, slender frame, green eyes, and Roman nose to our size eight shoes. But my red hair makes me stand apart from everyone in my brunette-topped family, not just my mom. My parents' recessive genes chose me, ironically the only introvert in a group of extroverts, to be the most noticeable.

"My favorite season has walked through the door!" My dad's booming voice unfailingly gives the effect of him standing two feet away, even when he's on a different floor of the house. He lumbers up the steps from the basement. Dressed in his signature flannel shirt with the sleeves sloppily rolled, blue jeans, and brown wool socks, he beckons, "Come here!" His long strides reach me within seconds as he hugs me with the same vigor Mom displayed. It's a far cry from their usual reaction when I visit. But I can't help but sink into his hugs, an aching inside knowing that my wonderful family has caused me to want my own as badly as I do.

"Rose, honey, did you have to use the handcuffs?" my mom asks.

Rose drops her bag by the door before closing it. "Nope. Just had to threaten her with the taser. She gave in pretty easily."

"Did you finally come to terms that this will be the best birthday you've ever had?" My dad squeezes me tighter as though that would convince me.

I envision all the times I've been forced to shake the maracas while wearing a sombrero at various local Mexican establishments to make all my birthday wishes of pure embarrassment come true. It's the way every birthday of mine has been spent for the past twenty-two years, the only changing variables are which restaurant wait staff sings "Happy Birthday" and in what language. I thought those moments were as embarrassing as it could get on one's birthday. But I was wrong.

"You guys are making me feel like this is the last birthday I'm ever going to have."

My dad chuckles as he lets go of me and rubs the back of his neck. "You're leaving for Paris soon. We know birthdays and visits won't be as frequent."

"A town in Italy, actually," I correct him, gauging whether he's being serious or facetious. "Paris is in France."

"'Atown', Italy doesn't sound very exciting. Paris sounds better," Dad adds his specialty: a cheesy joke.

My parents' obliviousness about various cultures once filled me with fear and partially contributed to propelling me out of Door County to follow Mark. It scared me to get stuck in the trap of this area and follow in their footsteps, never leaving my comfort zone to explore more. Both my parents were born and raised in Door County; my dad in Crimson Bay, and my mom in Ephraim. They're high school sweethearts, in love with each other as much as this state, and agreed there was nowhere else they'd rather live or visit. They rarely ventured outside of Wisconsin.

Being back in my parents' home, smelling the same flowery cinnamon potpourri that has welcomed me, my friends, and guests through the front door all my life suddenly is enough to make me ache at the thought of leaving them.

"Aunt Autumn!" My six-year-old nephew's bare feet slap on the hardwood floor while he runs to me, leaving little sweaty footprints behind that quickly disappear.

Surprised to see him, I open my arms as he jumps into them, momentarily making me forget any of my concerns. I lift Aiden off the ground and cover his head with kisses. "Hey, buddy. I missed these awesome hugs of yours."

His older sister, Olivia, isn't far behind him. "Hi, Aunt Autumn. Happy early birthday." She hugs my waist, her head ramming Aiden's dangling legs.

I vow to always be the crazy aunt, continually shoving my nose in the cheeks and hair of my nieces and nephews to breathe them in. One day they'll be too old to let me do it. I suck down longing of being a mother and focus on how these kids are enough to set my heart on fire.

Pulling back, Olivia hands me a small envelope covered in crayon drawings before running away giggling. Aiden leaps down from my embrace to follow her.

A secretive look is exchanged between my parents who are known for their silent conversations, a superpower that I suppose sprouts naturally after being married for so long.

I raise an eyebrow, unprepared for any more surprises. A dragon, bird, and something else I can't decipher with a form of "Happy Birthday, Aunt Autumn" is scrawled in colorful characters. An adorable handmade birthday card from two of my favorites. "If you two can hear me, I love the card!" I call out. Echoing giggles from another room answer. I flip it over and see written in my sister-in-law's handwriting,

Come to the backyard for a surprise so grand,
maracas and sombrero won't be had,
I'm trying to rhyme, but I'm not the poet,
so come on out before the kids blow it!

I look up from the card into the faces of my parents and Rose who are all smiling in a way that makes me immediately nervous. "What's in the backyard?"

Dad puts his hands on my shoulders to steer me through the living room to the back of the house. "I would think with the life you have lived you'd learn to trust more. You don't always have to know what you're getting yourself into before you take the first few steps, you know." Surprising words from my dad.

More anticipatory giggling reaches my ears, more voices than Aiden's and Olivia's. As soon as I pass through the threshold, "Happy Birthday, Autumn!" is shouted by my entire family as they stand in front of the sliding doors of the dining room, all wearing pointed paper hats splashed with confetti and blowing squeaky party horns. My brothers, Peter and Clark, my sisters-in-law, Beth and Tara, and my other niece and nephew, Juliet and Brantley run in from outside and join Olivia and Aiden in the line.

My dad hands me a shot glass, while Beth, a wine connoisseur, raises her burgundy-filled glass that matches her lipstick, "New decade and the golden birthday! Nothing but luck on your side!"

"Hear, hear!" everyone shouts, and we clink glasses with those standing closest to us.

I take the shot with my dad and Rose, and begin giving out hugs. I stop when I stand in front of my brothers, hair standing on the back of my neck when I see their faces side by side. I spent thirty years with these two. We were natural tricksters throughout childhood, setting out to play pranks and jokes on everyone we could. We were the kings and queen of realistic-looking plastic spiders and rodents, our chore earnings going into a collective pot for those specific purposes, put in the right spot to secure screams out of our target. They had poker faces to anyone who didn't know them, but I could see the twitch of Clark's upper lip and Peter's flared nostrils as he tried not to laugh, little nuances that told me when they were up to no good.

"Clark Kent and Peter Parker..." I warn, teasing them with

their namesakes. Both of my brothers were named after the true identities of Superman and Spiderman since my mom gave in to my dad's requests to name their sons. My dad was in his late teens when they were born and thought he was ingenious by calling them Clark and Peter. He later regretted it around the same time he realized that all of his 80s superhero and Dick Tracy figurines were better off donated to the local Goodwill. "Don't you two realize I know your 'tells'? Give it up."

Everyone looked at each other, unsure who should speak first. Then Brantley, using his plastic Tyrannosaurus to attack Aiden's Brontosaurus, roared out, "There's a stage outside! Rawrrrrrr!"

Beth bends to whisper something in Brantley's ear, his cheeks reddening. "I'm sorry, Aunt Autumn," he apologizes, before roaring again and chasing Aiden around the room with more dinosaurs.

"A stage?"

Tara plops a birthday hat on my head. "Well, that was short-lived. Did I not call it in my Pulitzer-prize-winning poem? Every surprise is like a ticking time bomb, waiting for a kid to set it off."

"A stage?" I repeat, stunned. "Did you guys forget about the time that I peed my pants when I was dragged on stage to fill in for Bobby's sudden asthma attack before the school-wide Spelling Bee in second grade? Or, when Rose and I were supposed to sing and dance to 'Hakuna Matata' in the fifth-grade talent show, and I completely froze, unable to move for the entire song? Are you waiting for a repeat performance?" I have a serious case of stage fright and every person who knows me is very aware of the fact.

Mom chuckles, "Oh, honey, you're much more mature now. You can't be scared you'll pee yourself again."

"The bladder only loosens with old age." I cross my arms over my chest.

Mom grabs my elbow, forcing me to uncross my arms and walks with me through the French doors leading out to the back-yard. All four kids squeeze past us to beat us outside.

"Ta-da!" Brantley, Olivia, and Juliet stand on the deck with their arms open wide. Aiden spins in circles around them.

Ignoring the bustles of random people in the yard below, setting up lights, tables, food, and more, I squint trying to find my bearings. Pointing to the deck, I stammer, "Th-th-this is a stage."

"No shit, Sherlock." Peter says as he joins us. He gives each kid a sparkler and lights them one by one. The kids take off running down the stairs and through the yard, with their lights barely making a dent in the early afternoon sun. "Dad, Clark, and I did this one. Pretty good work, huh? It needed an upgrade."

The deck had at least fifteen feet added to the front, extending it further out from the house. The same wooden steps that cascaded on the left side of the deck were now mirrored on the right side as well, with a portion of the railing removed to accommodate the addition. Strings of light extended from the roof of the house to the tall posts that connected to each corner of the front of the stage. At the top of each post was a giant stage light pointed to the deck.

Speakers were pushed up against the back of the house and stacked on top of each other. A giant X was marked out of white tape in the middle of the stage. "This is where I'll be?" I tap the X with my foot.

"It's exciting, right?" Beth stands next to me, her eyes lighting up as she watches the activity in the yard. She feeds off meeting new people, especially those who come from different countries or backgrounds. Peter and Beth met when she was sixteen, which left her with few travel opportunities since Peter didn't care for it. He was almost identical to my dad in looks and most other things, including a deep-rooted attachment to this tiny slice of heaven. Beth is the first one calling me after I return from every trip, demanding every detail and every picture of our travels, no matter how insignificant.

My head is spinning, struggling to wrap my mind around the concept, staring at my family's faces to see what sort of alien creatures replaced them to think turning the deck into a stage was ever a good idea.

Dad begins fanning me with the card the kids made. He asks, "Are you alright? You look pale."

A knock on the siding rescues me from my deepening hole of doubts and the internal flight reaction to run as far away from here as possible.

I turn around to see a woman dressed in black pants, a black button-down shirt, and a black headset on black curly hair, poking her head out to say loudly, "Okay, the first interview is in fifteen minutes." She's gone in a flash.

"Who is that?"

Mom explains, "That's Karen, the media producer for Bridging the Six Degrees. She'll be the one making sure the schedule runs as planned."

Rose covers her mouth and whispers in my ear, "If we were in Oz, she'd be the Wicked Witch of the West. I met her earlier, and she was a total—"

"One more toast before it begins!" Tara holds her wine glass in the air. "Happy Birthday, Autumn!"

"Happy Birthday, Autumn!" Everyone shouts and a few people from the yard whistle and clap, causing my face to burn with fire. I don't know who any of those people are.

Rose links her arm with mine as we walk back into the house. Following her lead, we arrive in the den that has been transformed into an unrecognizable space. The worn-down tan and floral, mismatched furniture my parents collected over the years has been replaced with brown leather chairs and couches that provide a rustic feel. The producers must have deemed the old, wood-burning fireplace acceptable because they lit a fire to set the mood, despite the lingering mid-80s temperatures outside. To offset the heat, someone stationed several fans spaced evenly throughout the room.

This Karen woman, dressed like a robber in the night, is waiting and directs me to sit on the couch, where a menacing black movie-style camera stares at me like it's instigating a game of chicken. Karen claps her hands so hard that it sounds like a gunshot and makes me jump. She announces that anyone who is not involved with the interview needs to exit "pronto, now, ASAP." Disappointment crosses Rose's face, followed by pure irritation, as Karen points to the door and says, "Go."

"See? I told you," Rose mouths before blowing a kiss to me, furrowing her eyebrows at Karen, and strutting out of the room in a very "remember, I'm the queen, not you" fashion.

A tall gentleman with wavy brown hair, defined cheekbones, and trendy glasses designed to give the illusion of intelligence and style appears out of nowhere. Seriously, his footsteps make no sound. "Hi, Autumn, I'm Kevin, the founder of Bridging the Six Degrees. Your husband is a good man for doing this. Thanks for taking part." He lowers himself into the leather chair next to the camera.

My mouth is dry, so I only tilt my head in response to his introduction. I reach for my water bottle and down half. I don't notice how loud my gulps are until my eyes find Kevin with a perplexed look and a tight, thin-lipped smile daubed on his face.

"Sorry, thirsty," I murmur an apology, twist the lid on, and stuff the bottle into the couch cushion. I'm sure he's wondering how I snagged a man as articulate and professional as Mark. I don't have any problem putting on a better performance when attending Mark's work events, but it doesn't feel right pretending to be someone else, here, as I sit in my childhood home. I'm having trouble marrying the two identities that I didn't realize I had so easily divided over the past few years.

"Sure, no worries." Kevin responds, swiftly averting his stare as though he'd walked in on me in the bathroom. Flipping through his notebook, he explains what to expect, "This will be quick. I only have a few questions to ask you. It's simply to gain a feel for what's going through your mind leading up to the party and how you became involved. We'll do a couple of brief interviews with you throughout the night. Then, we'll come back when you've completed your activities in ninety days to do a follow-up interview." Kevin adjusts his glasses. "Ready?"

"Yeah, I guess so." I need to pull together more intelligent sentences. This party is more than just a birthday celebration for me; it's a demonstration of Bridging the Six Degrees' potential success. I know how Mark's mind works; everything is business first. He knows this process entails parties and interviews and things that I downright prefer to avoid, yet here I am. This isn't about me. This is about his investment. I can be angry and shut down, or I can step up to the plate. Only one of these options is productive.

"Three, two, one..." Karen counts down as the red light on the camera flashes. She points her finger and mouths, "Action!"

Kevin's tone instantly changes. At first, I had the impression that he stepped off a surfboard in California before making his way to Wisconsin. Now, his voice is professional, polished, impressive. His sharp features give him an Adrien Brody look, where you want to keep looking at him to determine if he is, indeed, ridiculously handsome or merely mediocre with unique characteristics. He reminds me of pictures I've seen of Rose's dad.

"Today's featured guest is Autumn Goodfield, who is celebrating her thirtieth birthday party in the beautiful Crimson Bay, Wisconsin. Her husband, Mark Goodfield, partnered with Bridging the Six Degrees to throw her a bash in her hometown that she'll never forget. Happy Birthday, Autumn!"

"Thank you, Kevin. It should be one of the best birthdays thanks to all the outstanding and thoughtful planning by your company."

A wave of confusion crosses Kevin's face, as though she'd ruined his presumption that this interview would be agonizing. He needs to keep moving, though. Pauses will make me overanalyze my words, and then the nerves will take over, and the embarrassment will multiply.

"Well, we are honored to be a part of your special day. As you know, your husband chose our Celebrate Your Life package, one of five party variations we offer, which brings the Bridging the Six Degrees Senders who were selected to join you in the flesh. A record 436 members applied to your profile with their stories. Your husband and family went through every one of those applications and selected the best activities for you, allowing you to relate to the life of someone else who was personally impacted by that activity."

436 members applied to be a part of my party? Mark didn't tell me that. And no one mentioned they hand-selected these activities. My skin tingles and I sit up straighter to pay attention. *Maybe this was more personalized than I thought...*

"Today you will be given a list of thirty challenges from the selected Senders to complete in ninety days, while also getting to hear the stories behind each one. As you complete each activity, you will provide pictures and/or videos as proof, as well as a journal about your experience. Bridging the Six Degrees will cover all related expenses. Any questions before we begin?"

Only one of the biggest questions on my mind after seeing groups of people form outside. "Why do so many people want to travel far distances to a party that's celebrating a complete stranger?" It's not something I would do, so it makes me feel even more uncomfortable.

Kevin smiles gently as though he can see an insecurity from childhood bubbling to the surface. "We've found that through our application and screening process, we are able to vet the most genuine and wonderful people. They have varying degrees of individual reasons, but all are connected to the Universal Story, the joined human experience. Some are driven to build more lasting connections with other people through the sharing of their story. Others believe so strongly in the activity that has changed their life, that they are on their own mission to encourage others to do the same. Many people are looking for a chance to leave behind a legacy, and as their life significantly changes for the better, this form of paying it forward creates ripple effects in the world by helping others grow and enhance their quality of life as well."

I nod, my the tension in my neck relaxing a bit, feeling more as though I'm being welcomed into a warm light of global change, and not just people showing up for their fifteen minutes of fame or because they were paid to. It's definitely a more intimate level than any of Mark's other endeavors that we've taken part in, and intimate is something I can do.

"I'm wondering," Kevin continues, "what are you most looking forward to?"

I pause and consider what I just learned. "Well, the activities chosen for me have me intrigued. I want to know what they'll be, especially knowing that it will not only be a blend of what the members of your company want to challenge me to do, but in essence, what my family is challenging me to do as well."

Kevin chuckles. "That's a great way to put it, Autumn."

"Also," I keep going, surprising myself with my sudden energetic flow of words, "since I'm a writer, I'm interested in other people's personal stories. I love the concept of hearing about one event in a person's life that has changed them for the better. I want to know the details. I'm not sure how much information will be given to me, but that is the advantage of getting to meet those selected Senders tonight. It'll make the stories more real than sharing them online could ever be."

Kevin is beaming at my response, no doubt enjoying the extra plug about how powerful the upgrade packages can be. From everything I've witnessed so far, and as Rose pointed out, it can't be a small investment. Mark's investments are proportionate to his belief in the impact he thinks they can have, so it's saying a lot about this one.

"That leads me to ask, if you had to share the one event so far that has changed your life, what would it be?"

I don't hesitate for a second, "Marrying Mark. I wouldn't be sitting here right now, preparing for the most progressive social networking party that has ever existed if I hadn't."

Kevin jokes, "I suppose you wouldn't challenge others to marry him, though, to get the same life-changing result, huh?"

I maintain a bright smile on my face. "No, he's all mine."

"How sweet. Thank you, Autumn, for your time. We will catch up with you later tonight!"

"And... cut!" Karen calls out as the red light on the camera fades.

Kevin rises from his chair and holds out a surprisingly calloused hand to help me up from the couch. His grip remains around my hand even after I'm back on my feet.

"You were amazing. Truly amazing. I quite look forward to what else you have to say tonight. And, I have to say, you're absolutely stunning. Mark's a lucky man."

Is he hitting on me? "Thanks," I say awkwardly and quickly slip my hand out of his. I'm not used to hearing Mark is a lucky man. Usually, it's always about how lucky *I* am to have someone as great and giving as Mark.

Kevin's face flushes, and I get an uneasy feeling that he uses this program as a way to meet women. From the first time I saw him, he struck me as a womanizer. He carries the same demeanor as Justin, my high school sweetheart turned fiancé and then ex, who broke my heart before Mark came into my world—arrogance and narcissism frosted over with the charisma to make it look like confidence and humility.

Karen speaks before Kevin can get another word out. After barking commands into her headset and whispering into Kevin's ear, she grabs my arm. "Alright, let's roll. It's time to get you out there."

As soon as we step out of the living room, Rose rushes in right away, ignoring Karen's glares. "How'd it go? Are you doing okay?" I'm relieved to see her, a comforting body, especially since I can pass out at any moment because I know my next step is standing on a stage in the spotlight. Give me the chair across from the camera any day compared to a stage.

"I'm not sure I can do this." I stop and clutch Rose's forearm, the ground beneath my feet swaying. Maybe I have time to back out. There's a reason I'm a writer. I like to *write* the story, not be the star of it."

"But you were amazing! I heard every word!"

I whisper to her, "I had to *act*, Rose. I don't want Mark disappointed in me."

Karen taps the clipboard in her hands. "We've gotta go."

Rose puts her forehead to mine. "Breathe with me." I follow her breaths like I'm preparing for birth. She's been by my side for several of my nerve-induced panic attacks. "I know this isn't your scene, but this is incredible. Trust me. One foot in front of the other, okay? You'll see what I mean soon enough."

Together they steer me to the French doors that open to the backyard. Lacy curtains billow from the open doors, obscuring my view outside. They must be another addition that Bridging the Six Degrees added to make my parent's house 'show worthy.' This event is turning out to be more elaborate than my wedding day.

"Okay, when you walk out, stand at the edge of the deck. The deejay will make an official announcement, so everyone knows who you are."

"Wait—what? I'm going out there right now?" I self-consciously touch my hair. "Can't I run to the bathroom quickly to freshen up?"

"No, no time," Karen says irritably, lacking the understanding of why I'm not more excited to have the spotlight shine on me.

Rose whispers in my ear, "Just a few minutes longer. You'll be able to take a quick break once they get through the planned activities. It'll flow after that point." I'm grateful for her reassurance. At least she's seen the schedule. I wish someone had shown it to me.

"You, out of the way." Karen tugs on Rose's top to pull her to the side. I stifle a laugh as I see Rose's hand clench, clearly fighting the urge to hit Karen upside the head for picking at her Stella dress in that way. It's like a territorial dance between two lionesses.

Karen will not let Rose run the show, and Rose does not like being told what to do.

Even though they are only a few feet away, I feel completely alone and exposed, like a pig at a Luau. I've always been able to control the people allowed in my safe zone. Now, my security is being stripped away while thrust into a very public event for the entire world to see.

Karen reaches for the rope on the side of the curtains. "Okay, we gotta roll. Three, two, one..."

Three

ONCE THE CURTAINS ARE PULLED, MY EYES ADJUST TO the blinding lights. I resist the urge to lift my hands to block them out, aware that it would not be a good look on camera.

"Smile!" Rose and Karen urge in unison.

I bare my teeth to the colorful dots floating in my vision, the only things I can see.

"A little less!" Rose coaches like only a best friend can genuinely do. I must look as Frankenstein-ish as I feel.

Stepping outside, the enthusiastic clapping from the audience combined with the fast beat of the music from the deejay's speakers rushes at me and knocks off my equilibrium, and I stumble. When I regain my balance, the scene in front of me slowly comes into focus.

I had anticipated thirty strangers, my family, and maybe a few others to be present—fifty people max. It was a rationalization I used to calm my nerves. However, now staring at the crowd, I don't have to count them all to know a few hundred people are standing before me. My knees buckle. Nothing could have prepared me for this.

"Some of you are related to her, some of you grew up with her, but others will be meeting her for the first time. Ladies and gentlemen, I would like to introduce you to Autumn Lynn Olson-Goodfield!" the deejay announces, blending my maiden name with my married name to make sure everyone connects with all facets of my life—the past, present, and my near future. The crowd cheers and embarrassment flushes my cheeks. Being the center of attention has never been my idea of a good time.

The deejay continues, "Autumn turns thirty years old today, and we get to celebrate her! Let's all sing an oldie but goodie, 'Happy Birthday!'"

No, no, no... Please, don't sing to me. I am tempted to grab the deejay's microphone and tell him that won't be necessary. Instead, he takes the lead before I can react, singing, "Happy Birthday to you..." as the rest of the audience joins in. I freeze and fixate my eyes on the deejay's bald head. I hope I still have a smile on my face, but I can't tell. I'm numb.

Hundreds of strangers, some who traveled from all over the world, singing Happy Birthday to me as I stand on a makeshift stage in my parent's backyard is not how I expected to turn thirty. Especially as I prepare to be the first publicly filmed participant in the widely anticipated Bridging the Six Degrees social media experiment.

A short, common song turns into the longest musical in history. As soon as the deejay belts out the last note, a brief moment of relief comes, only to be quickly squashed when he snaps his fingers. Karen drapes a white sash across my body. Written in glowing black letters is, "Guest of Honor."

"Although there's no chance you will have trouble finding Autumn today—I mean, look how gorgeous she is with that fireball hair and stunning dress!" He whistles, igniting a few catcalls to come out of the crowd. I'm positive my face is redder than the Fiery She-Devil gloss Rose painted my lips with. The deejay continues, "To make it even easier, she will be wearing this white sash. The Senders of Bridging the Six Degrees are wearing blue sashes."

I scan the crowd, astonished by the number of blue sashes

mixed in with many other people who chose to be here for their own reasons. My stomach ties into knots as the reality of the situation strikes me. I had been selfish when the idea of this party was presented, thinking it was all about me and Mark's business venture. But after my interview with Kevin, and now sitting on this stage, it's like I am given a prestigious aerial view of humankind. I can see how I am such a small part of the grander scheme of Bridging the Six Degrees' goals. Each person will be spotlighted with a chance to share one of their most exceptional, eye-opening experiences while influencing others. The solidarity of it all is beautifully sentimental. Excitement begins to pump through my veins, replacing the egocentric dread.

The deejay proclaims, "Please, all you beautiful, blue-sashed people, go ahead and line up on the right side of the deck."

A flurry of activity and excited murmuring gusts through the crowd as the audience parts to allow the Senders to come on stage. Karen carries a white padded chair to the middle of the deck, scooting a wicker side table closer and placing a thick book on top.

The deejay nods in the direction of the chair. "Autumn, you sit there."

I oblige as Karen hands me the book. It has a beautiful blue velvet cover with "Autumn's 30th Birthday Party" embossed on the front in silver. I flip it open to see nothing but blank pages inside. Confused, I look to the deejay for answers.

He grins with kind eyes sparkling, resting the mic on his belly that hangs over his pants, like how a pregnant woman stands to protect her womb. Picking up the microphone to speak into it, he explains, "Every Sender will hand you a page to stick in that journal. The activity they are challenging you to complete and the story of how it changed their lives are listed on it. This is a keepsake for you, with lots of blank pages, so you can take any personal notes or store pictures in it as you process your experiences. However, you are required to detail your adventures in the online Bridging the Six Degrees portal using pictures or videos, which everyone will have access to and will be shared on all social channels. Remember, the more open you are to sharing your experiences, the more successful this experiment will be. Understand?"

I nod and grip the book tighter.

"I will call each Sender to the deck, one by one. Senders, you will state your name, where you've traveled from and what your challenge is. I ask that you refrain from sharing specifics of why it changed you, though. Autumn will discover that when reading the journal or through conversations with you. A brief intro is all we're aiming for here, friends. Everyone understand? Okay good." The deejay rubs his hands together as the crowd grows silent and says, "Member number one, please come on up!"

A lady in her mid-fifties regally floats up the stairs. I swear her feet never touch the ground. She has dark skin with dark eyes that are lit with passion. There is a visible fire to her. When the deejay gives her the microphone to speak, the whole crowd stops moving to listen.

"I am Nokutenda Marechera." I take note of the confidence in her voice. I want to speak like that, with such obvious conviction and power. All she has to do is state her name, and it transforms into an invisible arrow, striking you in the heart before you even know it's coming, leaving you breathless.

"I come from Bulawayo, Zimbabwe, Africa, beautiful Autumn." She turns, her eyes piercing mine, "You are a messenger meant to deliver packages to those in need. If you see someone without shoes, give them your shoes. If you have to walk barefoot for a few miles, do. Many do it all the time. You only gain when you free your body of the weight it carries. Give your shoes to someone who needs them more than you. You will receive more in your heart than the shoes you give away. We are all meant to be couriers in that way. I am Nokutenda Marechera. Thank you." She hands the mic back to the deejay and gifts me her page for the book.

I accept it, in awe that she traveled all the way from Africa to be here for me and this experience. "Thank you so much, Nokutenda."

She bows with a sparkle in her brown eyes, her lean body kneels so deeply her forehead nearly touches my knee, then stands and retraces her steps to join the crowd once again.

Everyone is silent. Especially me. I'm not sure anyone knew what to expect from these deliveries, and Nokutenda is a powerful force, setting the bar high. The deejay breaks the silence by yelling out, "You all don't have to be afraid to make noise after each one! Let's show our appreciation for Nokutenda!"

The crowd applauds, careful to maintain a level that would be respectful of Nokutenda's challenge. I slip her page into the journal, fighting the temptation to read her story.

"Okay, member number two, come on up!"

A young woman takes her turn in the center of the stage with a similar disposition to my own and even looks like me with the same height, frame, and facial features. The biggest differentiator is the shade of her light brown hair.

"Wow, kind of a hard act to follow, huh?" Intermittent chuckles rise from the crowd, as she flashes a smile that would make toothpaste companies fight to claim was a result of *their* perfect whitening solution. "Hi, everyone. My name is Alexis Winterland, and I'm from Minneapolis, Minnesota." Cheers ascend from a small group in the middle, which I assume are friends of hers. "Thanks, guys. So, mine is not quite as deep as the previous one. Honestly, I was shocked to be picked at all. It was cool to have something validated that means so much to me. So, thanks, Autumn's family." She points to the crowd as though she knows who and where they are. Maybe my family already met all the Senders.

"Anyway, what changed my life was the day I decided to dance out all my frustrations. I created a two-hour playlist, and I danced that entire time, alone, with no other cares in the world to weigh me down. All the great, empowerment tunes from Janet Jackson to Lizzo and everything in between, but it was one song in particular that got me moving first I was always too shy to dance before, even by myself. But I learned that day how freeing it can be. It changed me. I once struggled with being out in the open, as though I was constantly being judged but dancing taught me—" She caught the deejay's warning look the same time I did.

"Too much information? Sorry. There's more to the story, I promise!" She pushes the mic in his hands, ridding herself of the contraband, which elicits more laughs from the audience. Alexis hands me her page for the book and I mouth a sincere, "Thank you," over the noise of the crowd as she turns with a wave and exits the stage.

After the clapping dies down, the deejay makes the announcement for member number three to join us.

No one comes on stage.

"Uh, member three? You're being paged."

Still, no one.

"Did someone check the porta-potties yet?" the deejay jokes. He turns to look for Karen. "Should we move on to the next one?"

"Whoa, no, hey, I'm here!" A young man calls out with a thick southern accent, jogging to the deck while tugging up his loose jeans. He saunters up the stairs and grabs the mic out of the deejay's hands. "So sorry, y'all. I got all wrapped up in that gorgeous view these folks have out here. Someone is passin' out some pricey cigars, too, so that sure ain't gonna help anyone stay focused."

I join in on the laughter. This man had an infectious personality, with the southern charm to boot.

He runs his hand through his thin, brown hair. He is a couple of inches shorter than me, with a stocky build. "My name is Jer, short for Jeremiah Nation. I'm from the sweet land of Hereford, Texas. That's the United States of America, for those of you not too familiar with it." He pauses as his lighthearted conduct is replaced by a serious tone. "Miss Autumn, this isn't necessarily for me. It's for my late wife, the gorgeous June Bea Crawley-Nation."

The crowd falls into a hushed silence, sensing the weight that this young man is carrying. "I don't want to suck the air out, so don't y'all stop yappin' on my account. But, I want to make sure she's truly honored, which is why I'm here." He faces me directly, and I know that I am the only one privy to the sincerity in his eyes. "What changed June-Bug's life was spending full days pretending she was a kiddo again. She'd go to the zoo, swingin' and slidin' at the playground, buyin' a fun toy at the toy store, watchin' her favorite children's movies, whatever it could be. She lived for eight months longer than the doctors thought she would, and she said it's all 'cause of livin' like a kid again in those final moments of hers."

A tear slides out of his eye, that he is quick to wipe away with his large thumb. "Kids aren't focused on anything but the present, y'all hear me? We need to be more like kids." Handing me the journal page, he chokes out, "You can read about it. She sure would appreciate knowing her great idea is livin' on to help others like it helped her."

"Thank you, Jer. I promise to honor her legacy when I complete this."

He leans down and kisses me on the cheek. "You're as sweet of a thing as she was." Turning to the crowd, he thrusts a fist in the air and yells, "Free cigars for everyone!"

The audience hoots and hollers as Jer continues pumping his fist in the air. He forgets to give the microphone back to the deejay, who has to chase him down to retrieve it.

By the time the last Sender finishes, I am emotionally spent, yet desperate to get off the stage and join the crowd, so I can get to know all thirty more. Such a mosaic display of life-changing experiences, and although some were similar, the people and stories behind them are all vastly different from one another. An astounding seven countries and fifteen U.S. states are represented in the selection.

The deejay finally announces, "We'll take a brief twenty-minute intermission. Autumn will do a quick interview, and then she'll be out to mingle with you all! More food was delivered to the buffet lines, so eat up! Don't hold back! Get to know each other, too." He cranks the volume on the music, which is my cue to run back into the house.

Karen catches me the moment I enter the doors. "Let's go. We're ready for you in the living room."

"I have to hit the bathroom first." My bladder has become my ultimate sudden focus. I'm surprised it lasted this long.

"There's no time." She counters, snapping her fingers.

"Geez, lady. Do you not see her sash? She's the guest of honor." Rose is by my side, as always, quick to defend me.

"Okay, fine, but hurry up." Karen sighs a bit louder than is necessary before stalking away.

Rose rolls her eyes at Karen, then turns back to me. "How amazing is this?" She squeals before noticing the pained look in my eyes. "Oh, no—you go to the bathroom first. We'll talk after."

I sprint to the toilet, my bladder never so grateful to be released as it is in this moment. While I'm washing my hands, my wide eyes stare back at me—they're dancing, shining, reflecting. It's the happiest I've been in much too long—quite the opposite of what I had assumed today would be like.

A knock on the door reminds me there's a clock ticking, and once opened, Karen and Rose are shoulder-to-shoulder in the doorway.

Rose tattles, "I told her to give you a minute."

"Listen, *lady*," Karen enunciates the word to match Rose's use of it earlier. "We're on a tight schedule. It's my job to make sure everything runs on time."

"No, you listen—" Rose's voice rises in irritation.

I put my hand on her arm to calm her down. "I'm good, ready to go. Let's get this interview done with so I can get back out there."

Rose doesn't hide her surprise at my response, but I also catch a glimpse of her pride, like witnessing her child grow into a full adult. I put my arm around her shoulder as we head to the living room. "This time, though, she stays as I do this," I command Karen with the newfound confidence inspired by Nokutenda, not leaving any room for her to object.

Karen concedes. "Three minutes for the interview, and then we'll get you back out there. A few more announcements will come, and then you'll be set free to mingle for the rest of the night."

Being free from the strict agenda is all the motivation I need. "Let's get going then." I sit down on the couch and prepare myself for the second interview.

Kevin randomly appears again. I know this house like the back of my hand and cannot figure out where he hides between interviews. Rose leans against the end of the couch to whisper in my ear, "Ooh, who is that?"

"Who? Kevin?" I ask incredulously. Rose is perceptive. She has to see that Kevin is the spitting image of her dad, which should be a flashing warning sign to run the other way.

"If you're going to be here, you need to get out of the shot." Karen demands.

"Tell me later!" Rose calls out as she moves to the side of the room, slyly waving to Kevin and batting her long eyelashes at him. He takes several glances at her, as she leans her hip against the wall and seductively bites her lip.

Another man pops into the room as Kevin relaxes in his chair. "Oops, sorry—I must have gone the wrong way," the hint of a southern drawl emphasizes his gentle voice. A few inches shorter than Kevin, the man has sandy blonde hair and a build that looks like he does martial arts for fun.

"What are you looking for?" Rose asks.

"Bill said I could get a pen from his den. He gave me directions, and I thought I followed them..." the man drifts, flaunting perfectly straight teeth and dimples in his cheeks. He must be a dentist. Only dentists have smiles like that.

"Ahh, you turned left when you should have turned right. It's across the hall."

"I was bound to find it eventually, right? Sorry for interrupting!" Gone in a flash. He looks familiar, but I can't put my finger on how I know him.

I watch Rose, since she always did have a thing for perfect smiles. That's the type of man she should go for, but her eyes remain focused on Kevin, the man that strikes me as being the epitome of everything she's been actively avoiding her entire life.

Kevin follows my gaze and notices Rose's hungry eyes locked on him. He taps a pen against his bottom lip, almost like a bizarre seductive response to Rose's silent mating call. *Great, now I have a new problem on my hands.* Not even bothering to look at me, Kevin absentmindedly states, "Okay, let's get this interview started."

Four

To walk into the backyard again after completing the second interview feels like walking back into a dream you were sad to wake up from and are now happy to return to. Deejay Ben—I discovered his name from Kevin during the last interview—is lost in his zone. He's dancing with one side of the headphones to his ear, hitting on the eclectic tastes that represent everyone who traveled near and far to be here. Groups of people scatter throughout the yard. If bringing people together is what Bridging the Six Degrees wants to accomplish, this singular event is evidence of the significant impact they can make.

I stay in the shadows close to the house, absorbing the scene, before joining them. It is the first free moment I have to analyze the crowd. I recognize many faces as residents who live in this area, including a few childhood teachers, customers from my waitressing days, and members from our family church. Either people showed up, curious as to what was going on, or they had made an announcement in town to bring in a large crowd.

"Beautiful, right?" I jump at the sound of Karen's voice. I prepare to run into the audience, since I know she'll command me to do exactly that.

But instead of the tightly wound person she has been, a relaxed and calm Karen stands before me. A hint of a smile just barely turns up the corners of her mouth, making her look strangely awkward in the most beautiful way. Apparently not something she is used to doing, but definitely something she should do more.

"This is why it's all worth it," she continues, her voice soft and wistful. "We had an idea many people scoffed at, but we pursued it anyway. We've had to overcome a lot of barriers to make it this far. But look at the networking happening out there." She pauses, sucking in her breath and exhaling. "This is one of many parties we will host. People are connecting on levels that go much deeper than what's on the surface. They wouldn't be standing here together creating lifelong friendships without such a grand reason."

Karen's words sink in as I consider each person that stood on the stage tonight. Even the quietest of them displayed supreme confidence. They each shared a big part of themselves, and not one seemed fearful to do so. "There aren't many times you can be in an environment where you're encouraged to be vulnerable, and it's safely received." Karen's eyes widen, the only time I've seen a pleased expression from her.

"You get it. You should say that the next time you're talking to Kevin. He'd appreciate it." She glances at her watch which immediately conjures her all-business tone once again. "Okay, we have to keep rolling."

I remain by the shadows and wait for Karen's directions, realizing then that Rose never followed me outside. A groan escapes my lips. I already lost her to Kevin.

Karen hustles back to me. Before she can speak, I ask, "Have you seen Rose?"

She covers her headset mic and rolls her eyes, "When I left the room, she and Kevin were talking. My brother never makes the best choices in that department." As though remembering Rose is my friend, she lamely adds, "No offense to her or anything."

"Hey, you and Rose may not get along, but she's pretty damn great." Regret washes over Karen's face the moment she realizes she insulted a client. Since I don't want an empty, forced apology from her, I focus on the news she had just dropped, "Kevin is your brother?"

She clears her throat and straightens her back. "Yes, we started the company together. It's the two of us who do everything, with some part-time contractors on the side."

I am tempted to tell her that Kevin doesn't seem like the biggest winner, considering after the first interview, I am relatively sure he was trying to flirt with me, a married woman whose husband is investing in his company, but I respond with, "That's impressive."

"You don't know the half of it." Karen taps her clipboard, which apparently is the code to stay on track, and swiftly switches the topic, "Deejay Ben will remind everyone what the thirty activities are, then we'll send you down to the crowd. I know you have friends here, but try to keep your focus on the Senders first. Most of them should be around for most of the evening. We told them to make sure they talk to you before they leave, if they need to leave early. Any questions?"

I shake my head. "Nope."

"Okay, good. We'll keep the cameras rolling throughout tonight. Ignore them like they're not even there. No need to make eye contact with the cameramen, capisce?" Easier said than done.

Karen signs "okay" to the deejay as he fades out the current song.

"Ladies and gentlemen," deejay Ben announces in his radio-voice, the tempo reflecting that of a drumroll. "Soon, our guest of honor, Autumn Olson-Goodfield, will be joining the crowd. We know there are several people from Crimson Bay and the surrounding areas here to support her. We thank you for being here. But please, let the selected Senders of Bridging the Six Degrees, meaning anyone with the blue sashes, be the first to talk to her since they have traveled long distances to be here tonight."

He holds a typed sheet of paper in his hands. "Before we release Autumn, let's recap the thirty activities she's been challenged to complete within the next ninety days. And, in no particular order..." As he rambles off the list, the crowd stays unusually quiet. That is, until he gets to, "Don't wear any clothes for one full day."

Cheers erupt, same as they did when Margaret Brethner, a precious lady in her early eighties with white hair and bright blue eyes, hobbled to the microphone and made her introduction. Her face instantly reddened, as I don't think she was prepared for such an outlandish reaction full of whistles from an audience that had been drinking for a few hours. Everyone quickly hushed when she continued, "By freeing myself from clothes that one day and meditating on life, I was forced to become comfortable with the physical scars that decorate my body. A reminder of the hardships that have come my way. Now, I'm no longer ashamed of what I spent most of my life trying to hide."

Margaret had traveled from Nevada with her two daughters who were standing on the other side of the deck. They helped Margaret get down the stairs safely after she handed me her journal page. Their eyes glistened with pride from their mom's story and strength.

"Alright, let's slow down the flow of alcohol. There are a bunch of gutter-minds out there." Deejay Ben lowers his voice, "But for all you ladies out there, be sure to talk to me before you leave tonight."

A mixture of giggles and groans rise from the audience.

"Alright, let's continue. Number thirteen ..."

When he finishes, it's hard to tell whether deejay Ben is as moved as the rest of the crowd, or out of breath from covering the entire list in full. He lets the arm holding the microphone drop to his side in silence.

Hearing each activity separately had been emotional, but hearing them all at once intensified those feelings. When I first heard I would be completing random activities, I assumed I could do all of them in a few days if needed, and mock the ninety-day timeframe. However, now knowing the details, some call for a full week of dedication, and others require more consideration to complete. Regardless, all are a tender investment to honor each person who shared their experiences. I will need to outline a plan to complete them all by the end of October, while still trying to complete my first draft for my literary agent. It may be tough to balance.

After a few moments of peace, deejay Ben declares with a giant wave, "Autumn, you're released!" As I join everyone in the yard, the deejay calls out over the applause, "Somebody get a drink in her hands! She's gonna need it. Me, too!" The beat of the music follows my descent.

As soon as my feet reach the grass, nervousness strikes again as I'm enveloped by hundreds of people all at once.

My mom breaks protocol and comes to my rescue. "Autumn!" She embraces me. "How amazing! Do you love the activities we chose? We had such a hard time only picking thirty!" Before I can respond, she says, "I'm not supposed to be taking up your time, but I wanted you to get to know Nokutenda."

I noticed Nokutenda standing close by—she was impossible not to see—but in no way would I have put together the fact that she and my mom had been talking. I would have assumed my mom was entertaining the locals and not meeting people from other countries.

"Good to see you again, Nokutenda," I stick out my hand to shake hers.

"Likewise." She wraps both of her hands around mine and gives a nod of her head. "Happy birthday to you."

"I've been talking Nokutenda's ear off all night. She's a writer, too." Mom covers her mouth with a napkin. "Oh, goodness, you two are supposed to discover these things on your own. I'm stepping away before I say anything else." She gives an excited wave as she walks away.

"Your mom is a gentle soul full of love." Nokutenda states, her words as strong and powerful as when she stood on stage.

I agree, "Yes, I am very fortunate." I let my eyes drift away from Nokutenda long enough to catch my mom in full conversation with Sandra, a Sender from Ireland. It is shocking to see this side of Mom, especially when it's obvious how energized she is by it. Maybe my travel bug actually comes from her, a secret part of her that she has kept hidden throughout the years next to my dad.

"You're a writer, Nokutenda? Do you write stories?"

"No, *shamwari yangu*, I am only the teller of stories. I share the stories of people who are unable. Ones the world needs to hear."

I could listen to her speak all day, entranced by her ability to choose the most potent words that could concisely paint her point.

"Are these stories from others in Zimbabwe?"

"Some, yes. Others, no. The people I meet tonight may be stories if they so choose." She gestures to everyone surrounding us. "What do you write?"

"Stories that I create in my mind. Sometimes they're dreams, other times they're my take on how I wish things would be." I shrug, pushing my shoulders back to better reflect her level of confidence.

Nokutenda gives me a wide smile that displays a few missing teeth in the front row, a feature that went previously unnoticed, yet makes her even more stunning.

"You are a dreamer."

I laugh as I confirm, "That's what my husband says, too. He reminds me every day."

"Don't ever stop dreaming, beautiful one. Big things happen with even the smallest of dreams."

Chills skate across my arms, causing every hair to come to full attention. "Nokutenda, may I ask why you came so far to be here tonight?"

"Certainly." Her deep brown eyes travel to the evening sky,

and for the first time, I noticed the deep wrinkles set in her skin, making her look older than I first thought she was. "Many years of this life I spent on me. Selfish. I wasn't for others, only for me. You will soon read my story. My life was changed forever. When you believe in something great, the desire to share with others overwhelms all else. This program is a way. I hope your life will be saved from the years I wasted living the wrong way. As I shared, start by always giving your shoes to someone who needs them more. You gain the most when you give the most. Don't stop believing in greater things."

Nokutenda grips my hand with both of hers. "We meet today for a reason. You have my information. You need to go, but we will be in touch. Enjoy speaking with the others."

I don't want to stop talking to her, but she's right, there's only a limited amount of time I have to talk to everyone else, too. I put my other hand on top of hers. "Yes, we will be in touch. Thank you, Nokutenda, for being here tonight and sharing your story with me."

It feels weird to walk away, to know that people traveled to connect with me and being on such a limited clock to have the conversations I really want to have. After Nokutenda and I part, I decide to meet with everyone else in the order they were presented on stage, at least as best as I can remember. It doesn't go quite as planned, but it provides guidance as I seek each one out. Some Senders find me before I can get to the next, and others I have difficulties tracking down amid the large crowd.

Soon, I notice they must be regulated in their time spent with me because they abruptly stop our conversation, some more smoothly than others. When Naomi from Palm Beach, Florida pauses mid-sentence suddenly to tell me goodbye, I probe, "Did they give you a time limit or something?"

She chuckles, pulling back her long blonde hair, and pointing to a little black earpiece in her right ear. "They tell us when time's up."

I whip my head around the video camera shoved in my face,

and search for Karen. Sure enough, she's standing on the chair in the center of the deck, watching my every move, with her clipboard in one hand and a stopwatch in the other. I should have known.

"Don't worry, girl, this isn't the end for us. We'll chat more on the app." Naomi waves goodbye as she joins a group of other Senders having an animated discussion.

I have only a few more to talk to, but desperately need a wine refill. My first glass emptied two hours ago.

"Dry white, please," I request from the bartender. I'm a red drinker by default but want to refrain from purple lips and teeth while talking to everyone. Especially knowing every conversation is being filmed.

"Incredible turnout for you, huh?"

Preparing to respond to the bartender, I instead see the perfect smile from the man who was searching for a pen before my second interview.

He sticks out his hand, "I'm Nathan."

I take his hand and his grip tightens, warming my skin. I've been known, much to my dad's dismay, to date men who have smooth hands, more willing to pay someone else to fix something than to do it themselves. Sometimes, Mark's hands would feel calloused if he used a new piece of equipment at the gym, but it never lasted for long. Admittedly, it's always a turn-on to shake what Rose and I refer to as "true man's hands," and Nathan had the rough hands of a farmer that would make my dad proud.

Nathan laughs, which brings me back to reality as I realize I am still shaking his hand, far past the acceptable time to do so with a stranger. For a moment, I wonder if I called his hands "true man's hands" out loud, too.

I let go and wrap my arms around my waist, like a makeshift straitjacket. "Have we met before?"

"Oh, I just assume anyone from here knows me. You know, small area and all." He outstretches his arm to reference our little

Door County community. He must have grown up here too, which is why he looks familiar. We've probably walked by each other many times before. "I'm sure it's been a long night for you."

I only nod, struggling to speak as my brain disconnects from my mouth. Long day. Powerful night. The exhaustion is catching up to me and Nathan's eyes makes me want to share the intensity that has been burning through me since I woke up this morning, like a therapist hypnotizing me for the truths deep within. But profound statements are bound to come out in a blubbering mess at this point, and that's all a little too much to dump on a stranger. Silence is the better option.

"I've been waiting all night for a chance to talk to you, so I'm glad we both ended up here." Nathan leans into the bar, resting his right elbow on the counter.

"Here you go, ma'am," the bartender interrupts, handing over a newly poured glass of wine. I reach for it, relieved to have something I can use as a crutch.

Before I can ask why Nathan has been waiting to talk to me, Karen appears from whatever shadow she lurks in, annoyingly clicking the pen in her hand. "Is this a local?"

Shrugging, I answer, "I'm not sure, I just met him."

"Do you see a blue sash on him?" She motions to Nathan's shirt, making a needlessly flippant point.

I seize the opportunity to look at him again, even though I know he isn't wearing a sash. I already had his cobalt plaid button-down shirt noted, because it highlights the ocean blue tones of his eyes, providing a brief calming respite from the continual buzz I've felt all night. "Um, nope."

"Only blue sashes, Autumn. Not shirts. Sashes. You have three more to go. Then you can talk to whomever you want."

Nathan stands behind her with his finger pointed to his head, turning it in circles as if to say, "She's crazy."

I stifle my laugh, causing spittle to fly out of my mouth. I wipe at it with my finger, embarrassed. But when Nathan contagiously laughs, I can't help but join him, especially when I see the appalled look on Karen's face. She's concerned about the way everything looks. This is a big event for their company, and I recognize that, but I am also loopy from the enervation of the day and will not be able to hold a front for much longer.

She snatches the wine out of my hand. "Maybe you should wait on this."

"Hey! It's only my second drink of the night, I'm fine."

"Hmm," Karen isn't convinced. "Three more Senders, Autumn. Let's go. You won't have to see me for the rest of the night once that's done."

That is all the motivation I need.

"Don't worry," Nathan says, "I have nowhere else to be. I'll wait for you."

The mystery of *why* he wants to talk to me consumes me, but Karen jostles me away. "I'll find you when I'm done." I call out to him over my shoulder.

"You better." He winks, causing my heart to flutter ever so lightly.

The nostalgic music, soft lighting, and romantic atmosphere generated by the water's energy is the perfect brew for magnifying the most minor exchange between two people. Growing up here, I recognize that truth, because there have been many nights I've been swept away by the vibe, only to wake up the next morning wondering what I was thinking. Nonetheless, I can't stop replaying Nathan's wink in my head, even as I talk to the others.

If I were writing the fictional version of that scene, it would have gone differently. The girl would have played coy while radiating a subtle and alluring confidence—touching his arm as she laughs, holding her ground with flirting, wanting to know the answer but deliciously extending the anticipation of the truth, as though she's the one in control of everything happening next. The man would be playing into her every word and reeling in every minute she gives him. He would be purely captivated, his eyes drifting to her lips as much as they hold onto her eyes, knowing he found the type of girl he has always been searching for, and wondering how he could make her his.

I silently chide myself, knowing real life isn't like the novels I write. But sometimes it'd be more fun if it could be.

Five

THE POPCORN CEILING, WITH A REPUTATION FOR concurrently soothing and irritating me throughout the years, looms above. Multiple renovation periods in my parents' house, yet the sparkly bumps always survived.

Yawning, I pull the ruffled comforter closer to my face. When I found out I was pregnant with a girl, my parents redecorated my old bedroom with everything they saved from my childhood that I didn't take with me, imagining she may stay in this room on our return visits. An array of stuffed animals wave from their perch in a corner hammock, each labeled with a name in black permanent marker. I once had big plans to save every animal in the world. Since my parents never let me have a pet, I had to rescue what I could, found in the form of stuffed animals instead of real ones.

5:12 a.m. flashes in red from the retro rectangular clock on the nightstand. I had, at most, three hours of sleep. Despite the continued exhaustion from yesterday, electricity is still pumping through my veins.

Thirty people from around the world traveled here to share their personal stories, hoping I may have a similar life-changing experience from emulating it. *Wow.* I'll never enjoy being the center of attention, but last night was created with such care and intentionality that it remedied my stage fright.

At first, I doubted how well Mark knows me. The concept of such a large party thrown for an introvert was a lousy idea on paper, but in truth, it was so much more than that.

Mark. I check my cell phone for messages. There is only a text from him that reads,

> I hope it's everything they made it sound like it would be. I can't wait to hear what you think. I love you. My heart is there with you.

I exhale to push out the guilt that swells inside. With slow-moving fingers, I write,

> Just woke up, going to sleep some more. It was great, I'll call you later. Miss you.

Erasing the last two words, I replace them with,

> Love you.

I hit the send button and place the phone face down on the table, so the camera won't detect the wounded expression on my face. Remorse can cause paranoia.

Covering my head with my pillow, I attempt to block out specific guilt-ridden memories of last night. But the flashback comes rushing at me:

As soon as I said goodbye to the last Bridging the Six Degrees Sender, Jessi was waiting.

"A!" She ran to me, jumping on my back with a borderline chokehold. Jessi barely crosses the five-foot threshold. Self-conscious of her tiny frame, she displays her strength any opportunity she's able to seize, even in the form of a hug.

"I didn't know you could make it tonight!" I exclaimed.

"Sorry, I meant to let you know. It's been nonstop at The

Bridge. I've scooped up as many hours as I can while the season is hot." Jessi has worked as a waitress at Bridgette's Café—called The Bridge by locals for short—since she was fourteen years old. She swore she made better money than a regular full-time job so never saw a point in leaving. It was true. Money was flowing through the most popular restaurant in Door County.

"It's so good to see you!" She slid off my back, and we embraced in a real hug.

Once we let go, she dragged me to the bar. "You and I have some catching up to do! I've heard about all the drinking you've been doing with Rose. My turn!" She pounded her hand on the bar counter. "Bartender, I need four shots of whatever you've got back there. Pronto!"

"Jess, I've already had a couple glasses of wine."

"Now this is just you and me. You owe me." She shoved a shot glass filled to the brim with vodka in my hand. She held hers in the air, "Happy Birthday!" We clinked glasses and threw the liquor in the back of our throats. "Besides," she reached for the second round, "you're off duty now, right?"

My muscles relaxed. Everything planned for me was over; I could enjoy the rest of the party without Karen breathing down my neck. Even the cameramen stopped following me around. I reached for the second glass as we repeated the burning of our throats from our dear old friend, Vodka—a regular guest in our trio throughout the years.

Once that second shot kicked in, mixed with the wine and exhaustion of the day, the night dissolved into fragments. I remember hugging many bodies, although I'm not sure if I cuddled some people instead of hugging. Most of the Crimson Bay residents who attended stuck around late, taking advantage of the free drinks and food, and my parents' incredible view of the lake, as the water reflected shimmering crescents skipping throughout. Everything about the scene breathed comfort, child-hood, home, and summer.

Unfortunately, I also recall catching Rose and Kevin in the

middle of a heavy make-out session. I'm sure they didn't hear me walk into the living room, and I walked out muttering, "No, no, no, no."

I remember walking back out to the yard at one point to the emptiest it had been all night. Someone mentioned that it was already one o'clock in the morning. *Time to get home.* I believe it was my dad, who was urging me, and everyone else awake, to go to bed. I wanted to find Jessi though, so I ignored him and continued my trek through the dark backyard. I should have listened to my dad.

For whatever reason, after being unable to locate Jessi, the end of the boat pier beckoned me—per the vodka-induced part of my mind. I stumbled out of my sandals and managed to make it to the edge of the dock without falling into the water. Dangling my legs over the side, I reclined on the wooden slats to observe the clear night dotted with stars and a luminous moon—absolutely heavenly.

My eyes were closed. I was drifting into sleep, when heavy footsteps, vibrating the pier, caused me to open them once again.

Two water bottles were blocking the night sky. "Thirsty?" Blue eyes appeared over the bottles. It was Nathan.

He sat down next to me, pulling on my arm to help me sit up so I could take a drink. My body had failed to communicate how parched I was. I gulped down the bottle without skipping a beat.

"Whew, good thing I brought a second one." He chuckled as he sat it between us.

I yawned, unable to control my body. Making a good impression would not happen after mixing my drinks, and I wasn't putting up a fight.

"I'm sorry I didn't find you earlier," I said.

"Don't you apologize for a thing. There were a lot of people here to see you tonight. I didn't expect to be at the top of that list, especially when, as that bossy lady pointed out, I wasn't wearing a fancy sash."

Nathan was at the top of the list more than he realized. He

shouldn't be, but he intrigued me. Not to mention, the party ambiance, blended with a new, good-looking stranger had my fiction-writing-driven mind retreating to its dark corner of possibilities.

"Did you have fun tonight?" I was struggling to concentrate on anything other than the inside of my eyelids and the fact that he smelled so damn good. Spending many nights on this pier, I had become accustomed to the overwhelming aroma of fish. Now all I could discern was Nathan's cologne, intense hints of melon, suede, musk, and amber wafting, compelling me to lean in closer to him to breathe it in as subtly as someone clearly drunk could do.

"I'm sure everyone had fun. Such an awesome way to celebrate a birthday."

"So, you're from around here?"

"Lived in Ephraim since I was eight years old."

"What? How do I not know you? We're practically related then."

Nathan snorted in agreement. "You graduated four years before I did, so that played a part. Nathan Vertz."

Although the Vertz family was prominent in the area, I could only vaguely remember a Nathan Vertz. "Wait, weren't you..." I started that sentence before my mind could adequately formulate the rest to not be offensive.

"Heavy? Fat? Husky? Freckled-faced? So maybe that's the reason you don't remember me." He winked at me for the second time that night, making my stomach flip once again, although I'm not sure if it was from his wink or my embarrassment. "Yes, to all the above. I still did all right with the ladies, though."

I giggled. "Oh, I'm sure you did." Immediately, I regretted my flirtatious tone, and sat up straighter, willing myself to play it cool.

"I hope you don't mind that I dropped by the party. The news station gave an open invite to the entire town, and I was curious. Besides, I needed to meet you."

Now it made sense why there were so many other people

there. But why did he feel like he had to meet me? That was the second time he mentioned it, as though he was compelled, like he couldn't resist. Did the invitation have information about me that piqued his interest?

Before I could pose the question, nausea struck me in the gut. Everything had been happening in slow motion; suddenly, it was as though someone hit fast forward, and I couldn't keep up. Heat filled my body as I leaned over the edge of the pier. Vomit sailed out of my mouth, and I heaved and made noises that no one should ever have to hear. It was like a dying animal.

As sweat dampened my face, Nathan held my hair and rubbed my back. I was sure the puking would never end.

Finally, when nothing was left inside of me, I shoved my body back, pulling my legs up so I could hide my face in my knees, wholly embarrassed.

"Do you need anything? Take another drink of water. Don't drink too much, though." Nathan's voice filled with concern.

I obeyed and took a small swig, pausing to let it slide down my throat. I had another small sip for good measure to ease my burning throat.

"Do you want me to go get anything or anyone?"

I shook my head. "No, I'll be okay." Although I'd rather be alone to suffer in my humiliation and misery, I couldn't stand the idea of him walking away without knowing why he needed to meet me, even despite my dismal state.

"This will sound strange but try it with me." Nathan turned his body so that we were sitting across from each other, forcing me to look straight at him for the first time at the pier, the moon reflecting off his white teeth in the dark night. Sticking out his thumb, he directed, "Play thumb wars with me."

"What?" I didn't think I heard him correctly.

"C'mon, play thumb wars with me. My mom used to do this anytime I felt ill to get my mind off of it. Trust me, it works."

Reluctantly, I held out my hand as our fingers instinctively gripped each other's. Nathan's calloused fingers pressed into mine even more than our initial handshake, and the same warmth—a pleasant warmth this time—filled my entire body.

Together, the memories of the childhood game came back as we chanted, "one, two, three, four, I declare a thumb war," in unison. Our thumbs fought each other for several minutes, both of us proving to be quite strategic and competitive. We were grunting and laughing until finally, I pinned his thumb down.

Still grasping each other's fingers, I asked, "You didn't let me win on behalf of being sick, did you?"

He grinned. "It was the gentlemanly thing to do."

"Oh no, you don't let me win. Bring your best game, sir," I challenged.

"One, two, three, four, I declare a thumb war." This time, he pinned me within seconds.

"Geez, how in the world do you have so much thumb strength?"

"Daily thumb exercises," he deadpanned, bending his thumb back and forth for emphasis.

I poked him in the arm with my finger.

"I don't know. I help my grandpa farm, and I build furniture when I'm not working. I do a lot with my hands, I guess." His confirmation of everything I had assumed so far only heightened my attraction to him.

"I figured." I mumbled.

"What?" He was smirking, so I'm sure he heard me.

"You've got nice hands." *Autumn, shut your mouth.*

"Why thank you, but flattery won't help you win the next one."

We played several more rounds of thumb war. I'm not sure how many, but I know I lost more than I won, which propelled me to keep playing again and again, my competitive nature impossible to pacify when losing. By the time we couldn't pop our knuckles anymore, we had tears streaming down our faces from laughter.

Nathan positioned his body to sit next to me again, with the water as our primary view. Nudging my arm tenderly with his elbow he asked, "You feel better?"

It was the first time in twenty minutes I had thought about my mortifying vomiting episode from earlier. I had to give it to him. "You're right, that trick works."

"My mom was a master of distraction. She taught me about the power of the mind. It's a powerful tool at our disposal."

I was having trouble fighting my heavy eyes, ready to find my bed, yet there was a crucial question that needed answering.

"You said earlier you needed to meet me. Why?"

I prepared myself for a response that comes from romantic movies. The type when the man tells the woman he just knew he had to talk to her because something imperative was drawing them together. Despite knowing that he missed his chance because another man had already claimed her, he would forever cling to what little hope remained of the future because they were meant to be. I wasn't sure how I would respond after those words tumbled out of his mouth. There was no doubt I was drawn to him, especially in this quixotic air, which made it more challenging to block impure thoughts and what if's of an impulsive romance.

"Your husband is Mark, right?"

I nodded slowly. Mark. The one word from Nathan that could instantly sober me.

"He called a few weeks ago and said that you needed to sell your cottage. I've been in real estate for the past eight years, the best in the county according to most people here. I was hoping to schedule a time to talk more and snap pictures, so we can get the process started. I have no doubt it'll be swooped up quickly from the little I know already. Too bad the event tonight wasn't held there. Would have been excellent marketing."

My dry mouth drooped. It was a far cry from what I envisioned. This man had entered my life only to sell off a large part of who I am. There wasn't an underlying dreamy story; this man was motivated to meet me because he would earn money from selling my most prized possession.

The one that Mark wants to get rid of, not me.

I stood up and Nathan quickly followed, reaching his hand out to steady me.

"Yeah, Mark told me a realtor would call," I fought the disenchantment in my voice, saving face from the foolishness that had my mind summoning wild thoughts and premature undeveloped feelings. "You can come over Wednesday any time. I'll be home." Turning away from him, I stumbled toward my parents' house in my inebriated state, my bare feet smacking loudly against the wooden dock with every step.

"Do you need any help?" Nathan called out.

I waved a flailing hand in the air in a silent effort to communicate I was fine.

"Okay, see you on Wednesday! Happy Birthday!" he cheerily replied.

I had been disappointed that Nathan wasn't attracted to me like some stupid romantic movie. Even worse, I wanted to flirt and have this untouchable, exciting magnetism under the moonlight with a man that wasn't my husband.

Which is why this morning greets me with a heavy dose of mortification that seeps straight to the pit of my stomach, as though all my internal motivations could be seen by everyone.

I pull the pillow tighter against my face to hide my groans. *What is wrong with me? Why would I want that?*

A deep voice inside responds with the truth. Mark was supposed to be everything I could desire. A man that was a walking reflection of classic heartthrobs like Jimmy Stewart and Cary Grant, as they swooped in and saved the heroine from a life she didn't know she needed saving from until she met her man. A man that you know you need to hold on to because he's one in a million.

There was a moment in time when I could not get enough of

Mark. I had a history of dating Midwestern boys who I swear all had mamas linked together in the same club, because everyone knew everyone's business, sending endless juicy messages to my mom about every detail of my relationship before I had a chance to tell her myself. Not to mention the first, real heartbreak I ever felt when my first love decided to run off with my arch nemesis behind my back.

Then lo and behold, my mourning period was cut short when I scored a fresh part-time recruiting gig in Green Bay and was introduced to Mark. He is brilliant, constantly searching for ways to improve the world, and he truly cares about each person he meets. It's why his nickname is "Counselor," given to him when he was only ten years old, proving it's the way Mark has always been wired. His brain is always working to identify problems and discover a solution that would be just the ticket to fixing you, and therefore fixing the world. The only thing he didn't know how to fix was the brokenness between us.

I *thought* we talked about all the important topics in our heated dating days, but in hindsight, I can see all the assumptions I made with little verbal confirmation from Mark. He knew I wanted three kids, and he played into it on our third date when we brainstormed names for our future kids while eating sushi in the twinkling Manhattan lights after he flew me out to be at a conference with him. That's when I first thought this could be something real. Our future was already in motion with that conversation. He was great with my nieces and nephews once he met them, a natural dad in training. Then, when I discovered I was pregnant, we skipped the engagement announcement and immediately surprised everyone with a wedding. I was elated. It made sense. It felt right. Our tiny family—a beautiful fairy tale.

Then the sky darkened, crimson flowed out between my legs in the middle of the night, and we lost her before I could hold her, before anyone could know her. Amelia was her name. I waited a year before I brought up actually trying this time for another baby. It took Mark another six months to admit he doesn't want kids like I do, the truth of it converting into an acidic burn defacing my heart. Amelia wasn't an answer to a lifelong dream for him like she was for me. He doesn't want another child at all. "Isn't that the best part about being an uncle? About being an aunt? We can still love on the kids without having to stop our lives."

"That's your concern? You think our lives would stop with kids?"

Mark had paused on packing long enough to look me in the eyes and point to the suitcase open on the bed. "We couldn't do this. Leave on a whim to Bermuda. We couldn't see the world so easily. I couldn't run this company. Not as successfully without constant guilt, anyway." He took a step toward me just to rub my arm and say, "We have the best of both worlds this way. Surely you see that, too." Then he returned to packing and that was it. I left the room and tried to lose myself in a two-hour bubble bath, the agony of Amelia's absence surfacing again. My chance at being the mom I always dreamed about was gone. I was meant to have three —the clarity in my spirit for that is still so strong. She was one of three. I wouldn't have thought Mark didn't want kids; but he was right when he reminded me that he never uttered the words that he *did* want them. He just went along with my own dreams, knowing I would always be by his side while he chased his.

It hurts to think about those very first days because I miss him —the old him—and I miss us. To be honest, I miss the old me, too.

Henry had once told me that you can never escape who you were born to be. I've only just arrived in Crimson Bay and already I'm feeling the pull. It's like I've spent the past four years trying on several ill-fitting costumes for roles that I was never meant to fill. Thirty years old already feels different. Suddenly, I feel more ready than ever to shed those other identities, step off stage, and just be myself again.

Six

"You're not up yet?" My mom taps on the door before pushing her way inside. "What happened to you never wanting to miss a moment of daylight?"

The bed sinks as she sits down next to me. I roll over and glance at the clock, noting the time surged to 8:17 a.m. Mark never sleeps past five-thirty, so I had become accustomed to that over the years. *He's* the one who never wants to miss a moment of daylight; if I'm sleepy, I don't mind as much. "I've been staying up late since I've been back. Who knew Crimson Bay would tap into the party animal inside of me?"

Mom brushes my mess of hair out of my face. "I'm proud to declare that I've never had a daughter who is a party animal."

Snorting, I retort, "I'm not sure what your definition is, but it must not be drinking way too much, which is what I've done." I touch my pounding forehead, desperate for the nasty pink concoction that is stocked in my cottage and cures hangovers instantly. I can't drink like I used to. It's part of the maturity cycle. Now, I'm paying for it.

"If I know you at all, I have a feeling you're done with that for a while."

"You do know me because I would be if I could. But I have to drink a one-thousand-dollar bottle of wine at some point if you recall, so that won't last for long."

Mom reaches for Snorty, a well-loved brown stuffed pug sitting on the nightstand. "I'm hopeful that I raised you well enough to invite your mom to partake in drinking that fancy bottle of wine." She sighs as her gaze extends past the door to the empty hallway. "That was quite a party last night, huh? A lot of interesting people who have done amazing things came from all around the world for you."

I sit up in bed, leaning against the white framed headboard. "You sure came alive last night." My mom, the unforeseen social butterfly at the party, spent most of her time with all the out-of-towners.

"Your old mom still has a few surprises in her now and then." She says dreamily while petting Snorty's soft body. "Did you enjoy it?"

Taking a deep breath, I prepare myself for the "I told you so" that was bound to come as a response. "Surprisingly, I did."

Mom pats my hand. "Good to hear you admit it. I could tell you were nervous, but Mark knows you well. He's a good man." I can't count the number of times I've heard that throughout the years. It's as though the universe is continually reminding me that I scored big and should forever be grateful.

"Yeah, thanks for all your help, too. I'm sure you guys had a lot of work to do with Mark not being here."

"It was worth it, honey. We all had a lot of fun. We love you." Tears well in her eyes as she reaches for a tissue off the nightstand.

I cover her hand with mine. "Mom, I'm here for three months. No need to get emotional yet." I glance at the clock, "Besides, I'm supposed to be meeting up with Jessi and Rose. No goodbyes yet, okay?"

She wraps her arms around my shoulders. "Are you coming back for dinner tonight?"

"Sure, Mom."

She drags her hand along the wall of my bedroom as she

leaves, like the room will be moving to Italy, too. But maybe she knows it's finally time to redecorate the pink bedroom and come to terms with it as well.

Reaching for my phone again, I send Rose a text.

Breakfast, please.

It doesn't take long for my phone to buzz with a reply from her,

Already gotcha covered. 15 minutes.

I take a quick shower, pull my wet hair back, and throw on the wrinkled t-shirt and jeans stuffed in the bag Rose brought. I won't be the only disheveled one. After a night of drinking, Jessi will surpass me in that area. Rose, on the other hand, will look flawless as always.

As soon as I step out onto the porch, Rose pulls into the drive, perfect timing as usual. I jog to her car and slide into the passenger seat. Noticing the empty backseat, I ask, "No Jessi?"

"She hooked up with some guy last night. She won't return my texts, so I told her to meet up with us whenever she gets out of her drunken state of mind." Rose hands me a greasy, brown sack. "Breakfast, as you requested. Coffee is next to you."

I peer into the bag, the fatty, yet mouth-watering aroma filling my nose meant only one thing: breakfast sandwiches from Sunshine Café complete with greasy hash browns. My stomach growls and churns simultaneously.

"Thanks." I close the sack, preparing my stomach for what's about to visit. "I don't think she's the only one that hooked up with a guy last night." I raise my eyebrows at her.

"Oh, did you wake up with someone in your pink, frilly, little girl bed this morning?" She retorts, not missing a beat.

"Rose, I'm married," I reply, a bit too defensively.

"Geez, relax. I was kidding."

I take a deep breath, pushing thoughts of Nathan out of my mind. "I know, sorry. I'm a little tired."

"Don't make it a long day on us. Find your energy ball and squeeze whatever is left in it. Immediately." Rose readjusts her oversized tortoise glasses. "Anyway, yes, as you're so cleverly referring to, I had some fun with that Kevin guy last night. But no, we did not sleep together. I'm a lady, thank you very much."

I huff, "Since when?"

"Since last night! I know his type. I'm not the first girl at these parties he's tried to get with. But man," she grazes her cerise-glazed lips with her finger, "he's a great kisser."

"Did you make plans to see each other again?"

Rose turns the vehicle into a lake overlook, puts it in park, and rolls down the windows. She snatches the bag from me. "Bacon or sausage?"

"Bacon."

She pulls out the food before crumpling the bag and throwing it in her backseat. Pushing her manual seat as far back as it will go, she rests the back of her head against it as she unwraps her sandwich. "I went back to my place last night. Without him. He asked if I wanted to meet him for breakfast this morning."

"And you said...?"

Taking a bite of her sandwich and chewing slowly, she responds with, "No. Obviously."

Rose never reacts so sluggishly to conversations, even when sick enough to be on her deathbed. She's the most quick-witted person I know and continually in tune with how she thinks and feels. I admire that about her.

"What aren't you telling me?"

Watching the birds dip in and out of the water, she says, "Nothing. I don't know. Maybe something. That kiss..." She takes another bite of her sandwich and chews. "Well, all the kisses. They were different. Special. Made me feel things I haven't felt before. It sounds stupid, and maybe it is. I wish he weren't that type of guy."

I am shocked into a stupor. Rose picks this guy, out of all men, to think the kisses were special with?

"What type?" I ask, even though I know exactly what she means.

"A douchebag who knows he's on the verge of something amazing and girls will come running to him without him having to try at all."

And there's the root of all Rose's fears when it comes to relationships. It's why she keeps men at arm's length and bails before it can get serious. When her father walked out on her and her mom when she was eight years old, they both went through three years of individual hell before picking up the pieces and becoming the strongest women I know. Her father, Rick, had a string of repeating affairs on the frequent route of clubs his band would play at, from Minnesota to Wisconsin.

Rose tried writing him letters for years afterward, but he never responded. She looked him up on Facebook about ten years ago, saw he was now married again with two kids and the proud owner of a hundred classic guitars and three guitar shops in the Minneapolis area. She never talked about him again. It's why it scared me so much that Kevin reminded me of Rick, like Rose was unknowingly drawn to someone just like her dad, despite how careful she's been to avoid that exact pitfall over the years.

I'd already pigeonholed Kevin as the guy who lived for himself, traveled the world, and moved from one girl to the next long before Rose shared any of this with me. But Rose is the type where if I express my concerns, she'll set out to prove me wrong. I know I have to let her go through this her way if she decides to keep seeing him, and be there for her when it goes south.

After a period of silence, Rose slides her sunglasses to the top of her head and angles her body toward me. "Why in the world am I doing all the talking? How was last night for you? You were strutting around like a gorgeous movie star in the spotlight. I'm proud of you for embracing it." Her eyes dance with excitement, but I know her well enough to see the twitch of something—or someone—else plaguing her thoughts.

I blow on my coffee to cool it down. Sunshine Café makes the hottest coffee possible. It's a lawsuit waiting to happen, except that Mary, the owner for fifty-five years, always directly hands it to the customers, repeating the same thing every time with a twinkling smile in her Mary Poppins singsong voice, "Specially roasted just for you, darlin'." A person could have the worst day in the world, but that one interaction with Mary would turn it around. She is deemed the fairy godmother of Door County for a reason.

"Somewhat. Still processing. It was pretty incredible."

"Damn right it was! Now *I* want to find a sugar daddy who can throw me a party like that! I can't even imagine how much it cost!"

I cringe, sensitive anytime someone mentions Mark's money, as though it's the only reason I married him. I ignore her reference. "They have those online-only options. I'm sure those aren't too pricey. At least you'd still get the challenges portion."

"But to have people come from all over the world for me? That's so cool!"

"Well, if you'd have breakfast with the guy who created it, I'm sure he'd throw you your own party. Or, skip the breakfast and sleep with him."

Rose throws her greasy napkin at me. "Are we going to tackle this list or keep talking nonsense?"

I groan as I dig for the Bridging the Six Degrees list from my purse. "You can never chill for a few minutes, can you? Always whippin' the horse to go faster."

"I'm assuming you're the horse in this scenario?"

"You mounted a stallion last night. Now you're whipping a poor mare as a distraction."

"Ahh!" Rose groans as she forces the car in reverse. "You are not allowed to talk for the rest of the day!"

I hit a nerve with her and can't hold back my laughter. As

precarious as the risk he poses to break her heart may be, I've never seen her squirm over a man like this before.

We drive to Walmart in silence. I welcome the quiet to continue processing my thoughts now that I have a little fuel in me. Karen had compiled a list of suggested items that could be purchased for the challenges since, according to her, that can be the overwhelming part (although I would argue that the party and public interviews are even more so).

In the short distance walking from the car to the store, I notice not one, but several people pointing at me. I tug on Rose's sleeve and whisper, "Am I being paranoid?"

"Nope! You're a town-wide celebrity now!" She grins widely and pointedly waves at everyone we pass. "You were on the front page of the paper and on the evening and morning news."

I divert my eyes to the ground, proving I would be a terrible celebrity. On the contrary, the paparazzi wouldn't be able to get enough of Rose. I can only imagine her slinking into different poses as she saunters into Walmart.

As soon as I hear the "whoosh" of the doors as they open, I detour to the women's accessories before anyone else notices me. I set my eyes on an olive-colored, distressed baseball hat and pull it over my eyes.

"Would you like to check out the sunglasses, too?" Rose amusedly watches with crossed arms. "My goodness, Autumn. Some people spend their whole life searching for their fifteen minutes of fame. Here's yours, and you're hiding from it!"

"I write stories for a reason. I put characters in the spotlight and hide behind them. I don't seek attention for myself."

Rose juts out her bottom lip into a pout. "Are you saying I do?"

"You welcome it more than I do."

Rose uncrosses her arms and shrugs. "No denying that, I suppose. I'll get us a cart."

I hear Rose returning before I actually see her, steering this contraption that's falling apart. She's chosen a cart with the most rusted, rickety wheels possible to garner even more attention. Rose holds her head up high, a smirk plastered on her face, aware her intentions are known.

Attempting to be nondescript with the hat was pointless now. "You better be glad I love you more than I hate you."

"Our love-hate relationship is what keeps the passion alive, honey pie." She mimics a man's southern drawl, which eerily sounds like Nathan's, and smacks my butt for emphasis.

Pulling out Karen's list, we scour the aisles for something that could work as a time capsule and settle on a metal storage box with a lock. Following up with the stationery and baking sections, our cart is full in no time. At the checkout, I pay with the Bridging the Six Degrees prepaid card, which tracks all purchases made.

"It's like having a second sugar daddy, huh?" Rose comments nonchalantly as she picks through the magazine rack.

"Yep. You'll understand when you're using Kevin's credit cards for purchases. Or did he already transfer money into your account after last night?"

Turning red in the cheeks, Rose turns on her heel to head for the door, muttering, "Touché."

So far, the only thing I like about Kevin is being able to use him as retaliation for Rose's banter.

Not long after we arrive at my house to unload our Walmart haul, Jessi enters the front door and flings herself on a barstool at the kitchen island. She flips on the TV, muting it out of respect since we already have the radio on. It's her typical grand entrance.

"Where did you disappear to last night? I tried to find you again."

"Ugh," Jessi grunts. "One too many."

Rose wrinkles her nose. "You weren't stupid enough to drive home, were you?"

"Oh, I'm sorry, but the couch was taken, so I didn't have a place to crash."

That is all it takes to end Rose's role in the repartee.

"I had a ride, thank you very much. In fact, I didn't even make it home." Jessi lifts her head high with green eyes sparkling.

"Spill the beans. Who's the guy?" As tough as Jessi acts sometimes, she's a hopeless romantic like I am. Regrettably, she still chooses to occupy herself with man after man. We have come to expect the flavor of the week announcements and usually live vicariously through her sexual trysts, a selfish benefit of her state of wild freedom.

"No smart-ass comment from you, Rose. I actually like the guy. I don't know if you remember him from school, Autumn, but it's Nathan Vertz."

My heart beats faster as I focus on pouring the flour in the mixer for the chocolate chip cookie dough. I wonder if he said anything about me, or my embarrassing vomiting episode.

Jessi takes my silence the wrong way.

"I know, I know. He was such a nerd back in the day." She pulls wavy strands of brunette hair on her shoulder to braid. "But now, yeah, age has done him well."

"You're cougaring," Rose interjects. It now makes sense why Rose didn't react to Nathan the way I thought she would have when he walked into the room last night.

"He's not that young! And we're not that old!"

I act like I have minimal interest, even though I am desperate to know more. "So, a one-time hookup or been dating for a while?" I keep my eyes on the cookie dough.

"We've gone out a few times. Hung out. Dates, I think. I don't know. It's like we're testing the friendship boundaries."

Rose scoops in baking soda and heckles, "You'll be doing that for a while."

Jessi throws a chocolate chip at her. "I could be the one. You never know. Someone's gotta be."

I finally look up. "The one?"

"He's a virgin. Or claims to be." Rose rolls her eyes. "Jessi is targeting a twenty-five-year-old virginal man."

"Hey, he pursued me!"

"But you said you two stayed the night together," I point out as a surprising, twinge of jealousy shoots through me.

"They have junior-high style sleepovers." Rose barely gets the sentence out of her mouth before she's snorting due to stifling her laughter.

Jessi crosses her arms, pouting. Rose's laugh is infectious though, and I catch Jessi's lips tempted to curl up, despite her best effort to frown.

Rose sticks up her hands. "I'm sorry, Jessi. There's nothing wrong with his decision. In fact, I respect him. He's just the opposite of you in every way. I can't imagine you restraining yourself."

"Have you done anything physical at all?"

"She means outside of playing in that softball league together," Rose mocks, clearly finding humor in all her jabs.

Jessi positions herself so she's blocking Rose, suggesting the conversation is between her and me now. "Held hands, and he's kissed me a couple of times."

Apparently, Nathan likes her type, which is more proof that he was never interested in me, only in selling my cottage. My disappointment is annoyingly clear. I'm married, I know this. But being back home, away from Mark, I slip into the person I once was before he entered my life. Meeting Nathan at the party last night was a reminder of the electricity that once made flirting and dating fun, sexy, and enthralling. I miss those days. It feels good to feel wanted, and lately, I don't feel so desired by Mark.

Jessi never has that problem, hooking any man she's ever wanted. She has the "it" factor men crave with stunning good looks. I've always accepted it, but now envy stirs within me. Her freedom, her life choices, and now because she can openly pursue Nathan, a man I would shout "dibs!" on if I didn't have Mark.

"Do you think I'm crazy, A?" Jessi whispers, even though Rose can still hear every word.

"No." I reluctantly respond, as I swirl the wooden spatula around the bowl one more time to make sure the batter is mixed well. "He seems like a good guy."

"He is! You should hear the old ladies talk about him at The Bridge when he comes in. They're all in love with him. Daphne and Bridgett live down the street, so he'll mow their yards, shovel snow, bring in their trash cans, even go out hunting for Midnight each time that old cat escapes, which you know is every day. I wonder if Daphne lets him out on purpose now that I think about it…"

"Sounds like you've got a real Prince Charming there."

"Or, he *really* likes cougars." Rose teases.

"Rose!" Jessi exclaims with her hands on her hips.

I push the bowl of cookie dough towards Rose and try to shush her. "How about you start rolling the balls?"

Rose takes the bowl and flippantly says, "Jessi should be rolling the balls to keep her skills fresh since she won't be practicing on any real balls anytime soon."

Jessi stomps out of the kitchen, hurls herself on the couch, and picks up a magazine. Even if Rose hadn't offended her, she would have removed herself from baking cookies. She's more of a burnt toast kind of girl.

I squat by the couch. "Nathan introduced himself last night. Mark asked Nathan to sell this place. He seems like a nice guy."

Jessi sits up, exclaiming, "Oh he is! The nicest. And isn't he hot now?"

Nodding, I confirm, "Yeah. He's handsome."

"Thank you." She boasts proudly, as though she designed him herself. "But Nathan didn't say anything about selling your house."

"Maybe he doesn't want to mix business with pleasure?" I offer as a reason.

"Maybe…" Jessi hates being left in the dark.

"How many dates have you been on with him?"

She wraps her hair around her finger. "I don't know if you'd call them actual dates yet, per se. We watch a lot of movies. He's a big movie buff."

That makes sense. Nathan just doesn't seem to pair well with

Jessi's party-girl type. I stand again to return to the kitchen. "Well, keep me posted."

Jessi flashes two thumbs up with a toothy grin in return, which makes me a little sad, to be honest. In part, because their relationship doesn't sound like what she's trying to make it into, at least not yet. Also, because the idea of him being into her bothers me. A bit too much.

"Ooh, turn that up!" Rose shouts from the kitchen as one of her favorite songs blasts out of my vintage, green radio. I turn the knob further than I should to drown out the thoughts of Nathan from my mind, and my countdown to when I'll see him next.

Seven

Sunday evening dinners are an ongoing tradition in my family. No matter what we had going on through the rest of the week, we *had* to come back together as a family on Sundays. That still holds true anytime we are all in town.

I'm grateful for any extra time to spend with them, and after the wildly unpredictable party on Saturday, it's nice falling back into the warm embrace of familiarity and routine—part of the charm and comfort of returning to Crimson Bay.

"Aunt Autumn! You've made us all celebrities!" Ambushed as soon as I enter the house, I'm bowled over by hugs from all four nieces and nephews.

I ruffle the hair on tops of heads and kiss rosy cheeks. "Wow, what a nice surprise. What's been happening?"

"We were on the news this morning!"

"Eight people texted me!"

"They left so much food! We had to use both fridges! Yummy cakes and cookies everywhere!"

Beth appears from around the corner, a dishrag in hand as she crouches down to Aiden. "And you haven't stopped eating the cake even though I told you to stop." She wipes off the chocolate crumbs stuck to the side of his mouth.

"I'm sorry, Mama." Aiden has learned to perfect the pout with his bottom lip pushed out further than Pinocchio's nose. Beth bites her bottom lip to keep from laughing. A deep ache in the pit of my stomach gnaws at me.

Beth stands and hugs me. "I've been dying to talk to you all day!"

I gesture to the towel in her hand. "It didn't strike me until after I left this morning that there's probably a huge mess from the party. I feel terrible if you guys have been cleaning all day while I've been out."

"Oh, no, the house is spotless! The best cleaning this place has had. It was a good excuse for a deep clean, and we had a lot of volunteers who helped."

I smile. That right there is a perk of small town living that you won't find in too many other places. People won't just come to a party; they'll help clean up afterwards, too.

Beth keeps her arm around my shoulder as we walk into the den where all the adults are congregating. They brought the old furniture back in, which is oddly refreshing, regardless of the musty undertones that attach to outdated chairs and couches. I don't want that room to ever change. Everything has a 1980s cabin vibe; it's cozy and inviting, just like my entire family.

Dad and Mom look half asleep on the couch.

Beth whispers, "They might be worn out, but they'll even tell you the party was worth it, and we'd all do it again." She squeezes my shoulder and asks, "The question is... would you?"

I don't get a chance to answer her question because my parents pop up, wide-eyed the moment they see me. As expected, the questions about the party fire at me like missiles from everyone. I do my best to answer each one, reminding them that I have yet to dive into the challenges. The questions continue through dinnertime, my meatloaf and homegrown potatoes turning cold before I can eat them. When the questions turn to business, or more specifically, the financials, I tell them they'll have to save their questions for Mark.

Clark groans and wraps his arm on the back of Tara's chair. "Tell Mark thanks a lot for making the rest of us look bad. Now I have to pick up a second job to afford throwing Tara a bash. In about twenty years, I'll be able to afford it."

"Don't worry, I'll wait patiently." Tara responds sweetly and flicks his arm.

Peter says, "I'm not sure this town could handle another event like that. It hasn't seen this much excitement since that realtor kid almost won that show."

While building a tower out of magnetic tiles in the corner with Aiden, who lost interest in the conversation thirty minutes ago, I freeze at the mention of the realtor kid. "You mean Nathan?"

Peter shrugs his shoulders, "I think so. One of the Vertz kids. It was all anyone could talk about for months."

"Shot his realtor business through the roof. Smart move on his part. About the only thing reality TV is good for if you play your cards right." My dad adds, as though he has experience with reality shows when his television only plays black and white westerns.

Before I can ask what show Nathan was on, my mom speaks, "He's a sweet kid. Good family. His dad, James, was a star football player when we were in school. Everyone was shocked when he went away... where was it? Tennessee? Alabama?" She looks over at my dad for confirmation, but he shrugs his shoulders.

"Gosh, that was a while ago. Got married down there and had the kids before they came back up here. The kids shook their accents, but their mom, Rhonda, she's as southern as southern gets. Stands out every time she's in a room. She used to cater parties during the summer. I wonder if she's still doing that. I don't think I ever got to try her food. Anyway, I saw him with Jessi the other day at The Bridge. Do you know him well, Autumn?"

I shake my head, amazed that Mom can keep all the details straight about every family in town. "Not really. Met him at the party because Mark enlisted him to sell my house. Only found out afterward that he and Jessi are somewhat dating."

"Good choice." Dad affirms, and I wonder if he means for my cottage or for Jessi. "That boy will sell your house faster than anyone else in this entire state."

Which is precisely what I don't want.

Beth catches the look on my face. "How about you dads take the kids and let them burn off some energy out back before bedtime? We will clean up." No complaints come from the dads, and the kids are out the door before the men can follow.

"I can't believe you're moving to Italy soon. I mean, *Italy*." Tara sighs as she stacks the dirty plates.

Beth nods in agreement. "It's almost a better story than any of those romance novels I read while I'm locked in my bathroom, alone in a cold bubble bath, while the kids beat down the door."

Tara raises an eyebrow. "Almost? It's Autumn's reality. Not somebody's imagination."

"Well, my favorite novels involve a lot of sweaty skin-knocking. No offense, Autumn, but I don't want to imagine the behind-closed-door happenings of you and Mark as you explore the world. I've been married for fifteen years. We have two kids. I need the trashy fluff with as many juicy details as possible."

I almost add, "Hell, I'd even take the romance stories over my current reality," but don't feel like launching into the truth about our lackluster sex life.

"I'll miss things around here a lot." With falling back into old routines, like Sunday dinner with the people I love the most, the move is even more difficult to absorb.

Tara offers, "We can still do wine and game nights while you're gone! We'll prop up the laptop on the couch like you're right here with us."

I refrain from pointing out the seven-hour time difference. Wine and game nights won't be the same. "Of course," I say instead, smiling, doing my best to focus on the moment and not what's to come.

Beth puts her arm around me, not fooled by my act, "You're happy, right?"

My mom looks over her shoulder, the worry-creases above her nose unmistakable. Aware that I have little in life to complain about, I repeat, "Of course," while attempting to ignore the uneasiness in the pit of my stomach.

* * *

Our hard work on Sunday morning and afternoon to prepare for the Bridging the Six Degrees' challenges has an immediate payoff as Rose, Jessi, and I launch into my first activity the next morning.

"These are for you!" Rose sings.

"Are you serious? How many cookies are in here?" Michael, the first police officer to greet us, is peering into the tin, a look of astonishment on his round face. His wide, blue eyes and long eyelashes remind me of a porcelain doll on a broad-shouldered, G.I. Joe frame.

"About fifty or so. That'll be enough for you all, right? If not, we can bring more!"

Our voices are higher, sweeter sounding like Girl Scouts with a wagon full of cookies going door-to-door for deliveries. This is our third and final stop after bringing cookies to two fire stations and scoring an around-the-block ride on a fire truck. It feels good to pause and appreciate the men and women who put their lives on the line every single day for us, nameless faces they don't even know, without asking for anything in return. These are the people shaping our experiences and our lives without us realizing it or fully recognizing when it's needed.

Edna from New Jersey had a similar experience which led to this challenge. She wrote:

'Thank you' has become calloused throughout the years—planned, rehearsed, expected, forced. How often do we take the time to show our gratitude in unexpected ways? Appreciation is us acknowl-

edging that we can't do life without others. One random spring day, I had the inkling to bake cookies for the firefighters and police officers who protect my community. An act so simple changed me. When we are children, people are quick to praise; but as we grow into adults, people are swift to complain and hesitant to praise. These people are rarely thanked, especially not in the proportion that they deserve, for the selfless acts they do. Good deeds become expected; praise becomes foreign. Fix this wayward thinking with unexpected gratitude. It will change your perspective, welcome vulnerability, and alter your journey in this life. Whatever your or their love languages are, translate gratitude.

Similar to our previous two stops, word travels fast about our cookie delivery, and a rotating line of officers joins us. Rose comes alive as she does when people surround her, the haloed light standing in the middle of every gathering.

My eyes gravitate to Michael, who resigned to a chair in the back. The cookie is hanging in his hand with one bite taken out of it, his eyes zeroed in but also zoned out.

I lower myself to the brown, plastic chair next to him. "Not as good as it looks?" I tease him.

He startles, as though I jolted him from sleep. "Oh, no. No, I mean it's good." Michael exhales slowly, and I can sense his exhaustion like heat radiating from a fireplace. "It's delicious. Much needed today."

"Well, I'm glad to hear it." I prepare to stand when Michael places his hand on my arm to hold me in place.

He sighs again, holding the cookie in front of him, as though the cookie is the one talking back to him. "Nothing against the cookie. It's been a week, you know?"

"I can't imagine what you guys experience."

"Yeah, we see the full realm, some good, some bad. This week was one bad situation after another. It doesn't usually fall like that. From adults to children to pets..." He rubs his eyes and yawns, although I wonder if he's fighting back stronger emotions. "Sometimes, it's like no one cares that we do this. That we see these things. That we try to save everyone all the time, and that sometimes we aren't successful..." Michael takes a weakened bite. "Then these cookies come along. I don't know, I'm not very eloquent with my words, but the timing of this... thank you."

"You're not supposed to be thanking us." I put my hand on top of his. "More people than you realize appreciate you. Many people depend on you. Unfortunately, we go through life without recognizing it until an emergency forces us to. Your valor is admirable."

Michael opens his mouth to speak, but then presses his lips together instead.

Jessi waves her hands to get my attention. "We're out of cookies! Let these men and women get back to work. Otherwise, Rose will spend all day talking their ears off."

I turn back to Michael. "I hope you get some deserved rest. It's very nice meeting you."

He smiles in return genuinely, although still masked by exhaustion. "You too."

We yank Rose by her arm to force her to leave the police station. She has a knack for flirting with anyone who looks her way.

"That was so fun! Did you see their faces? We should do that once a month! What if we branched out? Every week we could bake cookies for a group of people around here. The Cookie Club!" Rose's entrepreneurial spirit takes flight. Soon, she's spouting details about a website that collects nominations with the most votes winning free cookies which naturally leads to us having a full-blown bakery that expands to locations across the United States. The business plan is developed within minutes.

Rose is a woman of ideas. Her contagious excitement persuades others to get on board, even if they have no clue what the ultimate mission is. It's one of many reasons she's so good at social media marketing, which she does for the Door County Tourism board. Her followers hang on to her every post, waiting to see what she'll recommend next.

Jessi swoops in to play devil's advocate as usual, challenging Rose on her crazy ideas with all the obstacles that would arise. I let them battle it out and check the trunk to make sure we have everything we need before we climb into the car.

We spent yesterday afternoon making one hundred origami cranes for the next challenge. None of us had tried origami before then, and the first two hours were spent in frustration, trying to figure out how to properly fold pieces of paper. It sounded simple until we started on it. Now it's evident why origami is considered an art. My patience was tested in new ways. Jessi even picked up a ruined piece of paper at one point and held a lighter to it after tossing aside thirty failed attempts.

The origami crane challenge was important though. It documented Natalie's journey as a child with cancer and her credit of a random stranger's delivery of an origami crane for her recovery.

The crane is powerful in Japanese folklore, a symbol of long life, happiness, good luck, and peace, believed to live for a thousand years. Natalie wrote that she would stare at her orange origami crane every morning and night, convincing herself that she was also a beautiful crane flying away from the hospital, stronger than ever. At eleven years old, she was declared to be in complete remission, and the cancer hasn't returned. Natalie has been making origami cranes for kids throughout England ever since.

We drive to St. Joseph Children's Hospital in Green Bay. Rose works the stereo, playing the role of deejay as usual. My mom's best friend arranged permission for us to visit the children. We considered doing it at a general hospital in Door County but wanted to pay homage to the experience that changed Natalie's life, hoping that another child in a similar condition could use the same message.

Nervous tension emits off each one of us when we arrive, all for different reasons, as we wash our hands twice before entering. My Amelia is heavy on my mind. I will spend every day of my life carrying the unanswered question of why she was taken before given a chance to breathe. Likewise, the kids here should be out living their lives but they're confined inside these walls instead, knowing more about the threat of death than they should at such a young age.

Sunlight pours through the floor-to-ceiling windows of the main lobby, a stark contrast to the gloom I had envisioned. Vivid and cheery artwork decorate the walls with cutouts of events to come, reasons to love summer, and an array of favorite cartoon characters. Private rooms for the kids exhibit different scenes, some displaying wild themes with the use of vinyl wall decals, from underwater exploration, to fairies in a pasture, even space travel. A community room rounds out each wing. That's where Heather, the Director of Nursing, guides us to set up. We are given an hour for each of the three wings, and I wonder at first if we created too many origami cranes.

It doesn't take long before they all disappear into tiny hands.

The kids seem ecstatic about our visit. Their smiles further illuminate an already sunny setting. The six hours we spent creating these suddenly doesn't seem like a long enough investment.

"Miss Autumn, can I color this?" I bend down to look into a girl's bright green eyes. About six years old, she has a white knitted beanie covering her head. I've never knitted in my life, but in that moment I resolve to learn.

I glance at her name badge. "Of course, Emmy. What colors would you like to make it?"

"Well..." She evaluates the crane in her hand, turning it over a few times before arriving at her answer. "Pink and orange."

"Ooh, like sunrise colors. The crane would look like it was flying every morning, first thing before anyone else wakes up."

Emmy's eyes dilate with a recognizable bond. "I wake up before anyone else!"

I smile, indebted to the universe for this one conversation, this pairing that has my heart aching but reminding me that it's beating, this chance meeting with this beautiful little girl. "The pink and orange crane would be a perfect match for you then."

She bounces on her feet and wraps her arms around my neck. "Thank you!" Emmy runs to find crayons at the creative crafting corner where several other children are coloring their cranes, smashing them into wrinkled pieces of paper we will have to fold again.

From the moment I saw Emmy, I could see Amelia. As she runs, it's like a bungee cord from my heart is hooked to her, and I expect her to bounce back into the safety of my arms. She is exactly the little girl I dreamt I would someday have; the one I thought would exist in this world with me. Sometimes I still see her in my dreams, convinced that Amelia is visiting me from another world.

The aching thoughts are too difficult to dwell on right now. I force myself to turn away from Emmy and focus on the other children. The energy in the room is palpable. Jessi sits at a small table reading a book to three kids, her face glowing with joy. Rose dances in the middle of the room with a group of girls. An audience of nurses and patients watch them, laughing, clapping, and dancing a little, too.

These kids aren't thinking about death; they're thinking about life. And they're living life. I'm not naïve to believe the air is always this cheerful, but I can guarantee that the moments spent here carry more energy than the seconds that tick away in my own life. Too many constant fears, worries, concerns, and pointless thoughts hold me back from living it to the fullest.

Our time limit at the hospital expires too quickly. Little voices inquire if we will come back to visit. A precious sweetheart named Connor asks if we can make balloon animals next time instead because he hates birds. We promise we will return soon. The realities of my upcoming move aren't lost on me, nor is the truth of how much can change between this visit and the next.

I murmur a silent wish that the cranes will indeed bring long lives filled with happiness to each one of these kids and affirm the power of the folklore. While with the kids, I wanted to drop to my knees and pray, dance with joy, laugh, cry, grieve, and celebrate, all at the same time. In a way, my body did all those things without me realizing, and it hits the moment we exit the doors, take a breath of fresh air, and sit on the bench.

"Three hours wasn't enough time," Rose complains.

"Time has a whole new meaning now," I say as I rub my eyes. The emotion is probing against the back of my eyeballs, and all I want to do is shut them to rest. "How are you feeling, Jess?"

Before we left, Jessi hugged each child in a way that shook my core. It was as tender as a bear hug could be.

She sniffs, her eyes watery and red. "They're amazing. Thinking about all their families..." She trails off, scratching at the red blotches dotting her face from her tears.

I put my arm around her shoulder. "Do you think you'll come back?"

She nods, "I spoke to a nurse about volunteering. She's sending me information."

"That's great, Jess."

"Yeah." She adds. "Yeah, I think it is, too."

We drive home with less energy than when we started the challenges. Rose hums softly to the music, Jessi naps in the back seat, and I make notes in my phone so I can upload the details of our experience to the online BSD platform later. While jotting down my thoughts, I watch the sun sliding down the sky, dipping in and out behind the gorgeous rolling hills. The trees are full and thick, lined shoulder-to-shoulder as though ready for battle, protecting the animals, plants, flowers, and mysteries of the forest behind them.

"Oh, shit!" Rose yells out, interrupting my dreaming as I'm thrown against the passenger side door. The oncoming vehicle's headlights give new meaning to "life flashing before my eyes."

My parents, nieces, nephews, Mark, Amelia, Henry, Nathan, the kids at the hospital—all of them I see at once.

"Shit, hold on!"

I cling onto the ceiling's grab handle as the car spins, a silent scream stuck in my open mouth.

My life suddenly becomes clear.

Eight

MY RIGHT SHOULDER THROBS WITH PAIN.

I look up in time to see the ass of a giant buck run by. Rose instinctively swerves to avoid an oncoming car, another car passing us and the guardrail.

Once the car straightens out with no threats, we all breathe a sigh of relief at missing the triple-collision threat.

"Shit, that could've been bad." Rose exhales.

Thump, thump, thump.

"Shit again."

Rose flips on her hazard lights and crosses lanes to pull over to the side of the road. We pile out of the car to survey the damage. No scratches or dents. "This thing is a beast," she boasts, patting the Civic like it's a loyal dog.

"But a leg of the beast didn't survive," Jessi points to the rear back tire, flat with a large nail sticking out.

"Dammit. Okay, don't panic. Roadside assistance to the rescue." Rose scrolls through her phone to make the call while Jessi and I climb over the guardrail to sit on the edge of Canyon Creek Hill. There's a short drop below us and then a much steeper one which flows outward to the tops of the trees and slopes to the forest behind it. This is a popular deer section and consequently known for numerous accidents, although I never understood how the deer crossed these sections as frequently as they did without near rock climbing abilities.

"Do you think the deer survived?" I ask as we look for any signs of life among the rustling branches while my heartbeat steadily returns to normal.

"I sure hope so." Jessi blocks what's left of the sun from her sight as she scans the scene below.

"A tow truck should be here in twenty minutes." Rose sits on the other side of Jessi, the flashing headlights of passing cars framing her body in the darkening sky.

The breeze catches the scent of wildflowers below, hints of citrus and mint, reminding me of early morning walks in Crimson Bay. A few glorious minutes, untouched by the concept of time, that seem to supply an endless stream of anxiety throughout the rest of the day. Even with a broken car, I'm overcome by peacefulness. There's no place I would rather be than right here with my two best friends, stranded in an area that we all love and have deep attachments to, as the night settles around us.

"It's great to have you back here, A." Jessi puts her head on my shoulder, clearly caught up in the same nostalgia as I am.

"I'm glad I'm back for a little while, too. It'll make the transition easier when we move." And *poof* the tranquility is gone. Why do I have to talk about that *here* of all places? It's like a defense mechanism when I'm feeling too comfortable here.

"Do you really think you're going?"

Rose casts Jessi a stern look that makes me question what's implied, while also wondering if my doubts are more obvious than I realize.

"Why wouldn't I?"

"I don't know. I thought there was a chance you'd stay here."

"In Crimson Bay?" I ask, feigning bewilderment when really it's just amazement that they seem to always read my mind.

"Yeah, is it really that crazy? You've been gone long enough."

Rose's lips press together as she shoots daggers at Jessi with her eyes.

"What am I missing here?"

Jessi opens her mouth to speak as Rose not-so-subtly shakes her head. "I feel like the old Autumn is back. It's been nice."

"Old Autumn? What does that mean?" My shoulder blades tense as I sit up straighter.

"The Autumn that isn't buying the newest technological piece or flying in a personal jet to Boston or going to fancy parties in fancy clothes." She ticks off the reasons on her fingers to prove her point.

I fold my hands together, my fingers firmly linked to push my frustration down. Jessi never bites her tongue. Rose calls it 'dirty, unfiltered foot-in-mouth disease.' You either love her or hate her for it. Right now, I'm not liking it much.

"You mean all the things that we do for Mark's company? All the things that we *have* to do for his success?"

"It's not you. I've never known you to care about any of those things, and now it's all you talk about." Jessi hasn't moved her head off my shoulder. I fight the urge to jerk my shoulder so she's forced off.

"I have to talk about it when it's our life. That job is our livelihood."

"Maybe. But is that the way you want your life to be? Mark's imprint is stamped everywhere. Where's Autumn in this?"

I refuse to admit the accuracy I feel in that statement. But Jessi isn't married. She doesn't get how conflicting things can become. Still, there seems to be more here. "Do you not like Mark? Is that what this is all about?" *Everyone* likes Mark.

Rose covers her head with her arms, pretending she's anywhere else.

Jessi answers, "I like Mark as a person, but not as your partner for the rest of your life."

Annoyance boils inside the pit of my stomach. "And Rose? You disagree, right? You're always gushing about Mark and how great of a guy he is." My mind prepares a list of all the things Rose has said about Mark to use as ammunition in case she denies it.

"Yeah, Mark is a good guy," she responds too carefully.

Suddenly, every feeling I've been pushing down is ignited with agitation from their comments—regret for never knowing they felt this way, and embarrassment for this getting brought up *now*, after all these years. "So, you don't think he's right for me either, Rose? You guys couldn't speak up when we were engaged or before we married or any of the other ample opportunities you've had?"

"You never gave us a chance, A. You were moving from one global trek to another after you left. We barely heard from you, and suddenly, you're getting married. When were we supposed to tell you what we thought?"

I stand up, my shoulder blade jutting into Jessi's cheek from the movement. "Any damn time! You're my best friends! We're supposed to have each other's backs!"

Jessi rubs her cheek while Rose's calm voice offsets the anger in mine. "And if we had told you our concerns, would you have made a different decision? Would you not have married him?" She pauses, letting her words seep in. She knows nothing would have changed.

And is she right? If they had talked to me, would I have listened? Right now, it's easy for me to say I would have. But at the time... at the time, all that mattered was Amelia. All I cared about was creating a family like the one I was lucky to be raised with. I wanted to hold her and hear her giggles and help her grow from a curious little girl to a confident woman. I wanted to witness Mark becoming an amazing dad, like I knew he could be, like his dad was to him.

I dreamt about her little hand in his as they walked together, so she could feel the sturdiness of him next to her, and know she was always loved, safe, and protected. It was a time when I still believed things could be the way I always imagined them to be. If Rose and Jessi tried to intervene, I would have thought they just couldn't see what I did. They couldn't understand the magnitude of the new life that was being born within me and how everything in my world was preparing for a light to radiate straight from heaven. I would have told them they were trying to interfere with every dream I've ever had. It could have put a strain on our friendship.

What I wouldn't have seen then, because only now am I able to see it, is even if I had Amelia in my arms, there would have been a disconnect with the dreams of my heart. We would have been constantly moving around as Mark acquired different businesses, trying to make the most out of every new location. We wouldn't have been here often at all. The kids wouldn't have been cooking the strange, yet delicious nacho chip chicken casserole with my mom in the kitchen or receiving scruffy raspberries on their cheeks from my dad or be confused that Aunt Rose and Aunt Jessi aren't actually blood relatives because they're ingrained in every day as much as the other family members.

We would have missed out on the fish boils and the lake floats and the town-wide Easter Egg hunts, where some unknown bunny hides thousands of eggs throughout the town, some that aren't recovered until months later. All the memories I had, that were being fused with the memories I expected my children to have, wouldn't have been the same with Mark. The truth hits me like a sheet of ice in my face.

Rose continues, "If you wanted that life with him, we wouldn't hold you back from seeking the happiness you desired, even if it was different from what we pictured for you."

I drape my arms over the top of my head, my hands pulling at the opposite ears, because I can't find the words to tell them everything that just went through my head, and I don't know what else to do. It's too dark to walk the side of the road in a frenzy. I'd either get hit by a car or fall off one of these cliffs.

An awkward silence fills the air.

"Where in the world is that tow truck?" Rose makes a phone call again. All we hear is, "You said they'd be here twenty minutes ago. Now another twenty minutes? Are they coming at all? Uh-huh. Yep. Okay." She hangs up. "We may be here all night."

I sigh, ready to be back in my bed. It's been a long, emotional day as it is, even without this conversation. I climb over the guardrail to appraise the flat tire, which is a dead-on description of the way my heart feels after Jessi's truth bomb and my revelation of how life would have been with kids—something I need to process more when I'm alone.

"Rose, do you have a spare?"

She shrugs while texting on her phone. "You can check."

I pop open her trunk and dig under the random assortments of clothes, bottles of water, and bags of chips. Constantly on the go with events, this is her mobile closet. Pulling up the carpeted floor of the trunk, the spare tire, jack, and wrench reveal themselves.

Leaning over the guardrail, I declare, "Screw waiting on someone else, you guys. We're strong, badass women. Let's do this thing together."

"I'm in!" Rose cries out as she bounces up to join me.

"Jess, shine the light on us and pull up instructions on your phone. Rose and I will handle the dirty work." I temporarily suck down the pain and frustration of their comments to push through this task.

Rose and I use our combined strength to pull the spare tire out and drag it to the road. We find large stones to use as wheel wedges, loosen the lug nuts, lift the car with the jack, unscrew the lug nuts, swap out the tires, tighten the lug nuts, lower the vehicle, and re-tighten the lug nuts. Afterward, we are sweaty, covered in sand and gravel, and out of breath.

"Did we do that?" Rose asks as we stand in awe, admiring the repaired car with flashing hazard lights, and all four tires ready to go.

"Damn right we did!" Adrenaline pumps through my veins.

Jessi asks the question that's on all of our minds, "Are we sure it's safe?"

"Only one way to find out!" Rose is the first in the car. As soon as we snap our seatbelts, the tow truck pulls in behind us with flashing lights.

Rose pops her head out of the window and calls behind her, "We fixed it! Thanks for making us wait an extra two hours!" She waves.

We endure the slowest drive possible without breaking the minimum speed limit for the fifteen miles back to Crimson Bay. The tow truck passes us with a flippant honk. No one talks as we listen for any signs of the tire falling off.

Once the car pulls to a stop in front of my house, we breathe a sigh of relief for the second time that night.

"We did it!" Rose pumps her fist in the air.

Sometimes, all it takes is surrounding yourself with people who believe the most in you to realize that you're capable of absolutely anything.

"You need to get that thing into the mechanic pronto tomorrow."

"I can drop it off on my way to work tomorrow," Jessi offers.

"Nah, that's fine. I can get Kevin to help me." Rose noticeably hesitates at the ease of Kevin's name flowing from her lips.

"You're seeing Kevin tomorrow?" I manage to keep the surprise out of my voice.

"Yes." She pulls her hair off of her neck. Even the dim porch light shows the redness in her cheeks.

"Is that the dude you were making out with at A's party?"

"Yes."

"Oh, cool." Jessi loses interest and turns back to me. "Are we cool, A? I mean, after all I said and stuff."

I unlock the front door and flip on the lights inside. My cottage extends the same gratitude for my return as I feel for it with a burst of welcoming warmth. Rose follows, but Jessi stays close to the exit as though expecting me to tell her to leave.

Rubbing my face, I respond, "I'm pretty hurt. I wish I knew years ago how you felt about Mark. But..." I rub my neck as I sit on an island stool, "I admit you're right in some ways. I haven't been too available since I met him." As soon as the confession exits my mouth, I immediately hate myself for being *that* girl. I got caught up in Mark's world. I dedicated my return trips to Crimson Bay to writing, but I'm slowly recognizing it was also so I could connect to my true self again.

When I'm with Mark at all his events, I'm pressured to uphold an image that proves I'm worthy of being the woman on his arm. I see how everyone watches us and the secret glances and whispers. Maybe I stuff the real me in this cottage, fiercely protected, scared that I could lose her forever if released into Mark's world. Maybe I'm scared of who I'll be if this cottage sells, my one physical reminder and anchor to the truth.

My head pounds. Rose stands behind me with her hands on my shoulders and says, "We may not agree with all the choices you make, but we will never stop loving you."

I lift my arm and motion Jessi to join us. "So does this mean you forgive me?" she asks as she enters our group hug.

"There's nothing to forgive." I kiss her cheek. "Love you, ladies. You will always be important to me. Always. I'll work harder at proving that."

"Even when you become an Italian diva?" Jessi nudges me with her arm.

I roll my eyes. "I'm still the furthest thing from a diva."

"Aww, look at these!" Rose flips through her phone to review the pictures from today. Grateful for the distraction from Mark and Italy-related conversations, our focus moves back to the emotional whirlwind of our morning and dipping our toes into the Bridging the Six Degrees challenges.

We only took a selfie outside of the police station with our tins full of cookies. Conveniently it's the shot where my neck is folded into a double chin, and my eyes are squinting in what Mark deems the "Olson Eyes." To get a good picture of me, I have to open my eyes wide the second before someone snaps a photo, as though I'm at the eye doctor preparing for the puff test. My dad's lineage is to blame for that pleasant trait.

Rose chuckles and watches my reaction, purposely stalling before swiping to the next. It's our only shot for that event, meaning it's the only one I can submit to the online BSD platform as proof of the completed challenge. Me, my double-chin, and my squinty eyes are now forever documented in that form.

The challenge that came from Callie of San Francisco is to learn to live in the moment and let pictures capture precisely how things are without altering. She despised her body after the birth of her second baby and fell into a depression, refusing to let people take pictures of her. While composing scrapbooks for that child's second birthday, she realized that she had less than a handful of pictures of her with her baby. All because she didn't like how she looked.

Callie wrote,

Accept yourself for who you are inside, regardless of what you think is reflected in pictures. Be okay with the first frame. A picture is to capture the moment you are in. It doesn't matter how dirty or messy you or the environment is or that it isn't the right angle or light. There is something about the moment that needs to be eternalized, so make sure it is replicated exactly as it is. Because that's what's most important, and what you'll miss the most one day.

Even with the challenge in front of me, I have to coach myself to accept the picture of my double-chin and squinty eyes. This picture isn't about me, anyhow. The focus should highlight how incredible that moment was to extend our appreciation to the people who risk their lives to protect our community. Bridging the Six Degrees is about the experiences—and the pictures are no exception. Vanity is not an option right now.

The following photos encompass that exact concept. The smiling faces of the kids at the hospital with cranes in their hands bursting through the camera. Funny how you think you're giving someone a gift, but instead, you receive one far greater in return.

* * *

The day was sentimental and special. We barely touch our pasta dinner, a rarity for us to not eat. We don't hold back on the wine, though.

Jessi calls dibs on the couch before Rose can, so Rose claims the left side of my bed instead. However, I can't sleep.

As I replay the day in my head, I keep analyzing how I am living. I am not brave like the police officers or firefighters we met, or like the kids at the hospital fighting to get well. Yet today, we all showed a bit of courage in our own ways by stepping out of our comfort zones and having unforgettable experiences because of it.

Restless, I dig through an old, wooden trunk that stores a motley assortment of pictures, souvenirs, and journals I've collected over the years. The journals contain my erratic, emotional, angst-ridden, joyful, and confusing thoughts from when I first started writing. These notebooks reflect my life, hiding my secrets, counseling me through tough situations, and acting as the other voice of the inner dialogue I have with myself.

Throughout each book are pictures, cut-outs from magazines, scribbled lyrics, poems, and quips. My dreams—all the ones pushed away to the dark corners of my mind, draped with cobwebs as I tried to live in the real world—still whisper longingly when the pages are turned. Browsing through these journals creates a deep longing for a life I never appreciated at the time and hope for a future that now seems too far out of reach.

My heart drops when I discover a collection of written dreams I had during one long, aspirational period. It's excruciating to reminisce on my plans to travel the world the way I envisioned, going from country to country, learning and absorbing new cultures in a nomad-traveler approach. I had planned to work the jobs of the country's people, eat what they eat, live the way they lived. I wanted to write about it all, document every experience, and capture stories of lives that few knew about. I was willing to be broke and homeless, as long as I could learn to love more and live more freely. Money didn't matter. Things didn't matter. People, experiences, and living were all that I cared about. That piece of my heart once ruled over all the rest.

There's something that happens to the mind as age progresses. Senseless fears enter. The mind, body, and heart become more guarded. Everyone becomes a danger in some way— whether to your heart or your life or to those in it.

I became scared.

Or, I found more of an attachment to the things I didn't think I once wanted.

Either way, I didn't become the person these journals described. My life didn't match the dreams of my heart that I wrote about so long ago. Yeah, I have gotten to travel, but it's been a rich and expensive way to do so, further removed from the journey and experiences I truly wanted to have. These journals contain a part of me that not even Mark knows.

Or does he?

The week that I put in my notice at work, since we finally came clean to management and our colleagues that we were in an official relationship, he came to my cubicle and whispered in my ear, "Just grabbed two extra sandwiches from the lunch cart as Debbie was loading it up. She let me score a bag of chips too, but only when I complimented her earrings. Want to hop out early and go on an adventure with me?" I only had time to nod before he rolled my chair all the way to the elevator with us both laughing, not caring for once that co-workers were watching us.

Five and a half hours later, we were at the Silver Lake Dunes in Michigan. I stepped out of the car, breathless. In front of me were giant sand mountains, one rolling right into the next, with the backdrop of the other side of Lake Michigan, that I normally don't get to see. It was like we were transported to the Arabian Desert with a mirage of water teasing us. "Mark, it's..." I turned to face him, and he was staring at me with a knowing smile on his lips. He grabbed my hand as we climbed a dune, slipping and sliding and eventually succeeding at getting to the top.

We laid on that dune for hours, and once the night fell, we witnessed one shooting star after another in the endless sky. It felt like a dream. I had been talking about the books I wanted to write and what I hoped to do as an author, when Mark said, "Autumn. You can do it all. Anything you want, you can make happen. You'll be published. I know it. Keep sharing your ideas with people. Your words will make a difference. People will connect with your stories. You've always wanted this for a reason, and it'll be yours. You're extremely talented."

The confidence he instilled in me that night was what fueled me to walk up to Nicole, the literary agent I met at a writer's workshop in Boston, who happened to be at the same charity event we were at three weeks later. With boldness that shocked me, I told her I felt like she was the right person to represent my book, and I would prove it to her. I then recited how my book connects to others in her portfolio that have seen success, and the unique edge to it that she has yet to represent but fits the current market and top trends.

All the words tumbled out of my mouth before my brain could make me doubt myself. The fact that Mark knows many impressive people who have accomplished big things and believed that I could do the same was exactly the validation I needed to make a life-changing move.

The dunes excursion is one of my favorite memories with him. It coincides with the last time I felt truly heard and seen by him since work has never stopped being busy for him since. The gap between us only grew once we lost Amelia, like he's completely disengaged from our conversations. Time after time, it's been proven as well, when I ask him a follow-up question and he doesn't remember our initial conversation. I chalk it up to his distractions at work and fatigue.

There's a better reason than his not being interested in listening, right? Sometimes he surprises me. Like with the party. Maybe it wasn't only about testing out an acquisition of his. Maybe he knows my heart better than I think. And even if he's not always listening, he can still read the dreams hidden deep inside. Because ultimately, Bridging the Six Degrees is a way to explore my limits through the experiences of other people.

Maybe Mark knew I needed this. Maybe despite the elaborate showmanship of the delivery of his gift (that is more his style than mine), I should appreciate being challenged to grow outside of my comfort zone. Maybe I don't give him enough credit for who he is and how well he balances me.

Or maybe, all these maybes have justified my life for far too long.

Nine

"ARE YOU HAPPY?"

My face basks in its own sauna, the steam from the coffee flowing around it. My eyes close as I inhale the heavenly, hazelnut aroma. I am in love with coffee. In love. I've never questioned it; I've never doubted it. 100% pure, unadulterated love with coffee —the smell, the taste, the comfort it brings when I wrap my hand around a mug filled with it. It is in me, and I am in it. We are one beautiful soul together.

I open my eyes, awakening from the romantic love affair with my coffee and squint at my mom from my hunched-over position in the booth. "Right now? Yes. Obviously."

"No, I mean, *happy*. Period."

"Like, with life?" I sip my coffee, delaying an in-depth conversation for as long as possible, especially after getting only one hour of sleep and waking up to my journal pages stuck to my face. My mom is relentless. I knew the question had been simmering in her since I left the house Sunday night.

"Yes." My mom is all too patient and would wait for weeks, if necessary, until I respond.

"Maybe be more specific?"

"Okay, fine. Let's start with the party. Were you happy with it?"

"Yes."

"But you weren't at first?"

"Right." Every time I respond, I reward myself with another sip of coffee. We could play twenty questions, or we could get to the point on her mind. "Astonished may be more accurate to describe the initial shock. It got better, though. What exactly are you digging for, Detective?"

"Okay..." my mom taps her mug of tea. "Are you about to do something drastic?"

Does she mean do something drastic as in move to a brand-new country, or do something drastic as in return to my home-town single? It could go either way, and I can't discern how much she's sniffed out with her mother's intuition.

I choose to remain silent. Especially since I'm not completely sure what I'm doing yet either.

Mom breaks her penetrating stare and shifts it to the view out the window. The Stella Café sits on wooden stilts at the edge of the rocks overlooking the water. It's one of the prettiest spots to be first thing in the morning since the sun rises directly across from the back dock, crystalizing the water. They even have an accessible rooftop for better views where a staggering number of proposals occur each year.

"I saw the look in your eyes, Autumn. It was back—that urge to mix up your life again, I could see it."

"Mom, I was uncomfortable at different parts. That's all. I'm not one for big crowds, you know that. But I enjoyed the party, and I'm loving these challenges."

"I don't think it was just the party," Mom mumbles as she watches the birds dip in and out of the water and chase each other. Finally, she turns her eyes back to me and continues her interrogation, "What else could you want, Autumn? Mark is great. You're moving to Italy for heaven's sake."

While the words tumble out of her mouth, each one slices off pieces of my heart that crumble in defeat. I fight back tears as I shred a napkin into tiny pieces. *I want a baby. I want passion. I want to have meaningful conversations about life with my husband. I don't want my only intimacy with him to be focused on earning the next buck when we already have more than we need. I want someone who loves being here as much as I do.* But the words don't come.

"I thought all you kids would stay here forever. That was my dream. But when I saw your relationship progress with Mark, I realized that this different life suited you, so I let that dream go. We can't keep one leg in and one leg out of our life. We have to commit to the decisions we make. You have everything you can ask for, so what's wrong?"

Even though my mom is offering a reprieve of the punishment my twisted gut has been dealing me by letting me confess my struggles, I bite my tongue. Why does she constantly have to say, "you have everything you can ask for" when is it not true? It's so layered between me and Mark. If it was easier, I wouldn't be struggling. I know these doubts won't make sense when I say them out loud because they don't always make sense in my head. On the outside, things are seemingly perfect. But inside, my heart is missing something substantial.

Mom is studying my eyes, which I'm sure are betraying me and revealing the words I can't speak. "It's about the baby, isn't it?"

"Amelia." I remind her. "She had a name."

"I know," Mom says while swiping at a tear that rolls down her cheek. "She was my granddaughter."

I shift in my seat. "Listen, Mom. I'm a writer. These thoughts, emotions, the wondering... I analyze everything because it helps me to write and understand life. I'm not reckless. Like you said, life is good. Mark is great. I'm not complaining. Lots of great things to come." Short, concise sentences to replace the millions of real thoughts swarming through my head.

Mom isn't buying it. "This life will go by quickly, Autumn.

Remember that. If you spend all your time caught up in the past or searching for the next best thing, you'll never remember what you had in the present that was so good. You're in a marriage now. It's not just you making decisions; you two have to make them together for the betterment of your lives, *together*."

She's right, and I know it. But I wish Mark knew it too. We should be making decisions together.

"So, you're happy, right?" Mom presses one more time.

"Yes," I succumb. Although my mind... it's somewhere else.

"Good." My mom stirs her tea and replaces the tension with a smile. "What's on the agenda for the rest of the week?"

* * *

By the time we leave the café, sprinkles fall from the sky, creating a synchronized *pff pff pff* on the sidewalk. It's warm rain—the kind that seeps inside my pores, wraps around my soul and hums along with the quiet song birthed from deep within.

Mom offers to drive me back to my house. She took my dad's truck so she can run to the hardware store for supplies. "The Bridging the Six Degrees production crew's critique of our house forced your dad to reconsider those remodeling ideas." She says it will be easy to throw my bike into the back and make a detour to my cottage before continuing on with her errands.

I insist on riding back. A challenge presented by Anna of Paris was to ride my bike for four days in a row to give up the notion that we need luxuries, like gas, to do such basic things in life. She conducted a study on World War II causalities and the effects of the war; as a result, she decided to live a more self-sustaining life. She sold her car and learned to rely on other modes of transportation, among forgoing other common, modern luxuries, testifying how much happier she's been from doing so.

"It's not bad and will let up soon." I give a little wave to the sky, a silent notion for it to ignore my words: keep the rain coming exactly like this.

My mom wraps her arms around me. "Okay, but call if you need me. I don't mind turning around."

I return her embrace. "Thanks for breakfast. I'm sure I'll stop by later this week."

"Good." She climbs into the cab of the truck, her petite frame consumed by the maroon beast.

Once she disappears down the road, I walk along the edge of the limestone cliff, surveying the water and enjoying the cool breeze as light gusts push strands of hair behind me. The proximity is intimidating, especially considering my fear of heights, but I have much trust in these parts, so much so that I'd feel comfortable walking around with a blindfold on.

I shut my eyes and breathe in the fresh air, appreciating the simplicity of this place, the views, the small community atmosphere, the pure wilderness of it all. I don't miss the hustle and bustle of Boston one bit. Why was I ever so desperate to leave here?

"Don't jump. It's pretty rocky down below," a gentle voice warns.

I startle, surprised to hear another person so early. Turning around, Nathan stands with a Tom's Produce paper bag in his hands and a coy grin on his face. My heart leaps.

"Well, good morning." I smile timidly, praying the spinach omelet I had for breakfast isn't revealed in my teeth.

"I didn't mean to scare you." He steps closer. "I thought it was you from the back, so I figured a lame joke was the best way to check. If it wasn't you, I could laugh with a stranger and keep on walking."

"And now that it's me?" I take a deep breath.

"I'm happy to see you and can sit for a while." As always, he's casual, even-toned, and doesn't match my flirting.

The breeze fills the air with Nathan's cologne. A man should never underestimate the power of scent. It brings back memories of the first night we met, especially combined with the water scene in front of us. It's turning into our thing, it seems. He sits down on the ground, sets his bag next to him, stretches his legs out and lets his sneakers dangle over the edge of the cliff.

I point to the bag. "That'll get soaked." I offer an excuse for him to leave as the embarrassment from the night of the party charges at me.

"Eh, it'll survive." Patting the ground next to him, he encourages, "Sit. Let's enjoy the quiet before everyone else ruins it."

I hesitate, then follow suit. It's another redemptive quality about this place. It's rare for someone not to recognize the importance of taking a moment to enjoy the view.

Nathan exhales as he lifts his head to the sky. Raindrops stick in his long eyelashes and slide down his face. "This is the best, isn't it? There are so few days like this that I have pity for all the people sleeping in and missing out on it."

Nodding, I agree, "When I lived here, I'd always wake up early and enjoy the silence of this town. I swear the warm rain would only come in the mornings, despite how hot it gets later in the day."

He chuckles. "I've noticed that, too." He props himself in the grass on his elbows and gazes at me with a raised eyebrow. "I'm surprised you and I haven't crossed paths more before."

I've also wondered that many times since I've met him. Instead of saying so, I pick a strand of grass and rotate it in my fingers. "Well, we were bound to eventually. I hear you're dating my friend."

Nathan reclines his body and puts his hands behind his head as he watches the clouds change shape. He closes his eyes any time a sprinkle lands on them. "Yes, Jessi. She's... nice."

"By nice you mean, beautiful, sweet, fun, and outgoing?" I smirk, a notable rise of jealousy catching in my throat.

His face doesn't change, he merely responds in a flat tone, "Yes." He peeks at me with a quick, lopsided smile before moving his eyes back to the sky.

A few minutes of silence pass between us. I pretend to watch a tree sway while out of my peripheral vision, I'm studying Nathan, searching for a hint of what may be rolling around in that mind of his.

"It makes you feel alive, doesn't it?"

"Yes," I murmur. I know what he's talking about without having to ask for clarification. The water beneath us, pounding against the cliff; the water dropping from the sky above us, gentle and caring. The warm sun heating the mixture as they collide together.

Nathan draws in his breath. It raises goosebumps on my arm. "Petrichor."

"What?"

"Petrichor. It's that wonderful smell that comes from rain falling on dry soil. There's nothing that compares."

I know the word, but the way it rolls off his tongue is even more beautiful. "It's glorious."

He smiles at me and moves his gaze to the water. "When everything is the same, it brings comfort and peace. When contradictory things come together, they generate excitement and energy. How can you possibly choose one feeling over the other? Everyone always forces choices down our throats. Do you want this *or* that? But I always ask, why can't we have it all? I want this *and* that. Isn't that the point of such an astonishing, fascinating, mind-blowing universe? Believing it's all possible? I choose comfort, peace, excitement, *and* energy. I get it all in moments like these."

Nathan is rambling, talking in circles. I like it. My mind works that way, too. It's like we're sitting in nature's church, listening to a sermon from the most natural elements that awaken my soul. Sitting on the same dirt I was raised on, it's confirmation of my sanity in such a chilling way that I almost call Mark right there and tell him all my things need to be shipped back to Crimson Bay because I'm never leaving.

Nathan squeezes his eyes and bites the inside of his cheek. It's a funny little look that makes me grin. With baby soft-looking skin, the tops of his ears are rounded into a point, the right ear with a tiny scar around the edge of the lobe. I wonder if he was born with that or if it came by accident.

After my visual dissection of his face, my eyes travel back to notice his blue irises locked on mine with a playful smirk twitching on his lips. We hold eye contact for what seems like an eternity. He breaks it suddenly by standing and dusting off his jeans, the wet sand relentless to break its hold. I immediately focus on the damp grass where his body once was, fighting the guilt because I'm so drawn to him.

"Here." Nathan holds out his hands to help me stand. I pull my legs from over the cliff and take advantage of his offer. The rugged patchwork of his skin leaches onto mine. Our hands are wet from the rain, but the warmth that generates between them once connected is like sitting next to a fire on a cold, winter day. The ultimate comforting contradiction.

Right as we release our hands, the last drop comes from the sky. We look up in unison.

"That's a shame," he mutters.

I nod, at loss for words for how bare my soul feels in his presence.

And in a flash, our private moment has ended. Nathan bends over to pick up his bag, holding the bottom to prevent the dampness from tearing it. His tone returns to business, "I planned to call you and set up a time to come by your house to take pictures. If tomorrow morning is still good for you, how's eight o'clock?" Another rude awakening to a whimsical fairy tale unfolding. "Sure, that works," I answer casually.

"Okay, great." Nathan hesitates and looks around. "Do you hear that?"

"Hear what?"

"Shh, shh... listen."

I hold my breath, expecting to hear a rumble coming from the sky, road, or ground, or some distinct noise that would cause him to freeze. I hear nothing. Except for the rustle of swaying grass, the sigh of the wind, the hum of bird wings flapping by, and the burble of the water.

Nathan whistles, perfectly mimicking that of a robin. I smile, catching on.

My heart flutters as he winks. "See you tomorrow." Nathan waves as he turns back on his trek. He doesn't get in a vehicle, but instead, continues walking. I like that he walks. I capture these characteristics and use them to envision the type of person he is to fill in what I don't yet know. In this case, a person that wants to take in the beauty of the world around him, which can only be done on foot.

Even knowing that Nathan will sell the most precious material possession I have, there's something about him that makes me feel serene, free, and excited, all at once.

The rain stopped, but I swear I can still feel the drops tingling my skin as I walk toward my bike. Picking it up, even the handles feel smoother, more relaxing, meant to be in my hands right at this moment.

I throw my leg over the bike rim, and as the pedals hook onto my feet, I prepare for the three-mile adventure back home.

The splash of cars driving by as the wheels hit puddles, the rise of voices as people fill the streets, the whizz of the breeze whipping by my ear, the swishing of the blowing trees—everything is louder, more intense. My senses are on full alert. They haven't felt this way in so long.

In Boston, I learned to drown things out—to ignore the preoccupations of the world around me. The sirens, the horns, the screams, they all put me on alert as though something terrible is bound to take place. "Do all writers have paranoid imaginations?" Mark asked me one day, noticing me often flinching while we walked the streets in downtown Boston.

"What do you think is the primary qualification to become one?" I snapped, my eyes hastily sweeping the busy scene in front of me.

Mark quietly chuckled in response, taking my hand in his.

* * *

When I arrive home, I place my bike against the siding and jog up the white stairs to the door. Once inside, I head straight for my laptop that's sitting on the makeshift desk I created, a wooden desk formed in the middle of the bay window alcove seat. I didn't want to lose the seat or the perfect view of the lake, so it was my only viable option for writing.

I grab a cushioned footstool to use as my chair. Electricity is pumping through me so much that my fingers are shaking, making it difficult to type. It is as though lightning struck and is snaking its way from the top of my head to the tip of my toes. I need to write, to channel it, but I have to do something else as well because my body cannot be contained in one area unless I burn some energy.

Then I think of the list.

Pulling it out from my purse, my eyes drift to two that are powerful by themselves, but combined, could be exactly what I need at this precise moment. They require a sense of vulnerability I have to discover again, after spending the past several years running away from it.

One by one, I shed every article of clothing. My shirt, shorts, bra, and underwear all come off as I kick them in a pile on the floor.

I reach for my book from Bridging the Six Degrees to find Margaret's story. She lost her family in a fire, spending her remaining childhood years in the foster system as she moved from home to home. She was abused in far more ways than any person, let alone a child, should have to endure. Patches of welts, bumps, and faded discoloration covered Margaret's body, each scar telling bits of her life story, which she spent most of her years hiding from the rest of the world.

One day, after too many years of avoiding short-sleeved shirts, shorts, dresses, tanks, or any garment classified as revealing in any way, she fought against her deep-rooted fears. She shed her clothes and modeled for a professional art class, letting talented artists build their own interpretation of her life based on the marks that covered her body. After seeing the images their paintings conveyed, ones that exhibited her as healthy and beautiful and not as broken and ugly as she always felt, her belief in herself was redesigned. Margaret learned how to see a whole, beautiful soul with a story that has shaped her, but not defined her.

Intending to blend two challenges together, I search for Alexis's story next, who was also familiar with hiding but for different reasons than Margaret. Alexis was an emotional teenager, getting lost in her own mind, confused about who she was, and embarrassed by the parts of herself she had come to understand. She hid from the world. Then one day, a song came on the radio that changed her life. "Stronger" by Kanye West.

Feel free to laugh at me. I would have been laughing, too, if I read this. But that song, the beat, the verse... for whatever screwed up state I was in that day, it's exactly what I needed. It was the rope to save me from drowning in quicksand. I don't have Kanye posters hanging in my bedroom, but that song made me dance. I kept it on repeat as I twirled about the room, swaying my hips... Hell, I may have even twerked. It freed me. So, I sat down and created a two-hour-long playlist, not expecting to dance the whole time after I hit play, but I kept dancing. I became addicted to it, and I learned I was good at it. I've since been doing competitive dancing, working my way up to eventually go pro. I know I will. I'm more confident than I ever have been, and it all started with that one song inspiring me to dance and let the rest of the world fade away. So dance, freely. Get lost in the music for hours until you can't move anymore. Just dance.

Opening my music app, I type in Dance. Everything that pops up seems too technical and not free enough. So instead, I type in what I should have in the first place: Rose's playlists. She is the dancing queen. I hit the shuffle button and crank the music. Loud.

Naked, I dance, and I give it my all. I focus on the energy that's pumping through my veins and how it amplifies as the music connects with it. I dance thinking about Margaret and how she bounced back from her hardships. I dance thinking about Alexis and how a random song helped her find who she was supposed to become. I think about my party and all the incredible people I met that night. I reflect on the moments I've shared with Nathan by the water.

Like Alexis, I even try to twerk, laughing at my efforts. I get low and touch the floor, I twist, I move my body in ways I'm sure I will never do in public but don't think twice about doing now. As I run my hands through my sweaty hair, one thought won't escape me: *What am I so afraid of?*

After three hours, I finally turn off the music, but it still fills the house like the walls are refusing to let go. My nerves tremble with equal parts adrenaline and exhaustion. My breath comes fast. Five of my thirty challenges are now completed. I already feel more alive than I have felt in a very long time.

I grab a glass of water and a sandwich from the fridge and sit on the footrest once again. The soft padded cushion cuddles my bare skin. There's something about being naked that makes me sit up straighter. Our posture reflects everything we hide and the proverbial weight we carry. It's clear now more than ever how much I needed to let go.

All my windows are open, and I refuse to care. No one will come by, no one will see. It's just me, in all my glory, as I was created to be. It's time to take all this energy, all this excitement, all these revelations, and put them into words. My fingers feverishly pound on the keyboard for hours on end. Writing is my therapy, a way to share how I feel and what's occurring in my life. My real-life emotions and questions are subtly weaved into the fictional story of Nicki, as her affair with a man that resembles Nathan steadily plays out.

Ten

I WAKE WITH A CHILL, PULLING THE COVERS TIGHTER over my body. I didn't put clothes back on when I finally shut down my computer at midnight. I hesitate to even put them on today. I could get used to this whole freedom thing. But with Nathan coming over to check out the house...

The clock flashes 6:30 a.m., just enough time to tackle an extra round of cleaning before he arrives.

I glance at my phone. Mark tried calling two hours ago. I hadn't stirred.

"I'm glad I didn't wake you. This is the only chance I'll have to talk all day, so I wanted to at least leave you a message. I miss you. I'll try again tomorrow when I know you'll be awake." My heart twitches at the sound of his voicemail as shame entangles with each beat. I haven't missed him. In part, I know it's because I've learned to swallow that emotion anytime it arises throughout the years.

There have been many nights I wouldn't hear from him until he stumbled home a day or two later, fried from paperwork and meetings. Friends ask if I worry about him cheating or spending time with other women, but I trust Mark. Early in our relationship, I concluded that he loves his company, and that's the closest thing to passion I've ever seen in him. Instead of getting upset that he spends most of his time there, I let it be without question, without demanding a deadline for when he has to be home or call. Maybe a bit abnormal, but it works for us and allows me the freedom to get lost in writing my stories.

I hop in the shower and quickly get dressed, adding yellow plastic gloves to my attire as I grab my bucket of cleaning supplies and get to work. Within forty-five minutes, my house is sparkling and ready for photos. Although in retrospect, I should have made it messier to detour potential homebuyers.

At 7:55 a.m., my phone rings. Though I am expecting it to be Mark, a local number displays on the screen instead.

"Hello?"

"Another beautiful day, huh?" the voice from the other end asks.

"Uh-huh…" I respond, attempting to place the voice.

"I didn't wake you up, did I? I assumed after yesterday you were an early riser."

"Nathan." I finally realize. "I didn't know who this was. You have a different voice on the phone." It's strangely more gruf, yet somehow sexier.

He chuckles and apologizes, "Sorry to throw you off. I forgot that you didn't have my number yet. How'd the rest of yesterday go? Did you get some good writing done?"

"How did you know I write?"

"Mark and Jessi both have mentioned it. With the way the morning felt, I can't imagine a writer not writing. It would have motivated me to write if I was good at it. But I'm a much better reader than a writer."

"It only takes writing down words," I say, stirred by his insight.

"I'm also a better speaker than a writer. Speaker, reader, writer. My time would be better spent on the two things that precede it."

"Writer, reader, speaker for me."

I can hear him grinning on the other side of the line. "I like that." He pauses as the faint sound of a woman in the background is muffled. "Hold on," he tells me before whispering to someone else and returning to the phone. "The main reason I'm calling is to reschedule our appointment today. Something came up, I'm sorry. It's not my usual way of doing business. Would tomorrow work instead?"

Instant disappointment strikes. "No worries, that's fine," I respond coolly.

"I'll bring the best coffee you've ever had to make up for it."

"Okay, sure," I grunt, skeptical since I've had coffee from every location within a five-mile radius and when it comes to flavor, none of them rank on my top three list. Service, however, is always incomparable. The nicest people live here.

"Thanks for understanding, Autumn. I'll look forward to seeing you tomorrow." He hangs up before I say goodbye.

I lay down on my bed, staring at the sloped arch of the ceiling, wishing I could have seen him. It's okay to have a crush even when married, right? That's what this feels like. A little schoolgirl crush.

I reach for my phone again and send out a text to Rose.

> Bored today? Want to join me on more adventures?

Less than thirty seconds pass before her text reply comes in.

> Live vicariously through you? Sign me up!

> Great! 9:00?

> Ugh. 10:00.

Rose is not a morning person.
I send the thumbs-up emoji.

Jessi?

Rose asks. My first thought is no, only because I hate how she makes me think about Nathan, wondering about the context of them together. But I can't let these foolish thoughts come between our friendship. Especially after her breakthrough at the hospital.

I'll text her.

And I do before I can stop myself.
Thirty minutes before we leave, Jessi's response arrives.

Hell, yeah! Be there soon. If I can get off the bathroom floor.

* * *

We take advantage of the sunshine and perfect eighty-degree weather with a day trip to Haven Beach.

Rose adjusts her pink sunglasses as she pulls onto Interstate 42. "Okay, read the challenge to me."

Sandcastles are built of dreams. You visualize the sandcastle. You personalize it with every grain of sand between your fingers. You battle the waves from tearing it down. Then, you realize the ocean isn't tearing your dreams down, but giving them space, air, and movement, so that all the world can see them.

My parents never gave me a cake for my birthday; I wished on a sandcastle instead. As I built one, I stored my dreams and hopes for the future inside. I watched with pride as the waves carried it away, making promises for the next year to come.

We didn't have many possessions growing up, but we had the memories of the beach and the sandcastles. I never had any sugar highs or upset stomachs from too much birthday cake. All I had was the ocean's whispers to dream big.

Make the biggest sandcastle you can, and make your wish for the next year to come.

"That's crazy deep," Jessi speaks up from the backseat.

"Definitely a new way of looking at sandcastles," I agree as I reread Carrie's letter, a Sender from Orange Beach, Alabama. I love the idea of wishing on sandcastles instead of cake, mentally adding it to the ever-growing "when we have kids someday" list before I have to scold myself. Old habits die hard, I guess.

"Let's build a sandcastle!" Rose snaps me out of my gloom. She turns onto the marked frontage road with a wooden "Beach" sign painted in white letters. Once she finds a parking spot, we fill our hands with every beach-related item that's in the trunk of her car: hats, sunblock, chairs, umbrellas, towels, coolers, and most importantly, cheap plastic tools to create the perfect sandcastle.

We locate an open spot on the sand, set up, and begin our castle construction. The last time I built a sandcastle had to have been when I was around eight years old, but my natural talent returns as I shovel sand into various-sized pails and carve intricate decorations with the tip of my shovel.

We craft a fortress that spans thirty feet of sand. Becoming more daring with our creations, we attempt to decorate with tunnels and doors. Our impressive work captures the attention of a few kids around Aiden and Olivia's ages, playing further down the beach. They creep forward slowly and observe before one of the boys steps forward and asks if they can help us.

Our fortress develops into a miniature, medieval city. As the kids dig a deeper moat, we snap a picture of us with the sandcastle in the background. It's the most magnificent thing I've created. I close my eyes and make a wish like Carrie does on her birthday. I wonder what she wished throughout the years and if those wishes changed throughout time. Mine is for clarity of mind and heart, and of where I'm meant to be.

When a young girl trips over a sandy tower, crumbling it to pieces, and breaks into regretful cries, we all follow her lead to comfort her, stomping on the buildings and rolling on top of the remains, turning her cries into giggles. Funny how you can spend so much time creating something, yet equally enjoy demolishing it.

After our hard work, we say goodbye to the kids and reward their service to the kingdom with our extra tools and buckets. Then we reward ourselves by relaxing on our nylon beach chairs and soaking up the sun.

Rose brings him up first, and I realize that it's the first I've thought of Nathan since earlier that morning. "Give me some updates, Jessi. You pop Vertz's cherry yet?"

"Not even answering that," Jessi replies, slathering more sunblock on her stomach, brushing the edge of her tiny black bikini barely covering the parts intended to be hidden.

"You gotta be kidding me. I mean, you were there again last night, right? Give us some dirt. Autumn is an old, married person, I'm single, you're somewhere in between, so entertain us with your frolicking joys."

Jessi's sleepover at Nathan's house must have been why he rescheduled this morning. She had to have been who he was talking to—which only makes my thoughts about him even more erroneous.

When Jessi refuses to say anything else, Rose tries again. "I promise I'll be nice. You know I love you."

"I thought it would happen last night," Jessi budges and spills the details as she braids her hair. "He was in such a playful mood yesterday. And happy. Like, ridiculously happy and carefree. Flirting and tickling me and laughing more than usual. I kept thinking: it's going to happen, it's going to happen." She throws up her hands. "But it didn't. Every time I thought it would go somewhere, he'd start talking about work instead. He's, like, crazy obsessed with your house, A."

"He hasn't even seen it yet."

"He has. Mark let him peek at it when they first talked about it."

"What the—" I glare at Rose, the only person with access to the keys when I'm gone. "Rose? You? Did you let him in to see it?"

Rose bites her lip and grumbles, "What am I supposed to do when Mark calls me up and asks me to show it off to Nathan? Say no? Call you first?"

"Well, it would have been nice to know! I can't believe neither one of you said anything about it!" Everyone seems to be plotting to sell my cottage without my approval, and no one understands how much I don't want to let go.

"Maybe I wanted to avoid the Wrath of Autumn."

"Okay, whatever. Go on, Jessi." Now I'm even more intrigued with what else Nathan has said.

"That's all. Anytime something would start up, he'd talk about work. And how great mornings are. I don't know what his obsession is with the morning." She shrugs as the night owl that she is. "It was all so flipping boring."

I stifle my grin. Nathan must have felt the electricity, too. Maybe he didn't go home and dance it off like I did, but he dealt with it in his own way. To have insight into him like this is thrilling.

"I drank two glasses of whiskey while he was rambling. He didn't notice. Next thing I know, I'm waking up with a hangover and puking. He's there holding back my hair like a gentleman would. Humiliating."

So that's the real reason Nathan couldn't come to my house this morning. He was taking care of Jessi, not tangled in the bed sheets with her.

Rose is shaking from holding back her laughter. She finally chokes out, "You may have just convinced him to stay a virgin forever."

Jessi pulls down the band of her bikini bottoms to lower her tan lines. "Pretty sure that's the end. We're too different. I'm over it."

"And you need someone to screw?" Rose lifts her sunglasses and bats her eyelashes.

"Well, I do have a talent that shouldn't go to waste."

I press for confirmation, "So, it's really the end? I mean, he did take care of you."

"Yep." Jessi sighs dramatically. "Friend zoned. Next. On to bigger and better things, I suppose."

"Maybe he was the biggest of them all..." I had been so tensely preoccupied thinking about Nathan with Jessi that now the relief of them ending things allows me to be back my wayward self. They were too odd together, anyway. And I hate feeling as though I am competing with Jessi for a man, even though clearly that's not the case. I'm married, after all.

Jessi giggles. "There could be some truth in that. I did get a little feel."

That's all it takes for my mind to wander into darker places than it should go. My imagination can work against me sometimes.

* * *

"Are we connecting? Is this happening?"

Mark laughs as much as a thoroughly exhausted person can. I imagine the dark bags under his eyes as he holds his head up just to talk to me. He is one of the hardest working men I know. "Hey, beautiful. How are you?"

I lean back on my bed to get comfortable. I had just gotten out of the shower, cleaning off the sand stuck in all the crevices of my body from our fun at the beach. When I called Mark, I expected to leave a voicemail and not have a conversation. It's close to midnight in Italy, and there's no doubt he is still working.

"I'm good. It's been a fun day. Rose, Jessi, and I went to the beach and built a medieval town out of the sand. A bunch of kids joined in, and then we all destroyed it like King Kong." The echo of laughter from the kids rings in my ear, etching the priceless memories in my mind even deeper.

"A sandcastle, huh? That was a Bridging the Six Degrees challenge, right?"

"Yep. Only twenty-four more to go."

"Wow, you're hammering them out. You're taking the time to appreciate the stories, right? That's your role in this. That's what you signed up to do." Mark sounds like he's talking to an employee and not his wife.

"First of all, I didn't sign up for this. But yes, Mark. These stories are delicate. I'm not taking this experience lightly."

"I didn't say that. I only want to make sure you're getting the most out of it. And you know, changing from it."

"Wait—the expectation is that I'm supposed to change from this? You got this for me so I would change?"

"No, I mean—" He shuffles papers in the background. I note the coolness escaping him as his voice shifts to an exaggerated tone of practicality. "Every experience provides growth, and every person grows from their experiences. So yes, this should be a great growing experience. If you don't change from it, that seems peculiar considering the full scope of what this provides."

"Okay, but can't I be positively impacted without changing who I am? Do I have to be a different person on the other end of this?" I shake my head, but it's more at me than him. I understand what he's saying, but it makes me feel like he *wants* me to change, stirring up fears that have been brewing under the surface since the beginning of our relationship.

I never felt like I fit in with his lifestyle. Mark compliments me at the end of every event, acknowledging that it's not my scene, and he appreciates how I'm doing it to support him. Every time we slide into the back of the car and get buckled in, I know what he's going to say. The words are automatic. Now, I wonder if it is more obligation than truth. I'm not sure I want to hear that everything I thought I was doing right over the past several years wasn't up to par with what he was hoping I would do as his wife.

Mark groans, and I can hear him impatiently tapping a pen against the desk. "Listen, I'm drained, and this seems to be leading into a fight. Can we table this for now?"

I take a deep breath, aware of my defensive mentality and disappointed with how quickly the conversation has turned when it's hard to find time to talk to each other as it is. "Yeah, okay."

"So, the family is good?"

"Yep, everyone is fine. No updates."

"Good."

"Any updates there?"

"Not yet. Working hard to make progress."

Awkward silence ensues between husband and wife.

His voice returns to normal in what I can only assume is an effort to placate me. "Well, I'm glad you called, babe. It's great to hear your voice. I have a few hours of work ahead of me tonight, so I should get back to it."

Afraid of hitting a nerve again, I debate saying what's on my mind but do so anyway, "One more thing about Bridging the Six Degrees, and then I'll drop it... These experiences are amazing. I'd love to share one or two with you. I don't care which ones, but to have you by my side would be such a great memory. Like the cliff diving one. I'm scared to death to do it. I'd love to face that fear with you." *And maybe it would give us something to bond over again,* I silently add.

"Autumn, this gift was about you doing the challenges on your own. I mean, I don't care if you do them with Rose or Jessi or your family. But challenging yourself is the goal."

"I can do these with anyone else except for you. That's what you mean."

Mark exhales loudly, the tapping of the pen more aggressive, and sternly says, "The answer is no. I won't be coming back to do any of those. I'm sorry." He softens again to add, "I want to hear about them, though."

"So you can make an informed business decision on your relationship with the company," I point out coldly.

"Yes, part of the gift is research. I won't deny that, and I don't feel guilty about it. You know how important these business decisions are. We have an incredible life, and a large part of it is floated by my work. I wish you'd appreciate that more."

Anytime I get angry, I cry. I hate that I respond that way and wish I could get it better under control. I bite the inside of my cheek for composure. He hit a sensitive note for sure. "I have never once taken advantage of our life together. I've always been grateful and tell you that frequently. I don't appreciate you making it seem otherwise."

He says nothing, and a full minute passes. I can imagine him leaning his head in his hands, eager to get off the phone and return to critical business matters. "Yes, okay. That wasn't fair, and I'm sorry. I'm under a lot of stress right now. Let's try this conversation again tomorrow, okay?"

"Okay." I'm quick to agree, although I know we won't be able to connect tomorrow. It'll be back to the game of tag via voicemail. Maybe it's better that way for now.

"Goodnight, Autumn."

I pause, hurt that he doesn't say "I love you" but ultimately decide to be as stubborn. "Goodbye, Mark."

Throwing my phone across the bed, I lean back against my pillow. I hate fighting with him. I stew on things and lose sleep, impatient for us to repair our relationship. While I grow angrier, he returns to whatever he was in the middle of doing with our argument far in the back of his mind. He forgets about it by the next day. It is like I am more invested in the relationship at times, which scares me.

I have to get out of here. I throw on a hat as though I'm a celebrity afraid of being spotted. Maybe no one will know me from the news or the newspaper article or being at the party itself, but perhaps they will. I want a few moments to be by myself in a public place, having a drink like any other person who would want to drown their frustrations in alcohol.

I grab my bike and pedal to the closest bar, one of my favorites, housing an endless supply of interesting locals for inspiration in the stories I write. Calhoun Bar & Grill, 95% bar, 5% charcoal grill; food comes fast, drinks come faster.

"Jack and Coke," I request from the bartender the moment I slide onto the stool.

This bar has two types of bartenders: older Scandinavians and younger Scandinavians, a display of this area's heritage. All from the same family, they spend their summer days working outside and welcome the cold air when it comes time to man the bar later in the night. The bartender tonight is one of the sons that local and visiting women tend to fawn over, due to his chiseled cheeks and broad shoulders, as though better designed to be a professional football player. He's quick to provide as he sets the drink in front of me and asks if I'd like to see a menu.

"Maybe later, thanks."

"The drink is on the house then," he adds with a bob. It's not flirtatious, but an act that suggests he knows who I am, and I'm positive it's because of the Bridging the Six Degrees hoopla. My hat disguise did little good.

My cheeks redden as I murmur, "Thanks." The truth is, free drinks always taste better, especially when desperately needed.

Preparing to spend a moment to self-counsel, I take a sip, a form of guilt beginning to replace the anger directed toward Mark. That man works nonstop every day. One of his primary motivations is to provide for me. Blending the BSD gift for me with work is a way for him to balance his two loves. I get it, and I appreciate everything about it in that aspect.

But I also long for a passionate relationship, one that I used to dream about when I was a little girl. I'm sure it's the fuel for my sudden interest in writing romance stories, a genre I never once cared to read or write, but now I can't get enough of it. It's easy to turn the longing into happy endings for the fictional characters I only wish I could embody, and therapeutic when I'm struggling with my relationship with Mark.

I know some girls want what I already have in Mark, the hard-working breadwinner with traditional values, yet with perks like worldwide travel and fancy events. But I can't help but look at guys like Nathan, who are open, receptive, attentive, and in tune with nature, and question if that's more of what my heart desires. Cinderella didn't need the glass slippers and fancy castle in the end; she loved nature and animals and didn't mind getting dirty. If someone else came along before Prince Charming, maybe the end of her story would have been even more fulfilling.

A voice interrupts my thoughts. "Joe, another round. Whatever she's drinking, and the usual for me, please."

"Nathan," I gasp, his name escaping my lips like it's my key to freedom. "What are you doing here?"

"Well, I'm a regular here." He slides into the barstool next to me and rubs the back of his neck. "Whether I should say that with pride or shame is the question."

"It's a good bar, so I'd say some pride is okay."

"How about if I told you I'm a regular at most bars and restaurants in Door County?"

"Do you have a running tab at them all?"

"Only about seventy percent of them."

"Ooh, well..."

Nathan scrunches his nose. "Pathetic?"

"Not the first word that pops into my mind."

He heartedly laughs, and I smile at how good his laugh sounds. "Well, have some mercy on me. I'm a businessman. I do a lot of business and meet with clients here. Also, I can't cook, so where else do you expect a man to eat?"

"Aren't your parents still around here? You're never too old to pop in for a good home-cooked meal from your mama."

"Oh, I do. Trust me. My mom fattened me up. She's the queen of southern cooking and could give Paula Deen a run for her money. Every day was full of homemade buttermilk biscuits, slathered in sausage gravy for breakfast or honey and butter for dinner, deep-fried vegetables, and chicken, followed up with some of the best damn pies you could ever eat."

I wipe at my chin. "You're making me hungry."

"Exactly. I had to stop going over there so often. Believe it or not, bar food doesn't impact my body the way her cooking does."

I put up my hands. "Okay, judgment is off the table."

"Great, then don't judge me when I do this." Nathan waves to the bartender. "Can we get a basket of cheeseballs and another of fried okra?"

"If you come here and order fried food, does it really offset your mom's cooking?"

"What does that tell you about how my mom cooks?" Nathan winks as my stomach growls with excitement that food is on its way, and I realize how little I've had to eat today.

"I'm getting ready to meet Rose and Jess for a girl's night," I say, using Jessi's name to build an immediate barrier between our barstools which are mere inches apart.

"Ahh, yes. Jessi mentioned karaoke was on the agenda tonight."

We only determined at the beach that we would do the karaoke challenge tonight, which has to mean that Jessi and Nathan talked in the few hours since. She said she would break things off with him, but he doesn't look too wounded if she did.

"So, it's your first time, huh?"

Okay, they must have talked in some detail for him to know that as well. Maybe she was just filling in the conversation before she delivered the breakup news.

"I'm not a big public display of *anything* girl. I don't do well in big crowds, especially when purposely making a fool of myself."

Nathan bats at a fly in the air. "Nonsense. That's what karaoke is all about. It's no fun if someone is *actually* good at singing. Where's the entertainment value in that?"

"Maybe I should rephrase that: I'm not great at *being* the entertainment."

Joe sets the food in front of us. Like the drinks, the food comes just as fast.

"Don't tell me you've never pretended to be some famous singer when you were a little girl. Like, make-believe that you were singing in front of people?"

The thought makes me blush as I recall memories of standing in my childhood room, singing my heart out to my biggest fans—all my stuffed animals—as though I was a Grammy-winning artist. In reality, I'm the furthest thing from it. Partially tone deaf. I even mouth the words when singing "Happy Birthday." "Sure, Mariah Carey and Paula Abdul were frequently rotated."

"Well, good choices at least. That's exactly what makes karaoke fun. You get to live out all those crazy fantasies."

"Do men do that, too? I have the feeling you may know a few Mariah Carey songs by heart."

Nathan pops a cheeseball in his mouth. "I plead the fifth."

As we snack, I have to fight the urge to ask him about Jessi. It's such an awkward line to cross, although the curiosity is burning a hole in the floor as my knee bounces.

We chat a while longer before I suddenly notice the time and immediately slip off of the barstool. I would have passed the entire night sitting with Nathan and talking if I hadn't caught a glimpse of the clock on the wall making its rounds and alerting me that it's much later than I thought it was. Rose and Jessi were set to arrive at my house soon.

I pull out my wallet from my purse to pay for my drinks when Nathan covers my hand with his.

"I've got the tab. Go enjoy yourself."

"I will not let you pay for this."

Nathan squeezes my hand. My heart thumps. "I've got it. Consider it a late birthday gift."

I agree, just to be able to slide my hand away. His touch has ridiculous effects on my skin, and I pull my sleeve down to hide the goosebumps that line my arm.

"Are we still on for tomorrow morning?"

"Yeah, definitely," I say, much too eager.

"Let me know if you need to reschedule after tonight. Have fun and hey—let go of whatever it is weighing you down. You deserve to be free." There's a deliberate gleam in his eyes.

I feel refreshingly better than when I first arrived at the bar. Nathan pulled me from my funk. I don't allow myself to reveal my enlarged smile until I'm back outside, feeling the urge to skip all the way back home.

Eleven

"The challenge is to sing a song that cracks open your heart," Rose coaches me as we browse through the song list. "Are you ready for this?"

"Am I ready to bleed my soul out on stage in a place where I probably know one too many faces? No. I've had enough stage action for one decade already."

KickStand Bar is only a half mile from my house, so this feels like a snippet of the Bridging the Six Degrees birthday event all over again. Except instead of them singing to me, I'm singing to them. On stage. With a spotlight.

"What if you don't cry?" Jessi asks as she licks salt off her margarita glass.

"It's the notion of singing a song that gives me all the feels. Actual tears aren't required. Being open and vulnerable are the only requirements."

"Two words that don't suit you."

"Thanks for the reminder, Jess." My family must agree, considering they hand-selected this challenge for me. I'm a reserved person, keeping my truest feelings and thoughts in my head. That approach is what helps me write, though. When the deepest parts of me are revealed through fictional stories and not real life.

Madison Gullings, a singer-songwriter from Nashville and the muse behind this challenge, was once known for doing entire sets on stage with her eyes closed. She wouldn't open them until her performances were over.

Call it stage fright if you will, but my songs became jarringly more personal when my eyes were open, which I couldn't handle.

I can relate to her fear, and it was ironic with her handing me this challenge as I sat on stage at the Bridging the Six Degrees event. One of her idols gave her the life-changing advice that, "No one will connect with you as an artist if you don't expose the things that connect and break you as a person." The next time she had a show, she put on dark sunglasses to practice singing with her eyes open, while still protected from the audience.

I lasted three songs before ditching the sunglasses. Some people didn't care about me on stage, which can be damaging in its own right. But then there were others who were right there with me, feeling my words and moving in motion with my soul. It's those connections, that feeling that you're not alone, that makes the risk worth it. It makes putting yourself out there worth it. It's good for you, and it's good for them.

I understand from my own writing how true that is.

Rose asks, "Do you want me to request *the* song?"

Am I ready for this? Can I do this? Sometimes the best way to get through the pain is to face it head on.

I nod silently.

Jessi hums along with the current singer, who is performing a hilarious one-person play while singing "Barbie Girl." It couldn't be more opposite from the path I'm preparing to go down.

"Did you break it off with Nathan today?" I go straight for

the question that's been plaguing my mind, a much-needed distraction for my nerves as my knees bounce underneath the table, the biggest giveaway of my anxiety.

"Why? Did he say something?" Jessi asks, bewildered.

"He knew about us doing this tonight so I figured you talked to him already."

"Oh." She takes another sip of her drink. "But *you* talked to him already? Does Mark even know you're here tonight?"

Her random inquiry is irritating. "What does that have to do with anything?"

Jessi shrugs her shoulders and doesn't say another word.

"Okay, you're up soon." Rose returns to the table, delivering a glass of water to help calm me. "The guy said it was a weird selection. I told him, 'Well, no shit. We have a karaoke virgin here. You either get all the ones people have heard a million times or ones you've never heard before. Which do you prefer?'" She scoffs as she replays her attack on him. "Don't question the choice, just play the damn song." For a woman who says she doesn't want to have kids, she sure has fierce mama-bear instincts when it comes to protecting her best friend. I love her for it.

"Your Winter" by Sister Hazel is my choice. Four minutes and forty seconds. I can do anything for under five minutes, right? That's what I remind myself as I walk to the stage, which is only three-safe-feet from the ground to mitigate harm from anyone who may pass out under the heated, colored lights. It takes longer than the length of the song to weave through the couches, chairs, tables, and people's feet. *I can do this. I can do this.*

This song was my therapist during my breakup with Justin and again when I lost Amelia to the point that I had it on repeat for five straight months, keeping me company through my earbuds during the most significant points of my heartbreak. In those first few months, I could only consider that losing her was my fault. She was in *my* body. It must have been something I ate or did, something that I *should* have been able to prevent. All I could say was "I'm sorry, I'm *so* sorry" to her and to Mark, sobs muffling the words.

I wailed with this song for hours in private and now here I am, sharing it with a public audience, exactly like songwriters do, exposing their deepest vulnerabilities through music every single day.

On stage with a microphone in front of me, Madison's stage fright competes with mine, my heart thrashing about so hard I swear it'll give out soon. I belt out the words, giving this challenge all that I promised I would. My first time singing in front of a live audience, and soon, tears dampen my face. The song resonates with me far more now than ever before.

I force my eyes open when all they want to do is close from intimidation. Scanning the crowd, I'm thankful there are many people not paying attention at all to this crying lunatic I'm personifying. Then my eyes land on one table comprised of two men and three women whose voices carry loudly to the stage and almost overcome mine. "Your Winter" wasn't a popular song, and it drifts back several years in time, but here they are, singing and connecting with me. It gives me the gusto I need to finish my first-time karaoke stint with a fiercer tone than when I started. Pulling the microphone away from my mouth, I lean back and round out the last verse with power that shoots from my core and through my mouth.

The song comes to an end so I do an undeserved and overexaggerated bow and jump off the stage, less emotional and weirdly more energized. I high-five the group who was singing with me as I pass them, on a high that I haven't felt in much too long. Madison summarized it perfectly. The few people who understand my song choice make up for all the ones who don't. Unexpected bonds with random strangers. Priceless.

Rose grabs my wrists and excitedly cries, "I can't believe you did that! I thought for sure you'd chicken out!"

"Thanks for the vote of confidence, best friend." I look over her shoulders, searching for an invisible man. "What, no music executive came over to sign me to his label while I was up there?"

"He ran when you started crying."

Laughing, I reach for my water to rehydrate and watch the next person prepare for their song. This girl is moving with more confidence than I could ever muster while on stage in front of a crowd. Some people can do this without thinking twice, but for me, it takes a lot more energy and force.

With my solo under my belt, it strengthens my nerves to do it two more times with Jessi and Rose by my side. We sing "Hold On" by Wilson Phillips and "Strawberry Wine" by Deana Carter. I wonder how we have gone so long without doing this before. Well, Rose and Jessi have done it many times, but I always opted out. I let the fear of embarrassment stop me from *this*. Lasting memories with my best friends.

We stay until close and even then they have to shove us out the door. The three of us walk home arm-in-arm, hand-in-hand, singing songs spanning three decades and a multitude of genres. As different as we all can be at times, I could not be more grateful for these ladies and the unmatched friendship we share.

* * *

The sun pours through the window much too early. I need to purchase darker shades for my bedroom.

If I stay here, that is.

If I stay here...

The thought jolts me awake. I reach for my phone, my eyes barely open, and scroll to the number that interrupted my dreams, making a mental note of the need to assign Nathan's name to it. Although I'm not sure if I want that kind of constant temptation. He strikes me as the type of person I could randomly exchange poetic lines or book excerpts with via text, and that's dangerous. It's something I could never do with Mark.

This may be the slowest text I've ever typed, my eyes straining to see, each letter a hammer to my pounding headache.

> Hate to admit, but can we reschedule? Late night.

Before I can set the phone down, it dings.

> No problem. Get rest. Text when you have an idea for rescheduling.

Then a second message from him,

> Hope you had a great time! I'm sure you put Mariah Carey to shame. ;)

I'm pretty sure I've drunk more in my short time back in Crimson Bay than I have in my entire life. The effects on my body are a screaming reminder that I am no longer in my twenties, and it's time I accept it.

Climbing out of bed, I almost step on a passed-out Rose on my floor, a string of drool connecting her face with the rug. Jessi has already left since she had the sunrise shift at The Bridge. She's the only one who can function as normal with a hangover, anyway.

I make a hot pot of coffee and pop sticky cinnamon rolls in the oven. As soon as the scent floats through the house, Rose stumbles into the kitchen, eyes closed, hands out in search of a mug and a plate. I place them in her hands and she retreats to the corner of the couch, throwing a knitted afghan my mom made around her shoulders as she hunches over, blowing the steam away from her coffee.

I rub her shoulder as I join her on the couch. "I know it's a busy time at work so I can't thank you enough for using your vacation to hang with me."

Rose grunts as she combs her hair over her face with her fingers. "They'll survive. You, however, are questionable."

"That's true." I pull the end of her afghan so it covers my cold feet. "Now that we're alone, will you finally spill what's going on with Kevin?"

She peeks through her hair. "I didn't think you wanted to hear about him."

"Maybe I'm not crazy about the idea of him, but I also know how it feels for your best friends to not be a fan of the man you choose to be with." I tap her leg with my big toe.

She scowls at me. "Notice your word choice there, Autumn. *Choose* instead of *want*."

I wince. "Caught it." I *want* to be with Mark, right? Why is it so hard for me to frame it that way?

"Kevin is... different. There's more to him than meets the eye. He's sweet, kind, considerate, and ridiculously smart." Rose's eyes light up despite her hangover, another telltale sign of how bad she has it for this guy. "Kevin will take over the world. You should hear all his ideas. He's bursting with ambition and creativity."

"Sounds like someone else I know." Ambitious and creative are two of the first words I would use to describe Rose, too. I've never heard her talk about a man in more ways than being "hot," yet in her description of Kevin, she didn't mention anything about his physical features. This may be more serious than I initially thought. "So, you like him?"

Rose leans her head back onto the couch and admits, "Yes. I like him quite a bit."

I nod, my lips pursed as I consider the possibility that Kevin isn't the man I perceived him to be. I owe it to Rose to be open-minded toward him. But why in the world does he have to carry the same demeanor as Justin and look like her dad? It's hard to shake the similarities now that I've seen them. It's surprising she hasn't made the same connection yet.

"You know how hurt I was when Jessi told me your true feelings about Mark, right? Do you understand how blindsided I felt?"

Rose lifts her head off the couch and wraps her fingers around my socked foot, gently squeezing it. "I know. That was a crappy way to deliver it. I'm sorry, Autumn. I should have brought it up before. You were so hell-bent on leaving the Bay that I didn't want to stand in your way. Not after what you went through with Justin. If Mark was the one to put you back together again, what could I say?"

My stomach clenches at the mention of Justin's name, a reaction that hasn't changed in a decade. Not only my first broken heart, but also the first time I truly lost trust in someone and witnessed the too-easy slippery path of staying in a toxic relationship. I thought we would get married—everyone in Crimson Bay believed it, too. But Justin had plans of his own with Holly, his temporary side action, turned into his now wife. They have three kids to boot.

Rose continues, "I actually ran into him the other day."

"Who? Mark?"

She rolls her eyes. "No, Justin. I still have to resist punching him when I see him."

"Oh." I take a minute to process it. I have avoided seeing both Justin and Holly in all my visits back, which is quite the feat for such a small town. "How'd they look?"

Roses raises her eyebrow. "How'd they look? They looked like a family advertisement for luxury yachts. Pretty sure they were headed to one and grabbing items for lunch. Annoyingly posh. Even the two little boys had loafers and button-down shirts on and were so well-behaved that I can only assume they were drugged. They're Justin's mini-mes. Hopefully they don't grow up to be little assholes like him," she half-snarls.

Rose almost murdered Justin when we found out about him and Holly having an affair. Cheating is an extra sensitive topic after what she and her mom experienced in Rick's Tour de Affair aftermath. I spent half that night making sure Rose wouldn't drive over to Justin's house to kill him, and the other half of the night with her wiping away my tears.

I can't help but envy that Justin's life progressed into the one I wanted to have. Despite all the terrible things he did, he still got it. He got the wife, the kids, the house on Lake Michigan. There must have been a part of Justin who thought Holly would make a better wife and mom. Why else go down that path with her instead of continuing it with me? We had spent years talking about how that's what we wanted most out of life.

If only I had dealt with that heartbreak better, maybe I wouldn't have been so blinded by Mark. He was a welcome reprieve from the shame I felt when everyone in town knew that I was cheated on, including some who were aware of the truth way before I was. Mark became my, "Let me show you that I'm okay and better than ever," but I lost sight of some of my biggest values as a result.

I roll my shoulders to shake off the lingering memories. "Do you think Mark is like Kevin, though? Like, maybe there's more to Mark than you guys realize?"

Rose tilts her head as she considers it. "I suppose you would know if that were true. But Mark isn't new. If there were more to Mark, we'd have realized it by now."

I ignore the reverberation of the truth shattering my heart. "So, to summarize your point, you don't think Mark is the right one for me?"

She stands and reaches for my mug to refill it, cupping my hand. "Do you?"

I don't answer. The "no" that enters my head is unwelcome. Too many layers to dissect; too many parts that comprise the core of my relationship with Mark, changing all at once.

When she returns to the couch with fresh coffee, she tentatively adds, "There is one thing about Kevin that is even more unexpected."

"I don't want to hear about it." I shake my head, assuming the reference is for something underneath his clothes.

"No, not that. Although that is..." She giggles and lifts her long eyelashes to the sky as though thanking Santa for the greatest present under the Christmas tree. Taking another sip of coffee to build the anticipation before continuing, she reveals, "This is a bit more serious. Kevin has a daughter."

Refraining from the dramatic antics of spitting out my drink in surprise, I steady my voice before asking, "That's a deal-breaker, right?" In our friendship trio, I'm known as the family-oriented one. My nieces and nephews leave me in a constant dream state of desiring kids of my own. I have baby names picked out, future family portrait poses chosen, and secret Pinterest boards filled with nursery décor ideas.

Jessi doesn't care either way if she has kids or not, but Rose never wanted kids. She wants a career-focused life with the ability to travel anywhere. Her and Mark are alike in that realm. *I* am the one who wants children. I am the one who *always* wanted to be a mom someday.

"I don't think it is."

I'm stunned, my stomach rolling for new reasons. "But you said kids would get in your way. If this turns into something, you know you'd be somebody's mom."

"Stepmom. Her real mom is out in New York."

"Okay, but still a mom. Still involved. Your life would still have to revolve around her."

Rose doesn't seem one bit phased by this. "I know. We've talked about it."

"You and Kevin have already discussed you possibly becoming his daughter's stepmom? Have you met her, too?"

"We've Skyped. Well, kind of. She's only eleven months old."

I rub my face with my hands, trying to wrap my head around *this* Rose, talking about being married and becoming a stepmom when spending most of her life not even wanting a boyfriend. "So you Skyped with his ex—or baby mama or whoever—to meet his daughter?"

"She called when I was with him. It wasn't pre-planned.

There are a lot of things you need to hold off on judging, okay? It's why I want you to get to know him away from the business stuff. Will you have dinner with us one night before you leave?"

"Can't I know more before agreeing to that?"

"Nope. Let me figure out a day that may work when he's back to visit and I'll get it set up."

I pull a throw pillow over my face and groan. A million thoughts swarming my mind and I can't verbalize any of them except, "When did things get so damn complicated?"

"When we turned thirty."

Rose has yet to know how true that is for me.

Twelve

Rose gets called into work for an emergency tourism presentation to fill in for a coworker with strep, so I embark on the next challenge by myself. I stop by Timber Creek Living, an assisted living home that I volunteered at during my school years. Carol will help with what I need.

Carol is my mom's best friend from elementary school and another permanent resident of Door County. As an only child, she took it upon herself to provide full care for her parents. When her parents went to live at Timber Creek Living, Carol decided that visiting wasn't enough. She secured a receptionist job at TCL to be close to them. She then earned her Certified Nursing Assistant certification to fill in around the home when needed. She reminds me of Mother Teresa.

"Hi, Carol." I hug her across the counter.

"Autumn! I didn't get a chance to talk to you at your party. That was mind-blowing! So much bigger than your mom thought it would be! How are the challenges going?"

"Good, good. Still working on them, which is why I'm here."

"Ooh, do we get to be a part of one? How exciting!" When people describe Carol, her enthusiasm and love for others are the two most consistently mentioned traits. She is a light in this world and frequently "adopted" by the residents, especially those with little remaining family.

"I hoped for a chance to get to know one of your residents. Someone who doesn't get many visitors but would be open to having one?"

"Oh!" Carol claps her hands. "I remember this challenge! I loved it when that girl presented it and love it even more now that you want to bring TCL into it! I know the perfect person. Her name is Marabelle. No family to speak of and very selective with the activities she participates in."

"Would she be up for having a stranger visit?"

Carol pauses for a moment before responding with, "I think so. We could always try, and if she throws a book at you..."

I laugh and then pause when Carol isn't smiling. "Wait, you're joking, right?"

"I hope so!" she giggles.

Marabelle is everything you'd imagine in a classic, perfectly-primped lady from the Upper East Side of New York. Except she is here, in Crimson Bay. Her hair is alabaster white, curled to perfection. A powder-pink suit jacket hangs on her small frame. Tan pumps and a white pearl necklace complete her attire. Marabelle is staring out of the window, her hands clasped together in her lap.

I am immediately drawn to her.

Carol puts her hand on Marabelle's shoulder. "How would you feel about a visitor today?"

Marabelle turns to study me, paralyzing me with the pureness of her crystal blue eyes.

"And who is this visitor?"

I stick out my hand. "I'm Autumn."

She encompasses it with both of her hands, just like Nokutenda did when I first met her. It's the type of shake you give someone when you're confident enough to share a part of yourself right away. "Red hair like falling autumn leaves. Pleasure,

Autumn." Marabelle turns to Carol. "Could we please have some tea, dear?"

"Of course. I'll bring a tray over shortly."

"Thank you, dear." Turning back to me she asks cautiously, "And why did you want to meet with me? Unless they solicited you? They're always trying to get me to be more social."

"No, I came on my own. It's a bit of a long story that I'd be happy to share." I'm not sure if I should sit down, feeling like I have to earn an invitation into her space first.

"I do enjoy a good story. What is it that you do?"

It's a question I struggle with when asked. I no longer work so I can travel with Mark. But I'm not a stay-at-home mom, which was the plan in the early months pregnant with Amelia. I'd love to say that I'm an author but it's hard to stand behind that when I've spent the past four years attempting to finish novels that have no endings. However, after these recent experiences, I've learned it's a part of me, regardless of the achievements I have or haven't made yet. I confidently—for the first time ever—reply, "I'm a writer."

"A writer, huh? Published books or articles galore?"

"Well, attempting to publish a novel currently. But I like to pretend I'm a writer nonetheless."

"Pretending can lead to becoming."

"That's sure what I'm hoping for."

A tiny smile appears on her thin, coral lips as quickly as it disappears. "Are you here to interview me for a piece you're writing?"

"No. Well, not exactly. I'm here to get to know you if that's okay."

"Why would you want to get to know an old lady?"

"To learn something from someone I don't already know." It seems too premature to dive into the BSD and how Lucy Danvers from Utah challenged me to

...learn the life lessons from someone who is older, wiser, and has lived a completely different life than you. It keeps you open,

grounded, and mindful of how precious time is and how little of it we have.

This challenge perfectly symbolizes my relationship with Henry so in many ways, it's already complete. But I figured I'd seek out someone new, which is a challenge since most local residents were either born in Door County, grew up here, or lived here for a good chunk of their lives. I doubted it would fulfill the "completely different life" portion of Lucy's request.

However, the moment Marabelle spoke with the undertones of a proper New York accent, I knew this was the right person.

"Have you learned anything from me yet?"

"Only that you're great with dialogue."

She chortles as she reaches to move the newspaper from the seat across from her and pats it. "Well sit, child, sit."

Carol returns with a tray of tea that she sets on the small table between us. She doesn't say a word as she walks away.

Marabelle and I talk about the weather and other nonsense topics while she directs me on how she takes her tea. I stir in half a teaspoon of sugar and a squeeze of a lemon slice before handing it to her.

She takes a sip and leans back in her chair as her pinky finger rhythmically taps the delicate glass. "Honey? A moment of honesty here."

I nod to her, encouraging her to go on.

"I hate small talk. *Despise* it. Would rather not talk at all than make small talk. If there are deeper matters you'd like to get to, let's go straight there."

I swallow the too-hot tea with a gasp and Marabelle looks at me curiously. I blow on the tea, leaning back in my own chair after realizing I was sitting on the edge, attempting to be proper for no reason. With a grin, I concur. "No small talk."

Mutually agreed upon silence settles around us as we drink our tea while gazing out the window. It obliterates the natural tension that sits between two people getting to know each other and creates a more relaxed atmosphere, like two old friends spending time together.

Once my tea cools to room temperature, I release the first question on my mind. "Are you married?" I don't have a predetermined plan for what I want to say to Marabelle; I'm letting my heart guide the conversation.

Marabelle stifles a chuckle as she sets her teacup on the table. "Oh goodness, child, no. No. No, no, no, no."

I can't help but laugh. Such an effusive reaction to marriage was not at all what I expected.

"Let's see..." She counts on her fingers until she ends with the number eight. "Eight proposals. Told them all no. I thought about one. I thought about it for fourteen days. Then he was foolish enough to demand an answer because he couldn't wait any longer. Well, he made that easy. An easy no," she scoffs.

My first question for Marabelle already proves how different we are. I was seldom without a significant other in some form. Whether it was drifting between dates or boyfriends, I was never alone, searching for the fairytale romance without considering my intention.

"They say you don't know yourself until you live alone with yourself. I decided that I really liked myself. More than I liked anyone else, in fact. Don't get me wrong, I like men a lot. But nothing lasting," Marabelle continues.

"So, you never had kids?"

"Goodness gracious, no." Marabelle reaches for her tea again. "That would have been disastrous."

"Do you wish that you did? Like in hindsight?"

"No, not at all. I know, I know," she says, gesturing to the walls decorated with colorful giant pictures ranging from piles of fruit to rolling hillsides. "You would think living here would make me wonder about the choices I made, and if I"d do them differently. But no. I stick by my decisions."

I raise my eyebrow, remembering my mom's similar reference

of the importance of being all-in on our decisions, as a question forms in my mind. Marabelle reads my thoughts.

"I checked myself in here. I don't need someone else to tell me what I already know. It was time." Marabelle leans closer to me. "I'm selfish. I always knew it. I like to do things on my own time. I had big goals. Having children was never one of them."

She reminds me of Rose and would have been the spitting image of Rose's future if it wasn't for Kevin's arrival shaking everything up.

Marabelle taps her teacup again. "Being a mother, a good one at least, is one of the most honorable acts a person can commit to. But so is admitting that you are too selfish to be a mother at all." She glances out the window again. "I prefer self-full. I traveled the world and met more people than most could ever dream. That satisfied me more than a family ever could."

A young Marabelle isn't hard to imagine. Similar to the famous Rose and Jack scene on the edge of the ship in *Titanic*, except Marabelle stands alone with her hands outstretched and the wind flowing through her hair—bold, inquisitive of the world, free.

"By your accent, I assume you're not from these parts."

"No."

"Was your family from here?"

"No."

I hesitate to fire more questions at her. Marabelle is watching with amusement dancing in her eyes. I finally concede, "Why are you in an assisted living facility in Door County, Wisconsin, of all places?"

Clearly pleased that I asked, she answers, "Redd Martin." Marabelle's blue eyes dilate with the memory. "The only man who could ever challenge me, and the only one who never asked me to marry him. The only one I would have said yes to. I came here almost six years ago—to the day—to be with him. I woke up one autumn morning and decided it was time. Donated almost everything I owned. Put on a lovely sage dress that I saved for the moment and hopped on a plane."

Even the selfish, or self-full ones, pursue love it seems. "What happened?"

"I found Redd's gravestone. He died five months before. Bastard couldn't wait for me." Her smile never falters even with the delivery of a sad ending. The *Titanic* image comes back to mind. Even Marabelle had a Jack. She wouldn't have been alone at the bow of the ship if he hadn't died first.

"And you stayed?"

"I made the decision to stay with Redd before getting on the airplane. I told you, child, I stick by my decisions."

I marvel at her character. This woman came straight out of the womb knowing exactly who she is and what she wants out of life. I wish I had the same strength to stand by my true self for all these years. If I had a little girl, I would protect her sense of worth and do what I could to instill confidence in the unique qualities that make her who she is. And hope that it would always carry forward in her life.

"What is it, child? Why did you get so sad?"

I pull my hair off my neck, heat rising in my body. As usual, my eyes make my truest emotions impossible to hide. "Sorry, my thoughts drifted."

"Never apologize for wearing your heart on your sleeve. In fact, wear it like the most exquisite scarf that has people bent with envy, no matter how psychotic those emotions become."

"Until they use that scarf as a straitjacket for me."

Marabelle's smile is equal to her wind chime-like laugh, and receiving one is like earning a high honor or receiving an elite award. I'm not surprised she had so many wannabe suitors in her life. "Please, do share. I believe you owe me a story since I've shared some of mine."

It's painful admitting to a lady of her stature, someone so confident in being alone, that my desire to not be alone is about equal to her independence. "I was thinking that if I had a daughter, I'd want her to be as self-assured as you."

She chuckles and offers, "Feel free to name her Marabelle. I never hated my name."

"We had a girl briefly. Amelia. We lost her during the pregnancy, though. And that was it for us. My husband doesn't want kids. Not anymore."

"Child, don't you ever let someone else determine what you have or don't have in life."

"My husband is kind of an important component in making babies." My voice chokes despite my attempt to keep it lighthearted.

"Perhaps. But if you chose him to do life with, then why are you so sad about this?"

"I didn't find out until after we were married. We rushed into marriage—for Amelia. If we waited just a little while longer, we would have lost her before being legally bound to each other. Having children was always part of my plan. I spent most of my life imagining beautiful kids, little reflections of their dad and me, running around, vacations, school plays, movie nights, holiday traditions surrounded by family. Now they're just that. Dreams. Not reality."

"Sometimes you have to embrace the life you are given, child. Too many people these days try to change the flow of the universe. They want to control an uncontrollable force. We are given the opportunity to make some choices—more choices than we deserve in all truthfulness. Once those choices are made, we need to see where life goes. Otherwise, you'll be too busy questioning everything and milking regrets rather than living a full life that embraces the present."

I nod while swallowing my sobs to prevent from releasing all my tears.

"You never know what life will bring in the future, as long as you stay open. If a child is what you want, you may still have one, just not in the way you originally dreamt. But never close doors that are meant to stay open."

My eyes drift close, letting Marabelle's words sink in and comfort my ache. It is the first time that a little hope and peace seeps through my bottled-up pain. Simultaneously, it makes me feel sacrificial, like I'm here on a path to give up having children just to continue living Mark's life.

We chat for another three hours. Marabelle is as fascinating as Henry. I wish they could meet. It's easy to imagine them as friends exchanging bits of wisdom and stories together. Her brief bursts of wind chime laughter combined with his hearty Santa-laughs would instantly cheer anyone privy to be in their presence.

I could imagine me and Mark with them, us falling in love with Marabelle as much as we have with Henry, adopting them both into our life. Maybe they could fulfill the aching for the family I wanted to create with Mark. Maybe I'm too focused on creating children with him when there are so many other people we could love and choose to be a part of our family instead.

I leave TCL for my parents' house to immerse myself in as much family time as I can. Marabelle reminded me of what's truly important. I hug my parents like I'm a little girl again. I bathe in the scents of my childhood home and hang all the details as permanent fixtures in my mind. Marabelle doesn't have the burning desire to surround herself with loved ones, but I do. I need my family. She reminded me there's nothing wrong with that.

Thirteen

Dark sky. Thunder. Lightning. Rain. Aggressive knock on the door. It's the perfect setup for a scary movie.

I close my laptop and jog to the door, opening it to discover a drenched man on my doorstep.

"Oh crap, is it four o'clock already?"

Nathan stands on the stoop wearing a navy-blue windbreaker with matted, blonde bangs pressed against his forehead under his hood. Drops of rain drip off his eyelashes.

"Should I leave?" he asks deadpan, turning his body to face the downpour.

Laughing, I grab his arm and tug him inside the house. "No, it's fine. I lost track of time."

He pushes his hood back, revealing a mess of hair ruffled from the windbreaker. "Don't let me block the creative juices from flowing."

"How did you know I was writing?" I always feel too transparent with him.

"You have a glossiness in your eyes, set with determination. That can only come from staring at the computer and writing." Nathan zips off his jacket to hang it on the coat rack. "Plus, I saw you through the window." He adds with a wink while wiping his shoes on the rug.

I shake my head at his reveal. "I was definitely in a zone."

"It's your passion, huh?"

Nodding, I reply, "Agonizingly, yes. Sometimes it's the only thing in the world I want to be doing, but life demands otherwise."

"Have you ever thought about running away, hiding out in a cabin on a remote lake, and writing until your fingers bleed?"

"Every single day." Our eyes fixate on each other. Despite being dressed, I feel naked in front of him. I can't disguise anything—not my thoughts, not my emotions, not my deepest dreams in the world. He would know them all, even if I pretended otherwise. I've never felt so immediately comfortable, so connected in the most profound way possible, with another human as I have from the first time I shook hands with Nathan.

He breaks the silence hanging in the air. "I wish I had something I was passionate about."

I gesture to the barstools by the kitchen island so he can sit. "There's nothing?"

Nathan slides off his muddy shoes before walking across the wooden floor to join me. No socks, just his tanned, bare feet, which convey a strange intimacy.

"Well, traveling, I suppose. And photography." He traces the lines in the granite island with his fingers. "I had dreams once of being this world-renowned photographer who would travel everywhere, taking pictures and creating insane works of art displayed in *National Geographic*."

I can't help but scornfully laugh, like a cruel joke being played. Nathan's dreams line up with the same ones I had when I was younger. Before I abandoned everything that made me, *me*, and followed Mark into a life that wasn't anything like I thought I wanted.

"What's so funny?" He raises an eyebrow.

"I once had similar aspirations. I wanted to travel the world, live among people of different cultures and write about them. I envisioned a photographer boyfriend who would capture the pictures of our experiences, and together we would publish articles in *National Geographic*."

Nathan stares back at me. My cheeks fill with heat. I might have overshared this time.

Clearing his throat, he states, "Well, apparently mine didn't quite happen. Instead, I get to use this camera to take pictures of real estate." He pats the brown leather bag in his hands. "Speaking of which, we should get these pictures taken so you can get back to writing."

As comfortable as I am with him, the same awkward feeling relentlessly surfaces at some point in our interactions. I need to stop saying so much. There's no good in divulging more information than necessary. It's like my overactive imagination strives to create a Harley Quin-style romance with Nathan as the star, and me as the innocent seductress in a plunging, too-tight bodice and 1800s-style dress. Clearly, it's far from that.

As I stand up, a loud boom makes the house rattle and the rolling thunder rumbles closer. The lights flicker out for a few seconds before returning. I point to the ceiling. "I promise those work."

Nathan grins. "I won't write that down."

"Well." I extend my arm, in true Vanna White fashion, to present the entire house to him. It's all easy to see from the kitchen island. "There's not much to it, as you can tell."

"Cozy," he mutters, distracted as he snaps pictures of the wooden beams that stretch across the living room and kitchen. Neither one of us brings up the fact that he has already seen it once before. I wonder if Rose and Mark told him to keep that information quiet.

Any time Mark was in my cottage, I felt restless as he walked around. Almost ashamed. It wasn't modern-looking and didn't have all the latest technology or updated appliances. He has never commented on it either, whether good or bad. Most people talk about my home's charm or the perfect views. Mark sees it as a random property we just happen to own, when in fact it is so much more than that. It's a part of me.

Nathan and I spend the next thirty minutes discussing business: the house, the market comps, setting the price, and open house information as he snaps pictures. We end the tour back at the kitchen island where Nathan digs in his bag and produces official documents. After filling in a few lines, he hands the pen to me to sign off.

I read the fine print in the documents, tapping the pen noisily on the counter as I scan the words. Before I sign, I look up at Nathan, his eyes scrutinizing me.

"You don't want to do this, do you?" His question falls sincere and gentle on my ears. It's the first time someone has cared to inquire as to how I feel about selling my house. Embarrassing tears spring to my eyes.

"No." The word comes out in a squeak as darkness covers us when the lights flicker out for good.

Lightning flashing through the window saves me from stubbing my foot while I cautiously walk to the pantry and stand on my tiptoes to reach the candles and matches on the very top shelf. I bring them back to the island and wait for another flash so I can see what I'm doing. Suddenly, I sense Nathan next to me in the dark. My body tenses.

He uses the flashlight feature on his cell phone so I can better see the candle.

"Thanks," I mutter as I light it.

Nathan remains standing close—close enough I swear he can smell my hair. Or, maybe he is actually smelling my hair.

"Reminds me of strawberry picking." He steps back to lean his body against the counter behind him.

I blush, thankful he can't see it in the dark. The one candle is barely giving off enough light to see his face once he steps away. I pull out a few more candles and use the original one to light those, placing them throughout the kitchen and living room.

Nathan is watching my every move.

"How have we never hung out before?"

I stop in my tracks, biting my lip before responding. "You don't know how often I've had that same thought. I don't know... It's strange though, right? This is such a small community."

"That it is..." he trails off.

"Especially if you know Jessi."

"Well, she is a little closer to my age."

I stretch to place the matches back on the shelf. "By two years? Do you think I'm ancient?"

"No, no. I didn't mean that. We were in school at the same time, and we've run into each other a lot since then. Only recently have we started hanging out."

"By hanging out, you mean dating."

Nathan stretches his arms like he just finished a workout. "I don't know if you'd call it that. *I* wasn't calling it that. But she's told me multiple times she can't see me anymore. And then next thing I know, she's on my doorstep. So, I'm not sure what it is."

"Wait, so you had no clue you two were in a relationship?"

He chuckles and dips his head. "We never went on dates or claimed to be exclusive. I wouldn't have blinked if Jessi dated someone else or *hung out*, or whatever she wants to call it. Besides, I hang out with a lot of people. Men and women. It comes with the territory of being a realtor and networking."

"Do you watch movies late at night with them all?"

"Believe it or not, I do! I love movies. I watch them with or without someone, so if someone wants to join me, I don't say no."

"Do you kiss them all, too?" I cover my mouth with my hands. I didn't mean to take it that far.

Nathan laughs in response. "Okay, not all of them."

I cock my head and analyze him. He could be a bit more of a playboy than he's letting on.

He continues, his voice lower, "Although, if you hung around here long enough, you'd hear rumors about me."

I wonder if he's referring to his virginity, which is crazy that I know such an intimate detail about him that never came straight from his mouth. "Are you a hot topic?"

"I'm not sure how I came to be that, but some days it sure feels like it. For years, many people didn't even realize my parents had a son because I was so quiet and shy. Somehow it went from that to what it is today."

I sense a touch of unease in Nathan. Maybe it's the environment, with the combination of the sudden darkness and storm. That can make people more vulnerable.

"People around these parts believe I'm gay."

That's not the confession I expect, but I breathe a sigh of relief. Is *that* the reason nothing more has happened with Jess? He did just say he hangs out with men and women. Even though there are already a handful of reasons I can't be with Nathan, at least that one eliminates my continual questioning of what my life would have been like if I'd met him before Mark.

Before I have a chance to respond, Nathan continues, "I'm not ashamed of being called that. People can believe whatever they want. It's their ignorant reasons *why* that make it sting."

I am all too familiar with the rumor mill. It's partially why I was anxious to leave the small community atmosphere and blend into a fast-paced city which is too busy to care what strangers are doing. After my broken engagement with Justin, I needed to be free from people who only knew us together and would question where he was when I wasn't with him.

I stay quiet and wait for Nathan to say more.

But he switches topics. "Is it strange that I want to unload everything on my mind when I'm with you? Sometimes it's hard to find people I trust around here. Every time I'm with you, I end up rambling."

"Unload away. Besides, I'm a safe zone, right? Not a permanent staple here. You're selling my home, after all, and getting rid of me." I point out to Nathan. *Although I want to be here. I don't want to give up my home*, I admit silently.

I think I catch a grimace, but his words contradict it. "Good point. Well, here's the straight scoop: I've never had a serious girlfriend. Truth is, I hardly date. I'm twenty-five, and people treat my status as though there's no feasible way that simply not desiring to be in a relationship at this point in my life can be the real reason. There *must* be more to the story."

I roll my eyes, although I've also questioned how he can possibly be single. He seems too good to be true. "People can be harsh."

"That's for sure. I'm grateful my parents instilled such a strong foundation in me. They raised me to live life to the fullest. To be the best version of myself before I share my life with someone else. It's rooted in my values. But it amazes me how many people think that's impossible. I want to get married someday, I do. But not until I'm ready for that person." Nathan nudges the island with his toe. "I work hard but instead of people respecting it, they call it a cover-up. Over the last few months, people have been trying to set me up with their sons, brothers, nephews, whomever. Simply because I've never had a girlfriend."

"So, when Jessi showed interest, you played it out to curb the rumors." Spotting the truth through his confession is easy.

Nathan closes his eyes and pinches the bridge of his nose. "Yes. I hate to admit that, but yes. Don't hate me. I know she's your friend. I like hanging out with her, don't get me wrong. She's a fun girl. I tried to stay open to the possibility of something panning out, even if it's down the road when I'm actually ready. But..."

"You're too different from each other?"

"Putting it mildly, yes. Although that's not always a bad thing, I'm not sure it's a home-run attraction, either." He drums his fingers against the counter. "But *you* even thought we were together."

"Well, that's because Jessi told me you guys were."

"Do you think she's my type?"

I look up at the ceiling to avoid eye contact. "In keeping with the honesty theme... no."

"Why?"

"Because you're a good fit for me." It sounded better in my head than out loud.

"What?" Nathan straightens his back. So do I.

"I mean, you're more of a fit for somebody like me. And Jessi and I are opposites. So, you're not Jessi's type, but more of my type. I mean, more of someone-like-me's type..." *Shit.*

My mind is racing and my stomach is tossing as though I could throw up. I take a towel to the floor to clean up a water spot my bare toes keep touching, which must be leftover rain dripping from Nathan.

Nathan stays mute, which only makes my slip-up more mortifying. I've had one too many embarrassing moments in our short time of knowing one another.

Finally, he sits down on the barstool again and asks, "Why did you leave the Bay?"

Instead of returning to the island, I slide down the wall to the floor. Although I'm grateful for Nathan's transitional topic, my new strategy is to keep as much physical distance as I can from him. "I spent my whole life determined not to be like my parents. I thought they lived in a bubble with fear keeping them rooted to one spot, which was the opposite of truly living, according to my limited definition at fifteen years old."

I play with the strings in the kneehole of my ripped jeans, wondering if it would have been possible *not* to be narrow-minded as a teenager. "But recently, I've been admiring the reasoning behind their decision. They knew what made them happy and they stuck with it. There's no shame in that. Their commitment to this area is admirable." *Especially for people like me who are still confused at thirty years old with no determined direction in sight.* I leave that last part out, though.

Nathan nods his head in agreement. "I understand that. After graduation, to avoid being stuck here I ended up on an excursion around the world. Twelve countries, five continents."

I giggle and pull my hair into a tighter ponytail. "You sound like *The Amazing Race*."

He hops off the stool and joins me on the floor, grinning, closing the distance between us, and not saying anything more.

"Wait—no way!" My mouth drops open when I remember my family referenced him on a reality show. "You were on it?"

"It's the reason I started working out and lost my eighteen years of baby weight." Nathan chuckles as he pats his stomach. "Came in third place. So close. Taxi issues, go figure."

"No way! That's awesome! I always loved watching the teams compete in countries all over the world, learning about the different cultures wherever they visited." I only stopped watching it once I moved into my cottage and couldn't afford cable. Then once I lived with Mark, the only thing that ever graced our TV was sports. Which was fine by me; it left me time to curl up on the couch and read.

"I'm surprised you didn't hear about it. It was all the rage around here for a few months. You weren't the first local celebrity." He taps my arm as though commanding goosebumps to appear, which they do. "But I think it's what fueled my early realtor boom, as bad as that might be. People say five minutes of fame can propel a lifetime of success and it's true. It's the strangest phenomenon, but I try not to lose sight of how grateful I am every day."

Mockingly bobbing my head, I say, "Okay, I get it, you're humble about it. Good job. Now tell me, what was it like being on *The Amazing Race*? What's Phil like? What was the hardest challenge you did? Who was your partner?" I move my legs to sit cross-legged and lean in to hear more.

Nathan laughs and I'm appreciative that he takes me with a grain of salt. He moves his legs to mirror my stance and leans in. Nathan is so close that I can smell mint on his breath, like he brushed his teeth right before he came over.

We sit in that position for hours as he describes his experiences on *The Amazing Race*, sometimes wildly moving his arms to emphasize his experiences and what he faced. The lights come back on too early, but we don't stop to acknowledge them. We each blink a few times as our eyes adjust but never skip a beat in conversation. Recognizing the lights are back on would be a reason to end the conversation and get back to business. It seems neither one of us wants that. At times, I am giggling so hard that I have to hold my stomach because it actually aches.

"You have the best laugh."

I abruptly stop. It wasn't his words, but his *tone*. The first outright flirting he's given into.

He's looking at me as though *I* surprised *him*, not the other way around. "I had to comment on it. People are afraid to laugh from deep within these days, or they force a chuckle to imitate a reaction. You don't hold back, though. It's carefree, and makes me feel the same, as cheesy as that may sound."

The room grows increasingly warm. My cheeks flush, and I wish the lights hadn't come on yet, so the darkness could mask what he's doing to my body.

"I snort more than laugh."

"That snort is my favorite. That's when I know I've gotten to you. I like it." He shifts his legs, so they're extended out. "How's the Six Degrees list going?"

His diversions are gold and advantageously placed. I corral my thoughts back to the PG zone. "Well, it's been incredible. Slowly working through it. Sometimes I'll make a plan. Other times I'll see how I feel that day and select a challenge that way. A few I'm putting off because I'm nervous about doing them."

"Would you mind if I take a look at the full list?"

"No, not at all." The deejay's version of the list is hanging on the fridge. To get to it, I regrettably have to break my little pow-wow with Nathan. I almost collapse when trying to walk. My legs fell asleep a long time ago.

I hand it to him, careful not to touch his fingers in the

exchange. I hate that I'm so vigilant around him but the magnetic pull constantly throbbing off him would lead me straight into his arms otherwise. "Want something to drink?"

"Sure, that would be great, thanks. Water is fine." Nathan scans the list. "This is pretty amazing. What a cool opportunity. I can help you arrange some of these activities if you'd like. Tap into some connections I have."

"Really? Yeah, okay. That would be a big help." It would save me the research and let me shift some energy back into my novel deadline.

"I'm happy to help. Any of these are fair game then?"

I set a glass of water next to him. "If they don't already have a checkmark by them, they're fair game."

Nathan pulls out his cell phone to take a picture of the list. "Okay, give me a couple of days to set it up. If you let me whisk you away from your housework, we'll be able to knock out a few and have a blast doing so."

I almost drop my drink. I place the glass on the island and sit. "You want to do them with me?"

"Oh, crap. Sorry. I assumed that was okay. Here I am piggybacking on your incredible opportunity. No, no—I don't have to. I can set them up and give you the information. Sorry, I jumped the fence there."

Reclining on the barstool while looking at Nathan on the floor, I consider how well he fits in here. He balances the ambience of my cottage, like something I would have picked out at the market that didn't necessarily match anything else yet it fits.

"I'd love it if you came along." The words are out of my mouth before I can shut them down.

Nathan's eyes are wide and shining as he stands, handing me his glass."Great! I'll get back to you in a few days with plans. I'll also get your house listed in the meantime."

"Okay, sounds great." I swallow the twinge of excitement and nervousness in my depths, along with the clashing sadness about my cottage being on the market, attempting to replace them with nonchalance instead.

I'm about to get to know Nathan even more. And the possibilities of what I will discover scare me like no other.

* * *

I don't touch the Bridging the Six Degrees list for a few days in case there is anything Nathan is arranging. I welcome the break so I can process what's already taken place and grasp the swing of disquiet growing inside my soul.

To pass the time, I write and focus on creating as many lasting memories with my family as I can. I take my nieces and nephews out for ice cream and swimming in the lake. I help my dad stain the new fireplace mantle and a coffee table he carved. My mom shows me how to arm-knit blankets, the first attempt wasting three skeins before I finally catch on. She's knitting them for the Timber Creek Living residents, each one taking her about an hour to finish. A single blanket takes me three hours since I can't figure out how to get the material tight enough around my arm without cutting off my circulation. In the evenings, we play board games until one by one, we drop off from exhaustion and admit defeat.

Work floods Rose's free time. One tourism season is about to end and they're already gearing up for the next. It's the most stressed I've heard her sound on the phone. The Queen of Texting now only sends a few messages throughout the day. Her replies take hours instead of her typical "reply within sixty seconds" habit.

Jessi is busy with work as well, squeezing in an overload of shifts before winter nears. She's distracted the few times we speak. Maybe it's me, caution underlying every conversation we have, wondering if she's still talking to Nathan and if she knows he's helping me with the challenges.

Mark and I have brief conversations, seldom lasting for longer than ten minutes at a time. We are further away in distance than ever before and it's reflected in our emotional state, too. I once prided our relationship on the independence that we extend each other, but these days I find myself longing for closeness, a dependency in the sense that we are affected when the other person is away. Not necessarily distraught or unable to function, but simply missing the other.

As much as I hate to admit it, I count down the days until I see Nathan again, and wish I felt that excited to see Mark instead.

I channel my dreams into my writing. It helps me work through the chaos in my head and my heart. Sometimes through my characters' actions I figure out how I can handle my problems better in real life. Sometimes, I write to live life in a different way than how reality dishes it out.

Currently, it seems I am caught in a recurring theme: debating loyalty toward an old love or the risk and reward of choosing a new one, which feels like foreshadowing as it comes through my fingers and onto the screen.

Despite how our relationship is these days, I sink into periods of longing, reflecting on a time when I was excited about Mark. I mean, *really* excited. Electricity. Fireworks. The typical rousing office fling, secretive and thrilling, hidden in tiny displays of affection, enriching an otherwise average workday.

Elevators and meeting rooms were our specialty. Mark was skilled at clasping his hands behind his back while his fingers found any inch of my exposed skin. Grazing my lower abdomen under the bottom hem of my shirt, or tugging at the waistband of my pants, playfully acting as though he would pull them down right then and there. My body would lean into his fingers, begging him to do it. I didn't care if we were surrounded by coworkers. He made me want to take risks. It was our private fun in a not-so-private situation.

When we were finally together at the end of the night, we couldn't keep our hands off each other. The anticipation had been building all day, foreplay could be skipped; we were always ready for each other.

Ugh, when did that end? When did we stop having the energy for each other? Why are we complacent with no longer being that couple?

I pick up my phone with the determination to light a spark again. I'll try Rose's suggestion of phone sex if that's what it takes.

"Hey, sweetie. I'm preparing to go dark, no electronics for a week, for one of the BSD challenges. I really want to hear your voice. Call me anytime today or tonight. I don't care what time, okay? My phone is turned up as loud as it can go. Otherwise, I'll be without access to phone or email until next Sunday. If you need me, you can visit." I force a laugh. "But seriously... call me today, okay?"

Is it possible for the electricity to strike again in the same spot after being stagnant for so long? Unfortunately, my phone never rings for me to find out.

Fourteen

"Will you *please* tell me where we're headed? Otherwise, I'm pretty sure this is borderline kidnapping." I swing my duffel bag in the back of Nathan's Jeep Cherokee, a similar model to mine, except midnight blue. After disappointingly not hearing back from Mark, I told my family, Jess, and Rose that I'd be off the grid without electronics to focus on the challenges for a few days. But I left out a significant detail. When Nathan called to set up a date for his plans, he confirmed that he hadn't heard from Jessi for several days. It meant one less possibility of someone finding out that I am, in essence, running away with him. Temporarily at least.

As I slide into the seat next to him, I take my first look of Nathan Vertz whisking me away. Dark shades cover his eyes and, combined with a black crew tee and denim jeans faded in all the right places, he looks like James Dean. *I. Am. In. Trouble.*

"Nope, no clues. You haven't completed anything since we last talked, right?"

I buckle my seatbelt. "Nope. Been too busy packing up my precious house that you're trying to sell." I glance at him sideways.

"Oh, you mean the one that you're *paying* me to sell. That one?"

"The one that my *husband* is paying you to sell, which was without my permission, if you must know."

Nathan raises his eyebrows. His mouth opens then quickly shuts, as he shifts the vehicle into reverse.

"Well, I have several activities lined up, so I hope you're ready for a jam-packed couple of days! We don't have to do them all if you'd rather not. Don't be afraid to speak up." It's the first bit of nervousness I've been able to detect in Nathan's casual demeanor. I smile, enjoying that spending time with me is causing it.

"I can't believe you've gone through all this work for me. I'm excited, so skipping any is not happening."

"Well, if it's too much at once, we can take another trip to do the ones you don't get to this time."

Nathan is confident in the way he presents this information, as if us spending more time in the future together is a given. The flutter of butterflies return; they come out of hiding anytime he's around. It would have been the ideal time for him to reach over and grab my hand if we were in a normal situation—as in, if I wasn't married. Ugh.

"I got you a gift." He interrupts my mental scolding by handing me a small, green gift bag with rainbow tissue paper hanging out of the top. "Call it another belated birthday gift, if you will."

I peer inside to see an item I thought had long since disappeared in our world. "I didn't know they made these anymore!"

"Disposable cameras will be around forever. They're way more fun." He adjusts the rearview mirror as he enters the highway. "I know you don't have your cell on you, but since you're still supposed to document your experiences with pictures, these were the obvious way to go."

Foolishly, I had yet to think that far into this trip. I meant to borrow Rose's Polaroid and forgot to ask her. Since my phone is currently under my bed, locked in a box to prevent the temptation to check it during this electronics blackout, his thoughtful gift is a necessity. "How do you think selfies look on disposable cameras?" I wrinkle my nose at the thought. There's a reason selfies had yet to be coined when disposable cameras were popular.

"It doesn't matter, right? The first shot is what counts."

"Dang, you really studied my list, didn't you?"

"This whole social media-party-planning-concept is fascinating. I'm jealous I didn't think of it before the guy who did!"

Refraining from making any snarky comments about Kevin, I tear open one of the boxes and reach in for the camera. "Smile!" I lean in closer to Nathan, our arms touching on the armrest, and snap a picture. Maybe not the smartest idea for burying evidence that he's with me, or that we're in a car, alone together road tripping.

"Am I hearing this right?" I reach over to turn up the volume on his stereo. "Are you playing Taylor Swift? Are you a *Swiftie*?" His phone is hooked to the system so "Wildest Dreams" playing can't be blamed on the radio. The song is uncomfortably representative of the situation we're in.

Nathan chuckles. "Hey now, I'm not afraid to admit it. She's a damn good songstress. You're about to discover that I have quite a diverse taste in music."

There's no denying that. For the next hour, he dabbles in every musical genre from the past four decades. We have our own private karaoke jam. I don't hesitate to sing, which is new for me considering I don't even sing in front of Mark for fear of judgment. Maybe the karaoke challenge changed me. But I also don't feel self-conscious around Nathan at all.

The hour-long trip seems like only ten minutes. Too soon after our departure, he pulls into a parking space in downtown Lemonsa.

"Welcome to our first stop." A white painted brick building stands out among the sea of brown traditional structures with colorful scalloped banners and lettering on the windows advertising a variety of candy and ice cream.

"Great, you're allergic to candy?" Nathan teases when I stay rooted next to the car, confused.

Scrunching up my nose, I respond, "I'm trying to figure out which challenge this fits. Did I have a stuff-yourself-with-incredibly-sweet-foods one?"

"It's the 'be a kid' challenge! No better way to be kids than to fill our pockets with sweets first thing in the morning, right?" Nathan's interpretation of Jer's wife's request is perfect.

"I love it! But they don't look open." Everything inside the window is dark.

"Come on." He gestures, dangling his keys. The largest one on the hook unlocks it with a click.

"Great, so you're Willy Wonka on the side, too?"

"I can be Willy Wonka if you want me to." He winks. Confusing, yet heat stirs down below. *How can I possibly be turned on by that?*

Nathan opens the door and flips the switches next to it as bright lights flood the store one by one. It's reminiscent of a candy shop in the 1950s, even down to a milkshake bar.

"Where in the world are we? Did we step back in time?"

"Welcome to Tinkerton's Candies."

"You work here? You own this? What's the deal?"

"My Uncle Jeff owns the place. I help when I can, weekends and whatnot. I've been doing it since high school."

"This would be ridiculously tempting." I walk down the aisles, peering into the bins and surveying the candy selection. They have everything from modern candies to the colorfully-wrapped, old-fashioned ones I remember choosing when my dad would take me every Saturday morning to get treats as a little girl. I was given fifty cents to spend any way I wanted.

"This may have also contributed to the heavyweight version of Nathan that I spent most of my life battling."

"You were at a major disadvantage between the southern cooking and delicious candy selections."

"That's what I blamed it on, too." He throws me a small, white bag. "Fill 'er up! Anything you'd like, toss it in."

I catch the bag with one hand. "Seriously? Okay, now I *am* a kid in a candy store."

"Ironic, right?"

By the time my bag is full, Nathan had made us chocolate shakes. "It's eight-thirty in the morning!"

"There's no time like the present… to have a shake." He points to the slogan painted in bright rainbow colors on the wall that says, *There's no time like the present…*

I take the Styrofoam cup and slurp through the straw. "Okay." I lick my lips to scrape the remains of the thick chocolate, "This may be the best shake I've ever had."

"I have mad candy and shake-making skills. I will impress you by the time this trip is finished."

"You already have." I drag my fingers along the rows of pixie sticks and foot-long gum rolls, obsessed with the magical atmosphere of this little shop.

Nathan jots inventory notes on a sheet of paper and locks the store doors before we get back in the car. By nine o'clock, I'm on a sugar high and ready to run in circles when we hit our next location: Franklin Zoo in Green Bay.

"Nate! I heard a rumor you were coming by today." A lady that reminds me of a young Princess Diana reaches through the white-pane ticket window, squeezing Nathan's hands. "You look terrific!"

He beams with obvious adoration for this woman. "Thanks, Betty! It's great to see you. We're on a strict schedule, but if we finish up early, I'll stop by again. I want to hear how Brent and Lyla are these days."

"You never forget peoples' stories, do you?"

"Never." He gives her a knowing smile and introduces us.

Betty gives us permission to forge ahead. "Nothing has

changed, so you know your way back there. Martha is expecting you. Have fun!"

We step through the turnstile and are greeted by the smells of wild animals, hay, and manure. I ask, "Did you work here as well?" There seem to be no limits to Nathan's various side jobs.

"Kind of. I went to school to be a zoologist. Did an internship here. It seems most of the people I worked with are still here, as I figured they'd be. Once in love, it's hard to break free."

"You were planning to be a zoologist?" Just when I didn't think I could be more intrigued by him, I suddenly am.

"It was my initial backup plan to being a travel photographer. I have a soft spot for animals. Thought I could save them all by becoming a veterinarian or zoologist."

"What happened? Realty is a far cry from animal science."

Nathan leans his forehead into the protective fence two feet in front of the Gibbons cage as they swing from rope to branch chasing after each other. "Sammy happened."

"Girlfriend gone bad?"

"Giraffe that died."

Chalk it up to another ill-timed joke from me. "Oh. What happened to Sammy?"

"A pregnancy complication. She was twelve months along. Beautiful, full belly, we were all ready. The zoo had an ongoing contest for staff and visitors on what the baby's name should be. Everyone was invested. *Everyone.* But I was the one who found her."

I wince at the pregnancy complication reference, but I'm soon distracted from my pain by the grief that clearly scorches Nathan. It's strange seeing him with anything other than a smile or wink. I tenderly touch his back and it contracts under my fingers. Nathan takes a deep breath which causes my hand to quiver. It must have really affected him for him to still carry the weight of it and change the course of his life. I wonder if there's a lingering sting of regret riding the grief.

"You don't need to know the depressing details. Bottom line,

Sammy died. We couldn't save her baby, either. The name would have been Ash or Hazel. Fall baby. Anyway..." He continues walking so I follow him. "I had a hard time bouncing back from that. I ran away instead of stepping up to the plate. Some days, I wonder how life would be if I never gave up. Being a realtor is great for the money and satisfying when I can help people find their dream home. But it's not anywhere close to how gratifying it would have been to be a zoologist instead."

Nathan displays more emotions over a lost baby giraffe than I've seen in Mark our entire marriage. I spent years feeling like I was the only one who felt Amelia's absence. I once thought the difference was that I could feel her inside of me. Mark never even got to hold her so maybe she never seemed real to him. But here is Nathan, more wrecked over a baby giraffe he never held than Mark over our lost child.

"You once told me there wasn't anything you were passionate about. Sounds like animals may be your thing. Is it ever too late to let a dream die?"

"You tell me. Do you think some dreams never come true, or is there always hope?" His words hang thickly in the air with underlying implications. I understand more than I wish I did.

"Kind of hard to say never. As long as there's still life to live, everything is hopeful."

"Hmm..." He moves strands of hair from my shoulder, and I turn my face in response, my lips inches from his fingers. "I like that. I'll have to remind myself of it."

Why does he have to have those dimples?

Nathan glances at his watch. "Oh, we have to go if we want to feed the river otters."

"What? We're feeding river otters? Are you kidding me? They're my favorite animal!" I bounce on my feet with joy.

Nathan taps the side of his head. "All a part of my plan. Women can never resist the cute river otters."

What plan? What are your intentions with me, Nathan Vertz? I'm not sure I can handle knowing.

We take a loop, passing penguins, monkeys, turtles, bears, owls, eagles, wolves, pandas, and bobcats. They all seem excited to be outside today, moving about eagerly in their display cages, waiting for feeding time.

"So, now that you fell into real estate, is it the field you want to stay in?"

"I don't plan for it to be my only identity but sometimes it seems that's all people know about me. I want to be and do so much more. I want to know I'm making a difference in peoples' lives on a deeper level, helping them see their worth and value so it doesn't go without acknowledgement."

"You should talk to Kevin about Bridging the Six Degrees opportunities since they're growing and hiring. It could be a good fit."

"Hmm." Nathan seems to truly consider it. "Their mission is incredible, but I'd worry about how much travel is associated from what I've witnessed. I want to be a dad in a house full of kids and a husband that is home every day, partnering with my wife to take care of the family. Not traveling without them all the time."

Of course that's what he wants. Because it's what I want, and it's becoming increasingly painful that we want the same things.

"And I want a dog named Sammy," he adds.

It's as though I can feel my heart literally melt into a puddle. "Aww, that's sweet. To honor your giraffe."

He nods. "I want to do something with my hands, where it feels more like I'm contributing physically. Like build dog houses for rescue organizations, or maybe I'll still become a photographer, or yet, a zookeeper. All I know is I'm happy with my life today, but there are still more things I want to achieve and become."

I listen quietly, fighting envy over Nathan's freedom to make that choice. In the early days with Mark, it felt like the world was filled with possibilities because of our frequent travel on Neigelman's dime. But throughout the years, it's become confining. We don't go places because we *want* to. We go places because he *has* to for work. I feel like I'm pouring into his dreams instead of my own.

"We're here," he announces as we stop at a pebble-filled path leading up to an unmarked building. There's a sign stopping us, hanging in the middle of the path, connected by a rope attached to posts on both sides of it, warning visitors that it's an "Employee Only Zone." Nathan lifts the sign and we both duck to go under it.

"Ooh, I feel official." I tease.

He says, "Just you wait. You'll never look at a zoo the same again."

We walk around to the back of a massive, steel-framed building that is much bigger than it appeared from the path angle.

Nathan pulls open the door and encourages me to walk in. As it slams behind us, I notice there are several large buckets stacked in a corner, a wide industrial-sized sink, boxes of gloves, several pairs of galoshes and steel-toed boots on the ground, and brown, plastic aprons hanging from a wall.

He knocks on the door next to the sink. After a minute, it swings open. "Nate Vertz!" A woman with curly, red hair in her fifties reaches up to hug Nathan, standing on her tip toes as he bends down to return a hug on her short frame. "Out of all the ways to be blessed today, this is one of the best!"

"Martha," he says with a smile. "This is the one I was telling you about. Meet Autumn."

"Come in, come in! We've got a lot of work to do so I'm grateful for the extra hands."

The second room we enter is more the size I was expecting to see. Easily the span of two high school gymnasiums connected with a domed ceiling and dotted with singular lights hanging from cords. Massive shipping containers stacked on top of each other are strategically placed throughout the room, with restaurant quality walk-in freezers and refrigerators which are surely responsible for the temperature drop.

Martha and Nathan introduce me to a few other people who

come over to hug him, all former coworkers. I can easily see the zookeeper version of his life if he kept going down his original path. One that all the other employees admire and respect, turning to him for guidance when they need it.

But if he chose that path, we wouldn't be here together right now. Life is funny that way.

Martha guides us to two shiny, metal tables and hands us oversized goggles that we pull over our eyes. She sets three gigantic buckets of fish by our feet. "Okay, cut them up! You remember what to do I assume, Nate?"

He holds up a gloved thumb. "We got it, Martha!"

"I'll be back in a few minutes to lead you guys out. Have fun! You'll get used to the smell, Autumn, I promise."

Nathan reaches under the table and pulls out two gleaming butcher knives, carefully passing me the handle of one. "You'll want to grab some of those plastic gloves, too. It can get messy. Let me show you how to do it."

I gag with the first slice of the fish.

Nathan points out the obvious. "You look like you're going to get sick."

I lift my arm to wipe my nose with my bicep. "I never did well in biology class for this exact reason."

"You just have to keep your mind off of it."

"I don't think your thumb war game will work here." I lift my hand and wiggle my fingers in the glove that isn't holding the knife.

He chuckles. "Fair enough. Well, ask me a question instead."

"Okay." I try to reset my thoughts on anything other than the squishy sound that happens right before the knife hits the board underneath. "Why do they call you Nate here?"

"That's not a distracting question. It'll take thirty seconds to answer."

"I'm waiting."

"Okay, I went by Nate for most of my life. Probably would have kept it if I became a zookeeper. The realtor route felt different. Like going by a formal name would help my credibility. Sounds stupid saying it out loud, now, but the logic was there at the time."

"I like Nate. I like Zookeeper Nate even more."

He grins and glances over at me. "You can call me anything you want."

"You're right, though. That wasn't a distracting question." I am tempted to resign from fish cutting. Eating all the sugary foods right before this wasn't the best idea with the nausea coursing through me.

"Okay, let me ask one. If you were a kid and got a free pass to do anything you wanted in this world, what would you do?"

I pause my cutting to think it through and then say, "Feed and play with the river otters at a zoo."

"Ooh that was a smooth answer. Now tell me the truth."

My fish-slicing sickness is soon forgotten as we debate what we would do as children if we had free passes in the world. We quickly realized we were answering the question as experienced adults instead of children with no boundaries. We had to reframe the question, adding in fantastical elements, like we have super-powers that prevent us from getting sick if we ate too much sugar or the ability to be transported from one location to the next or invisibility rays when we didn't want to be seen. By the end, we are laughing so hard, I can barely see the fish in front of me through my tears.

When Martha comes back in to check on our work, she says, "I've never heard happier people slicing fish." She guides us to fill our buckets with fish meant only for the river otters, leaving the other bodies behind to feed other animals. We follow Martha to the cages where my all-time favorite wild animal awaits.

"Babies!" I cry out, in awe to see so many tiny river otters running around.

Martha grins with pride. "Born only a few months ago!"

An adult river otter climbs up on the rock in front of us, his little nose sniffing the air, knowing what we brought him. "Okay, little buddy. This one is for you." I throw a fish like a baseball, and it flies over his head to a lucky otter behind him.

He watches as my terrible attempt feeds another otter and turns back to me with a glaring look.

"I think he's judging my throwing abilities."

Nathan laughs. "Pitching fish is a little different than throwing a ball. Watch this." He underhand flicks his wrist, and a fish flies up in the air, landing perfectly in the river otter's open mouth.

"Okay, show off. I'll stick to feeding the babies." I throw another, and it lands right where the little ones are waiting. "I wish we could play with them."

Martha says, "Not smelling like fish, you don't."

Being this close to the otters for the first time is thrilling. It's like being up-close in a nature documentary. I'm on top of the world. The worst thing about it is when my bucket empties.

"That was amazing," I sigh, as the otters scamper back into the water to play. We stand and watch them for a few more minutes before returning to the food building to rid ourselves of our gloves and wash our hands. "I'm sad that's over."

"It's not the last of our adventures here. We're just warming up." Nathan nudges me with his elbow as he soaps his hands.

"Are we feeding more animals?" I've been to the zoo a hundred times before, but never on this side. Behind-the-scenes is a totally different experience that I wish more people could see. My nieces and nephews have a set of children's books showcasing ideas of what you can be when you grow up. A zoologist is one of the cutely illustrated themes with funny quips and endearing drawings of the real-life version. The books make it so probable, the ability to become anything you want with a snap of your fingers. You decide to be something, and you're it. If only it were that easy in real life.

"We're not exactly feeding them, but we get to play with them."

"Ooh, how fun!"

Nathan shushes Martha who is suppressing a laugh. "I hope you still feel that way soon."

Nothing prepares me for going into the Amphibian house next. "This is the part of the zoo I would be happy to avoid," I point out as we walk through the doors.

"You did mention you weren't a fan of spiders."

"Yes, maybe my highest-ranking fear."

"Why do you hate spiders so much?" Martha inquires.

"Because I swear, they are everywhere. On the floor, on the walls, on the ceiling, hanging in midair by a web you can walk through at any time." I shudder at the thought. "No, thank you. They are terrible, terrible creatures who haunt me." I look up in time to notice we are walking directly to the spider display. Then I remember why we're here. "No...."

Nathan confirms the bad news. "Today is the day you get to face your biggest fear."

This is the challenge I cringed at when being presented with it at my party. Ironically, it was also the story I was most captivated by. Nadia Antos from Poland presented this challenge through a fascinating story about her grandma's time in a Nazi concentration camp during World War II.

I was impacted by the importance of not fearing the things that are in your control. Because suddenly, you realize there are greater things to fear that fall outside of your control. Those things will always be far more life-altering. So, if there are minor fears, face them. Show them that you're bigger than them. It will only strengthen you should you face anything greater someday.

I become more empowered each time I read her story. I had yet to consider what I would do to complete it. But now I'm standing here as Martha shoves in my face what must be the biggest tarantula that's ever lived.

"You want me to hold that? Are you out of your mind?"

Nathan shakes his head. "You can either hold it or let it crawl on you. Your choice."

"I regret ever answering your question about what my greatest fear is. I thought we were getting to know each other." My hands claw at my neck as I envision spiders crawling all over it. "Isn't this supposed to be a childlike day? Facing my worst fear on a fun day seems a bit contradictory. Let's go back to the river otters."

"Don't you think as a child you'd be more willing to let a spider crawl on you? That a part of you would have found it kind of cool?"

His words trigger a memory of being at the laundromat with my mom when I was only four or five. While I waited for her to finish the laundry, I stood outside playing with daddy long legs crawling on the posts. I let them walk on my arms, and I named each one, spinning tales about adventures they were embarking on. I'm not sure when my spider fear became extreme, but next thing I know, I'm older and can't stand the sight of a cartoon spider in a kid's book, let alone a real one in front of me. Chalk it up to yet another irrational fear. Some come from nowhere in particular, but they stick around and latch on deeper throughout the years like a tick.

Nonetheless, a tarantula is a far cry from a daddy longlegs. "I mean, there has to be another way to do this challenge, right?"

Nathan taps his chin. "Do you remember that show *Fear Factor*?"

"Don't tell me you were on that one, too."

Nathan snickers. "No, but I always wanted to be. Anyway, do you remember where they had people stick their heads into a glass box filled with spiders that crawled all over their head, face, and shoulders?"

I involuntarily shudder again. "Why in the world would you tell me that?"

"To prove we could have taken it a step further." He gently slaps my shoulder and grins. "Time to play ball."

"You need to work on your comforting skills," I call over my shoulder while I reluctantly stand next to Martha.

She handles the spider with grace as though it is nothing more than a hamster. It is furry, but no hamster. I wait for it to sink its fangs in her, but it waits for me.

"Put out your hands. I'll give Frank over to you—"

"Frank? His name is *Frank*?"

"Makes him a little less scary, right?"

No. No, it doesn't. I stare at her.

"We can spend all day here if you want. Or, we can move on after you conquer this fear and enjoy the other things I have planned. I'm not in any rush, so it's all up to you." Nathan uses the same parenting technique that Beth uses to coerce my niece and nephew to do the things requested of them.

"Ugh, fine. Give me... Frank." Bile rises in my throat.

Martha's eyes dance with humor as she brings the spider to me. "Breathe normally and don't make too many quick movements. Spiders can be laid back, but you have to be as well."

I liked Martha up until this whole spider situation.

I try to take calming breaths but when the spider's spiny legs land on me, I instantly tense. Martha puts the spider on my shoulder, although I'm not sure why. This thing could latch onto my face in no time.

I never get comfortable with the idea of Frank on me, but I do eventually breathe normally. The trick is keeping my eyes open. If I close them, my mind runs rampant with crazy ideas of the intentions of this spider. He is curious at first, exploring my shoulders, then strutting down my left arm and back up again. Apparently I bore him because soon he stops moving.

"Is he dead?" I block the hope from rising in my voice.

Nathan snaps a picture right as Martha reaches out and takes Frank, who wakes from his trance. "Nope, he's ready to go back to his cage. Congratulations! You did it!"

Nathan gives a slow clap. "You survived! Frank survived!"

I am rooted in the spot afterward. *Did I just let a spider crawl on me?* My mind may have shut down to allow it to happen. But I did it. That's the thing with all these challenges, the high that comes after they're completed. *I did it.*

"Now you get rewarded!" Nathan says.

"I'm sugared out if that's what you're referring to." We have been snacking on our sugary treats from the candy shop all morning. The threat of a sugar crash is very prominent.

"Nope! Follow me." He grabs my hand as we yell, "Thanks so much, Martha!" in unison behind us.

We jog across the yard, and I find I'm eager to see what he has in mind next.

Nathan is giddy next to me, still celebrating my feat. "You had a spider on your shoulder and you just *stood* there. You didn't freak out. You didn't scream. You faced a really big fear!"

I shake my head, almost unable to accept that it happened. "I can't figure out if it was a dream or a nightmare."

He stops jogging and faces me, putting his hands on my shoulders. "Autumn, you're amazing. Do you know how many people would have walked out? No one is forcing you to do these things. You're willingly choosing to do them every single time. This isn't easy. But you're doing it and giving yourself wholly over to these experiences."

My head is nodding on its own as it listens to him, and eventually I give in to what I know is true: he's right. I could choose not to do any of these, but I do them because thirty amazing people shared their stories with me and I want to honor that. This may have started out as something I was being forced to do, but now I want to and feel committed to it. I'm all in.

"And this," Nathan cocks his head to the side, "is our next step."

A giant, gold-painted carousel. The laughter of kids fills the air while they ride on giant, ceramic animals that endlessly circle.

We stand in line and hop on it the next turn; Nathan selects a giraffe, and I choose the polar bear next to him. The last time I rode a carousel was when I was seven years old at the county fair. It isn't the most thrilling ride, but it's fun. Most of all, I feel like a child again. Each go-around, we take turns challenging each other to do things like lean as far back as possible or ride with no hands. I'm sure the parents standing around aren't too pleased that we are an anti-safety billboard for all the things *not* to do when on a carousel. Especially when we are boisterous and jubilant, like it's the best time of our lives.

Afterward, we visit all the animals we had yet to see and take turns reading the fact boards in front of each cage. I love that he is as big of a nerd as I am and equally in awe of the knowledge discoveries, despite his zookeeper education.

Everything we do and say comes naturally. It's hard to ignore the increase in physical touches as the day goes on. They may be simple exchanges of light arm touches, but they're comforting and exciting all at once.

"I have one more idea that we should do before we leave to really get the most out of today."

Squinting at him, dubious after the spider encounter, I ask, "Should I be scared?"

"I hope not! Let's go. It's an easy walk."

The Adventure Park connected to the zoo turns into our next destination. "How do you feel about zip-lining?"

Truth be told, I have a fear of heights, too. But I'm much better at handling that one when strapped into a safety harness. Zip-lining has always been on my list of things to try. "I'm up for it!"

We are two of twenty people in line. Nathan's zoo connections can't help him on this side of the park. The struggle with waiting is that it allows more time for my nerves to kick in as we climb higher and higher.

"Heights don't bother you at all?"

Nathan adjusts his helmet. "They once did. But we had to zip-line over the Grand Canyon, so anything less than that doesn't feed the nerves."

"Maybe I need to get on *The Amazing Race* to conquer my fears."

"Don't you think you're getting a mini version of that with these Bridging the Six Degrees experiences?"

I hadn't thought about them in that way before. He makes an excellent point. This is my own little amazing race. I beam at the correlation.

Zip-lining is an addiction. The first time is scary, and I worry I may truly end up childlike and pee my pants. But the wind, whipping through my hair as I slide down the rope like I am flying, is exhilarating. It's exactly how Nathan makes me feel.

When Nathan takes off his helmet after we finish the last leg, his blonde hair is windblown and his cheeks are red and chapped from the wind. I reach out and smooth his hair down as he grins back at me.

Our detour to the adventures course made the zoo trip longer than Nathan allotted time for, so we grab a quick bite through Chick-fil-A on our way to the next destination.

"I noticed we stayed away from the giraffe exhibit all day," I comment while chewing my chicken sandwich.

"Ah, and here I thought I was stealthy."

"You were deeply affected by that, huh?"

Nathan shifts in his seat. "I know it's something I should be over by now. But I've always loved them. The first stuffed animal I ever had was a giraffe so I have these early memories of them being a comfort to me. Any time I was presented with choosing an animal for whatever reason, it was always a giraffe."

"Like the carousel."

"Exactly."

"So, a giraffe is like your spirit animal?"

Nathan glances at me with confusion. "I still have no clue what the hell that's supposed to mean, but sure. It's funny how many people ask me that. What's your spirit animal?"

"River otters." I smirk with a mouthful of chewed fries.

Laughing and clearly pleased, he says, "Happy I nailed that on the head then. So, was the mission accomplished? Did you feel like a kid today?"

"Yes, absolutely. Hopefully I did Jer's wife justice."

"If you saw the smile on your face all day, you would say you accomplished it. I'm sure she'd be quite proud."

That response warms my heart. It would have been a dream day as a child: getting to hang out with animals, feeding my favorite ones, and eating more candy than I typically consume in one year. My body still buzzes from the sugar. My teeth, too.

"I smell fishy." I sniff my shirt. "Yeah, I'm pretty sure fish guts are clinging to me."

"Ah, that's why I couldn't shake the zoo smell."

"Hey!" I lightly punch him on the shoulder.

"Well, you might be able to take a shower here." Nathan pulls into the circle valet of the George F. Nathaniel Hotel.

My mouth drops open. "Is this our next destination? Isn't this where all the famous people stay?" Not to mention, it's the location where three of my favorite romantic comedies have been filmed.

He turns off the car. "Sure is. I'm guessing they have decent showers, too." The valet, dressed in a suit that could have come straight from Mark's closet, opens my door. He completes a smooth transaction with Nathan for the keys and a tip while grabbing our bags from the car. We walk through the automatic doors to see a lobby so grand that it could have been painted in gold for all the shine that radiates from it. Floor-to-ceiling Roman columns, white granite floors, and the most beautiful Romanesque artwork, in frames taller than my cottage, grace the walls with statues of Roman gods and goddesses spaced throughout.

"This is unreal," I mutter in complete awe.

"It's supposed to be the best spa north of Chicago so you should get the kind of pampering you're supposed to."

"I get to do the pampering challenge here?"

"You sure do. Only the best, right? I'm sure that's the way Mark would have wanted it, anyway." Nathan's use of Mark's name after such an intimate day together feels like a punch in the gut, if not the reality check I needed. "I had an appointment set up for you. Luckily, we made it in time. It starts in ten minutes so let's get you in there. I'll check us in while you're at the spa."

"We're staying the night here, too?"

"Of course."

I wonder whether we'll have a room together, or adjoining rooms connected with a door. Surely he wouldn't do that. He seems too gentlemanly, plus he just mentioned Mark's name, for heaven's sake. I shake my head as I reprimand myself. He's just here to help me, that's all. It's innocent.

The spa receptionist stands to greet us, perfectly manicured from head to toe with a pressed, black pencil skirt, white blouse, and open-toed heels that add another seven inches to her small frame. This is a far cry from the places I'd pop into every now and then for a thirty-five-dollar manicure or pedicure.

"Autumn, we are fortunate to welcome you to the Dei Consentes Spa. I must admit, I researched you after we heard about your challenge. What an amazing program! I sent the news link, the application, and a reminder that my birthday is around the corner to my husband."

I smile at her. "It's been pretty fantastic, that's for sure."

"Well, what can we do for you today?" She returns to the other side of the desk and slides an open pamphlet towards me, listing the available spa services. The list is extensive, endless variations of each pampering service. "You have five hours to fill with two attendants dedicated to you."

Five hours? I glance around the spa, expertly designed with its white walls and fluffy everything to reflect a peaceful oasis. What does someone do for five hours? "I was thinking a regular pedicure or something..."

Nathan interrupts me. My sense of wonderment must be evident. "How often do you get pedicures as it is?"

"I don't know. Maybe a handful of times a year. For special events and whatnot." I just had one last week, but he didn't need to know that.

Nathan clears his throat and turns back to the receptionist. "She'll do this package." And points to one in the pamphlet.

I stand on my tiptoes to peek. "What did you select?"

He places his hands on my shoulders, apparently his go-to stance today, and dips his head to peer into my eyes. "Autumn, you're supposed to really pamper yourself, right? I think the words were 'let yourself remember all the reasons you're worth it.' A pedicure would go by too quickly before you have a chance to consider all the reasons. Five hours still isn't enough time, because you're worth a lot."

I'm stunned by his assessment. "How do you know which one to pick?"

"I grew up with sisters, remember? Trust me on this. Relax, enjoy, have fun. I'll drop the key off once I get us checked in. I'll be working in my room and have reservations at the Rock Restaurant at eight o'clock for dinner. If you want to join me, I'd love it." He then retraces his words and quickly adds, "In the restaurant, that is. It's through the main corridor. You'll have to eat dinner sometime."

The receptionist leads me to the changing area, pointing to a locker to store my clothes and a shower area to wash before starting. For a moment, I wonder if she can smell the fish on me, too. "We want everyone to feel completely clean and relaxed before starting their spa services. One of our attendants will retrieve you in fifteen minutes. If you need longer, take your time, she can always come back. There's no rush. Your husband chose an excellent package. Attentiveness is the sign of a great man."

"Oh, he's not—" but she turns away before I can finish.

I rub my hand over the white plush robe, brushing the delicate fibers with my fingers. I can't believe this is happening. I already feel like a princess. The first step, though: scrub this awful fish smell out of my pores.

To say it is the most relaxing five hours I've ever experienced in my life is an understatement. I am treated to a full body, hot-stone-massage, facial, pedicure, manicure, and hydrotherapy bath.

After the first thirty minutes, I finally learn to let my thoughts go and focus on... nothing, the epitome of pure bliss.

Tara Jackson submitted this challenge, and her reasons were simple:

As women, we feel a lot, do a lot, demand a lot, love a lot, work a lot, learn a lot, and live a lot, but we don't pamper ourselves nearly as much as we deserve. Recognize the beautiful soul that you are, think about all the reasons you should celebrate yourself every single day, and spend at least one spa day thinking about all the reasons why you are worth it.

Even though I'm supposed to spend this time reflecting on my value, my mind and heart fill with gratitude. These Bridging the Six Degrees challenges have connected me to people I wouldn't have otherwise known. By performing an activity that holds strong significance to them, learning about their story and experiencing it too. *Who gets to live like this?* Me. Right now, in this moment, *me*. I am so, so grateful to Mark for this.

I should call him and tell him that I'm sorry for ever doubting him. That he was right, and I am changing from this. That this was exactly what I needed without knowing it at the time. That maybe he can sometimes see what I need before I see it myself. I reach for my phone and forget it's locked away for the next week.

Time disappears too quickly as I sip on bubbly champagne and eat the freshest fruit. This spa sets a whole new meaning to quality pampering. I only wish that Rose and Jessi could be here with me. They would love it.

Except that would mean Nathan wouldn't be here, waiting for me to join him for dinner at one of the most romantic hotels in the world. He takes over my thoughts, and while I close my eyes and sink deeper into the hydrotherapy bath, I wonder *what if...*

By the time I get out, my body is tingling and ready to see him again.

Fifteen

"You're glowing." Nathan pulls out a chair for me. Although I'm continually putting myself in temptation's way, meeting him for dinner didn't need to be debated. He arranged these activities for me so it would be rude to decline his invite.

"It was incredible. Thank you for pushing me to take the extra services. I don't think I would have otherwise."

"You mean you *definitely* wouldn't have." He pours me a glass of wine from the opened bottle already on the table.

"These activities are revealing how small my comfort zone is... nearly every one of them has fallen outside of it."

"I was looking over the list again. You've done a lot of them already. You can't tell me your comfort zone is the same size now as it was when you started, so that has to feel good."

I reach for a piece of bread from the basket, my hunger hitting hard. "I *was* feeling good about it. But Mark said I must not be appreciating them if I'm doing them this quickly."

"Hmm." Nathan spreads butter on a slice. "I don't mean to disrespect Mark's opinion because he must have had something in mind to set this all up for you. But does the time spent doing each activity reflect the amount you're gaining from it? You have to journal about each event, right? Journaling is time spent reflecting and letting everything sink in. It's not like you're knocking them out and moving on."

"Exactly." Though I value Nathan's words, an ache forms in my heart, wishing that Mark could see it that way too. "I don't think he's ever journaled a day in his life. He doesn't know what it's like to reflect in that way and what it can do for the mind." The bitterness about Mark has staked a permanent residence in my voice since our sour phone call and him not calling me back afterward. Maybe the bitterness began long before that, if I'm being honest.

"Besides, some of the challenges are a bit of a given, right? By doing most of these, you can automatically do others, too. The 'embrace every opportunity' one, for example."

"That's the way I'm looking at it. Naomi's challenge was to say yes instead of no, which is what I'm doing by tackling the twenty-nine other activities. Having that push is nice. I'm an introverted writer so I tend to stay in a little bubble."

Nathan looks genuinely surprised. "But it sounds like you've had a lot of travels and adventures already."

"I travel mostly because of Mark's job. If I'm being honest, I'm exhausted with all the trips. *He* feeds off it, but I just go along to support him."

"But isn't that the life you wanted? Traveling to different countries? Being able to write about the cultures?"

I rub my hands together, smooth as butter from the spa treatments, and admire my newly painted nails to distract myself from the despair rising in my voice. "The reasons we travel are different than the purposes I thought I'd be traveling for. They're financially-driven above all else. But his reasons get me out to new places, so I'm grateful for that. It's partially why I write fiction now instead of the travelogues I thought I would. I can live through people who are much braver than I am. People who can fulfill their dreams and redeem their mistakes." That facial must have opened more than my pores because I'm pouring everything out to Nathan.

"Don't be so hard on yourself. Some people can go out and tackle all the things they wish for their lives without blinking an eye. Others need more support or a push in that direction. It's not about the how. The important thing is doing it, so you don't have those regrets later. Why do you think *The Amazing Race* works so well? Partners. Otherwise, fear can latch on and prevent you from pushing yourself, despite the drive of the competition."

"Partners only work when both are striving for the same goal." I avoid eye contact with Nathan and push around the bread on my plate, watching as it soaks up the oil and parmesan cheese.

Nathan tenderly touches my hand and waits for my eyes to meet his again. "You're incredible and brave, Autumn. Everyone else seems to realize it except for you."

I roll my shoulders back and hold up my wineglass. "Well, cheers to incredible experiences today and more to come tomorrow."

Nathan clinks my glass with his and waves the waiter over. Nathan is as much of a foodie as I am, ordering the full list of small plates for us to try, which is exactly what I would have done. The food is as good as the spa services. The wine may be even better. The conversation flows, so I don't even notice that we are two bottles in before Nathan requests the check. We are also one of two tables left in the restaurant. We missed the cues of closing time.

I sway as I stand up, and Nathan catches my arm.

"Are you okay?"

I touch my warm forehead. "I think it's a rush of all the activities today mixed with a heavy dose of delicious treats, food, and wine."

He smiles sympathetically. "You need a good night's sleep."

After he pays for dinner, he keeps his hand on my arm and gently steers me to the elevator. I like how he takes care of me. Especially as the lights in the hallway burn exceptionally bright, and I want to close my eyes. It makes me want to sleep. All I can think about is sleep.

That is, until Nathan moves his hand to the small of my back, which sends a sudden jolt of electricity through my body. Once the elevator dings on our floor, he walks me to my room door. My knees weaken. This has felt too much like a date all night. The ease of our conversation, the way we lean into each other, the constant pulse of my blood as the night comes to an end. If it were a date, it would have been a perfect one.

We get to room 1232, and I brace myself for a goodbye. "Thanks for walking me to my room, Nathan." My trembling hand fumbles for my room card in my purse.

"It's the least I can do. You shouldn't be walking the halls of a random hotel by yourself so close to midnight."

"I was wondering what time it was."

"Flies by when you're having fun, huh?"

"And when you're without a cell phone for distraction."

"There's that." He smiles, seemingly close. In fact, he's very close.

My hands gravitate to the crook of his arms. "Nathan, thank you for everything you've done for me."

"Don't thank me. I'm lucky to be here with you."

I don't want to take my hands off his arms. I can claim that I'm using him for balance, but I am also incapable of walking away for other reasons.

"Here, let me get the door for you." Nathan slides the card out of my hand and into the door. It blinks green and clicks to unlock. He turns the handle and reaches into the room to find the light switch.

"Be sure to check out the view in the morning if you haven't yet. It should be pretty spectacular. Get some rest. I'll pop by around seven so we can grab breakfast." Nathan kisses my cheek, lingering like he's caught in my earring, but I know better. I can feel his warm breath on my cheek and the energy of his lips only millimeters from my skin.

All I would have to do is slightly move my face for his lips to end up on mine. My breath hitches, anticipating. When I finally inhale, rosewood, cardamom, and amber drift through the air, a different cologne than the one he usually wears, exposing secrets of the words that we avoid speaking. All I want to do is breathe him in. Mentally, I'm begging him to do it—to take control of this moment, of me, of my body—my mind manifesting the darkest desires I hide.

Somehow the door closes behind me, separating us–Nathan on one side, and me on the other.

I don't bother to change my clothes. I fall into bed and into the deepest sleep I've had in years.

* * *

The sun filtering through the curtains is bright enough to wake me up. I groan and search for the clock to verify how early it is. My body feels like a limp noodle. Those spa services did me in. I don't think I moved at all during my sleep.

But I feel renewed, all because of yesterday. And because of Nathan; his smile, his laughter, his easy conversation, his touches, his immediate reactions to serve my needs without me having to express them.

I force myself to take an unbearably cold shower to wash away the fervor as a punishment. But cold showers are horrible, so it doesn't last long before I crank up the heat.

Unsure of what Nathan has planned for today, I dress in jeans and a basic t-shirt to play it off as casual, but it feels too casual in such a fancy hotel. I grab a cardigan to throw on over it to make it dressier.

At seven o'clock on the dot, there is a knock at the door. Prompt as always. I open the door eagerly, only to discover a room service attendant with a pushcart full of breakfast dishes.

"Good morning, ma'am. Where should I place this?" he asks.

"There must be a mistake. I didn't order food."

He checks the card on the table. "It was ordered by a Nathan Vertz. Does that sound right?"

Nathan did this. I wonder if he is planning on joining me. Nathan... in my room...

"Set it right here, please." I point to the foyer. As far from the bed as possible.

Once the table is in place, he bows as he exits, which is great since I have no cash to give him a tip.

My hotel phone rings ten minutes later. "Hello?"

"How's breakfast?" Nathan. Maybe he's avoiding me after last night. Perhaps he's preparing to call everything else off.

I hadn't started on breakfast because I was convinced that he would show up at the door. "It all looks delicious. Thank you for ordering it."

"I promised you breakfast this morning, so I wanted to follow through. Unfortunately, when I checked my messages last night, I missed a bunch of important calls. I have some work to do this morning. I'm so sorry."

"Oh." I can't mask the disappointment in my voice. "No, it's fine. Do we need to head back home?"

Nathan chuckles. "Our adventure is far from over. I'm only asking for a couple of hours to work before we continue. So no, you're not done with me yet."

I'm not done with him yet.

"No problem. Call me when you're ready."

"Well, one thing on the agenda isn't far from here. If you have sweatpants or something comfortable along those lines, I'd recommend changing into them. It starts in two hours, so I'll stop by a quarter 'til."

"No hint?"

"What's the fun in that? See you soon."

With newfound ammunition to fire at my work in progress, I grab the plate of food off the table and find a pad of paper in the drawer. I snack on fruit and convert this crazy state of life I'm in to the fictional, comedic lives of Nicki and Quinten, and their romantic affair as he secretly chases her across the country while she goes on a chaotic hunt to discover who she truly is.

The knocking on my door startles me. I had been so absorbed in my words that I lost track of time.

"Hi!" I say a bit too enthusiastically when I open the door to finally see Nathan. Dressed in black track pants and a navy, cowl neck, athletic sweatshirt, he looks like a runway model on his day off.

"I'm guessing you forgot to bring something more comfortable than jeans?" He's assessing me as much as I am him. I forgot I needed to change.

"Oh, crap. I was busy writing. Give me five minutes!" I leave the door open and run into the bathroom to change into my yoga pants. As I head out of the bathroom, I nearly run into him standing in the small foyer of the room. I ask, "Do I need to grab anything else?"

He reaches for the door. "Nope! You look great. We need to hurry to make it in time."

We half-jog to the elevators. Nathan is purposeful in keeping distance between us. Maybe he has qualms about last night, too.

"You were writing?"

"I was."

"I love to hear that. I knew you would be."

"You've got me figured out, huh?" I pull my hair back in a ponytail. "Still no hints?"

The elevator dings, and the doors open. We arrive on the bottom floor of the hotel, a dull, white hallway with numerous conference rooms on each side.

"You're right. We didn't have to go far."

Nathan steps closer, finally closing the gap between us, and leans into my shoulder, pointing to a giant banner standing in the middle of the hallway. "That's what we're doing."

"Seriously?"

"It's on your list, right?"

"Yes!" I exclaim, my veins alive with energy. "Oh my God, a

meditation class—with a real Buddhist monk! How in the world did you track this down?"

"This event actually helped me target an area to do these activities in. Good meditation classes aren't easy to come by around here. This is supposed to be one of the best. He comes once a month."

Nathan seems relaxed around me again, or perhaps the anticipation of the event takes over. Either way, I breathe happily that the tension has been removed. He puts his hand on the small of my back to steer me to the registration table. I revel in the return of his touch.

We walk into the quietest room I've ever been in. I am afraid my breathing is too loud, let alone my footsteps. A giant, white platform stands in the front of the bare room. Blankets and cushions are placed strategically across the floor. We choose the two remaining ones, which puts Nathan behind me at a diagonal angle. I won't be able to see him, but he can see every move I make.

After a few minutes, the monk walks onto the platform. If I thought it couldn't have been any quieter, I was wrong. Somehow, even more of a hush falls over the room.

A discussion about the history and importance of meditation, to become comfortable with the concept, fills the first twenty minutes. The monk then launches into tips on how to clear our minds to meditate effectively and teaches us that it was initially created to spread kindness and love by removing negativity from the thoughts we have of other people. It is our time to focus strictly on positive things and direct the resulting flow of energy out into the world.

The official meditation period begins. Sitting in a quiet room and digesting everything I just learned, acutely aware that Nathan is right behind me, makes my initial attempt challenging. I visualize pushing thirty years of collective negative energy out of my body and seizing the positive power that remains. Gradually, I become calmer, steadier, and stronger mentally. I begin to feel at ease with life as it is, without answers, without the need to know more. That's a feeling I don't want to let go of, acknowledging the rarity of its existence in my life.

The monk walks by, as though floating on a cloud, and whispers to each of us, "Stay or go, it's up to you. The class is over, but there's no pressure to leave." I don't open my eyes. It's as though I have fallen into a deep sleep, yet I remain conscious.

I'm not sure how much time passes while my body remains frozen in the same pose, but I eventually succumb to my full bladder's call for a bathroom break. I half-expect all the lights to be out and the door locked, but the monk had returned to his place on the platform. I rise and peek around, noticing four other people remain, but Nathan is not one. I slide out the back door as quietly as I can, realizing I heard no one else leave; that's how deep in it I was.

Jane Murgowsky, a former attorney from Chicago, suggested meditation as a Bridging the Six Degrees challenge. She once loved being immersed in the busy life of a big city. An unscheduled corporate retreat that her boss forced her to attend led her to discover meditation. It took her about six months before she started incorporating it in her everyday life. Jane's story points to the unique ways our lives lead us down the right paths without our awareness.

Her last-minute work event led to the exact thing that showed her she was in the wrong profession. Jane soon retreated to the suburbs for a chance to separate herself from the "hole that can be easy to fall into when living a busy, somewhat unfulfilling life." Learning how to meditate helped her discover true happiness and more of her life's purpose.

As soon as I exit the conference room, I spot Nathan pounding away at his phone.

"Hey, you." He shoves his phone into his pocket. "What did you think?"

I touch the smile on my face. "Amazing. Absolutely amazing."

"That was the goal!"

"How did you feel?"

Nathan bobs his head. "It was cool. I mean, how many people can say a monk taught them how to meditate? I may need a little more practice. Couldn't quite shut off my mind."

"Things going okay? We can head back if you need to. Don't put me first over your job."

"No, we're good. You're more important." He touches my arm innocently, but it's enough for me to fight back tears. I've been desperate to hear that exact line from Mark. *I'm more important than work.* "I have something big planned."

"Bigger than meditating with a monk?"

"Okay, *as* big. Go back to your room and grab a change of clothes, a towel, and a swimsuit, then meet me in the lobby in fifteen minutes. Sound good?"

"We're going swimming?"

"Close. Cliff diving."

Sixteen

"No, no, no, no, no, no." I shake my head violently. "I can't do this. Cover me with one hundred spiders. This is so much worse." Standing at the top of Briar's Triangle Cliff, my knees shake. One arm is holding on for dear life to the rocks behind me while I wrap the other around my stomach, like a hook pulling me back. I didn't realize how harrowing my fear of heights is. Until now. When I'm standing on a ninety-foot cliff, hyperventilating as the waves below me hammer the jagged boulders scattered throughout the coast.

Our drive to get here was spectacular. With the too-fitting playlist Nathan chose as our soundtrack, the serenity still lingering from the meditation session earlier and the ride through heavenly rolling canopies of orange, red, yellow, and green had me euphoric. With the window rolled down, I stared out in amazement that life could be this beautiful, the breeze gently rolling across my face while I dipped my hand into the air to the beat of the music. Nothing else mattered except the moment I was in. The tranquility faded when Nathan guided me to the cliffs. At first, the height, size, and magnificence of them stunned me into reverence. Until it sunk in that we would be jumping from them, at which point my peacefulness escaped like air deflating from a balloon.

Nathan leans over the highest cliff a few feet above my head. He squats down, his feet tottering on the edge as though he's a well-balanced monkey, to touch my shoulder. "You don't have to do this, you know. But I promise you, if you choose to, this is a safe place to do it in. There are two rock formations down below. Each one is comprised of three rocks that form a triangle. You simply have to avoid the triangles. You'll be fine."

I shut my eyes to push out the image of my head bouncing off the rocks, or my body lying broken on one as I misread my jump. "Hence the Triangle Cliff," I mutter.

"Exactly." He gives one more quick squeeze before pulling back his arm. "You've got this. If you want to embrace every opportunity, that is," Nathan adds, a sly reference to the challenge we discussed last night.

I take a deep breath to steady my nerves. I consider for a moment walking away from it.

But then I think about Ben Nepture from Washington State. He attempted to take his own life by jumping off a rocky cliff. By some miracle ("a wave reached out and saved me"), he survived. As Ben was falling, he realized how much his life was worth living and that he was capable of more than he had given himself credit for in the past. After ten months in the hospital recovering and relearning how to use his left arm and both legs, he changed his life.

Ben became a motivational speaker and a professional cliff diver (jumping into the water now instead of rocks), traveling globally to do so while speaking to various groups of adolescents who may struggle with suicidal thoughts. Ben says every time he jumps off a cliff, it's now a reminder of how precious life is and how grateful he is for every single moment, good or bad, because he gets to breathe air for another day.

If I don't jump, I won't be honoring Ben and his story.

I bring my feet closer to the edge.

"Woo-hooooooo!" A shouting figure jumps from over my head and flashes before my sight, plummeting into the water below.

"Nathan!" I screech as I peer over the side, anxious for his head to resurface.

After much too long, he finally pops up with his hair matted to his forehead. He wipes it back with his hand and clears the water from his eyes. "It's a bit chilly, but it doesn't take long to adjust!" he calls back up, the whiteness of his teeth noticeable even from this distance. Nathan paddles out of the way, patting the water in front of him as encouragement for me to take the plunge.

I don't allow myself to think about it for another second and meekly will my body to jump. *Just jump.*

It happens fast, yet my mind slows down enough to process the little details. The cold wind whipping through my hair and stinging my ears. The top of the trees as a bird flies out, terrified by my shouting. The tingling of my toes when they first touch the completely under-described freezing water. Watching Nathan's eyes enlarge as he witnesses my fall.

I hit the water hard and it burns my back as I sink, sink, sink. The water progressively grows warmer the further down I descend, and I enjoy the pull of it. Then my mind clicks back on and reminds me that I need to swim to the top, to breathe and to live. I could have dissolved into nothingness right here.

Popping out of the water, I gasp for air. As soon as it fills my lungs, I swipe the water from my eyes and cry out, "I can't believe I did that! Look how high that is!" I point up to where we were once standing as if Nathan didn't know where we came from. *I jumped from that!*

Nathan's entire face sparkles with his smile, now mere inches away. "That was awesome, Autumn! You soared!"

He makes me sound like I was a bird, and I like the visual. I jump into his arms without thinking. "Thank you for pushing me. Thank you, thank you, thank you."

His arms wrap around my waist, his warm touch a reminder

of how little we are wearing, a fact that went unnoticed when we were changing earlier. I was so nervous about cliff diving that I didn't think twice when Nathan took off his shirt, and I discarded my clothes to reveal my bikini underneath.

But now, with his fingertips grazing my hips in the chilly water, trembles rock my body.

I push back from him and float on my back, squashing the incessant flutters of my stomach and the desire to stay in his arms, peaceful and happy.

I can hear him wading next to me, soft paddles of his hands hitting the water.

Nathan exhales a groan. "Can you imagine if this was your life day in and day out? Always out in nature and enjoying this world the way it was meant to be appreciated."

"Surrounding yourself with the important things in life."

"Exactly. Watching you jump off that cliff was like viewing a meteoroid with the way your red hair was flying. I won't forget that. Like a once-in-a-lifetime phenomenon that I can brag about witnessing."

I try to deflect the sweetness of his words and how each one makes me long to be closer to him. "Everyone makes redheads seem like a different species. Although, here's a fun fact for you. Redhead emojis were only added to iPhone options after they decided the llama and toilet paper emojis were essential, too. How's that for species order of importance?"

He doesn't latch on to my diversion. "If you could see what I saw, you'd understand. I've witnessed a hundred falls, but none like yours. If only you could see you through my eyes."

I squint my eyes, shielding the sun with my hand and glance at Nathan. "You've been out here before?"

"It's my favorite place to come. I'm not exactly a cliff-diving virgin."

I disregard his virgin reference since it makes me think of Jessi and less innocent things. "I noticed! Do you have any fears? There seems to be nothing you won't do. Did the big *Race* conquer all?"

"I have a few fears." His voice is barely audible, contradictory to his typical air of confidence.

"Oh yeah? Like what? The Loch Ness Monster? The Abominable Snowman?"

Nathan moves on his back to float alongside me. "Finally falling in love and having it be with the wrong person."

I fall quiet, wondering if he's putting it all out there. Questioning if he has the same thoughts as me. Doubting decisions that have been made and pondering if this moment could be different. *What if I had met him first...*

A large splash a few feet away soaks my face and ruins the mood. We shift to a treading position. A young man in his twenties had dived headfirst off the cliff. Three others stand at the top yelling down at him and catcalling at us.

"Well, that peace was short-lived. I think our time is up. Follow me." Nathan's face reflects his disappointment; I'm sure mine does as well.

I swim behind Nathan until we reach the shore, where we pull ourselves on the bank. We climb several rocks to retrieve our items, which luckily went untouched by the newcomers. Nathan paves the path to a large rock encompassed by the sun. He throws me a towel and we lay out in the warm sun, letting our bodies soak up the heat.

As my skin finally dries, I replay the view in my mind as I fell from the sky, and the thrill that electrified my body.

Nathan asks, "Would you do it again?"

"I don't know. The one-time experience was so special. It seems like a travesty to try and replicate it."

I can tell he's smiling without having to look. It's like my body can sense him without seeing him. I sit up and braid my hair, so it has hope of looking decent again. "This place is gorgeous. It's been nice doing these challenges with someone rather than alone."

"Life isn't about being alone. Other people enhance all the

great feelings that come along with living and ease all the bad ones."

I sure wish Mark felt that way. It stings that he outright refused to take part in these with me.

"I was engaged before. Before Mark, that is." The unpremeditated words are quick to slip out, another defense mechanism. *Let's ruin this magnetic pull with reasons why I'm tainted goods.*

"Oh, yeah?" Nathan's eyebrows raise but he doesn't look shocked, only interested.

"He was the first man I thought I could be with for the rest of my life. At least, that's the direction we were headed in after years of dating."

"What happened?"

"I wasn't enough. He was cheating on me with a girl who is now his wife."

Nathan sits up straighter. "I doubt you weren't enough. My guess is you were too good for him."

I snort, flicking water drops off my arm, avoiding eye contact, "I tried to tell myself that, but it took a lot of hurt before I finally started to believe it. My mom was actually the one who told me he cheated. Isn't that wild? She found out through the girl's mom. They were playing cards and the lady just casually mentions, 'Oh, Holly told me that she went out with Justin last night. She stayed at his place afterward. For the past two nights, in fact.'" I repeat what Mom had told me verbatim.

"Ahh, there's the county-gossip train in motion again."

"Exactly. I swear my mom always knew more about my relationships than I did." I grab a small stone and play with the edges, my voice breaking while the old emotions pound through me. "Then Mark came along."

"And he was different?" Nathan asks.

"Yes, very different. I didn't have to talk because he never asked a lot of questions, which at the time was strangely comforting. Vulnerable parts of me were closed off because I was scared to reveal them to another person again, and Mark didn't need me to. So I kept them here, locked in my cottage."

"That's why you're reluctant to sell your home. Not only does it reflect you, but you've been hiding in there even when you were thousands of miles away."

I eye Nathan apprehensively, wondering how he can see through me so clearly. "Yeah, that's a part of it."

I hadn't revealed details about my broken engagement to Mark. He didn't want to know about it. Deep hurt that severely impacted me yet was never adequately dealt with still lingers. Instead, I flung myself in Mark's arms knowing full well how much of myself I was burying, and finding comfort in that, when I should have felt anything but.

I trusted him. I didn't think I could trust anyone ever again but with Mark, I don't have to worry that he will cheat on me. He is who he is, readily transparent. When I had yet to heal, that characteristic was what I cared about the most. But now, experiencing an even more tragic event without any support from him, I crave more. He will constantly choose his work over me. I've learned you can be with someone and yet still feel alone.

"You do know you don't have to hide anymore, right?"

"I'm learning." I'm finally embracing that I deserve *more*.

"What's clicking for you?"

I rub my eyes, confident that my makeup is washed off my face. Bare. Nathan is seeing it all. "Being back now. This trip has helped. Maybe it's the threat of leaving it all behind soon. Maybe it's the Bridging the Six Degrees challenges. Maybe it's you." Those three were the only differentiating factors from this trip to previous visits. It felt unfair to not add that last point.

Leaning back on the boulder, I let out an exhale louder than I mean to. Instead of questioning it, Nathan leans back too. We sit in silence, the sun's rays drying the remnants of our time in the water.

My fingers pulsate when Nathan's fingers graze mine. The touch is noticeable only amid certain breaths. I don't know if it's on purpose or by accident. I refuse to open my eyes to check. I lie as still as possible.

Within minutes, his fingers inch closer and link with mine. The heat from Nathan's skin is warmer than the sun. The nerves are steady, making it hard to breathe, as though someone vacuum-sealed us in a plastic sack.

My mind is blaring a horn to get my attention about how wrong this is, but my body is comforted. Mark rarely holds my hand these days. We walk next to each other, but we don't walk linked together. Not anymore. I opened a Dove Chocolate wrapper a few months ago that said, "Hands are meant to be held," and I broke down in tears. Holding his hand was once my favorite part about being with him. I couldn't wait to hold his hand wherever we went because it would engulf mine, warming it and steadying my nerves when we walked into one of his events.

"How do you think your life would be if you had never left Crimson Bay?" Nathan asks the question that has been tossed around in my own head repeatedly since I've returned.

What if I had never left...

I avoid the first image that enters my mind. The one of Nathan and me running into each other at an earlier point in life. We are both single. I never leave. We are carefree. There is no tension in the attraction between us. We would take early morning walks before anyone else wakes. We'd dance in the rain. Our hands would never stop touching each other.

"I'm not sure I can go there right now." I let go of his hand and cross my arms, suddenly much more emotional.

"Autumn, I'm sorry. I didn't mean to..."

"There's a lot I've been trying to figure out, Nathan. Even before you and all of this. Nothing is clear. If anything, it's morning-Bay foggier. I've been consumed by regret and guilt since I've been back. I'm overwhelmed and can't decide to save my life."

"I would argue that you've made a lot of decisions lately. Great ones. No one is forcing you to figure out anything on a deadline,

Autumn. You have plenty of time. That's what life is all about. Making mistakes, bouncing back, fixing them, getting lost, and finding the right path again. There's nothing wrong with that."

"Don't you think that stuff needs to be figured out before you get in your thirties? Explore life in your twenties. Settle down in your thirties. Yet I can't get my heart and head there…"

"You just turned thirty. Shouldn't there be some grace in that reasoning?"

I thinly smile, appreciating Nathan's kindness. "Sure. Except I feel nowhere near where I need to be."

"According to what standard? Live your life. You won't be happy if you're always focused on other people's expectations."

I know how right his words are. But there are still facts that exist that I can't change, decisions already made that are now concrete footprints in my life.

We stare ahead in silence, watching the water, the trees, the birds, the squirrels—nature in its place. It all knows where it belongs and it gravitates there without a second thought. A stark contrast between nature and man—nature goes and trusts, man hesitates and doubts. Both make their own mistakes in some ways. But how would it feel to be more instinctive and rooted than in a constant guessing game of what's right and what's wrong?

Nathan touches my shoulder. "It's okay. We can go."

As usual, he's reading my thoughts. "Thanks, Nathan. I just need to be back there right now."

Home.

We quickly stop back at the hotel to shower and change, grab our bags, and check out. When we get back to the car, Nathan throws me his hoodie. "It'll be chilly by the time we get back. You'll want this." It's why September is my favorite season; warm days but around four in the afternoon, the temps start dropping fast. I haven't had a man give me his sweatshirt to help me stay warm since Justin and I were Juniors in high school. I snuggle up in it as I buckle in, wondering why men's sweatshirts always smell and feel like heaven.

Despite what could have been tense, an easy silence fills the car ride. And I hate it. I long for it to be uncomfortable between us to make it easier to push away and shut down. *Give me an excuse to leave you, please.* I can't be feeling like this around him.

Nathan shifts the gear into park when we arrive at my house.

My hand slides to the door handle, but I don't know how to exit the car. My time with Nathan needs to end. I need to say goodbye.

"How about I make dinner tonight to say thank you for being there when others were too afraid?" The words are out before my willpower kicks in. My legs are dangling outside the car. I was *this* close to being in the clear.

Nathan grins. "Wusses."

"Does seven o'clock work?"

"Definitely." Relief washes over his face. "See you then."

I start to pull his hoodie off my body, but he says, "No, keep it. I've got plenty. You look better in it than I do."

I watch him drive away, biting my thumb to hide the smile that wants to push through my clenched jaw. It's the lightest I've felt in so long. But the invite is risky. Nothing with Nathan is innocent, as desperate as I am to pretend that it is.

Partially skipping to the door, I stop short when I see it's cracked open. I know I locked it before I left.

Peering through the front door, fearful of who or what may respond, I call out, "Hello?"

A matted ball of brown hair rises from the couch. "Hey," Jessi murmurs.

"Jess! You scared me. What are you doing here?"

She slowly sits up as though she's an eighty-year-old with arthritis. The mascara smudges and streaks down her face are the first things I notice.

"I quit The Bridge today."

She's damn near hyperventilating. I fill a glass with water and join her on the couch, sliding my arm around her. "Drink."

Jessi takes the glass to her lips and sips, with water dribbling to her chin.

"Do you want to talk about it?"

"Not really." She exhales as her shoulders shake, and the words spill out of her. "I was bringing Jeffrey his usual order. Two slices of extra crispy bacon, eggs over easy, wheat toast with butter and grape jelly, and coffee with one tablespoon of cream. I dropped it off to him as I have a thousand other times for ten years. He responded with his typical, 'Thank ya, bunny.'"

She looks at me as though what he said was the most incredulous statement I could ever hear. I don't understand what she means, but it could be my selfish preoccupation with how close I was to being busted with Nathan. She could have been looking out the window when we pulled up.

Jessi shakes her head in disgust. "It's the same thing he says every time. He comes in twice a week. I've waited on him every damn time for the past ten years. That means he's called me 'bunny' one thousand forty times!" She throws the check pad paper at me with her math scrawled on it. "I hate being called bunny!"

I nod to empathize, although her primary point evades me. Jessi loves The Bridge and loves Jeffrey even more. He's an elderly man born and raised in Door County who walks everywhere with a crooked back and a cane, wholly genuine and sweet with everyone. Bunny may not be the ideal nickname, but he means well.

Jessi paces the room with heavy steps. "I walked straight up to Sam afterward and told him I quit. Sam laughed. He thought I was joking. Until I threw down my apron and walked out."

"Jess, you know Sam will let you come back. Everyone has rough days. You're allowed yours now and then. You're the most loyal employee they've ever had."

She throws up her arms. "Don't you see that's the problem? I'm the most loyal waitress that Bridgette's Café in Crimson Bay *has ever had.* I don't want to be that person!" Jessi turns on her heel and marches out the front door, leaving it swinging behind her. I'm not sure if she wants me to follow but I do.

Jessi stops at the water's edge with her hands on her hips. I stand next to her, waiting for her to continue if she wants to. I know better than to urge Jessi to talk. It will only shut her down, with a higher risk of a dramatic ending.

She eventually whimpers, "It freaks me out, A. I have these desires of travel but have no clue what to do with them. I envy the shit out of you for being able to do it all."

I shake my head at the irony. "That's funny. Lately, I've been envious of people like you and my parents who stayed dedicated to one place. I don't know why I wanted to run away from here. This is home."

Jessi whips her head to stare at me, her drama momentarily forgotten. "Are you thinking about staying?"

Oh, how I wish that question could be that simple. "Ha, it's not so easy. I'm a two-person deal."

"But you don't have to be," Jessi whispers. "You can do it without Mark."

"Are you saying if I were to leave him?"

"Exactly."

I bite my bottom lip, struggling not to admit that I've had those same thoughts.

"Why not, A? I don't see why it's such a bad thing to admit you guys want different things out of life now." Jessi throws a rock in the water as her eyes narrow in on the created ripples. "People are too focused on regulating each other, concerned with what others will think about them. It's bullshit. And such a screwed-up way to live. Most of the time we do the things we do to stay within the lines that some unspecified person drew."

I don't like that a part of me agrees with her so strongly. It's the same side that's wondering about what-ifs—the dreamer, the overly optimistic believer in freedom and endless opportunities.

"Where's this coming from? I thought you were content with where you are."

Jessi turns to face me, her eyes blazing with enough force to make me take a step back. I poured fuel on a flame I didn't know was burning. "Do you know the number of times I've seen you and Nathan together? People don't hang out with their realtor like that, A. You two, there are feelings there. I can see it a mile away." She sits down on the ground and glares at the water.

"Don't give a shit about me, A. I'm serious, and I'm not saying it because I'm hurt. Well, I am hurt because I liked him. But if you guys are looking at each other in those ways, don't let me—or anyone, for that matter—stop you. I've been searching for that for years and wouldn't care who got hurt if it meant having that for life. And I know that's one of his favorite sweatshirts."

I'm confident my mouth is hanging open. I can feel the wind and a nagging water gnat enter. I'm caught... busted. My face flushes with confirmation. I can't find the words to deny it. All I can say is, "Jess..." with a half-hearted reach as I sit down next to her.

Jessi rubs her hands down the side of her face. "I'm not judging you, A. I'm not. I'm the last person to judge anyone. I don't make decisions that would be labeled right by everyone else. But I follow my heart. I thought you were like that, too. But you're not the same since you married Mark."

Her words fall like a rock in the pit of my stomach, worse than when we were beached roadside and she first shared that she wasn't a fan of Mark. Silence ensues until I finally allow my mouth to verbalize the broken thoughts drifting through my mind.

"It's so screwed up at this stage of life. Thirty years old. People have expectations of who you should be by now. Settled, married, maturely happy with the highs and the lows that life deals you." I dig at the sand with a stick. "My life with Mark is what I *thought* I should want. He seemed like the ultimate fairytale."

"So now that you have it, is it still what you want? You staying together as a couple doesn't memorialize Amelia any more than your love for her already does. You realize that, right?"

I inhale the truth, swallowing a sob that catches in my throat. When I can speak again, I raise my eyebrow at her. "Since when did you become a shrink?"

The corners of her mouth turn up, and it's the first hint of a smile I see Jessi crack. "Who knows? Maybe that's my calling after all."

"Maybe that's why you waitressed all these years. How well can you read people? How many problems have you listened to? How many words of wisdom have you passed on or had passed on to you?"

Chuckling softly, Jessi shrugs her shoulders as a trace of hope glimmers in her eyes. "I'd enjoy being a therapist."

I pick up a rock and attempt to skip it across the water. It jumps twice before sinking. "I found a bunch of old journals while I was packing. One entry was written right after my broken engagement with Justin. It was my newfound declaration of what I wouldn't settle for moving forward. I outlined what I wanted in a future husband. Mark fits five of the eleven traits. *Five.*" My heart splinters as I voice it for the first time.

Jessi nods and bites her lip. "And you're feeling discontent."

"I think it's a combination of a lot of things." I drag my fingers in the sand making random lines and circles that, in many ways, symbolize my life. "Mark is such a great man. Objectively, I know this. But you're right, I'm not sure if he is the one for me. I got wrapped up in the idea of this fantastical, adventurous, fast-paced life and how it was the complete opposite life from what my parents had. I'm a different person when I come back here and he doesn't understand that person."

I take another deep breath. "We're both envying the paths we've not taken. You're doing it the right way, Jess. You're living life. You have never done the things expected of you. That's about as admirable as it gets. Don't regret your choice today."

"Argh, I have no clue what I'm going to do now, though." Jessi holds her head in her hands. "I have enough saved up so I can take time to figure it out. If it gets bad enough, Sam will take me back, right? I mean, he'll have to take me back."

Sam views Jessi like another daughter of his. "Yeah, I'm sure he would. But don't think of it like that. Don't have your contingency plan in place before you have your actual plan set."

"What do you think I should do?"

"Well, if I gave you any suggestions and you ran with them, that wouldn't be a very 'Jessi way' of handling things now, would it?"

"Touché." She stands and dusts the sand off her pants. "Thanks for making me feel better, A. I had a moment of doubt, but I'm glad I did it. Now, I need to figure out what in the world I want to do instead." Reaching out her hand to tug me to a standing position, she adds, "And maybe you should do the same, huh? Live life for you, A. 'Tis the season." She waves her hand to the autumn sky.

I am blown away by Jessi's courage. Even if it was brash in the moment, it was overdue. I always thought Jessi would be a staple in this town, as did most people. Jessi is like nature, though, relying on instinct above all else. She effortlessly sorts through the overwhelming number of thoughts that can confuse a matter or make the deciding ground murkier.

Jessi would move without a plan, without a job, without a house. People would say she's crazy, but it would all work out for her. It always does. Because she relies on instincts and intuition as her compass, and, like nature, she knows precisely where she belongs and when.

Seventeen

With only a few hours before seven, I debate whether I should cancel. If Jessi has noticed Nathan and me together, I'm sure other people have as well. It's not people *knowing* that worries me as much as other people making assumptions before I have any conclusions of my own.

I clean the house and run to the grocery store, replacing his sweatshirt with one of my jackets, paranoid that someone else may recognize it as his sweatshirt as well. I return home with a few essentials to start prepping for dinner. Soon after, Nathan knocks on the door.

"Come in!" I call over my shoulder.

His cologne that I've been smelling all afternoon on his hoodie fills every molecule around me before I even turn to look at him. When I finally do, his blue plaid button-down shirt, untucked over a pair of distressed jeans, makes his eyes pop and shine. Second to a great cologne, I'm weak for blue eyes.

"Mmm, smells good," Nathan comments as he leans across the island to see what I'm working on.

"It must be the candles because I have yet to start cooking. Running a little behind."

"Anything I can help with?" He steps around the island, stop-

217

ping only inches from me, the pull stronger than ever before, as though the few hours apart supercharged the natural electricity between us.

My body automatically tenses as if I need to defend myself. "Can you open up that bottle of wine?" I nod to a dry red sitting on the counter to get him further away. "We're having pasta, so it'll be a good match."

"You've got it." Nathan opens the bottle like a master.

"You typically choose wine over beer, huh?"

He laughs as he pockets the cork. "I've never thought about it before. Why?"

"You're a pro at opening it. Quicker than anyone I've seen."

He shrugs. "Just good with my hands, I suppose."

The connotation is not lost on me. My body temperature rises a few degrees, no matter how hard I try to regulate it.

He pours a glass for both of us, handing me mine as our hands graze. I'm certain the skin-to-skin contact was intentional, on both sides.

"What did you do for the rest of the afternoon?"

"Napped."

I glance up from dicing tomatoes. "Seriously? I thought you were going to work on whatever chaos you had going on."

"I did for a while. But then I fell asleep on my couch. Didn't sleep well the night before."

"Why's that?"

"Thoughts kept me up. You know how that goes."

I do. I return to the sink to wash the parsley.

"Put me to work, chef."

"I swear I'm almost done. I only have a few more veggies to cut up, and then I'll throw it in the oven. You just sit there and enjoy the wine." *In other words, drink up so you don't remember if I say or do anything stupid.*

"Do you have *any* dishes that match?"

I freeze in motion, my arm in midair from reaching for a bowl in the cabinet. "Um, nope. My dishes represent little moments in time, and I like that about them."

Nathan runs his hand through his hair with a sigh. "That's crazy endearing."

I gently shut the cabinet door since it has the tendency to send shock waves through the dishes. With none of them being alike, they don't stack correctly and rattle loudly anytime there are vibrations in the house.

"Endearing, huh? That's not usually what people call it." Mark hates that I collect mismatched dishware, which is why my collection wasn't allowed to travel with us to Boston. Which was fine since each piece belongs in this cottage exactly as they are.

Nathan reaches for a green bowl on the counter. "Where'd this one come from?"

"Passed down from my great-grandma, Patti. She always used it for salad so I continue the tradition."

"And what about this one?"

"That came from the flea market. It was the first time I took Mark there. He bought it for me when I couldn't stop looking at it."

"I see." Nathan's eyebrows furrow as he rotates it. "So, what did you do after I dropped you off?"

"Well, I thought a burglar broke into my house but it only turned out to be Jessi, so we chatted for awhile. Then I wrote for a bit before trying to get dinner thrown together."

"I can always tell when you write. Your eyes lighten. Like they shine more of a sage green color."

I freeze in the middle of cutting peppers. No one else has told me that before.

"It's a high for you. It stands out. The first time I saw the change in your eyes, I thought it was the lighting. But I noticed it again this morning when you said you had been writing before the meditation class."

To hide the blushing of my cheeks, I turn back to the cutting board and murmur, "Holy crap, we meditated with a monk today." The memory rushes back. Even though it happened earlier this morning, it feels like a dream. "Isn't that crazy? An actual monk."

"We did, indeed. Pretty incredible."

"Think you'll put any of it into practice?"

"I'd like to say I'm going to. It takes commitment. Twenty-one days to form a habit, I suppose. What about you?"

"Yes, for sure. I need as much positivity in my life as I can get."

"Speaking of..." Nathan places his elbows on the island and leans into them. "Listen, our last talk today, out on the rock..."

I don't know what's coming but a knot forms in my stomach. I don't want to hear whatever he will say. No matter what, the result can't be positive.

Instead, I blurt out, "You should give Jessi another try. There's more to her there than people realize."

Nathan hesitates before responding, his words slow, "You want me to date Jessi?"

I shrug and return my focus to the pepper. Halve it, core it, then slice it. "She was here earlier and I don't know... she has layers. They're worth exploring. Her walls can be up with men. Maybe she didn't show you her true colors." I mean none of it. Nathan and Jessi are not a good fit, even with my feelings put aside, but I must find a buffer. Something else to detract from whatever he planned to say. From whatever I may say in response.

"Hmm..." Nathan sets his wineglass down and appears next to me, leaning his waist against the granite only inches from my arm. His familiar heat radiates off him to my skin as my heart speeds up. "Do you think I'm a good fit for her now? After spending more time with me?" The same question he asked me before when I so ruefully claimed he's a better fit for someone like me.

I want to scream no but I attempt to form a different reasoning. "Jessi is a great person. Big heart, smart, romantic, deep when she trusts you enough to open up... layered. I thought guys kind of like that." I joke, raising my eyebrows at him.

He doesn't take the bait. Instead, he moves his hand until it's covering mine. I drop the knife. His hand slides up my arm, trailing goosebumps, and down my side to gently grip my waist. Slowly, he turns my body to face him. "I asked if *you* thought she was a good fit for me."

My breath catches in my throat. Nathan's eyes travel my face, searching for an answer that we both already know, but he's waiting on me to say it out loud. His eyes rest on my mouth.

"No..." I finally exhale.

"Why?" Nathan captures pieces of my hair, runs his fingers down the strands, and pushes them behind my ear.

"Because you're a good fit for me, which means you're not for her." Our exact conversation from last time repeated, except now with more force and meaning after our time together. My body is curved out, my hips jutted forward, as though fighting the resistance to fill what little space remains. One shuffle, that's all it would take, and my hips would be pressed against his.

A coy smile crosses his face. "Explain."

I sigh, exasperated by the constant battle of my heart—and hormones—when he's around. "You're the perfect fit for me. And I don't know what to do about it. I can't do *anything* about it. Not yet." I grip the sink in defeat, tears fighting to wash me away, when all I want to do is tug on the waistband of his jeans to connect his body to mine.

Silence. Nathan gazes at me. I take a deep breath, lift my head, and steadily return his look.

Nathan inches closer, closing the gap between us. "I've been wondering if this is reciprocated."

"It doesn't matter. Don't you see that?" I won't cheat on Mark like Justin cheated on me. *I won't.* I turn my back to Nathan because my willpower is losing steam. Nathan's breath tickles my nape. How badly I want to give in a little, only a taste, just to know what it's like.

"I know..." The air of his words blows hair off my neck, the nakedness beckoning him. "I replay these imaginary scenes in my mind of you never leaving Door County, of us running into each other at the bar and having the same conversation we had that night. How easy it all would be."

"I'd be lying if I said I didn't think about that, too. But Nathan…" I struggle to grasp a coherent thought while my body is screaming to take the damn risk already. "My life is… confusing right now. That's what I was trying to say on the rock. I don't know if I'm at liberty to stop and think that way. Not right now."

"Then when? When do you question whether you're making the right choices? What if this is happening for a reason, you and me being here. Like this." The back of Nathan's hand slides down my cheek as I suck in my breath, thinking about what would happen if I gave in to his touches. *Would he kiss me? Would I kiss him in return? Then what?*

"Autumn!" The front door bursts open. Nathan and I break away from each other like a bomb exploded between us, prepared to be faces of innocence, but my rising chest gives me away.

Panic fills Rose's eyes. I've only seen that look once before when her beloved rabbit escaped through an open window. She was convinced it would get hit by a car before we found it.

I immediately cross the room and put my hands on her shoulders. Her eyes dart from me to Nathan and back again, undoubtedly confused with an edge of disappointment that only I can detect.

Before she speaks, I note the figure that's now standing behind her. "Kevin," I acknowledge, startled to have yet another person witness me with Nathan, especially one with direct contact to Mark. Rose's cheeks redden, as I'm sure mine are.

"I've got Mark on the phone." Rose's voice is barely above a whisper. "Something happened to Henry."

My heart pounds out of my chest as I tear the phone out of her hands. "Mark! What happened? What's wrong with Henry?"

"He had a heart attack, but he's okay. You know the old man is a fighter." Mark yawns, and I realize it's the middle of the night there, but that's still no way to respond to the news.

His cool manner may aid him in business, but as his wife, it pisses me off. Major life events demand a bit more care, especially knowing how much Henry means to him. Mark already lost his dad; he would be crushed if he lost Henry like this. To this day, Mark struggles to talk about his dad, marked by a fear that the more he shares, the more those memories will no longer be his, as though opening his mouth will cause them to escape forever. Every now and then, he'll mention his dad's love for Skee-Ball and their frequent trips to arcades to compete against each other, or his dad's obsession with making pasta from scratch, yet with minimal talent to produce noodles that were rarely thin enough or tasty. I've learned that asking probing questions will immediately shut Mark down, but by stilling my body and holding my breath, Mark will speak about his dad— until he catches himself and stops, usually leaving the room soon after.

But Mark will talk about Henry nonstop, and I'm shocked he's so nonchalant right now if Henry is hurt.

"He's being monitored for a couple of days at Mass Gen. Thought you'd want to visit him. I can't get Griffin out to you until the morning, though. But he'll be at the hangar right at seven if that works for you."

"Yes, of course. I want to see Henry."

"I'm having Griffin bring you a temporary phone. I don't want you in Boston without one."

I shake my head even though he can't see me. "No, Mark, I have three more days to go without it. I don't want to break the challenge."

He yawns again. "Can't you put a pause on that and pick it up again? Or start over when you get back? I don't want you to be in Boston without a cell. It's not like being at Crimson Bay. I have no way to get a hold of you if I need you."

"I'll be fine. I'll plan a time to meet up with Griffin again. He can text you and let you know that I'm safe."

I hear the springs in his bed as Mark adjusts his body.

"Autumn, I have to put my foot down here. You need to take the phone when Griffin picks you up."

"Mark, I'm a big girl. I can handle myself." I turn my body so that everyone else doesn't hear my tone change.

"It would simply make me feel better if you would take a phone with you."

"I appreciate your concern," I state calmly, "I've committed to this challenge. I'm almost done, and I don't want to regress. People have survived for years without technology. Thank you for letting me know about Henry. I will make sure Griffin stays in contact with you throughout my travels. You can also reach me at the hospital." I pause to wait for further disputes.

Instead, Mark angrily resigns and through gritted teeth says, "Be careful, Autumn. Love you."

I glance over my shoulder at Rose, Kevin, and Nathan chatting together before responding, "You, too."

As soon as I end the call, Rose is next to my side, whispering, "Is everything okay?"

I take a deep breath to swallow the tears. "Yeah, I'm headed to Boston in the morning to see Henry and make sure he really is okay. We're the only family he has. I hate that he's alone tonight." Struggles with Lenora's health before she died contributed to the primary reason she could never bear children, which had troubled her for most of their marriage. She felt as though she kept Henry from being the family man he was always meant to be. They couldn't adopt because of the financial strain of her ongoing treatments.

"But I loved her." Henry shared with us the first night we invited him into our house, as he provided marriage advice from the telling of his own story. "This life was for her. No kids, that's okay. My life and her life together, that's all that mattered. It'll be fine. Everything always turns out fine."

Everything always turns out fine, I remind myself, using Henry's words for comfort.

Nathan catches my eye and asks with genuine concern, as

though he knows Henry as well as I do after all the stories I've shared, "What happened?"

"He had a heart attack, but it sounds like he'll be okay."

"That's good. Or good in a bad situation, at least."

"Yeah." Emotional exhaustion ransacks my body.

Kevin looks at Nathan, then grabs Rose's hand and says, "We should get going before we're late for our dinner reservations."

"Do you need me to stay?" Rose clearly doesn't want to leave. If Kevin wasn't standing next to her, I know she'd demand answers on what was going on with Nathan in my house for what is clearly dinner plans. Since I'm not ready to answer those, I am relieved for Kevin's presence.

"No, I'm fine. Thank you, though."

"Okay," she relents. "Call me or find me or whatever you have to do to..." she glances at Nathan. "Update me. On Henry."

Not like everyone doesn't know exactly what she means. "Will do. Thank you for getting the message to me."

Rose gives Nathan one last curious look as she descends the steps, Kevin pulling on her hand to navigate her out.

I leave the door cracked open instead of shutting it and suggest a rain check. "Dinner may have to be postponed. I need to pack. And honestly, I'm not feeling all that great."

"I totally understand. No worries. I have my tabs at the bars around town to add to anyway."

I force a chuckle, anxious to lay down all of a sudden.

Nathan pulls me in for a hug, and I seize the opportunity to breathe him in, once more for comfort.

"Hey." I pull back from him. "Out of curiosity, if we didn't come back today, what else did you have planned?"

"You sure you want to know?"

"I do."

"There's a Hot Air Balloon Festival in a couple of weeks. They do pre-runs for the weeks leading up to it. I know a guy who owns one. I figured if you could conquer cliff diving, we could then move on to the next big height and do the hot air balloon challenge."

I picture a hot air balloon traveling over the park where we went cliff diving. To see the place we dominated cliff diving from an aerial perspective would have been incredible. I don't know if I could handle doing that with Nathan. It all sounds so romantic, so tempting.

"Nathan..."

He leans his forehead into mine. "No need to say anything. You have a safe trip. We'll talk more when you get back."

When the door closes, I feel more alone than ever.

Some people wait their entire life to meet the right person. What if I finally met mine, but while he was waiting for me, I didn't wait for him?

It's time to sort out my heart, and I'm terrified at what I may find.

I TOSS AND TURN. I GET UP FOR A GLASS OF WINE TO SEE if that helps. Then warm milk. Then warm tea. But then I have to pee ten times from drinking so much so late at night, which doesn't help me sleep either.

I'm thinking about... well, everything. Life. Love. Henry. Death. Life. Moving. Mark. Family. Friends. Nathan. Love. It's all just a skipping record on repeat. When I try to write my thoughts down, I'm unsuccessful. I can barely keep up with them as they're zooming through my mind, one after another, like shooting stars, impossible to catch.

My eyes are still wide open when my alarm goes off. It doesn't take much effort to bounce out of bed and hop in the shower. I'm ready to get on the plane and be closer to Henry. I hate thinking of him all alone in a hospital room. Although, there's no doubt he's been charming the female staff with that accent of his; he seldom realizes he's doing it.

My drive to Green Bay is in silence. It may be the first time I've driven this route by myself without music blaring. I can't turn off my thoughts. My worry about Henry, my wonder about Nathan, my conflict with Mark, my evaluation of my life. *What if I had never moved out of Crimson Bay...*

"Griffin, hi!" My thoughts finally come to a halt when I see his military, steady-as-a-rock frame and demeanor. I'm waving my hands in the air, garnering the attention of the other eight people sitting in the small terminal. His presence brings a sense of calm to my nerves, and I need it like medicine.

The last time I saw Griffin, one of Neigleman Tech's pilots, was when he was putting my bags in my Jeep for what we thought was the final time he would be flying me to Green Bay for my three-month stay. As the only private jet pilot assigned for Mark's needs, we had clocked many hours together in the sky. We seldom held long conversations because we are both quiet people, but we didn't require many words to understand each other. That trip was supposed to mark the conclusion of our time together. There was no point in false promises that we should keep in touch because we weren't the type of people who made those efforts. So saying, "See you soon" was the best form of goodbye I could muster at the time. He had tipped his hat in a nod and replied, "Ma'am," with his thick southern drawl, which was the perfect response. He could read my eyes and I could see my feelings reflected in his own. That silent language between two people can be the most meaningful.

I didn't expect to see him again, especially so soon.

Griffin tilts his head to me in a nod. "Miss Autumn. Let me take your bags." There's a glint in his eyes. I know he's as happy to see me even when he doesn't use words to say it.

"Thanks, Griffin."

"We are on time for take-off and should arrive in Boston by ten-thirty. Weather looks all clear, although we may hit a few rough patches. I'll keep you updated."

We climb into the cabin and I find my favorite seat with two cold bottles of water ready in the cup holders. We're back into our flow. Even though it's only been a couple of months since the last ride, it seems like much longer. So much has occurred in a short time. I'm a different person.

We rise over the fields of Wisconsin and as I look out the

window, I try to imagine how I would feel knowing I'm not returning, that I'm off to Italy instead.

It doesn't feel right in my bones. A cold feeling settles there so I close my eyes and try to nap instead, pushing away the dread that rises.

Once we deplane in Boston, I pull open my carry-on and grab my coat and scarf. It got cold quickly here.

Griffin waves over a black Town Car. "We received special permission for the flight today and tomorrow since I am no longer assigned to Mark. Due to that, I have to fly out to my next assignment right away. Mark said it was imperative you take this." Griffin holds a pre-paid phone.

"Please tell Mark that I decline it, just as he and I discussed last night."

Griffin nods uneasily. "He warned me. I'll let him know I tried. Here's the phone number for the Town Car driver, William, and your hotel information."

I glance at the sheet in his hand. "I don't need that. I plan to stay at Henry's."

"Mark said he would prefer that you were closer to the hospital since that's the purpose of the trip. It also gives him a place to call if he needs you." A brief look of pain crosses over Griffin's face as he winces, waiting for my reaction. He's caught in the middle of a marital spat so I can't blame him for feeling uncomfortable. Griffin is the type who avoids drama at all costs. It isn't fair to put him through any more of what Mark and I should personally discuss with each other.

I spare him further agony by taking the paper without complaining.

"I'll be back here at four tomorrow for a five-o'clock takeoff. If you could be here by four-thirty, that should allow plenty of time. Call me if there's anything else you need." Griffin opens the door to the car for me.

"To the hotel, miss?" William asks from the front seat.

"Yes, please."

Once we arrive, I relieve William of his duties. I'm eager to walk around Boston anyway. The constant sirens and honking and swarms of people are a stark contrast to Door County; I welcome the jolt this time. I was falling into comfortable, old patterns back home, and a little shakeup may be what I need to get my head on straight.

As soon as I get settled into my room, I head straight for the hospital. When I request to see Henry, the sour-faced front desk attendant laughs and slaps her knee. "Oh, that man, bless his heart. We are all in love with him. We get some good-looking fellas in here, but none are as charming as Henry. Are you his daughter?"

"A friend. But he's basically my adoptive second father."

"Oh honey, I'd adopt him, too. I'd marry him even, despite the age difference."

She has me laughing and feeling a lot better about Henry's condition before I see him. Once I lay eyes on him, though, a sob catches in my throat.

This is a man who rarely sits down, even with a walking cane and a limp. He is so active, always striving to get out and about and "live as much as possible," as he always says. To see him restrained to a bed, hooked up to a monitor and IV, is heartbreaking. It's as though an entirely different Henry lies here, and not the one I've come to love.

"Henry." I kneel by his bedside and reach for his hand. It feels cold to the touch as the dry wrinkles press against my skin. "How are you?"

"Autumn wind," he sighs my name, relieved to see a familiar face. "You came to visit!" His voice is bold, which both elates and surprises me. My overactive imagination makes me paranoid, especially when it comes to losing the people I love the most.

Henry's blue eyes twinkle as always, and that charming smile of his uplifts my soul. Pictures from his younger days prove he has always been handsome. It's part of why I was smitten with his love story with Lenora. There's no doubt he could have had any woman he wanted but he was loyal to Lenora his entire life, even after she passed.

"What happened, Henry?"

"Oh, the world spun and stopped. That is all. My trusty cane was not so trustworthy. I saw the floor and—poof, no more. Then I woke up here."

"Are you in a lot of pain?"

"I do not remember what they are pumping into my old body, but it is good, like a good wine. Hard to feel pain when you're drinking good wine." He pats my hand. "I have been with myself for far too long. Time to hear about you. How's home? You happy to be back? Mark said he had a very big surprise for you."

I pull up a chair next to his bed. "It's good, and he did. Surprised me with a big birthday party that was led by one of his newest companies."

Henry wrinkles his nose. "You, parties, businesses? Not such a good mix."

I chuckle and grab his hand tighter. "Sometimes, Henry, I swear you know me better than anyone."

"I only listen. You learn people when you listen to people."

I missed this man and his wisdom so much. I wish I could pocket him and carry him with me wherever I go.

"What is sitting heavy on your mind?" Henry peers at me with suspicion. "I have seen that look before."

I lean closer to him, resting my chin on his bed. Henry and I were never big on small talk. That's one reason why we know each other so well. No fluff, only intentional words. "I've been wondering..." I outline his knuckles with my thumb while forming my thoughts. "Do you think there's one place that we're meant to be? And if we're not there at the time we're supposed to be, that we will forever be dissatisfied, wondering and searching for something else? But if we are where we are supposed to be, then we are content, happy, and fulfilled?"

Henry is quiet for a moment, and I wonder if I confused him

as much as I almost confused myself trying to explain what's itching deep in my soul.

Finally, he speaks, "Do you want there to be only the one place?"

I snort before responding, "No, I suppose that'd be like jail. Feeling captured and stuck, hoping you're someday freed to go elsewhere."

"You are where you are meant to be. Now. Tomorrow. Always. Happiness is found where you want it to be seen. Not happy where you are? Your eyes are looking somewhere else. Not where you are. Look where you are *now*." Henry could give Confucius a run for his money with philosophical wisdom.

"But what about with people? Does it work the same way? Doesn't saying you're only meant to be with one person limit the possibilities of living life?"

Henry shrugs, which makes his hospital gown swallow him up. "Only if you believe sharing life with someone limits the possibilities of living life."

"That's exactly what I question sometimes. What if in the middle of being with one person, you meet someone else who actually wants the same things that you do?"

"Beautiful Autumn. You surprise me with your naiveté." Henry shakes his head, as though disappointed with my line of thinking. "Do you actually think sameness brings contentment? Will you be content with someone who dreams like you, thinks like you, feels like you? You only need to be with someone who is exactly like you if you need confirmation of who you are; confirmation of your thoughts, confirmation of your feelings, confirmation that you are who you see when you look in the mirror. But you, my dear one, are much stronger. You don't need confirmation of you. You have you for that."

I hadn't thought of it like that before. But still, there's a pull with Nathan, strong, urgent, yet delicate and soft.

"You're doubting your move to Italy, yes?"

Without preparing for it, tears freely fall from my eyes. This trip has made me incredibly emotional. Soon, I'm sobbing into Henry's shoulder, and he's patting my hand.

"I'm sorry, I'm so sorry. This visit is about you, not me."

"This world is never about one person. What is on your heart?"

I test the words on my lips, pushing them through for the first time, "I don't know if Mark and I are good together. Not anymore."

Henry wrinkles his forehead, and it's my exact fear coming to life: disappointing him.

"But..." I sniff and try to reel back the emotions, to smooth over the terrible truth I just voiced. "Together, we're a family. You, me, him, and I love that. I can't imagine not having that. It's what helped me survive Boston and... everything. I'm just confused being back home and all. I'm sure it'll be fine once we're all in Italy together."

Henry is quiet much too long. Finally, he speaks.

"I'm not your child, Autumn wind. I am fond of you and Mark, and I would miss you very much if you were not in Italy. But I'm not your child. You must not worry about letting me down. You must not worry about breaking your family. Once a family, always a family."

I choke back sobs. We had adopted Henry as the child we never had, despite the fact that he could be our grandfather. We cared for him, cooked for him, and took him on as many trips as he was willing to go on with us. The truth is, we tried to replace Amelia with Henry, a necessary bond that keeps us together. We needed him for us to stay together.

Henry, in his wisdom, just released me of my self-imposed obligation. I didn't realize what we were doing until he spoke it out loud.

"You are very much like my Lenora. Both free souls, relentlessly chasing fluttering ideas. Dreams that only you can see. I spent a lifetime chasing her. She was my dream. I'd spend many, many more lifetimes doing it over again." Henry pats my hand again and leans back in the bed, closing his eyes. I've seen this look hundreds of times and know he's about to drift into sleep. This man could nap anywhere. "You and Mark... both very independent. No matter who you choose in the end, you will spend a lifetime having to chase each other. No wrong in that. But you have to be willing to be caught, Autumn. Never forget that."

Henry's eyes grow heavier, and his breathing deepens, seconds away from falling asleep. I lean over the bed and kiss him on the cheek. "I'll stop by later tonight. I love you, Henry."

Snores are his reply.

I close his door quietly and lean against it, staring up at the fluorescent lights. If I never left Door County to follow Mark, I would have never met Henry. And that man, all that I've learned from him, has shaped me and will, without a doubt, continue to do so for the remaining years I have with him. I can't regret my path with Mark. I had Amelia with him, for however short she was with us, and later, Henry, both people who I've been so lucky to love.

Henry's words stay with me as I walk seven blocks to pop into one of my favorite coffee shops, Houndstooth Coffee & Books. After ordering a coffee with a splash of oat milk, I sit down to pull out my journals and pens that are stuffed inside my messenger bag.

I try to write, but I'm restless. My knees jiggle under the table. Would Mark be heartbroken if our marriage ended? I'm not sure. Sad, of course. Heartbroken, though? He didn't even stop working for a day after we lost Amelia. I was paralyzed, chained to the floor by grief. I assumed our coping mechanisms were different, but when he doesn't tell me how he's feeling, how am I supposed to truly know? I don't want to experience anything near that earth-shattering pain again. I don't want to feel as though I'm completely alone when I'm supposed to have a partner who shoulders the good and the bad throughout life with me. The thing is, I know that if anyone else in his life experienced a hardship, he would be there for them. He was always showing up for other people, knowing his presence sent a strong message. But home seemed like the last place he wanted to be.

Since my initial visit with Henry went much quicker than I had planned, I decide to walk the city. Rarely did I walk the streets here alone, as I always had Mark or Henry with me. I need to start exploring what it feels like to do things without them.

I rifle through my Bridging the Six Degrees journal and analyze the list of remaining activities. One immediately stands out as something I had contemplated doing while living here but I was too intimidated. I'd stalked this place online, scouring pictures and social media to work up the guts to walk into it someday. I believed, for too long, that my abilities were lesser than those who were already doing it, so I never worked up the nerve.

A lengthy taxi ride later and I'm standing in front of Max's Boxing Ring. It is a rough-looking gym built around the idea of boxing, but has branched out to Krav Maga, Brazilian Jiu-Jitsu, and Keysi fighting classes. They're all activities I consider relatively badass and I admire the women who kept up with the men.

The challenge from Coby Kensington, who traveled all the way from Ireland, was to do something that makes me feel strong, to connect with the strength inside of me, whatever my definition of that is. Coby had committed to training for the Ironman Triathlon after winning his battle with cancer, which strengthened him not only physically but mentally and emotionally as well. It gave him a newfound purpose and mission.

Max's Boxing Ring is a converted Speed Lube business, with frosted garage doors as floor-to-ceiling windows. When it's hot outside, they prop those open, letting people get a peek into the trainings they hold. I've seen the videos posted by watchers with comments like *"Ooh shit, don't want to tangle with her," "Did you see him go down? He hit the ground like all his bones got crushed at once,"* and *"How is this legal??"* It's exactly why I've been too intimidated to get this close. Until today.

I take a deep breath and step through the regular door, the bell ringing behind me.

The gym is raw compared to any other workout facility I've been to. The vast open space is decorated with piles of jump ropes, punching bags, and free weights. There's one cheap looking treadmill in the corner and a rowing machine next to it. Large HVAC vents run across the high ceilings, maintaining the garage-feel.

"Can I help you?"

A bald man in his fifties wearing a tight black crew tee and cargo pants appears from a back room while pushing a cart full of glistening boxing gloves. Colorful tattoos snake around his biceps and a giant silver ring full of keys jiggles as they hang over his left pocket.

I clear my suddenly dry throat. "Yeah, I was hoping to try out a class."

I expect him to look me up and down, scoff, and make judgments about what I wouldn't be able to handle. Instead, he wipes his hands on his pants and saunters to the counter in the corner, where he waves me over. Pulling out a registration form, he instructs, "Fill this out. Which one?"

"Are there any classes starting in the next couple of hours?"

"Not today. Team trainings have the gym booked. Our next one isn't until seven tonight. It's the Keysi, if you're interested. We've got space."

I weigh my options with seeing Henry tonight. I told him I'd be back and I want to honor that, but this gym is a good forty-minute haul from the hospital with traffic. There'd be no way I could do both.

The man notices my internal debate. "Nerves?"

"That, and time constraints unfortunately. I won't be able to come tonight. I just moved out of Boston but had to come back for a friend today. I spent about two years looking inside this gym but always staying out. Finally wanted to face my fear."

He studies me and I try not to squirm. "Which class interests you the most?"

"Any of them. They're all frightening."

He chuckles and sticks out his hand. "My name is Guy. I own this place."

I shake his big and calloused hand wearily; I'm pretty sure it could crack me in half with one squeeze. "I assumed a Max would be the owner."

He snorts roughly. "Yeah, I get that a lot. I was told calling it 'Guy's Boxing Ring' made it sound sexist, like a men's-only joint or whatever. Apparently, Guy isn't common enough of a name for people to see it for what it is. Whatever. My middle name is Max. Maxwell, actually. So, I went with that when we had to put up the name. Pacified everyone enough."

Pointing to the form I'm filling out, he commands, "Finish that up. Make sure to sign the consent form. I gotta finish a few things in the back. Go find gloves that fit you from that bin there and meet me in the ring. I have some free time so I can teach you a few things from each session, okay? The only catch is, if you find you like it, make sure to find that class or a version of it wherever it is you've moved to. No sense in teaching someone something they'll never apply again. Also, leave a review on that Facebook thing."

I can't believe he's being this generous with his time. "Thank you so much, and yeah, I will do that. Both of those things."

"Great. Make sure to stretch and warm up. I'll be out in a bit."

It takes a while to find gloves that won't devour my hands. There's a large container of hand wraps next to it that I don't know what to do with, so I leave it alone for now. I climb through the ropes of the boxing ring, grab a jump rope hanging from the side and do intervals to warm up.

"You're pretty good with the rope."

Guy returns, startling me from the zone.

"How long have you been doing that?"

I stop to catch my breath and shrug. "Since I was eight or nine." A Jump Rope for Heart fundraiser during elementary school kickstarted my jump roping obsession. We held contests and I won just about every one except the double Dutch because, like most things, I mess up when someone else gets involved. Great on my own, unable to find a rhythm with others. Typical.

"You're good. Real talent there. I see a lot of ropers, but few do it with as much grace and skill."

The compliment catches me off guard. Jumping rope isn't something I'd typically list as a strength. I do it to burn off anxiety or stress, or when I need a quick break or brain boost from writing all day.

"You may be better at what I'm about to show you than I originally thought."

"Because of jumping rope?" It's an odd thing to realize about myself after many years of doing it without a thought, especially to know it could aid me in an environment like this that I've avoided for too long.

"You'd be surprised what I can pick up from people's warm-ups. Been in this business for a long time." He grabs a roll of tape from the corner. "Alright. Rope down, fists out. Let's get you wrapped. We'll lead with boxing."

The afternoon produces one surprising, new discovery after another. I find out I'm pretty decent at instinctual ducking.

"That's part of those jump rope skills," Guy says. "I knew you'd avoid the strikes."

I'm afraid to punch him at first, even with his mitts on, but I get over that fast. It's liberating to have the free reign to do that, to know someone will be fine afterward no matter how hard I hit. It also turns out that I have plenty of pent-up emotions I need to punch out. Shocker.

Guy explains the art of Jiu-Jitsu next, which is an intense change. Suddenly, we're more intimate with increased physical contact. Guy talks the entire time, coaching and stressing the importance of using these moves in self-defense. With zero initial experience, the intentional violence surprises me at first when he points out how to break a person's limbs at the joint.

"Think about some asshole attacking you or a friend on the street. They're out there. You read the stories; I know you do. Someone sneaks up behind you, has a knife, tries to assault you or your friend. Will you give a damn about breaking his arm? Hell, no. You'll do what it takes to stop him. Gouge out his eyeballs if need be."

We end our session with Krav Maga, which wins as my favorite since it relies more on instinct than skill. "You don't give the person time to attack because you're striking at the same time, while simultaneously protecting yourself. Elbows up. One more time." I'm addicted. Even though my arms are shaking from the work, I find the strength to keep pushing.

By the end, all my nerve endings vibrate, my muscles ache and tremble, and I am drenched in sweat. I down my fourth water bottle refill like it's air. But I feel empowered. Almost like I can go out and kick some serious ass as a superhero. Or at the very least, defend myself if needed.

Guy wipes away sweat from his forehead with a towel. He picks up his camouflage canteen and takes a swig, "Whaddya think?"

"I wish I hadn't waited so long to try this."

"Yeah. You could be real decent if you'd been practicing all this time." I almost take offense to it, until he follows up with, "Like entering our tournaments, representing your age group for the women. Yeah. You could have been an asset, I think."

Moved by his compliment, I say, "I'll try to locate Krav Maga classes when we move. Or maybe I'll start with boxing, then Krav Maga. Or both."

"Yeah, I could see that. That's good. I'm glad you want to keep going. Where you moving to? I might have contacts there. You want good coaches. None of these all-encompassing fitness instructors who don't know what they're talking about."

I hesitate for a moment and almost say Wisconsin, but then correct myself before opening my mouth, "Italy."

"Like Italy a town in some state?"

I shake my head. "The country." My stomach rolls at the thought.

"Well, shit." Guy takes a swig out of his canteen. "Can't help you out there. Don't know anything about that. Are there gyms? Or do they squash grapes and drink wine for exercise?"

"What about Wisconsin?"

"That's a long way from Italy."

"Any there?" I press.

"Sure, Milwaukee, Green Bay, and Madison. Take your pick."

"Green Bay." My voice is steady, assured.

"Bobby McAllister. Let me jot his info down. He's scary, but a big teddy bear at the core. Make sure you tell him I said that."

THE HOT WATER ON MY MUSCLES FROM THE HOTEL room shower is exactly what I need. It's reminiscent of how I felt after my pampering session. Similar relief, two different experiences. It also feels like two different time periods, even though only a few days separate them.

By the time I get out of the shower, there's a blinking light on the hotel phone. I listen to the message. Mark had called and said he'd try back again later but wanted to let me know that he had checked in with the nurse and was happy to hear Henry was doing well. "Give that old man a hug for me and tell him he needs to take better care of himself."

Afterward, I stop by the deli to pick up Henry's favorite sub sandwiches, which are, ironically, the classic Italians. I add a few bags of his secret craving: Sun Chips. Lenora had a strong hatred toward his loud crunches and would hide the bags or "forget them" when grocery shopping.

As soon as Henry sees me, he breathes out a sigh. "I can smell the meat. You have come to save me, my dear Autumn."

"I'm hoping you haven't eaten yet?"

"I have. But I have the room to eat more. Always."

He has quite the appetite for a man his size. I pull out the bag of Sun Chips. "Room for these?"

Henry's pupils enlarge. "Please."

I open the bag and pour them on Henry's tray. He pops one in his mouth, savoring it before the big crunch comes. "I said a prayer to my Lenora that she may forgive me, that I may be deserving of these. Crunching and all." He wrinkles his nose as he takes another one, imitating Lenora as though to bring her presence closer.

I convey Mark's message, and we chat about Henry's progress and his expected release date from the hospital. Then he makes me turn on the TV to his new favorite show, *House Hunters International*, quite fitting considering the upcoming move.

Once Henry finishes eating and a commercial break comes on, he leans closer. "I am rude. Here you came to visit me, and instead, I am looking at the TV. What did you do today while I slept?"

"Well, I took an interesting self-defense class. It taught me a little about boxing and various other street fighting arts."

Henry raises one of his bushy, white eyebrows. "Street fighting?"

"I know, it sounds rough, but it was amazing."

"Self-defense is good. You are strong, but more strength can only help. I am glad. I hope you do more."

Henry is such a peaceful man, I worried he would criticize it. "It is addicting. I'd like to continue it if I can find a similar place."

"Oh, all those things are popular. Some very good fighters have come from Italy. You will be fine. I will help you find ones. Many private instructors. You will be just fine."

How do I tell Henry I was dreaming about continuing it back home more than in Italy?

Henry watches my eyes and pats my hands. "I have a feeling you are sorting lots in that mind. I am here if you need me."

"I know you are, Henry. You always have been. I'm very appreciative of you."

"And me of you. And of Mark. You two are what my life need-ed." He pauses a moment before asking, "Why did you wait until you returned to do the fighting?"

I pick at the blue blanket on his bed. "I couldn't persuade anyone else to go with me and didn't feel comfortable enough to go on my own. It's not exactly the most welcoming environment if you've never stepped into a place like that before."

"But you went today. Alone?"

"I did."

"What changed?"

Sure, I was given the challenge to complete and a limited timetable to do it in since I'm only back for a short time. But there was more to my push.

"I've finally come to terms with the fact that life shouldn't be full of fears. It's full of choices, and I'm ready to be bolder in the ones I make. I'm ready to embrace my own strength and value."

Henry's eyes sparkle. "Why do you think I take so many walks by myself? It is a reminder, in my age, that I can still do those things on my own. Some days can be scary if my muscles ache. But like this fall, I survive. And like you, you survived. You choose to hold the fear, or you choose to let it go."

As always, Henry is right.

I'm ready to let my fears go and stop wavering in the choices I make.

* * *

I wake up sore. But it is a powerful soreness. One that I don't mind feeling because it's a result of doing something remarkable. I already want to go back to Max's Boxing Ring and will be calling Bobby the moment I get back to Crimson Bay.

After showering and getting ready, I pack my bag to end what may be my last visit to Boston for a while, barring no more Henry-related injuries. I check out of the hotel without another call from Mark, which doesn't exactly surprise me, but it does agitate me that he was so set on me staying at the hotel to only call once.

I plan one final walk around downtown to burn off my frustration. After an hour, I end up cold to the bone from the windchill. I warm up with coffee and breakfast at my favorite pancake joint which never disappoints, especially because they serve a sizeable homemade biscuit with every order. Each bite melts in my mouth.

Being without a phone is growing on me. As I pass by people on theirs, missing beats of conversation with others, overlooking the hidden beauties of this city as their eyes are glued to their phone instead, I vow to be on mine less once I have it again. It's liberating. Like being restrained in handcuffs for most of life, only to be completely free now.

I arrive back at the hospital by ten in the morning and stay until Henry falls asleep in the early afternoon. We have lunch and play backgammon. Henry wins each game. He is a self-proclaimed board game-aholic. It doesn't matter if it is Chess, Scrabble, Yahtzee, or Monopoly, Henry is unbeatable. Somehow, he draws on the right amount of skill and luck to be on top.

When the time comes to leave, he promises, "I'll be a new man when you see me next."

I've been skirting around the topic and now time has run out. There's no way to lessen the blow, so I come right out with it, "Henry, I'm not sure I'm ready for Italy. I think Mark and I have some things to figure out first in our marriage."

Henry's eyes remain on mine but he doesn't say anything. Finally, he inquires, "But Mark is going, yes?"

"Yes, Mark will be in Italy regardless of my decision. Business first with that one. You know that."

Henry nods solemnly. "Good. I'm ready to return. I will miss you, Autumn wind, but you need to do what is best for you. The time we've been gifted in life is too short. Follow your heart. I would want that for my own children. I want that for you."

I hold his hand and kiss his knuckles. "I'll miss you, Henry. I'll get Mark to set you up with a video call once you settle in Italy." He starts to argue, but I interrupt him. "You don't have to use it all the time. But I want to see you and video chats, regardless of your resistance, can bridge miles. I will also still visit you no matter what. You're important to me." I kiss his cheek and warn him to stop flirting with the nurses or else he will break many hearts when he leaves. He waves me off, although grinning, knowing the extra pudding cups on his tray gave him away.

I manage to hold my tears back until I exit his room. Then I sink into a waiting room chair with a mixture of relief from coming to a decision at last and heartache at what it means—no longer seeing Henry regularly and having to soon break the same news to Mark. Telling Henry was my way of testing it out to see if I'm ready for it and it feels right, regardless of the remnants of fear on my heart.

With two hours to burn before Griffin expects me at the airport, I continue my mini tour of the city. I'm anxious about what's to come when I return home. After a few miles my legs cramp, so I find a bench and sit down to rest my feet. The streets are growing louder and more active as area schools let out and work shifts end.

Across the street, a lady dressed in a long-sleeved grey shirt and khaki pants leans against a brick wall, her legs bent with her head resting on her arm, strands of bleach-blonde hair falling over her face. She sits on a sleeping bag surrounded with brown paper sacks and odds and ends. Her other arm wraps around a gorgeous beagle mutt, tri-colored with big brown eyes.

Since moving to Boston, I learned to avoid eye contact with the homeless. Somewhere along the line, I became more callous than generous. My justification was that it can be difficult to discern who is in need and who is abusing a good heart, so it's easier to avoid them all. I don't know when I decided that it was up to me to make the choice of who is worthy and who isn't, but I don't want to be like that anymore. As soon as the cars clear, I cross the street.

Dipping down by the dog, I scratch his long ears. He immediately licks my hand and rolls on his back. "Oh, you are such a sweetheart!"

"Benjamin." The lady speaks as she slowly lifts her head, her voice low and raspy. "Benji for short."

The most piercing blue eyes I've ever seen. If she were walking down the street, I would have been convinced that she was from the future. Behind the dirt streaks, her skin is perfect, almost doll-like, possibly ageless if it wasn't for the hardships she is clearly experiencing. Deep wrinkles are etched into her forehead, an out-of-place feature, as though drawn in by a makeup artist turning a beautiful, young girl into an elderly woman. Her magnificence is captivating despite the elements surrounding her.

"How old is Benji?"

She doesn't speak for a moment. Before I can repeat my question, she murmurs, "I say six, but I dunno. Either he found me, or I found him. I don't remember. But we found each other, and I keep saying he's six."

"Well, he's a beautiful dog, that's for sure. What a heart of gold, too." Mud gummed into his fur sticks under my fingernails as I scratch his ears. Drool drips out of his mouth as though my touch is the greatest massage. I turn to face his owner. "What's your name?"

"My name?" She crosses her hands in front of her, suddenly protective. "I don't want no shelter or anything. I'm only here to take a breather. We are walking. We are walking a lot. We won't be here long." Her paranoid eyes dart behind me.

"No, no. I'm not here for any reason other than Benji catching my attention." My words tumble out to reassure her. "I love dogs. I'm sorry, I was curious about your name since I know your dog's now. But I don't need to know it."

She examines my face, the sunlight turning her eyes translucent. It's easy to imagine her stepping off a spaceship.

Finally, she speaks again, almost a whisper. "Marlena. I'm Marlena."

"I'm Autumn." I smile at her, hoping to receive one in return. She doesn't react. I stand when she shifts her legs back and forth against the ground with unease. "Well, it was nice to meet you both."

Benji senses my departure and sits up, puts his paws on my knees, and whines. My heart breaks. I want to cuddle him in my arms.

Marlena doesn't acknowledge me.

I grab my bag and get half a block down before a knot tightens around my heart. It is already cold and will only get colder in Boston. She didn't say where they are headed and made it clear that she's not big on questions. But they need more than the grubby bags sitting next to them if that's all they're taking.

I return to them and hand Marlena my carry-on bag, keeping only my messenger bag with my purse contents. "Here. There isn't anything for this little love bug." I reach down to pet Benji again, "but surely some things that will come in handy on your trip. Sweaters, jackets, toiletries, there's even an envelope with some extra cash."

"I don't need nothing." Marlena's eyes lighten more. Agitation edges her voice at my return. But I know I'm supposed to give her the satchel. It becomes more than another Bridging the Six Degrees challenge, more than Nokutenda's story at this point. It is merely something I want to do, to lessen what I don't need, to clear my head of the things that are no longer of importance. I'm ready to remove the weight.

I bend down to place my bag next to her. "That's fine if you don't. Use what you need or don't use it at all. I'm getting on a plane to go back home. You, however, seem to be in the middle of your journey. If you don't need it, give it to someone else." I pat Benji's head one more time before turning.

"You take him." It's the loudest I've heard Marlena speak. I wonder, yet again, if I've upset her. She repeats, "You take Benji."

I shake my head, unsure if I heard her correctly. "Marlena, I didn't want an exchange. You take my bag. I don't want anything in return."

She slowly slides her back up the wall as she stands. Benji looks to her and then at me, as though he understands everything we are saying. When Marlena straightens her back, I'm now looking up at her. She nears Griffin's height and has a sculpted body most athletes would kill for. The desperation to know her story fills me, and it takes every ounce of control to not ask her more questions.

"I want you to take him. He would be better with you than where I need to go. Take him. He needs warmth."

"Marlena, please let me help you. If you need to go somewhere, I can help with that."

She shakes her head. "No. Take Benji. That... helps."

I stick my hands in my pockets, unsure of what else to do. I don't want to take her companion from her. "Won't you miss him?"

Marlena pulls a tattered red leash with a collar out of her bag. She stoops down and gently places it around Benji's neck. Rubbing her face on his neck, Benji's tongue laps her cheek. She's softly crying. "Take him. You will help me. More than this bag. You'll help him."

I can't imagine how they will both survive the harsh, New England winters without proper shelter. I also know that some shelters won't allow animals, which could contribute to part of the reason Marlena is still on the streets.

My voice shakes with the sentiment she's extending, the protection of the dog she desires. "If you're sure... if you promise you won't regret it..."

"You'll give him a good home, right?" Marlena's gaze into my eyes is the most intense it's been. She's searching for confirmation of her own, that what she's doing is the right thing, and that I'm the right person to help. Maybe it's what she's been waiting for.

I start to reach for her hand but refrain. I have such an urge to comfort her, but I know it won't be warmly received. "I promise, Marlena, I will. Benji will have the greatest home he can have."

She nods and wraps her hands around Benji's neck one last time. She whispers something in his ear which gets his tail wagging. Scooping up her items from the sidewalk, including the bag I gave her, Marlena hurries away, not looking back. Benji watches her leaving and lurches, whining until I pat his head and assure him that he's in good hands, while keeping a tight hold on the leash.

I need to find a phone and call for the town car. I am vaguely familiar with this part of the city and recall stores down the street that may have a decent supply of pet products and a phone I can use.

Sure enough, we hit the jackpot. Or at least a dollar store with a small pet aisle. I purchase a new leash and a collar to replace the tattered one around Benji's neck. He seems well-behaved but I want to make sure he won't make a run for it if he sees a squirrel.

I also buy dog food and dishes and a squeaky toy. Because every dog needs one, right?

It only takes William fifteen minutes to show up. He seems both surprised and annoyed that I have a dog with me unexpectedly. Sifting through his items in the trunk, he drags out a mini tarp that he spreads across the seat for Benji to sit on. I can't blame him since the poor dog doesn't look the cleanest. I'm sure he will fluff right up as soon as I can get him bathed.

Oh, the soul in this dog with his big brown eyes. I can't fathom the loss Marlena must be feeling. By the time we arrive at the airport, Benji is curled asleep in my lap. I'm already in love with this sweet dog.

We pull up to the terminal precisely one minute before Griffin had requested. Griffin does a double take when he sees me step out of the car. He immediately bends down, patting his knee, and Benji doesn't hesitate to run right into his arms.

"Well hi there, little guy." I didn't expect Griffin to be a dog guy but should have known that there'd be one weakness that could get past that professional demeanor of his. After years of traveling with him, I may have finally discovered what it is.

"His name is Benji. He's in need of a bath and a quick trip to the vet. I'm not sure if he's had shots or any veterinary care in his life."

Griffin scratches Benji's ears. I've never seen more than a neutral expression on Griffin's face in the years I've known him. To witness him on the ground, sitting cross-legged with a thirty-pound dog jumping all over him, is shocking. It's even more startling when he laughs.

I sit across from him on the ground while Benji hops back and forth between us. "I'm guessing you're a dog person?"

Griffin's ears turn pink at the tips. I knew he'd be uncomfortable with any personal questions. He was probably coached to never become friendly with his clients. I can't resist, though. We thought we had our last ride together before but then this emergency trip occurred, and it is providing Griffin and me one more chance to get to know each other.

"Yes," he finally admits. "Very much so. We had several dogs while I was growing up. Farm dogs. We were told to not get too attached, but I was never good at that." He rubs Benji's belly. "We lived out in the middle of nowhere so it's easy for the animals to become your closest friends. I had a special touch with dogs. I should have done something with them. But I also learned how to fly when I was a young boy. My dad said I should be a pilot since my brother was getting the farm, so that's what I did."

"Have you owned a dog since?"

"No. Thought about it. I visit animal shelters wherever we travel. I've been tempted more than once to help fill the silence at home. But it wouldn't be fair to the dog. Me leaving as much as I do, that is." Griffin confirms what I always wondered, whether he had a significant other at home. He didn't wear a ring on his finger, but that didn't rule out a serious relationship.

"What about traveling with you? Is it possible for pets to tag along in the cockpit?"

A brief glimpse of hope glimmers in Griffin's eyes. "I guess I've never been one to ask. I do my job as I'm told and don't push the boundaries."

"Maybe there aren't any boundaries for flying with a dog. I'm sure Mark could look into it."

"Yeah... yeah, maybe." Griffin warms to the idea. It speaks volumes about his character that he is one to stick to the rules, do his job well, and not ask a lot of questions. The typical farm boy.

Benji had fallen asleep under Griffin's hand. It is the first time Griffin doesn't seem concerned about sticking to a strict schedule and is reluctant to leave.

"Griffin, would you like to keep Benji?"

"Aww, I can't do that. Isn't he Henry's?"

"No. It's a strange story but he doesn't have an owner now. I haven't claimed ownership of him. I promised his previous one that I would find a great home for him. *You* would be a great home."

Griffin's walls break for all of thirty seconds. His steady composure quickly replaces the hint of emotions. "I would love that. What do you say, boy? Want to come home with me?" he whispers as the dog sleeps, with gentle strokes of his fur.

The ringing of his phone breaks the tender moment, frightening Benji. "Mark must be wondering where we are. Excuse me, Autumn, er, Miss Autumn. I need to answer this."

Benji jumps off Griffin when he stands up and joins me again with another whimper. "We'll get some food once we board, buddy, I promise. Your life is about to go from the ground to the sky." He licks my face in excitement.

Hearing Mark's voice over Griffin's phone makes my stomach pinch. I'll have to talk to him soon. Saying the words to Henry was one thing, saying them to Mark will be something totally different.

Griffin returns with a hop in his step. "Mark said to call him as soon as you get back home. Also, he was pleased I found a copilot in Benji. He said he didn't think it'd be a problem."

The timing was something majestic. Benji found a new home, and Griffin finally got the dog he always wanted. "That's terrific news! Let's get this guy some water and food, huh?"

As soon as we climb aboard, Benji does his "dog due diligence"surveillance of the plane then jumps into the co-pilot side of the cockpit. He knows that seat is made for him.

"We'll have to get you a proper seatbelt, little guy," Griffin comments as he rubs Benji's head.

There's no doubt these two are meant to be paired together. I can only hope Marlena will be okay, and that someday, she will be rewarded for such a sacrifice—giving up something she loves for its own well-being.

Without intending to do so, I completed another Bridging the Six Degrees challenge: fulfill someone's wish. Rachel from Oklahoma worked closely with the Make-a-Wish Foundation in granting wishes to children with serious illnesses. I thought I would do something similar. It seems that the more I embrace life and the opportunities it presents, the more it seamlessly aligns with Bridging the Six Degrees. For the first time, I'm realizing all the ways people's lives are connected and then transformed by those links every single day. The more we take time to truly relate with each other, the more united we are to the purpose we're here to serve.

My goodbye to Griffin this time is even harder than the last, especially with Benji added.

"I won't be able to thank you enough for this gift." Griffin's voice is thick with sincerity. "There was a reason we had one more flight together, Miss Autumn."

I smile at how right those words are. "You guys take good care of each other."

Griffin salutes. "Absolutely."

I bend down and give Benji another good scratch on his head. "You are a miracle dog, you know that? I'm not sure what your life was like before, but you have an incredible life ahead with lots of love and plane trips."

Benji puts both of his paws on my shoulder and licks my cheek. I melt. I just met him but I'll already miss him too.

I wave one last time as they head into the hangar. Hopping into my Jeep, I prepare for my short drive back to Crimson Bay.

I'm ready to return home.

Twenty

My first stop is Jessi's house. I'm excited to tell her about the experience I had with Guy. In my temptation over the years to enter Max's Gym, Jessi was the person I had wished could be by my side. She wouldn't have let me hold back because she never does.

The first thing I notice when I arrive at her house is Nathan's face. On a sign. In Jessi's yard. Those dimples of his make my heart flutter, even on a sign.

As soon as she opens the door, I exclaim, "You're moving already?"

"Autumn!" She hugs me tightly. Piles of moving boxes are stacked behind her.

"Jess, I was only gone for two days! What in the world have I missed?"

She closes the door with a flushed face. "I'm going for it. I'm not waiting."

"What? Where?"

"Chicago, to start with! It's close enough with lots of opportunities."

"Wow." I lean against the wall. "I can't believe you're going."

"You think it's a good choice?" Jessi pauses, then continues before I can respond, "You know what, don't answer that. I don't want to know. I feel like it is so I'm running with it."

I laugh with her. "That's good. That's the way it should be." Instinct like nature. I love that about her. It seems fast, but what does she have to lose?

"I tried calling you to let you know but I forgot you were doing the crazy no electronics thing. Rose told me about Henry and your trip. Is he okay?"

"That man is resilient. I'm convinced he could walk out of fire unscathed."

Jessi rolls tape across another box to seal it shut. "I've never met him, but I like to imagine he's the type of man I'll end up with."

"Except sixty years younger, I hope?"

"Eh, I'm not so picky these days."

I join her in wrapping newspaper around the items from her bookcase. Jessi is bouncing and can't stop humming.

I shake my head as I watch the happiness radiate on her face. "It's wild, Jess. Look at you. You have fun with life, you make a difference in the lives of others, you never let yourself get weighed down by superficial things, and you've always stayed true to who you are."

Jessi picks at fingernails, her cheeks pink. "Thanks, A. That means a lot to me."

"I've been running around trying to live a life that isn't true to me. I've been fueled by thoughts, not by heart. You're all heart, Jess. I admire that so much."

Jessi sobs out of the blue, a total 180-degree change from a few moments ago.

"What did I say? What's wrong?"

She sniffs and grabs a tissue from the bookshelf. "I'm relieved to hear you say that. I mean, it helps, you know? I'm blindly jumping off a cliff, and most people would call it senseless."

How ironic that she chooses cliff diving as her analogy?

"You will be great in Chicago, Jess. They're lucky to get you. Anywhere would be."

Jessi holds up a framed picture of me, her, and Rose from five years ago when we attempted camping (or glamping in Rose's case) in the National Hills. It was one of my favorite trips with them. "I'll miss us, though."

"We'll always be us. It won't matter where we are."

"Yeah." She kisses the frame before wrapping it. "I sure hope so."

After a moment of only the sounds of bubble wrap and paper, I remark, "I can't believe you asked Nathan to be your realtor."

Jessi's merriment through her tears is such a beautiful sound. "There's no denying he's the best around. I need this place sold."

I help her pack a bit longer before leaving. We promise to save our goodbyes until the last night she's here.

Waiting for the final 10,080th minute of my electronics challenge to end, I drive to my house next to grab my phone and see what messages await me. As I get closer, my anxiety increases, thinking about what I've missed after a week without it. However, once I arrive, another Nathan surprise greets me.

"Sold" now plasters the sign that once so innocently expressed "For Sale."

"What the hell?" I mutter as I swing the car into park. Apparently, the universe shifted entirely in the past two days. Once inside my cottage, I crawl under my bed to grab the box I threw my phone in.

It takes longer than it should to power on. After a few seconds to connect with service, the phone overloads with missed calls, voicemails, texts, emails, and all sorts of social network notifications. I flip it over to catch my breath from the overwhelming inundation of information that hits. An immediate headache instills, and I wonder if I could always be without my cell phone. I didn't miss it when it wasn't around. I felt more in tune with life and more trusting that things will happen as they need to. The cell phone brings out this sense of control, like I need to know how everyone is, that everyone can reach me, and what random people are posting on social media, as though all of that summarizes what life is about.

Ugh, I kind of want to throw it against the wall and watch it shatter. The bombshell that my house has sold is contributing to the rage, which I would have known about if I had my phone. Maybe this is the universe telling me that I shouldn't stay after all.

I flip my phone back over and scroll through the texts. There are several from Mark and Rose the night that Henry went into the hospital. Some from family members saying they are thinking of me and not to forget about them while I am on my electronic hiatus. There are random drunken ones from Jessi that make me laugh. A couple from Rose. But nothing from Nathan.

I switch to the voicemails, and that's when I see five from him:

"Hey! It's Nathan. I hope everything is okay. I know we ended, uh, abruptly last night. Listen, the timing is bad, but I just received an excellent offer on your house and want to run it by you. I hope you get this soon and will reach out to me."

"Hey! Thinking about you... and really hope everything is going okay and that your friend is good. I'm not sure if I'm presenting good or bad information here. Wish I knew how to get a hold of you. Hoping by chance you check your voicemail. I'd like to talk to you before I talk to Mark."

Then they progress into professionalism.

"Hi Autumn, it's Nathan again. I'm sorry to call so many times, but the person who placed the offer bumped hers up to asking price. She doesn't want to wait much longer. I know Mark said that if that price was met, then it's a done deal. I don't want to lose out on this buyer but hate to do it without your permission. Let me know soon."

"Autumn, it's Nathan Vertz. I got off the phone with Mark, and he said to go ahead and move forward. We'll need you to sign off on the papers once you return. Give me a call once you're back in town. Thanks."

Then back to his normal voice.

"Hey, Autumn, it's Nathan again. I put the Sold sign on your house. I was reluctant to do it because I knew it would feel overwhelming if you hadn't heard the news before seeing it. Maybe Mark will contact you or you'll check your messages before you get home. I'm sorry this happened while you were gone. The timing is terrible. Call me so we can talk it through. I've been thinking a lot about you. More than just the house. Call me when you get back, okay? I'd like to see you."

I lock the phone screen and hold it against my chest. It's thumping in beat along with my heart. Nathan's voice buries itself deep in my mind, soul, and parts of my body that haven't felt alive in far too many years. I've always blamed the way my body and mind shifted in lack of sexual interest on my miscarriage, yet here I am, *feeling things* once again.

The phone rings and I jump out of my skin. I prepare myself to answer Nathan's call. But as I flip the phone over, Mark's name appears.

"Hey!" I shout too loudly.

"Hi, beautiful. You made it back safely then."

"I'm sorry I haven't called yet. Just got home and opened my phone. Trying to go through all my messages now."

"No problem. How's our Henry?" *Our Henry*. A phrase that once used to make me smile now pains me.

"All the nurses are smitten over him."

"That I can believe." Mark chuckles so sincerely that I long to see it in person. With all the recent tension, I can't remember the last time I heard his laugh, so pure and not forced just to pacify me.

"He's good. They're keeping him one more day, but he's ready to leave. He's not looking forward to the plane ride, but he's excited to be back in Italy."

"I'm glad to hear it. I'm calling him next. I have arrangements set to get him over here in three days if he's willing and if the doctor signs off." Mark clears his voice as though preparing his defenses for an argument. "On another subject, I'm hoping I got to you before anyone else. Nathan found a buyer for your house. They sealed the deal on the asking price we set."

I sigh loudly, a much better response than the anger tempting to leash out. "I saw the sold sign outside and was listening to voicemails when you called. I guess that's what you wanted, right?"

"I'm hoping you mean *we*. It would have sat empty for months with us in Italy."

"Mark..." I didn't expect to have this conversation yet. I'm not prepared. My thoughts aren't completely worked through, but here's my chance. "I don't want to sell my house."

He's quiet as he processes my words. Mark can't be completely oblivious to my desire to stay. "It's been nice being back..." I'm struggling. I don't want to do this over the phone.

"I can only assume it's because you've been more present this trip."

I hold my breath and release it slowly. "What exactly do you mean by that?"

I can hear the tapping of a pen on the desk in the background, an indication of his own anxiety. "It's partially why I believed the Bridging the Six Degrees experience would be a worthwhile experience for you. When you return to Crimson Bay, you never seem present. You go there to write your stories, which I understand, but I feel like you use it as a catalyst into daydreams, fantasies, and different lives. I had hoped I could give you time to be present, live in the days, in the moments, and say goodbye."

I pull my lips back together again once I realize my mouth had dropped open during his little speech. Sure, some of that may be true, but I wouldn't have thought Mark would be the one to call me out on it. On one level, I'm hurt, but on the other, it's gratifying to realize Mark pays more attention to me than he lets on. "How do you know how present I've been?"

"Because you admit it's nice being back there. Every time I ask you about your trips, all you tell me is how much writing you've done. You seldom mention anything else. I've been reading your online journal entries through Bridging the Six Degrees. You're changing."

I groan and pull my hair off my shoulders. "Why does it feel like you want me to be someone else?"

"No, Autumn. Your perspective is changing. How you view your life there is changing. I know you're a dreamer and I love that about you. But I don't want you to be like Henry someday, looking back at the life that was home and having regrets. That's been my biggest fear, especially with this move. It'll take you further away. I'm not sure you'll find happiness in me or our life together until you learn how to be content with saying goodbye to the life you once had. You need to be ready for the new things coming our way."

"So, Bridging the Six Degrees was more than an acquisition test or a birthday gift?"

Mark whistles through his teeth. "It was a combination. People from all over the world submitted challenges. We could have selected ones that said scale the Great Wall of China, touch the Eiffel Tower, skinny dip through Costa Rica—whatever. But we chose challenges that would keep you connected to the Crimson Bay area. It was the best idea of a send-off that I could think of, and your parents were on board with it."

"Weren't you scared I wouldn't want to leave here?"

"Sure, that thought crossed my mind." Mark clears his throat again. I wonder if he's not coming down with a cold from working as much as he does. "If you want to stay in Crimson Bay, I'd rather know now than after we get settled in a different country."

He is reminding me why I married him. It was more than just because of Amelia. Even though we are vastly different, there's an underlying understanding that exists without needing to divulge all the deep secrets of my past. As Henry said, I chose someone who would challenge me.

"Do you miss her?" I choke out.

Mark is quiet. He knows what I'm asking. Finally, he responds. "Of course I do. I don't talk about her because I know what the memory does for you."

I settle on my window seat and look out at the water. He feels open for once, ready to talk, as though the time and distance between us has been eye opening for him too. "What's the real reason you don't want kids?"

"I told you, work—"

"No, Mark. The real reason."

Several minutes of silence flood the phone. "I didn't want my kid to hate me like I hated my dad," he says flatly.

I stand and pace the room. That's not the answer I expected. "You always speak so highly of your dad! You loved him."

"I spent most of the time he was alive despising him. He was always choosing work first. I told him I hated him more than I ever told him I loved him. I felt like he didn't want to be around me. It wasn't until I took on this COO role that I understood him more, but it was too late to tell him that. My dad was providing for us and he was doing something that served a bigger purpose within him. When he was home, he focused his attention on me, but I didn't see it like that. I was always thinking about when he would leave next so I assumed that's what he was always thinking about, too. Like he couldn't wait to leave."

"Oh, Mark... You were just a child. You couldn't understand all of that. You have to forgive yourself."

"I believe I have. But I know any child I have will view me the same way I spent my younger years seeing my dad, and I can't bear the thought of them constantly disappointed in me. I can't stand knowing that I'm causing them pain every time I leave for long work trips, or having the same regrets if something happens to me before they realize the truth."

I take a deep breath, wondering why he never shared that with me before but knowing it doesn't matter now. "You can choose a different life, if that's what you're worried about."

Mark clears his throat. "I did choose a different life. A life without kids." And somehow, despite not being news, hearing it again causes my heart to shatter even more. "I know how to make other people happy through business deals and initiatives. I'm good at that. There's a time limit on those, though. They have a marked beginning and a marked end. I can show up and fulfill any expectations within that time. There's a lot more to being a dad, and there's never an end to what they expect out of you."

"You don't think you'll regret not having kids?"

"I'd have more regrets having kids and not being what they need."

My chest aches for him and the potential of the dad that he could have been for some lucky children. I don't think they'd see him like that, but how do you talk someone out of a belief they've held onto for most of their life and have used to shape their choices and worldview?

"I'm really glad you finally shared the truth with me." I pause before adding, "You do know I really want to be a mom, though, right?"

Mark doesn't respond, but he doesn't have to.

"Being a mom and a writer are the two things I want more than anything. You knew this."

"I did. And I do," he admits quietly.

My breathing speeds up, whether from anger, surprise, or heartbreak, I can't tell. "Then why dream with me about having a family someday on our first dates? Why not tell me you don't want kids?"

My body is shaking involuntarily. My skin is cold. I wait for his response. Finally, he says, "I just thought if I could give you everything else in this world, you'd be happy."

"You thought material goods and a fancy life would fulfill me instead? So when you say you wanted me to come back here to say goodbye to the life I once had, you mean to finally let go of my deepest desires as well."

"I just thought it could be enough. That *I* could be enough."

How does he not see that he put our relationship in a place

where he gets to live out his dreams while I am forced to lose mine? Quietly, I say, "Mark, I have a few challenges left. Do you mind if I take the next few days to work through them without us talking?"

"Oh." He sounds shocked, and falters. "Sure, okay. But I need to know, are you serious about not wanting to sell your cottage?"

I don't hesitate. "I don't want to sell it." It's the one fact I know for sure.

I swear I can hear his heart beating in the silence that follows. Or maybe it's mine as I hold my breath, wondering if he's coming to the same conclusion I have.

"I found us a house here," he murmurs. "I emailed you pictures. You would love it. There's a giant second-story room with a window overlooking the water and a ladder that leads to a rooftop view. I thought it'd be the perfect place for your writing. The rest of the house is nice, too, but it was the closest one I could find that reminded me of your Crimson Bay cottage, and it's only a couple hours from Montone."

"Is that why it was taking you so long to find a house? You were searching for one to resemble my cottage?"

"I know it's a big transition. I wanted to make it as comfortable as possible for you."

"Oh, Mark..." I shake my head. It's a sweet gesture, but he doesn't realize that it's not about what my cottage looks like. It's not about anything materialistic. It's about the memories and how I feel when I'm in my cottage. It's about the people who come into my cottage. It's about how every piece of life it holds within represents the parts of me I love the most. This revelation, on top of the fact that he's never liked my cottage, makes me wonder if he ever really understood. And if he never understood me, did he ever really love *me*?

"Listen, I know there's a lot to think about. Do me a favor. If you like the house, let me know, so I can make sure we don't miss out on it and can get all of our things from Boston shipped out there. Sending me a quick email will do. Then give me a call when you're ready to touch base again, okay? Take all the time you need."

The moment he ends the call, I stop fighting the tears and let them flow down my cheeks as a sob escapes my lips. I slide to the floor with the phone pressed against my chest, processing all the information he divulged.

Once the tears subside, I sit up, wiping my face with my sleeve, feeling so drained that I'm unable to stand to get a tissue. I return to the missed texts on my phone. One from Rose says,

> Would love to see you, call me when you get
> back.

The wording is different from her standard texts, which pairs paranoia with my sadness. She could be mad for what she witnessed the last night we saw each other. The night I was growing closer to Nathan than I should have, feeling more understood by a man than I ever have in my life.

I see the house pictures from Mark in an email, but I can't will myself to open them. Not yet. Instead, I call Rose, expecting to be yelled at—as I deserve—by someone who can see the truth, even if she doesn't know the details. I have been walking on a dangerous tightrope with Nathan.

The phone barely rings before she picks up. "Autumn! Welcome back to the new age. How's Henry? Is he okay?"

I manage to smile at the sound of her voice. I miss her. "He'll be released soon. Thank God. Mark is flying Henry to Italy sooner than he originally planned. It's nice knowing one of us can keep an eye on him."

"Oh, that's great news. I'm relieved. I love that little man. You probably got my message, but I wanted to invite you to join us for dinner Friday night at seven. Me and Kevin, that is."

It's strange hearing an "us" come from Rose's lips. She sounds nervous, which is also unlike her.

"Okay, that'll work. Your house, I assume?"

"Um, actually... we are on his houseboat."

"Houseboat?"

"Yeah, it's on the lake. Meet us at the Grandview Pier. We'll pick you up. The views out here are incredible." *Here* implies that she is currently on it. She rushes through the rest, avoiding an interrogation from me.

"I can't wait to see you, Rose." I mean every word, pushing all thoughts of Kevin aside.

"I've missed you!"

I take a deep breath. I knew things would shift with my return to Crimson Bay, but I underestimated how significant that change would be. I have big decisions to make, and soon.

Twenty-One

THE NEXT MORNING, I WAKE WITH A SURPRISING BURST of energy despite my looming choices. I grab a granola bar and make a quick cup of coffee before bundling up in the chilly morning air to take a walk.

Soon, I'm standing in front of Evergreen Cemetery, an unexpected detour. I push open the gate and step inside. Gorgeously landscaped with white gates stretching out along the front entrance next to the road, and the rest surrounded by evergreen trees, marking the edges of where the living resides from the dead. A faded white bench rests under one of three giant willow trees in the center of the cemetery. Once I reach it, I sit down and breathe in the fresh air, which has dropped a few more degrees in such a shaded area.

One of my favorite places to visit in Italy is the cemetery in Manarola, perched on a hilltop with dazzling views of the Ligurian Sea. Fresh flowers decorate the marble walls lined with coffins. Outside of each loculo is a picture and carved images or words to describe the deceased. It is such a beautiful memorial to those who have passed. Walking by the pictures makes it feel like I am at a unique party to honor lives, which is quite the contrast to the mostly faceless headstones that cover many of the cemeteries in the United States.

I pull my Bridging the Six Degrees challenge book from my satchel and read the one from Kevin Mandalay, a Montana man, who now resides in British Columbia, Canada:

I grew up terrified of all things "after-life": ghosts, spirits, cemeteries... strange considering I was surrounded by magnificent wildlife like bison, moose, and wolves on our family ranch, which were more realistic fears. But even the most intimidating forms of life never scared me as much as death. Forty-five years into life, and I finally embrace death-related concepts. Some may call it a mid-life crisis; I call it a future investment. I'm not sure why the idea came to me at first.

Whatever the cause, I walked into a cemetery scared and walked out as a braver man. What changed? I got to know the people in those graves. I stooped down and read each word engraved on their tombstone, said their name out loud, thought about their life, and sometimes I would place a flower on it. I wonder if their full purpose in life was achieved. I won't let them be forgotten. Perhaps some of them lived horrible lives and were evil people. It doesn't matter. Everyone is on equal ground in those cemeteries. They're all in the same spot.

If I were in one of those graves, I would love it if someone came by to say hi now and then and get to know me, too. That way, my life in this world, whether ever completely accomplished, is still recognized long after I'm gone. So, take some time to get to know the people at a local cemetery. It's not as scary as it seems. And maybe someday, someone will keep your memory alive, too.

I take my time walking up and down the rows of tombstones in Evergreen Cemetery. Some are pieces of art, others are basic; some are new, some have been around for decades. My breath catches the most when I see one dedicated to a baby or young child, one who never had a chance to do much with their life.

What their loved ones would have given for them to have more life to live. What a shame that we aren't more motivated to live life in a greater way, to honor those who didn't have the same chance. Like my Amelia.

The tombstones with details are as fascinating as the ones along the Cinque Terre's hillsides. They are glimpses into who these people were. If I were to die today, what would my family put on my grave?

"Hey, you're the cookie lady, right?"

I look up into familiar kind eyes. "Michael the policeman, right?"

His lips curl up in what looks like a forced smile, but his eyes are shining as though he is legitimately happy to see me. He has the disposition of Eeyore. Not in a pitiful way, but in a "I'm carrying the weight of the world on my shoulders" way. You immediately want to reach out and hug him.

I stand to shake his hand instead. "I didn't expect to run into you again, here out of all places."

Michael chuckles. "It may be the first time I've seen someone else out here in all my visits, actually."

"Oh, did you know Jameson?" I nod to the grave I had been kneeling by. It was a young death, only thirty-three years old, which rings a little too close in age and occurred only two years ago. There wasn't anything else written on this one.

"Not personally, no. I was on the scene when he was found, though." Sorrow once again dimmed the natural twinkling of his eyes. "I'm so sorry for your loss."

"I didn't know Jameson. No, I'm just here visiting graves." I scrunch my nose. "That sounds a bit morbid, huh?"

"Nope, since that's what I'm doing, too." He places his hand on Jameson's gravestone. "He died from a car accident. Left behind a wife and a little girl. The wife is remarried now. All bits and pieces I pick up from hearsay. I like to come here and honor the ones I've watched pass. Let them know they're not forgotten."

Chills ripple through my body. It is exactly what I read in

Kevin's letter. It's reassuring to think that people are doing this everywhere. If I had to bury a loved one, I'd find comfort in knowing someone else was stopping by to remember them, even if they didn't know them personally.

"Do you do this often?"

"I've been doing it monthly for eighteen years. It's how long I've had my job, standing on the sidelines with a prime viewpoint of life fighting death. I struggled with it in the beginning. Had a few bouts of depression, to be honest. It's hard not to." Michael takes off his hat, holding it solemnly in front of him. "I've realized it's not my job to save people. Don't get me wrong, I try my hardest if I'm there. I'd sacrifice myself in a heartbeat if it meant saving someone else. But ultimately, it's God that saves or doesn't. He has his reasons. I've learned to trust those. Though it can be hard at times."

"It's hard letting go of control," I mutter.

Michael nods in agreement. "It's hard admitting someone else may just know better than you."

"I'm glad we have people like you."

Michael glances down at his feet before returning his glossy eyes back to me. "Thank you... um, cookie lady." I let out a giggle as he gives me a sheepish grin. "I'm usually great with names, but I had very little sleep the day we met. What is your name again?"

"Autumn."

"Ah, how could I forget that? The season that's falling among us right now. As someone once said, 'Autumn shows us how beautiful it is to let things go.' You're in the right place for that."

Goosebumps line my arm. *Am I letting go like Fall inspires us to?* I survey the scene, the splendor of this cemetery, a place that could so easily be dark, yet there is beauty all around. Letting things go in life doesn't have to resonate with disastrous, negative connotations. It can be a beautiful thing. A time for rebirth.

"I should get going and let you have your time with Jameson. It was good to see you again."

Michael crouches down next to the grave. "You too, Autumn."

I walk a few steps before turning around again. I'm tempted to ask Michael if he would like to get coffee sometime. The matchmaker in me considers how great of a fit he'd be with Jessi. But I stop before I say anything. Jessi is on a path of self-discovery. I can relate to that now more than ever before. I don't want to add another distraction and give her a reason to stay where she's always been, instead of moving forward and exploring new territory.

I am confident I will see Michael again in some way. It could be through Jessi, or on a different path. You never know how life will lead you to cross paths with others on their journeys. But instead of forcing it and shifting Jessi's focus to love instead of herself, I trust that it will happen on its own.

* * *

I spend the next morning eating breakfast with my parents. Mom makes a variety of pancakes which my dad and I devour. Afterward, we sit outside on Adirondack chairs bundled in blankets, drinking coffee, and watching the water.

Mom watches me suspiciously. Finally, she speaks, "You look refreshed."

"Well, I completed the pampering challenge. It gave my skin some much-needed color."

"I read about that in your online journal."

Of course she did. Mom probably refreshes it a hundred times a day to stay posted on what's occurring with the challenges. That's what moms do after all.

"What will you do when I'm done with that journal?"

"With any luck, I'll have phone calls from my daughter to fill me in on what's happening in her life! Although I doubt I will learn as much straight from your mouth as I have from these secret insights. Things written and not written, for that matter."

Dad stands, stretches his arms, and says, "I'm making a fresh pot of coffee." As usual, he bails at the first sign of an emotional conversation.

"What do you mean by that?" I sit up in my chair and turn to face Mom directly.

"Who did you do those challenges with when you went to the southern parts? You disappeared. No one knew where you were."

I shift uneasily in my chair. "Does it matter? I had challenges to complete and was able to do them in enjoyable ways. I had help in some, but I did others by myself."

"I only want to make sure you're careful." Her voice hints at a warning that has me wondering how much she actually knows.

"I'm good, Mom. I can take care of myself, I promise."

"You'll understand when you have kids someday," she mumbles, pulling her blanket tighter over her shoulders.

This trip seems to be a constant reminder of my loss.

I scratch at the mud on my armrest with my thumb and confess what I have been holding back from Mom for too long, "Well, with Mark, that won't happen." There. I said it to the one person that I was the most afraid to say it to. Telling my mom somehow always makes things more valid, real, and distressing.

"Oh, honey." Mom reaches for my hands. I'm sure the wavering of my voice and the tears that line my eyes are all she needs to know it isn't my choice. Besides, she knows better than anyone that starting a family was what I was looking forward to the most when I married Mark. Some girls dream of weddings, I dreamt of having kids. "Is it because you lost Amelia? Does he not want to go through it again?"

"No, it's because he never wanted kids. He doesn't want to try."

"You didn't talk about that before you got married?"

"I just assumed it was part of his desire. Amelia was on her way."

"Oh, Autumn. You should have talked about it."

"I know that, Mom." I try to shrug off her comment, but cracks form in my heart and the floodgates open before I can stop them. In no time, my entire body shakes. Mom puts her arms around me, bringing me closer to her. Which makes me cry harder.

"I can still see her. Every day, I can see her with hair that starts dark red but then gets fiery as her personality grows with it in each passing year."

Mom sniffs, brushes my hair with her hand, and whispers, "I can see that, too."

"When I married Mark, all I could think about was that she'd be here soon. Nothing else mattered."

I bring my knees to my chest, hugging them. "But she's not here. And Mark and I... we don't know how to be married without her. We don't know how to be a couple anymore. I don't think we would have gotten married if it wasn't for her. The fun would have faded eventually and we would have broken it off."

"Oh, Autumn." Mom hugs me again, her own tears slide in my hair. "Are you sure Mark feels that way? He went through an awful lot for the Bridging the Six Degrees event. You don't do all of that if you don't love the person it's for."

"He loves his company, Mom. Yes, he loves me but not to the same degree."

"Maybe you should try marriage counseling."

Everyone assumes there are other options. But it doesn't mean other options work for every couple, especially when they want different things out of life.

She lets me sob and quietly hands me tissue after tissue until my tears subside. After a moment, she asks, "So, you're unhappy with Mark?"

I had a sneaking suspicion that question has been on her mind for a while. "I think we're unhappy with each other and just forcing it to work. I'm not sure his lifestyle is for me. What if I was always supposed to stay here and never run off with him?"

Nathan's face is like a hand clutching my heart. What if I was supposed to find Nathan before Mark?

"I don't believe in life being anything other than it is. You were meant to do exactly what you did because you made the decision to. I want you to understand that."

"Mom, no offense, but it's hard to take that advice from someone who has been in one area her whole life with limited decisions to make."

Mom shakes her head. "Autumn, I am here because I made the choice to stay here."

I raise my head and look at her. "You and Dad always said there's nowhere else you would choose to be."

"Yes, because we *chose* it. Your dad was the one who never wanted to move or travel anywhere outside of the state. He doesn't have the desire or interest, but I always did."

"No..." I'm suddenly questioning everything I thought I knew about my mom.

"It's true. I spent the first seven years of our marriage sneaking away, looking at issues of *National Geographic*, dreaming about living elsewhere, being elsewhere, and tasting food from all over the world. I was always snapping at your dad and your brothers when they were young any time I had my nose in those magazines. I was living one life and allowing myself to crave a completely different one, and it was making me miserable.

"One day your dad found me reading one and said, 'If you want to go, go. I won't hold it against you. I want you to be happy. Everything I could ever want is right here and I'll be here if you decide you want this too.' Seeing him standing there, so committed and happy with his life, rooted in the fact that everything he needed was around him, it was admirable.

"Not too many people feel that way, and it reminded me of what I knew when we were teenagers—that he was a very special man who I never wanted to lose. I had to choose, for the sake of my own happiness, and I chose to be right here in these moments with him, and be all in. I've never looked back, and I can truly say I've been happy ever since."

I touch my throat, searching for the right words. "I never would have guessed."

"That's because I made up my mind, and your dad and I have been a united front ever since."

"No, I never would have guessed you and I are so much alike."

Mom laughs and I join her, allowing the laughter to take over my tears.

"Listen, honey. Mark shouldn't fulfill you. You should always find that within yourself. But if you aren't seeing eye to eye on important life decisions, then I understand having to step away. I've always known your love for kids, Autumn. I was thrilled when you found out you were having Amelia. If you are ready to try for a baby again, it's not fair for Mark to hold you back from that. Likewise, it's not fair for you to impose children on his life if he doesn't want that experience."

"I know." I sniff, wiping my raw nose on another tissue. "It's hard letting go." Mark was my everyday connection to Amelia. I know I'll always have my memories of her, but knowing Mark will soon be only a memory for different reasons is too much. It feels like I'm losing her all over again.

What Henry told me at the hospital, about how alike Lenora and I are, clicks for the first time. They were unable to have children as well despite wanting them, and they still shared a wonderful life together. But Lenora's inability to have children is vastly different from Mark simply not wanting them. That's a difference in desires and life values, not circumstances.

Mom pulls my hair from my dampened face. "Thank you for sharing that with me, Autumn. I had no clue the depth of your pain."

I wipe my eyes one final time. "Things you won't read in that online journal."

She leans her head against mine, and I link my arm in hers

while my dad joins us again. "It's these conversations I'll always hold close to my heart."

"More coffee?" My dad holds the carafe to fill our mugs. We sit, listening to the serenade from the crickets and the birds, watching the ripples of the water, enjoying the moment together, and appreciating what family is all about, a support system when we all need it the most.

Twenty-Two

Turns out I am an excellent knitter, and the entire process is quite therapeutic. It may have started out a little rough when I was arm-knitting with my mom—a cat batting at a ball of string would have had better success than me.

Following my failed attempt at arm knitting, and after admiring Emmy's knitted hat at the Children's Hospital, I began researching how to knit. I started watching YouTube tutorials on regular knitting and was encouraged to try that route. To my advantage, Hobby Lobby was having a great sale on skeins so I purchased twelve, unsure of how many I would need.

I mentioned to my mom that it would be great if I could tie it in with a BSD challenge from Abby Keptler from Portland. She started crocheting blankets for the homeless and discovered it was a skill she was good at and that relaxed her. Abby's challenge for me was to learn a new skill that could benefit others. I loved the idea of being able to make something to keep people warm. Living in the cold eight months out of the year in Wisconsin and Boston, I wasn't a stranger to how a warm hat, scarf, or blanket could go a long way for someone in need.

The concept thrilled my mom who said Carol teaches knitting classes once a month at Michael's, which doesn't surprise me one bit. Carol also spends most of the year knitting clothes for the residents at the nursing home.

My knitting excitement deflates after several attempts. But not long after, the action clicks. I move my hands like I have been knitting my whole life.

Carol laughs at me as I lament having waited thirty years to learn this skill. "Goodness, dear, I didn't discover it until I was fifty so you're ahead of the game!"

I'm about to finish a kid-sized crimson scarf when Carol asks me about the time I spent in the nursing home. "How was your visit with Marabelle?"

"Oh, I learned so much from her. I could have talked to her for days."

"You know what's strange about all of this? I have thought of you many times throughout the years while talking to Marabelle. I was pleased to finally introduce you two."

I raise an eyebrow. "Really? Why have you thought about me? We're so different."

Carol clicks her tongue. "Not at heart. You're both strong, confident ladies who know what they want. That's something people admire more than you know. The boldness to put everything else aside and go after what you set your sights on."

I stop knitting and assess her, waiting for her to admit she's being facetious. But her expression doesn't change. "That's sweet of you to say. I don't know if I agree with that, though. I would consider myself quite reserved and indecisive. Mom would agree."

Carol links a new skein and glanced over her glasses at me. "Oh, honey, you haven't been scared to fail. Do you realize how big that is? Many people aren't brave enough to do that. They'll continue down the path they are familiar with instead of discovering a brand new one."

"I'm guessing my mom told you what's happening with Mark." My mom plays as big of a part in the gossip train as everyone else.

Carol chuckles as she licks her finger and rubs two strings

apart. "Your mom and I talk every night. I hear it all. Everyone has to choose their own paths. But you and Marabelle, you're the brave ones. You both deserve to have incredible opportunities because you seize them. You've wanted to broaden your world and that's exactly what happened. Not always in ways you would have penned or predicted, sure, but by taking chances, by exploring, by living, by saying yes. There should never be regrets in that, only learning opportunities."

"You make it sound like a very romantic notion. It doesn't feel quite so pleasant or rewarding."

"You're the writer. Don't all love stories have discord because that's what makes the ending worth it? You're in the middle of your journey still, not the end. It doesn't have to always be happy in the middle." She hums Billy Joel's "Vienna" and the meaning is not lost on me.

After I complete my scarf, Carol promises next time she'll teach me more advanced techniques to create the fancier-knit animal hats I'd love to deliver to the Children's Hospital someday. I ask if we can do that while having tea with Marabelle and she claps her hands with her typical Carol-level enthusiasm, plus a bonus squeal. Kissing my cheek before I leave, she says, "I know it won't always be easy, but you have a lot of people who are here to support you. I, for one, am excited to see more of you again."

Once I leave Carol's house, I make my way to Grandview Pier, unsure of what to expect from my dinner date with Rose and Kevin. Because of my first impression of him, I envision a huge, white yacht that would be a sore sight to anybody who calls Door County home—despite Rose's use of the word "houseboat." But once I park and exit my car, as the only houseboat in a pier full of fishing boats and canoes, it is easy to spot and surprises me with how basic and semi-run-down it is, as though originally purchased in 1980.

A squeal comes from the boat. "Autumn!" Rose runs down the dock, arms outstretched. She's gorgeous in an off-the-shoulder, knee-length, pink dress, with her hair tied in a bun, rosy cheeks, and a smile that lights up the pier. She strikes me as a modern-day fifties housewife, and I mean that as a compliment. My distressed jeans, Boston Harbor sweatshirt, and flats seem inadequate.

Rose embraces me as though it has been years since she last saw me. "I missed you!"

I can't help but laugh. "We saw each other a few nights ago!"

She dismisses it with a waved hand in the air. "I want to show you our boat." She grabs my hand and pulls me on deck.

Our boat?

The inside meets more of my expectations than the outside. It had been completely gutted and renovated. Everything is shiny, confirming my initial assumptions about Kevin. Her reference, like she owns this boat too, disturbs me, as if they are married and both have ownership.

I whisper, "This is Kevin's, right? You didn't like... go in with him on this or anything?"

Rose's eyes open wide. "Do you think I'm crazy?"

"I don't know! Not that you're crazy, but I have no clue what's going on with you and this guy. Everything you say is always 'us' which is unusual with you."

Her eye twitches, the same look she had when she caught me making Nathan dinner. The guilt sits hard in my stomach as I prepare for her to clap back with that ammo. Instead, she drops her shoulders and says, "I don't know. It's different. I can feel it. Instead of fighting it, I'm going with it. It's been fun. He stuck around so we could explore things. That's pretty romantic, right?"

I can't argue with that. "Yeah, it is. He must really like you."

Rose rubs her hands together. "I think he does. You can judge for yourself. Here he comes."

Kevin climbs aboard with his boat shoes, white khakis, plain navy sweater, and a grocery bag. I am surprised he didn't add a captain's hat to his ensemble, which are the thoughts I need to stop having if Rose does indeed like him as much as she's hinting.

Rose links her fingers with his.

"Hi, Autumn. It's good to see you again." For a brief second, it looks like he might try to hug me, but then he doesn't, and I'm relieved. I'm still dubious about this one.

"Thanks for inviting me to have dinner with you guys tonight."

"We hired help so we can sit out on the deck and chill. I've got heaters out there to help us stay warm." Kevin turns to Rose who is already rubbing her arms. "Speaking of, you should grab a sweater. You look gorgeous but I don't want you getting sick."

"Good call. It's colder than I thought out."

Kevin kisses her cheek before she disappears below deck and watches her walk away before turning back to me. "Let's grab a seat. There's wine on the table already." Tealight candles, wine glasses, and four bottles of wine decorate the dining table outside the cabin. He pulls out a seat for me then sits down across the table. "I wasn't sure what kind of wine you liked. Rose said you aren't picky but I know everyone has a preference."

"Any dry red is great."

"Perfect." Kevin pours me a red blend, then picks a white for himself, pouring it in Rose's glass first, then his own.

Rose returns before we are alone for much longer, probably not trusting that I'd be civil. She didn't just add a sweater to her outfit but changed into a cardigan and jeans instead. I know she did it to make me feel more comfortable. Sitting down next to Kevin, she immediately grabs his hand again. I've never seen her be this affectionate with a man before. Usually when Rose dates someone, she keeps some distance between them, treating them more like a sibling than a romantic interest.

"I have to ask." Kevin apologetically glances at Rose. "How are things going with the Bridging the Six Degrees challenges? I've been reading the platform entries. You've had incredible experiences so far."

Rose presses her lips together, and I wonder if she asked him not to bring it up. I don't know how much I'm supposed to reveal when we will be sitting down for a final interview in only a few weeks' time. "It's been terrific. Exactly what I needed when I didn't know I needed it. I'll expand more during the interview, I promise."

He winks. "Fair enough, fair enough." Ugh, I hate that wink. It's part of what I despised in the first place. Funny how Nathan winks all the time too but it's endearing when he does it and not akin to a used-car salesman.

I need to be more cordial with Kevin to be fair to Rose, so I ask, "How did you come up with the idea? Mark and I haven't had a chance to talk much about it."

He swirls the wine in his glass. "Do you really want to hear it? Once you get me started, it's hard for me to stop."

"I can attest to that." Rose lifts her glass as Kevin shoots her a grin. "But I love his passion for it."

Did she say *love?* "Well, I'm all about passion." I settle in my chair, preparing to bite my tongue.

"Alright, then. Don't say I didn't warn you." He sits up straighter and plants his elbows on the table. "Bridging the Six Degrees was a concept I had when I was around ten years old, as crazy as that sounds. I noticed the way technology was changing the world and, in some ways, it was great. It could bring people together who wouldn't meet otherwise and I liked that. The core of BSD is founded in providing virtual parties for people everywhere in the world. My family was constantly moving since my dad was an entrepreneur himself, buying new franchises in areas that he thought they'd most succeed in. We never had family nearby and rarely made friends. I spent most of my birthdays alone."

Rose rubs his shoulder. The way she is gazing at him makes the hair stand up on my arms; I adore seeing her like this but equally want to protect her. I doubt I am hiding the confusion on my face. It feels like the apocalypse is happening, something I never thought I'd see in my lifetime.

"At first I thought, let's have a virtual party where everyone can log in and practically be there, regardless of distance. I envisioned cameras providing a live feed to communicate back and forth to all the guests. Obviously other people had that thought too because that technology now exists. But as the years went on and social media shifted, my vision for BSD did too. Social media seemed to be driving people further away from each other instead of bringing them together. It was putting chasms between meaningful interactions.

"People were talking about what they were doing but they weren't talking about how what they were doing was changing who they are. I wanted a platform that focused on celebrating our growth and transformation, not hiding or minimizing it. Still using the party idea as the base, it eventually evolved into how you know it to be today.

"We are still working out the kinks, and it will only get better from here, but we strongly believe it will help people connect on deeper levels and challenge growth as a community, bridging souls from all over the world together, so we never feel like this life isn't worth the experiences we go through, and we know that we're never truly alone." Kevin shrugs at the end, and for the first time, I have insight into the way Rose views him: a humble man with a genius idea who is seeing his dreams come to fruition.

"In time, we will create levels that work for all socioeconomic groups and make it accessible to everyone. Right now, it costs a lot because we have to invest a lot, but eventually, we should be able to offset that more. Your husband's company taking interest is one of the first steps in making that dream a reality." His eyes flash with excitement, revealing his passion for what Bridging the Six Degrees will achieve.

"I love how impact-driven it is. No one can deny it's a unique business model," I say approvingly in response to his Bridging the Six Degrees origin story. "I'm sure Rose already told you that I'm not one for large social interactions so it was overwhelming at first. However, I'm extremely grateful for the experiences and the lifelong friendships that have bloomed."

Kevin squeezes Rose's hand. "I love to hear that. You're our first self-proclaimed introvert, so honestly I've been nervous about how you'd hold up during the process. Especially with this being our first publicly-broadcasted event. But you haven't retreated, and all the footage we have of you is beautiful."

I laugh nervously as I imagine him and a crew of people scrutinizing footage they've taped, editing it, catching all my looks and comments, editing more, and analyzing everything I'm writing in the online platform while I go through my adventures. Between that and Rose, I'm sure Kevin knows more about me than I know of him.

"How did you come up with the term Senders and Targets as the names of those involved?"

"They're based on the original research and successful testing of the Six Degrees of Separation theory. It's all quite fascinating. The first theory was proposed in the 1920s—" The sound of a crying baby interrupts him.

I pop my head up to search for the source in the dark night, expecting it to come from a nearby boat. Rose holds up a monitor, showing a little baby thrashing about in a crib.

"I'll go check on her." She kisses Kevin's cheek before she leaves and glances at me with concern. She clearly had a plan arranged to bring up the child topic and this wasn't it.

Kevin dives right in. "I understand Rose mentioned I have a daughter."

I had been warming up to him, but now I regress to cynicism again. The jealousy sparking deep within isn't entirely fair, but it's there whether or not I want it to be. "Yep."

"Would you like to know more about her?"

If his relationship with Rose becomes more serious, he and his daughter will both be in my life. "Sure," I respond, firing mental judgments before he even has a chance to share his story.

"Shannon is her name. She's the light of my life. She primarily resides in Manhattan with April, her mom. It isn't the most conventional family, but we are happy and we make it work."

I bite my lip to maintain a neutral look, knowing my feelings show on my face too easily.

Kevin continues, "April has been one of my best friends since I was three years old. She was a huge motivator in me taking the risks I did to get Bridging the Six Degrees up and running. Unfortunately, she ended up in a bad situation a couple of years ago while on a girl's trip to Cancun. I'll spare you the details, but unfortunately, she," he clears his throat, "was sexually assaulted and later discovered she was pregnant. April didn't want to raise the baby alone and was considering terminating the pregnancy.

"That's when I stepped in and offered to be the father, legally. After some convincing, she finally agreed. No one except for Rose, and now you, know the truth. I was there with April in the delivery room, I'm on Shannon's birth certificate, and I'll continue to be every bit of the dad Shannon deserves to have, and a partner in parenthood that April deserves."

I swipe at my eyes, taking a deep breath, my chest heavy with the story he delivered. I did nothing but judge Kevin from the very beginning. There is much more to this man than my first impressions.

"Why haven't you told anyone else the truth? That's incredibly selfless of you to protect April and Shannon."

"No." Kevin leans in closer, his voice low. "It's not about what I did. It's about the family we've now created. That's what matters. No one needs to know the reasons. I'll be honest, Autumn, I wouldn't have told you. Rose begged me to, though. She's a tough one but your opinion of her decisions seems to carry weight. I want to be with Rose so if that's another step, I'll do what I have to do."

This man poured everything he has into creating a company with the sole purpose of removing loneliness and building lasting connections between people all over the world. And he saved a good friend and her baby. I've been too harsh on him. I assumed he was hitting on me during our first meeting but I see now he was just as nervous as I was, wanting to make sure the guest of honor was happy and that everything was going to run smoothly. He had a lot riding on me and I didn't realize it. Everyone says first impressions are what sticks but that's only if you have a narrow mind and aren't open to a new perspective.

"I'll keep it to myself." I promise him.

"It's part of why I'll never give up on the Bridging the Six Degrees mission. I know that if we can stop and really see each other for who we are and take the time to form meaningful connections, this world could be a much happier place. People would operate more from love instead of fear. It's my tiny part in making sure Shannon grows up in a happier world."

For the first time since I met Kevin, I give him a genuine smile. "I'm glad you're in Rose's life."

Even in the darkened night, I note the delight on his face. "I'm even happier that she's in mine."

Excusing myself from the table to find the bathroom, I slide below deck and immediately crash into Rose on the stairs. "Oomph!"

"Shhh." Rose pulls the monitor out of her pocket to check on Shannon. "She fell asleep again but I'm not sure how long it'll last. We think she's teething again."

Rose with a baby monitor and in full mother mode is the strangest sight. But at the same time, it is a great look on her with her independence pushed aside and the needs of this baby as her focus.

I start to open my mouth, but she cuts me off. "Listen, I know when Kevin is in business mode, he can come off as cocky. But it's a front he carries to protect himself from the anxiety of his dream crashing down around him. When you have him by himself, you see how sincere he is. Like tonight. Tell me you've seen *him* tonight." She is all but pleading with me. I'd say she was a little deeper than the "like" territory with this guy.

"You don't have to beg me to see it your way. I understand. He seems like a solid, great guy, Rose. I'm surprised, but in a good way."

She hugs me, proving what Kevin said about my opinion on her decisions. I wouldn't have thought Rose, in all her individuality, valued my thoughts to that extent.

"So, this is the real deal, huh?"

She gently touches her gold necklace with a diamond-encrusted R resting against her neck. "Yes, I believe it could be. Kevin is the first man I've met who has shown me what a real man can be. I feel safe with him. Emotionally, spiritually, mentally, physically. That's the best way I can describe it. I feel safe. Like it's okay to believe a man will say he'll be there for you, and he'll show up."

"Rose, that's big." I can't find a better adjective. We're both looking at each other with tears in our eyes, a silent understanding of the impact that this shift in her actually fills. How a belief she's held onto since she was six years old is now shattering in front of her, allowing her to fearlessly love a man and trust that he won't break her heart.

"I have to ask… Are you worried at all about him and April with their history and having a family together?"

Rose snorts and rechecks the monitor. "Goodness, no. Not only do I trust Kevin, but I'm more of April's type than he is. Besides, we bonded like sisters right away. I'm excited for you to meet her someday."

Rose takes a step back and looks me up and down. "Speaking of types… you and Nathan looked pretty close the night we popped over." She finally addresses it. I'm sure it's been eating away at her, so I give her credit for lasting this long.

I shake my head. I don't want to dive into the details now. "Let's just say it's been a time full of discovery and introspection since I've been back here."

"Just be careful, Autumn. Kevin's camera crew was everywhere that first night. They captured some footage of you two on the dock. It looked intimate then and you didn't even really know who he was."

The cameras. I didn't consider those. I wonder how much

feeds back to Mark. "I want to talk to you about it, but let's not ruin tonight."

"You promise? I can come over tomorrow."

"This is one of many reasons I'm grateful for you." I give her another hug. "But I need to locate a bathroom pronto. It's turning into an emergency."

Rose points to the direction of the bathroom. I dart in as fast as I can. As soon as I flush, the crying begins again. I must have woken Shannon up. I quickly wash my hands and tiptoe to her room, expecting Rose or Kevin to be there. When the crying intensifies, I push open her door and peek inside. It's a small room with a crib-changing-table combo, wooden rocker in the corner, bags on the floor filled with baby items, and a flashing green turtle displaying rotating star-shaped lights on the ceiling and playing soothing lullabies.

Sneaking to the side of the crib, Shannon's eyes lock on mine. Her crying stops as she evaluates me with curious brown eyes. Her arms shoot out like she's requesting that I pick her up. How can I resist? I lift her tiny body out of the crib, forgetting how it feels to hold such a little baby. It's been years since my nieces and nephews were this small. She grips onto my shoulder and snuggles her face in my neck, her thin black hair tickling my skin.

Sitting down in the chair, I rock in tune with the lullabies, soothing her. Shannon's breathing becomes heavier and right as I'm building a plan for how to get her back in her crib, the lullabies stop. The turtle must have been on a timer. That two-second pause is enough for Shannon to begin screaming again.

I rack my brain to think of how those lullabies go but my brain bolts into panic mode with the shrillness of this little girl's screams. Instead, I default to the only song that comes to mind: the alphabet song. As soon as I get to the letter K, she stops crying. I sing it repeatedly, waiting for her to fall asleep.

The feel of Shannon's heartbeat against mine, her light snores, the twitching of her hand as it continues to grip my shoulder, and her heavenly scent are enough to break me. I sing the last two rounds of the alphabet through tears and a strained voice. *This is what I wanted so badly for so long.* I had glimpses of it with my nieces and nephews, nights where I would drop everything to help out with babysitting whenever I could. As much as I love them, I wanted those experiences with children that weren't on loan, ones that were mine. *Someday,* I would think to myself.

I breathe in her scent once more, allowing myself this time to mourn what I could have had. Sometimes it's the only way to move forward. I place Shannon delicately in the crib.

"Goodnight, sweet girl," I murmur, gently brushing the hair off her forehead.

When I return to the deck, Rose and Kevin are snuggled up next to each other watching the water. It is the sweetest scene I've ever seen Rose in. For a moment, it triggers a need inside for someone to be next to me as well. The environment is intoxicating with the chilly night sky lined with stars and little candles all around the deck. As soon as Mark crosses my mind, Nathan does, too, with memories of the first night we met and our secret trip together. Remorse replaces them both.

Once I sit back in my chair, Kevin and Rose respectfully part but remain holding hands on the table.

"Not to bounce back to business-talk specifically, but..." Rose trails off. She glances at Kevin as he gives her an encouraging nod in return. She continues, "Kevin asked that I take the lead on the marketing of BSD. It's why I've been so busy lately, to make sure the Tourism Board is in a good spot before I leave. I'll move to Manhattan as soon as I'm done."

"Wait. You have to move from here to do that? Isn't this an online company? Didn't you just buy a houseboat here?"

Rose doesn't answer right away. She looks at Kevin and him at her. They're having a silent conversation, and it's driving me nuts.

"Rose, what does this mean? You're leaving?" I ask again, more insistently this time. *I'm staying right as she's leaving?*

Another glance at Kevin before she answers, "I am. I think it's time. Kevin wants to open the headquarters in Manhattan so they no longer have to shuffle Shannon around different cities. I've always wanted to live in New York. I'm ready to take on something bigger. Connecting with people around the world will be the big thing I've been looking for. You saw it at your party. I want to be part of that more."

I want to ask her if she knows how big of a risk that is, to leave a stable company she's been with for years to go chasing after a startup company. To pack her things and move halfway across the country because some guy won her over. But to knock the future of the company was, in essence, bashing Mark's judgment and investment. Not to mention I had also moved for a guy, so who was I to judge? Rose needs something bigger than Door County. She always has. Whether it'll be this startup company or merely being in NYC, *something* will give her more of what she deserves.

"Sounds like the perfect fit then."

Rose slams her hands on the table, startling both Kevin and me. "That's not the reaction I was prepared for. I have a speech outlined to convince you this is good for me!"

I chuckle, half embarrassed that I'm *that* friend, but also concede to the truth. "I trust your decisions. It's your life."

Kevin kisses her cheek. "See? All great things occur as they should."

That comment just makes me like him more.

"The real question is, does Mama Ackerman know?" Rose's mom is one of the sternest women in Crimson Bay. An administrator at the high school, who has inspired numerous memes and caricatures with her wide mouth open in a screaming fashion and a giant rolling pin in her hand. She also bakes the most delicious famous pies that have won nationwide ribbons. Everyone is always shocked to learn that the free-spirited Rose is her daughter since hardly anyone remembers her father, who was much more of a creative nomad.

It's even more shocking to see Rose and her mom together; the only time that Mama Ackerman will reveal a smile, and a hint that there is a lot more than what appears on the surface between them, an unmistakable bond, strengthened through an early hardship that brought them closer. Now, two independent, adult women chasing their dreams in life and never letting anything stand in their way, cheering each other on through it all, friends as much as family.

"She scares the living daylights out of me." Kevin admits.

"Hey!" Rose swats his shoulder. "That could be your future if you play your cards right!"

Through the course of the night, I learn that Rose is planning to leave sometime within the next six months. It gives Kevin and Karen ample time to get the headquarters set up and everything squared away with Neigleman Tech, as they hire more permanent employees rather than using contractors everywhere they go. Rose plans to rent her own place; although, if it is still six months down the road, there's no telling how much more can change between now and then. I don't have the heart to tell her yet that I plan on staying. I don't want it to affect her decision.

"Are you sure you can handle seeing Karen on a regular basis?" As soon as the words are out, I cover my mouth, remembering Karen and Kevin are not only business partners but siblings, too.

Kevin pulls his fingers through Rose's hair and says, "The problem is, they're too much alike. They'll butt heads."

"Well, Rose likes to argue so at least that gives her someone else to do it with other than you."

"Cheers to that!" Kevin lifts his glass.

"Hey! I... eh, I can't argue that one." Rose reached her max on wine a while ago, but she clinks her almost empty glass with ours and flashes her million-dollar smile.

I return to my cottage with my heart overflowing on love. Everything in Crimson Bay is changing quickly. Although sad in some ways, there are so many new adventures being taken in the pursuit of happiness. This place won't be the same without Rose and Jessi but I still know it's my home. It's the choice I'm choosing to make.

Twenty-Three

MARK IS A ROMANTIC IN HIS OWN WAY, CATCHING ME off guard, which is part of what made the beginning of our relationship electrifying. He wouldn't do things when I expected them or when the timing was right according to the rest of the world. Valentine's Day for example: no dates, no flowers, nothing. March 4th, however? A beautiful bouquet of flowers that stood three feet in height. Just because. He had his own timing for romance and the thrill was like standing outside in the middle of a lightning storm, waiting for the bolts to strike.

Here's a truth that no one except us, plus a random man and a little girl knows: we married before our wedding ceremony.

We were lying in bed one night, in a state of euphoria from intimacy so intense that it now seems like a long-lost dream since I can't recall the last time we felt like that. Mark's words interrupted the silence. "Would you marry me with no one present?"

I tilted my head from his chest where I was resting so that I could look up at him. "You mean without friends and family? Elope?"

"Yes."

"Don't we need a witness?"

"Those things can be arranged."

I closed my eyes, thinking about his words. "Are you serious?"

Mark angled my chin so my eyes were looking into his. "I am. We both don't care to be the star of the show. A wedding would be more to appease everyone else. Let's just get married, you and me. We can still have a ceremony. But this way we can focus on us, and no one else has to know about it."

It sounded so romantic; how could I say no? Instead of responding, I kissed him and he gently placed his hands on my growing baby bump. I wasn't sure if he was caught up in the moment or if it was something he actually wanted. Not until he brought it up the week of our wedding while eating dinner.

"Are you ready to get married before Saturday?"

I paused with my fork in the air. "You were serious?" By then so much time had passed, I had chalked it up to a joke.

He reached over to grab my hand, running his thumb across my knuckles. "Yes."

I raised my eyebrow, still doubting he'd go through with it. "I'm up for it if you are." Mark was a man of tradition, not one of impulse. But I wouldn't be the one to back down.

"Okay then."

The following morning, Mark woke me up at 3:30 a.m. I thought there was a fire or emergency. Instead, he held up a beautiful ivory sundress with a generous amount of stretch and asked, "Would this work?"

"For what?" I rubbed my eyes, trying to see out the window for a glimpse of the sun. But it was pitch black.

"We're getting married today, my dear." It was his terrible Rhett Butler impression. He used it each time I picked up *Gone with the Wind* or when it came on TV.

"You're joking."

"Nope! Your lovely ass needs to get in that bathroom, so we can be on the road in thirty minutes."

"Words I'll never forget my husband said to me on our wedding day," I mumbled as I stuck my tongue out at him and sleepily sauntered into the bathroom to get ready.

I don't think it hit me we were actually doing it until we arrived at the location.

Sunrise. Overlooking Cape Cod. Those were Mark's wishes from the beginning, and he timed it perfectly.

The minister was a retired employee of Mark's. The witness was his little granddaughter playing the flute. I'll never forget the way the pink ribbon tied around her ponytail fluttered loosely in the wind while I said my vows. She was so giddy during the ceremony as she held on to her grandpa's leg and watched Mark and I become husband and wife. It was precious. I had daydreamed of Amelia playing the flute someday.

It was a much different point in life where the innocence of the future settles on your shoulders and brings hope and optimism of things to come. Before reality, both gently and harshly, blows that innocence away. A time when anything feels possible and no obstacles cross your mind. The beginning of our life together.

Our impromptu wedding wasn't the end of Mark's surprises. After we had a delicious breakfast with mimosas to celebrate at his favorite restaurant, The French Hen, which overlooks the Cape, he announced that we had one more stop to make.

I stumbled, in shock, across the threshold at the tattoo parlor he chose. Mid-morning on a Wednesday, I didn't even know those places were open during the day. I assumed they were only open during the late-night drinking hours as people stagger in drunk from the bars down the street, finally brave enough to either get whatever mark they've been eyeing or create something on a whim. Clearly that's how little thought I had given to getting a tattoo. I definitely wasn't prepared to do it at that moment.

"Why are we here?" I inquired, having to do a double take to ensure the grin on Mark's face was real, one that very rarely surfaces, excitement lighting up his eyes like a kid looking at a Christmas tree filled with presents underneath.

"We should get tattoo rings."

"Instead of our regular rings?" I adjusted the silver band on my finger, admiring the simplicity of it.

"No, we'll still wear these rings, too. But the tattoos can be our little secret, hidden under our rings to symbolize our true ceremony that no one else knows about."

Mark is about as clean cut as it gets. Never in my wildest dreams did I think he'd want a tattoo. We hadn't talked about it, but I knew he was conscious of the image he sets for other people, and no matter how much our society changes, tattoos are still a questionable trait for many.

He didn't ask what I thought about it or if I would do it. The tattoo artist came out and said that he was ready for us, and that was it.

I went first. My heart sped up, and if it wasn't so cold in the studio, I'm sure sweat would have been lining my forehead. I couldn't believe he wanted to do this.

After several failed attempts (and a knee that I couldn't settle), the tattoo artist wasn't able to keep my finger steady.

I knew the truth: it wasn't fear of the tattoo.

Mark must have known, too. He never expressed his disappointment. He supported my decision to walk out that day without a tattoo. The same way he supports all my decisions.

The door chimes when I walk through Hepburn's Tattoos, the only parlor in Door County. Etta Derring's challenge rings in my ear as I sit down in the chair, *Limit your regrets in life. Do something you always knew you should have done.*

* * *

My alarm rings hours before dawn. Ten minutes later, I'm out the door in the dark, throwing supplies in my Jeep, and getting back on the road that leads to the Triangle Cliffs.

The drive is one of the prettiest routes through Wisconsin. When Nathan was driving, it gave me a chance to look around and take note of things previously unseen. I had detected a patch of land close to the Cliffs that stole my heart the moment I saw it. A giant hill was beckoning me to climb it and see what was on the other side. I'm glad I didn't tell Nathan because I'm sure he would have stopped so we could explore. But I need to do this by myself.

Before I pass the last exit for breakfast options, I stop by a diner that opened only minutes ago to order a sausage biscuit and a coffee.

"Up early, honey," the waitress comments while shoving my money in the register.

"Sure am." I can't contain my excitement.

"Big plans?"

"Only to breathe in nature."

She snorts and slams the register shut. "Oh, to be young again."

Yes, I'm thirty and young. I take pleasure in that. *Lots of life left, Autumn. Lots of time to get your life on track.*

The light breaks over the horizon as I slow the Jeep to find the exact spot that demanded my attention last time. I pull over into a break in the trees and haul my items out, attempting to balance my coffee without spilling it. I'm running out of time to set up.

I hike up the hill fast while carrying an extra twenty pounds of supplies. I set up the easel, canvas, and paints right as the sun rises. A Sender from Australia, Gavin's challenge was to paint the sunrise and then paint the sunset on the same day and look at it as a way to reframe your thoughts about whatever is resting the heaviest in your mind and on your heart. It's the same sun both times but presents different colors and emotions. He says he uses it to start fresh in the morning and let go of daily weights by the time night arrives. Instead of journaling, Gavin has books full of watercolors, his visual versions of the state of his mind and heart on each of those days from the very beginning to the end.

I'm a terrible painter but you'd have to be a brick to not be motivated by a sunrise bursting with yellows, oranges, and pinks climbing behind a field full of trees. Lighting up the world as though it was born today, magnifying beauty of all nature's greatest gifts that man could never manufacture. Only the truest artists can capture the details and do it justice.

I can't paint well but I can follow my feelings. Each stroke of paint on the canvas and each choice of color is tightly wound with the emotions I've had since I've been back in Door County.

Two Bridging the Six Degrees challenges go hand-in-hand, so similar that I am surprised that Mark and my family chose them both. Vicky from New Jersey recommended that I spend one day by myself amid nature, journaling from sunrise to sunset in solitude, not speaking to anyone, and reflecting on life. She was infatuated with writers who would do that for months at a time and later share their most private journal entries. So, she embarked on that challenge herself.

Vicky had to gradually build up to doing it for an extended amount of time,

For solitude can be challenging in a world where we are inundated by noise from others—whether from other people in our daily lives or even the voices that carry through the radio and TV. Not having someone else's voice in some format or another can shake the soul. It takes time to let go of the feeling like we're not entirely alone, even if all we desire is to be alone sometimes.

Vicky suggested starting with one day of it, and then if I were as impacted as she believed I would be, to incorporate it slowly for greater periods. She is a teacher and started doing it during the summers until she met her significant other, *which makes it harder to leave and express my need for solitude without offending him.*

Once the sun moves higher in the sky, I place the final touches on my painting with delicate strokes of the paintbrush. It will never hang in an art gallery, but it without a doubt reflects the hard truths deep in my heart.

I eat my now-cold breakfast sandwich while watching the field below. Since it's a weekday, my hope is that there will be few visitors so I can honor the challenge of total solitude. I already feel myself reaching for my phone several times—which I purposely left in the car—to turn on music to fill the silence.

A family of deer trot into the field. Serene, peaceful, graceful. I suck in my breath, taking in the grass-scented air when I do. Tiny bugs keep appearing, some buzzing around my face, and others climbing on my legs, and I try my best not to swat at them, letting nature be exactly as it should be, and not interfering.

All these observations I scribble into my journal. And when nothing new comes into view, I dive into a full dissection of my time in Crimson Bay—how my trip started and the impact on who I am today, and what that means for my future. An outpouring of words, and as each one connects with the paper, I free myself from my attachment to them. I stay focused on who I am in this moment, and it's someone who, perhaps for the first time, I'm learning to love exactly as she is.

I finally put the journal back in my bag, whisper goodbye to the grazing deer, and return the heavy items to my car to retrieve them later. I choose a path through the trees that should, in theory, lead me directly to the Triangle Cliffs.

It doesn't take long to find them. The rushing flow of the water hits my ears first, and then a few steps later the trees part, as though announcing that the spectacular view has arrived.

Memories of Nathan and me here together, touching, tempted to do more, both my mind and body demanding to be freely handed over to him. My heart swells with heat, happiness, comfort, joy, and appreciation of getting to do something new with someone who valued it too.

I close my eyes, focusing on the sound of the water, meditating on where I've come from in this journey and valuing every step and misstep. The joys, the grief, the challenges, the unknowns, and the surprising clarity. The result of it all: happiness. Each puzzle piece connects naturally, but only when I let go of control and have faith in the full puzzle designed for me.

The sun makes the temperature feel ten degrees warmer than what it was predicted to be. I confidently strip down to my tank and boy shorts and walk around the man-made path that leads to the edge of the second-level cliff. I lift my arms above my head, tilt my head to the sky and breathe in the pure air. Without another thought, I jump.

The water proves to be much colder than the outside air. The sun has yet to warm it, making the shock of the jump alarming. I kick back to the top of the water and emerge with a shriek. "I did it!" All by myself. All without the need for someone else to encourage me. All without my mind taking over with unnecessary fears.

I am brave. I am courageous. I am enough.

Best of all, this is now a *me* memory that no one else is privy to.

As I dog paddle around the triangle rocks, it's impossible to keep Nathan from my mind. That day with him here was special, but even from the moment he first spoke, I was hooked. The more I got to know him, my heart became deeply attached. Despite not being born here, Nathan still embodies everything I love the most about Crimson Bay. He gets it.

Mark, however, doesn't understand the appeal of this place or my cottage, and instead of trying to find pieces about it he likes, he simply avoids it, despite how much it means to me. When these are the things that symbolize my heart and soul, it's quite telling of the path we'll continue to walk down at this rate. Nathan, however, values the way of living here and the closely-connected family and community that is etched in my being.

Nathan. I still need to call him back. I need to deal with the cottage. But there's so much more I want to tell him as well, and I know the moment I hear his voice, I won't be able to resist.

Like bursting out of the cold water into the warm air after sinking from such a steep fall, I am learning that all the highs and lows combined are necessary for a meaningful life. They work together to create this journey. The low times will force me to recognize my strength, courage, and abilities when I succeed in getting through to the other side of the darkness. The highs allow a celebration of who I've become and offer a chance to love myself more, so I can better love others and equally accept them for who they are.

Mark doesn't have to change what he wants out of life.

I don't either.

Floating in the water on my back, I stare up at the boundless, blue sky while I bask in gratitude of it all. I'm ready to let go of the grief and guilt. I'm ready to be free.

Once every inch of my skin wrinkles, I paddle out of the water, grab my clothes and bag, and sit on the rock exposed to the most sunlight, so I can dry off while writing in my journal. I write about all the things I've come to realize lately, all the things I've been able to do, and all the things I want to do from here on out.

In a way, I have been baptized by the water, cleansed and ready to start anew for the final time. Finally at peace with my decisions, comfortable with who I am, and willing to be steady and committed to my word. Even though coming to terms with it all at thirty years old seems overdue, I have a full life ahead to become the best version of myself.

After hours of hiking and exploring, I return to my place on the hill with my art supplies and wait for the sunset. The purpose of the challenge is to see how one's perspective could change within a day. In the morning, you have the impression of a brand-new start. By the evening, you're usually more weighed down, burdened by the trials and exhaustion of the day. My experience for the day was reversed, heavier burdens when I started than when I ended, but the application remains the same.

With a day like today, a chance to clear my mind, to challenge myself in my own scope alone, my sunset is brighter than my sunrise. Those two pictures will forever set the bar for how I shall spend my days, remembering the power and gratitude in simply feeling *alive*.

Twenty-Four

I'm swimming in a pool of empty, brown boxes. Flaps open, calling out to be filled with my unwanted possessions. I'm amazed at how much is still in this cottage. It's like a part of me knew this is where I would come back. Or I was afraid to mix too much of my flea market finds with Mark's modern and refined Crate & Barrel aesthetic.

Rose and my family all offered to help me pack but I knew the time would be spent answering questions about why so much is staying. I have yet to talk to Mark. No one else can know anything until I speak to him first.

I grab my challenge journal and skim through the Senders' stories and my pictures that captured my experiences. To say my life has significantly changed in eight weeks is an understatement.

I had planned to do one of my final challenges while packing for Italy, but even with my change of plans, it's still relevant. *Dare to get rid of what you don't need.* In Adam Shaw's case, he forwent a large family inheritance by giving it, and all his possessions, away. He chose to live in a small shack in Hawkes Bay, New Zealand instead, to pursue his love of wine by working in a vineyard. He could have bought the vineyard and the finest wines in the world with the money he inherited, but he chose a different life, a life that filled his soul.

What don't I need and what do I need? Things. Those are easier to discard. Yes, I love this cottage and everything in it. But how much of this represents who I am now?

If there has been a clear, consecutive message in the Bridging the Six Degrees experiments, it is this: material things do not matter. People and experiences are what this life is all about. I'm fortunate to have the most incredible people surrounding me, especially after this event. I'm learning to shift my focus from dreaming of how things could be to realizing how amazing it all already is.

Walking around the house, I pull pictures out of frames, placing them in a pile on the counter—all of them are pictures with Mark. For now, they'll go in my memory box. I don't want him permanently removed from my life but I want to avoid the natural ache these pictures will elicit after we end.

I also remove any item I bought in an attempt to fit into his life, rather than fit into mine. I strip my bed of the pure silk linens and comforter I bought the first night Mark stayed here and replace them with my old flannel sheets and a red and black checked quilt that is about twenty years old but still brings me comfort.

I remove the fancy kitchen gadgets he bought the first time he tried cooking in my house when his lack of patience for my old-fashioned knives and spoons was vocalized. I like using basic methods when I'm cooking. It soothes my mind. All these contraptions do is take up counter space when he's not here, so into boxes they go. Some lucky people will discover these for cheap at a thrift store.

The slam of a car door grabs my attention and interrupts my flow. I glance out of the kitchen window and see the edge of a Jeep hood. Those are abundant in Crimson Bay but I'd know that one anywhere. Nathan.

I walk to the door and open it just as he rounds the corner. His hands are gripped around the for sale sign.

"I guess I can officially remove this, huh?"

"Yeah." I wrap my hands around my body to hold myself back from the desire to hug him. "I'm sorry I haven't returned your calls yet."

He waves off my apology. "No need. Mark updated me." Pointing to the boxes behind me, he asks, "But you're still packing?"

I bite my lower lip. I want to tell Nathan everything. But I can't—not yet.

He nods once as though he understands but what he's deduced is not the facts. "Italy," he murmurs.

No, no, no. I want to tell him. *That's not it at all.* My stomach is a rolling pit like I will be sick at any moment. I can't tell if it's the thought of Nathan assuming things that aren't true or the realization that I need to call Mark as soon as Nathan leaves and finally speak the words I've been avoiding.

My phone rings, and I answer before looking at who is calling, my eyes focused on Nathan.

"Hello?"

"Hi, sweetheart." It's Mark.

I wouldn't have picked up the phone if it was him. Not yet. Not until Nathan leaves. "Hey." I turn my back to Nathan. "How are you?"

"I'm good. Missing you, but good. I know I said I'd wait for you to call, but I have something to share with you." Doors slam in the background and air moves through the phone. An engine starts.

"What are you doing?"

"I'm tr-... but didn't-... calling first and..."

I interrupt him. "Mark, you're breaking up. I can't hear you."

The phone beeps, signaling the loss of a connection. I sigh and lean my head against the threshold. Glancing in the foyer mirror, I push a few stray hairs out of my face and pause to make sure Mark isn't calling again before turning back to Nathan.

He's moved closer, now standing on the doorstep in his classic, cerulean polo that makes his eyes pop and chinos that I know make his butt look good because I've glanced a few times before. The sun shines down on him as though he's a walking golden trophy, waiting for someone to snag.

He hands me a nondescript cup he must have retrieved while I was on the phone. "A long time ago, I promised you the best coffee you've ever had. Here it is."

I laugh as I hold the plain, brown cup in the air to analyze it. "I'll admit, I doubt you now as much as I did then."

Nathan tenderly grabs my hand, guiding us to the steps to sit. As soon as our butts hit the concrete, he lets go, and I'm grateful. A tingling remains on my skin where his hand was. If he didn't let go, I wouldn't have either.

We blow on our coffee and watch the birds fly over the water. The leaves in the trees have changed since the last time he was at my house. Red and brown are mixed with the fading green.

"How's your friend doing?"

"Oh, Henry's better. I missed him, so it was good to see him. Even if not under the best circumstances."

"I'm happy to hear that. I wasn't sure how long you would stay with him."

"It was only two days."

"I see." Nathan flicks an orange leaf off his pants. "Well, I have a fun story for you."

"Oh, yeah?"

"Do you remember your junior year homecoming dance?"

"That's a funny question." I set the coffee between us while it cools and lean back on my hands to recall distant memories—ones I pushed away out grief once my relationship with Justin ended. "I vaguely remember wearing a shimmery blue dress, putting weird tiny flowers in my hair like it was cool and eating more than dancing that night."

"Well, let me help." Nathan digs into his pocket and pulls out a black and white picture copied from a yearbook.

"Oh, my goodness!" I exclaim as I bring the picture closer to survey the details. Sure enough, there I was with miniature, white roses decorating my head with Justin to my left, and on my right were Jessi and Mikey, her date, and Rose making her usual statement by going stag. We all wore big smiles with arms wrapped around each other like we were having the time of our lives. "Where in the world did you get this?"

"My sister, Jennifer. Do you remember her? She was a year older than you. Anyway, I was at her house for dinner and asked if she had her old yearbooks. I was curious about what you were like back in the day." The tips of his ears are red like he's embarrassed to divulge the information. It's sweet, though, to have someone *want* to know those things about me.

"Do you remember this kid?" Nathan taps the far-right edge of my shoulder in the picture where the pudgy face of a younger boy could barely be seen as he stood behind the giant cake.

The memories of that night thirteen years ago come flooding back. Justin and I had one of our many fights. He wanted to leave the dance, go watch football, and drink with his buddies. I wanted to stay and have a real homecoming dance experience. I thought it was romantic and Justin thought it was lame. He left me, and I stood by the snack table stuffing my face, attempting to focus on anything other than being dateless.

The boy at the table said, "Here's a napkin. Also, here's a pile of Onion Blossoms. My mom made them. I know it's not like slicing an onion, but you can still blame them for why you're crying."

I took the napkin from him. "Thanks." I patted my eyes.

"You don't have any mascara smudges. You also don't have food in your teeth in case you're wondering." I gave him a questioning look as he shrugged. "I have sisters. I get asked those things a lot."

I remember little else, but I know I talked to him for a long time because he made me laugh and was the best distraction from everything I was feeling.

Staring at Nathan in awe, I say, "You gave me a detailed food tour of everything on that table. You were helping the caterer."

"I told you my mom was a great cook."

Shaking my head, I respond, "I can't believe I forgot that."

"Well, it wasn't long before your boyfriend came back. You walked away without saying goodbye."

Justin was dragged back in by Mikey. It wasn't even his own choice to come back for me. Someone had asked us to take a picture together so we put on our happy faces, but I was miserable for the rest of the night. *Funny how pictures don't always reflect the truth.* If only I gave the boy in the background more attention than I did. Everything could have been different.

"Can I keep this?" I hold up the picture, knowing right away the home I have for it.

Nathan puts up his hands. "By all means, yes. Please take away my evidence of stalking."

I slide it in my back pocket and take the first sip of my coffee, my eyebrows rise in surprise. "Okay, I give. This *is* the best coffee I've ever had. Where's it from?"

"My house." He gives a sheepish smile.

"Mmm," I acknowledge, keeping my lips firmly together to refrain from everything else I want to say. I'd be okay with him making this for me every morning.

Minutes pass with neither of us saying a word. Nathan eventually rests his chin on his arm and sighs. "I figure this is probably my goodbye to you. I know this hasn't been good... for either of us."

I start to protest, but he interrupts me.

"No, it *was* good. But not right. I missed you while you were gone. A lot, actually. I loved spending time with you. I haven't felt that way in... well, probably ever." It is the most ineloquent I've heard Nathan, and even more upsetting to know I feel the same way and can't say a thing.

I picture that scene in *Indiana Jones and the Temple of Doom* where the crazy ceremony leader wearing the horns reaches through the man's chest and pulls out a thumping heart in his hands. I'm not sure if it's happening to my own heart or Nathan's at this point. I'm confident we are both feeling the same way. A perfect dream fluttered around us in the sky for the past few weeks, crafted by intense conversations, incredible experiences, and a rare magnetic connection. He sees it as flying away. He doesn't see that the string to it is still tucked safely in my hand.

"Timing is everything, huh?" Nathan mumbles while I stay silent.

I nod. An act we're both doing to save ourselves the agony of more words, if for different reasons.

Nathan sighs as he comes to terms with his own resolve. "Well crap, okay then. I should go before I can't pull myself away again." He stands and extends a hand, offering to help me up.

I take it, letting the warmth soak into my skin. I'm not sure I can let him walk away. Not like this.

"Nathan—" I start.

He stops me by shaking his head and pressing his lips to my hand. When he pulls away, he gives me a dimpled smile that makes the goosebumps threaten to return to my arms. But his sad eyes contradict it. Chills cover my body. The effects from the lake aren't helping much. It knows before anything else that the seasons are changing. Like it's preparing for a brand-new chapter in life, and so am I.

Another sound of a car door and footsteps follow. Nathan drops my hand as we both wait for who it is.

Still wearing a business suit as though he stepped out of a meeting, my husband appears. Nathan and I freeze.

"Mark! What are you doing here?"

He strides across the lawn with his long legs and a brown leather duffel bag in one hand and hugs me with just enough might to not squeeze me to death. Pulling back, he kisses me on the lips and then on the forehead, lingering for a few seconds before whispering in my ear, "I missed you."

Mark is wearing a different cologne, unfamiliar to me yet clearly higher priced and foreign, probably straight from Italy.

When we part, I catch Nathan with shoulders uncomfortably hunched. The disgrace of us pushing things too far is hitting him as solidly as it is striking me.

"Hey, Nathan, right?" Mark extends his hand, and Nathan shakes it. Nathan and Mark. Standing side-by-side outside my home. An ache settles deep inside me. This is what growing up is all about: learning to let go of the past and trusting yourself enough to commit to future decisions. "Nice to finally meet you in person. Thanks for all your hard work with the cottage. I'm sorry about..." he trails off and gestures to me and the cottage, implying the confusion that was caused by my indecisiveness. Confusion that should have never been if he had listened to me in the beginning. Yet it wouldn't have led to me meeting Nathan, or having the experiences that I had, proving again that the steps and missteps all work together exactly as they should.

"It's been no problem at all. I was just stopping by to pick up the sign. Thanks for trusting me with the listing. If you need me again, you know how to find me."

"Will do. Thank you. I hope you got the check I sent. I want to make sure you're paid since the outcome wasn't your fault."

"Yes, I appreciate that, thank you." Nathan clears his throat. "Autumn," he says with a nod. "Take care. Enjoy Italy."

Mark might not detect the melancholy in Nathan's voice, but I sure can. I don't understand how my heart can break at the same time as it's being mended. I wave, because I have no suitable words for him and am at a loss for what else to do, especially with Mark's hand on my hip. We step into the house and I fight off the immediate surge of sadness when Mark closes the door. Nathan and I had grown close and comfortable with each other in such a short period. Surely he can feel that it wasn't our last goodbye. People like us, we don't end that way.

"Italy." Mark repeats once Nathan is out of earshot. He nods to the boxes, visibly relieved. "You're packing. Does that mean...?"

I look into his innocent brown eyes and touch just above his right ear at the gray patch shaped like a foggy lake in a field of brunette hair. *How do I tell him that this isn't going to work? How do I express that I'm relieved he's here, not because I missed him, but because now we can talk in person to finalize our years together?*

"I'm sorry I've been so distracted. I wanted to get as much settled as I could before you came out. It's been on my mind constantly." He was taking action for me. Mark is always doing things for me, and I see that now. He wants me happy, but we find happiness in different things. "You will love it over there." Mark kisses my nose.

"You're incredible, you know that?" I mean it. He is incredible. Maybe there's hope we can still be friends, but I doubt it, unless Henry can still bond us in that way. I'll have to visit Italy to see Henry and it seems strange to not see Mark while I'm there. I'm not good at saying goodbye to meaningful people in my life.

"I'm also in dire need of a shower. It's bizarre having to use a commercial plane again. I forgot how dirty they can be." He steps around me to pick up his bag and disappears into my bedroom.

I stay rooted in place, still taken aback that he has come to Crimson Bay. Is he trying to prove to me that he's willing to fight more for our relationship?

The spray of the water hits the side of the tiles as Mark steps into the shower. I walk back to the bedroom and close the bathroom door and return to my spot on the floor where I was before I had visitors to continue boxing.

Soon, a wonderfully familiar soapy scent fills the air. Mark's lips press against my neck, water from his hair drips on my shoulder. "Now that I'm here, I'm all yours. Are there any remaining challenges you want me to be a part of?"

My heart thumps against my chest. I turn to him, "Mark..."

He kneels in front of me and wraps his hand around mine. I can't deny how good it feels to hold his hand again. "Listen,

Autumn, it's been rough and I know that. We've had a lot going on. Let's just spend some time together, okay? That's all I ask. I told Todd I'm off the grid for the next two days. I'd like to get to Boston within the next few days to get Henry and I want you to come with me. But let's focus on *us* for now. Can I get that? Please?"

His eyes are begging for a chance. The emptiness of Nathan is still settling in the air but Mark is my husband. "Yeah, okay," I concede.

Mark kisses my head and returns to the bedroom to unpack his clothes. I look at the spot on the floor where Nathan and I talked nonstop the night of the storm, aching for that moment again.

Twenty-Five

"WHAT THE HELL?" I HISS INTO THE PHONE, GLARING AT a sleeping Mark. "Does that man not learn?"

Apparently when Mark stopped by my parents' house, he arranged a going away party to be held at my cottage. My mom had called me in whispers asking if this was a smart idea.

"Of course it's not a great idea!" I was angry again at Mark for jumping the gun but he had already set it in motion, including inviting Rose and Jessi. I was trying to keep an open mind to honor our marriage, but that move had me pulling away from him in the middle of the night when he sleepily reached out for me in bed. His version of being sweet is different than mine.

By the time the morning greets me, I've decided to take the reins and turn this into a going away party for Jessi and Rose instead. I made several calls and sent out multiple texts inviting everyone in Crimson Bay with a connection to them, including Sam, Jessi's old boss who I knew she would want to see again, and Kevin.

The only person I didn't invite was Nathan, even though I desperately wanted to.

As soon as my parents step through the door with trays of appetizers in their hands, my mom whispers in my ear, "You're standing up straighter. You're more rooted. You've made your decision, huh?" She's always the first to observe even the slightest change in my demeanor.

I nod and lean the side of my head against hers. "I have but it's still a work in progress, if you know what I mean." I gesture to two bottles of Chateau Latour on the counter. My mom's eyes open wide. She has been waiting for this moment. "I can't imagine anyone better to share this challenge with than you, my biggest cheerleader."

The wine was inspired by Laraine's story. As part of her husband's travels, he would bring home exotic wines from all over the world, stocking their two-hundred-square-foot wine cellar. During a party they were hosting for close friends and family, Laraine went to get another bottle of wine from the basement. As she was drinking it at the table while playing cards with friends, Steve walked in and immediately his eyes went to the bottle of wine. He darted to them, picked up the bottle and exclaimed, "Laraine! This is a $1,000 bottle of wine! It's the most expensive one in there!"

After the initial shock wore off, instead of Steve being angry about it, he poured himself a glass and toasted, "At least it was tonight. There's not a better group of people to share it with."

Even the most financially-uptight person could come to terms with a bottle of expensive wine being worth a night that will forever symbolize love, friendship, and memories that will never be forgotten with those that you care about the most. Splurge on those you can't imagine living life without. When you spend that money, it helps ingrain the memory in your mind even more, and you'll never forget it.

There is no better time than now to share an expensive bottle of wine while surrounded by my family and friends.

"Let's pop this baby open!" my mom's voice is raised high as we all laugh and crowd around the island with our glasses.

My family fills the giant picnic table outside and everyone else takes over the smaller ones and the random assortment of popup chairs that guests brought. With patio heaters surrounding us, my family asks questions about the challenges I've completed since I saw them last.

I glance at Mark and answer truthfully, "It is the best gift I could have received. Especially during this period in my life." Although each person sitting at the table may have a different insight into what I mean, the only person who knows all of it is me. "I was given experiences that pushed me along in a leg of my journey that would have otherwise taken years to reach, if ever."

I choke back tears, comprehending how lost I was only a short time ago, yet how much stronger, braver, and settled I now feel. Thirty was once intimidating; now I was only a couple months in and knew it would be the best decade of my life thus far. I lift my glass and declare, "Cheers to the best people in my life. I am blessed by the way you've stood by my side throughout the years and been there for me in my best and worst moments. Thank you for your love and support. Cheers to new memories but to never letting go of the old ones, too." Glasses clink all around the table to a chorus of "hear, hear."

"You didn't have a favorite challenge?" Beth asks, pressing for more information. "I mean, you had *thirty* to do! Tell us more about what you loved."

"They were all magical in their own right. I know that's not the answer you're looking for, but they were. I don't think I could rank one above the other."

Beth grunts. "That's what we tell our kids too, but that's not true now, is it?"

"Mom!" Olivia cries out.

Mark speaks up, "Well, I know of at least one person you made happier through this process. Griffin has not stopped talking about Benji. I've seen pictures of them hiking together, traveling together, even sleeping in the same bed together."

My heart warms. "If there are doggy soulmates, Griffin found his. It was one of many ways this experience brought people together without my doing. There's a powerful force behind it all."

Tara nudges Clark. "Seriously, I expect this for my birthday next year."

"Rose is dating the owner so maybe he can get you hooked up for a good deal." Jessi moves her eyebrows up and down for everyone's entertainment. For the first time, maybe ever, Rose doesn't have a snarky comment in response. She sits in her chair, smiling with flushed cheeks, enamored as she watches Kevin mingle with other guests.

Mark holds my hand under the table, playing with my wedding ring as he always does. I grimace, fighting the urge to slide it off.

I pull my hand from his and say, "I have yet to put this on the BSD platform because I wanted you to see it first." I slide off my ring enough to show him.

His voice is tender, "You got one." He traces the cursive *Amelia* that I had tattooed rounding my left ring finger.

Moved by the emotion in him, I swallow. "Yeah. She joined us together. I thought it was a fitting place for her to be."

"It's perfect," he whispers.

"We were committed to her."

"We were."

"I'll always be grateful to you for her, you know that, right?"

He nods once, his eyes downcast. I know he's feeling what I am but now isn't the time to talk about it.

I kiss him on the neck softly.

He squeezes my hand once and lets go.

I grab the Polaroid camera that Rose brought over and the time capsule box from the ground and slide out from the picnic table.

"Okay, let's see if we can get a good selfie!" I station myself at the head of the table, lifting the camera, knowing my angle is the worst, but it's worth it to capture the beautiful faces behind me.

Mark stands up and reaches for the camera. "No, let me. You all need to be in this picture more than I do."

As innocent as it sounds to anyone else's ears, I know right then that we are on the same page. It's a silent truth moving between us. I let him have the camera, mouth a "thank you," and return to my place at the picnic table, putting my arms around Rose and Beth as we all say, "Cheese!" like only Wisconsinites can mean.

When the picture slides out of the camera, Mark shakes it and smiles fondly. "A good-looking group of people here." He hands it to me. "I'm not feeling the greatest so I'm going to sneak back and lay down for a while."

"Okay." I squeeze his wrist.

He walks around the table to shake my dad's hand and hug my mom. Tears slide down the bridge of my mom's nose. She can sense what's happening, too. "Goodnight everyone," he announces. Ruffling Aiden's hair, he saunters through the dispersed groups back to my cottage with shoulders hunched. I'm tempted to follow him, but there will be time for us to talk later.

I catch my mom's eye, and I send an inaudible question whether I'm doing the right thing. She gives me a tense smile that tells me it's going to be hard, but it's right.

Dropping the picture in the tin box, I pass the time capsule around the table. I requested that everyone bring two small pieces to put into it, commemorating what Door Country is all about today, to be put into the ground and discovered in the future.

The challenge was set by Leo Creed, who is now living in an RV while he treks across North and South America. A sensitive boxer-turned-poet, buying time capsules everywhere he went became a part of his travels. It started when his metal detector discovered a time capsule buried in the Smokey Mountains that forever changed him. It was from a period thirty years prior. Leo was moved by the way that it captured exactly what was happening at the time: the good, the bad, the mundane.

Anytime Leo would stay in a place for longer than two

months, he'd set out to do research about the area. He would record local events through printed articles, usually from help at the library who would sometimes guide him toward artifacts he could use as well. Then he would bury them. Leo had a notebook with details of all the time capsules he's ever buried and the exact global positioning of them. It reminded him about the importance of living in the now and the sentimentality of reflecting on the past.

I force myself to turn away from peeking when each person throws in their items. I am determined to not know what is in the time capsule until we open it years down the road.

The copy I made of my Bridging the Six Degrees challenges is my most significant contribution to the capsule. If someone finds it before me, I want them to know about what I had the privilege of experiencing. Surely, Bridging the Six Degrees will still be around then, and if so, I can't even imagine how much more it will have evolved. Reaching into my pocket, I pull out the folded copied picture of Rose, Jessi, and me from homecoming years ago. Not only was I grateful for having the greatest friends, but that picture would also secretly tell the story of a man named Nathan, who came to my rescue twice in my life in ways that no one else will know.

After each guest contributed their pieces, Rose and Jessi help me dig a hole with shovels from my shed. We make sure it's deep enough to keep the time capsule covered and well-hidden, protected by potential weather elements that could chip away at it over the next several years.

"We should make a pact to come back in twenty years to see if we can find it again and open it up.

"Yeah, your fiftieth birthday party, Autumn!"

"I love that idea." I glance over my shoulder at my cottage, yellow light glowing warmly from inside, knowing that no matter how life may develop, I'll still be here. There's plenty of room for additions.

I look around at the faces of these people who have helped

shape me. This moment, where all of them are together, these are the memories we are meant to hold on to, to implant in our brains forever. It may not ever be the same; the people who I thought would always be rooted here will have moved away, and my memories of Crimson Bay will be reframed and changed again as life moves on. But it will always be my home.

The sentiments expressed through sweet toasts for Jessi and Rose for their upcoming moves are bittersweet. I can see the apprehension and sadness that comes with any new transition, but they make promises to everyone to come back often, and I know that they will. I'll also be a frequent visitor to Chicago and Manhattan and anywhere else they decide to go. Friendships like ours will last until the very end of time.

After most of the other guests leave, Beth and Tara walk up to me in tears. I have to explain that it's not an actual goodbye party for me, like Mark had originally implied. I'm staying. When they begin to question why, my mom steps in and saves me. There's a man in my cottage I have to talk to before I can explain it to anyone else.

I take my time cleaning up the yard after everyone leaves. My mom helped with most of it, but there are still stray remnants of food that I don't want to use as bait for the neighborhood raccoons that have been known to roam. I'm also stalling, and I know this. When all is clean, I shut off the outside lights and step inside. Mark is on the couch with his laptop fired up next to him, the screen darkened, proving he fell asleep a while ago.

I sit on the arm of the couch and watch him breathe, his beautiful lips parted ever so slightly. I know I still love him. I can feel it. But I want children of my own, and that's simply too big of an issue not to see eye-to-eye on. We'll always have Amelia between us, Henry too. That's history that will never be erased and a deep part of our joint souls that neither time nor distance will ever replace.

I pull the quilt from my bed and cover him with it. He doesn't stir. I kiss his cheek and turn out the lights.

In my room, the quiet hits hard. I dress for bed, brush my teeth, and let my tears carry me into sleep. Closing a chapter is hard no matter what the situation is, and I will miss him greatly.

* * *

I am awakened by Mark tapping my shoulder. "Autumn, wake up, we have to go."

I groggily open my eyes. "Go where? What time is it?"

I peer past him to the window that displays a darkened sky, the sun not yet risen.

"I have somewhere I want to take you."

"Oh, Mark." I pull myself into a sitting position and rub sleep out of my eyes. "Can you just sit here next to me? We should talk." I thought last night we were on the same page, but apparently not.

He glances outside and back to me. "I know, but let's do it later, okay? Please. There's something I want to show you."

This is the second time he's begged me to do something since he's been here, and that's a rarity for Mark. I can't help but give in, curiosity winning out. "Okay, give me five minutes."

I push myself out of bed and hurry into the shower to get ready. Mark is all but shoving me out the door, handing me a banana and a protein shake. "We can grab something once we get on the road if you need more sustenance."

"Can you at least tell me where we're going?"

"No."

I sigh and follow him to his sleek black Lexus rental, sliding into the heated leather seats. This is a bit too similar to our surprise wedding. I hope he's not trying to recreate the moment. I glance in the backseat to confirm that no ivory dress is hanging in the back.

Looking over at him driving, he's nervous. Tapping the wheel. Restless. That's not like him. This must be something big.

As we get on the interstate, he says, "I know you wanted me to help with your challenges."

"Yeah, I did, but listen, Mark—"

He cuts me off, "No, don't say anything. Not yet. I want to do a challenge with you. I want to be a part of this. I know I brushed it off earlier and I'm sorry. I was stressed about a deal and it was terrible timing. I'm only asking to be a part of one. This one."

A siren inside of me is blaring how terrible of an idea this is. I've already made my mind up. He knows it, too, I can tell. So, what good can come out of this?

I stay quiet and watch the sun slowly work its way up over the horizon. Finally, Mark pulls into a familiar town. Lemonsa, where Nathan's family candy shop is.

I sit up straighter. "What are we doing here?"

"Apparently they do a hot-air balloon festival here each year. Nathan called me last night and asked if he could set a ride up for us as a send-off. Unfortunately, since it's windy, we have to be tethered. But it'll still let you experience the challenge."

I have trouble focusing on Mark's face through my blurred vision. It feels like Nathan's goodbye gift to me. He had this planned for me and him to do; instead, he is letting Mark be the one to do it with me.

But Nathan doesn't need to be the one saying goodbye.

Mark turns into the fairgrounds on the edge of town and parks. A line of large balloons greets us, some already inflated with the smell of propane and the hiss of the burner filling the air.

Mark grabs my hand. "Are you scared?" He misinterprets my tears.

I shake my head. "Surprisingly, not this time." Mark may never understand my full reference behind those words.

While we walk across the flat cornfield toward the green and yellow streaked balloon reserved by Nathan, I think of Stephanie Pfitzer, who became engaged in one. She said it was more the ride than the actual engagement that left such a lasting impact on her.

It gave her the strength to accept a new life and trust in the man standing next to her, which was something she struggled with after being sexually abused by a trusted family friend during her teen years.

As we passed over the houses and land below, I realized that I didn't have to let myself drown in hatred, that I didn't have to stay stuck in this mental jail that always told me I wasn't worthy of more. I could soar. I could soar higher than my past, see new things, and have a brand-new life by letting go of all the pain that weighed me down and accepting the true love that's being offered and the beauty of what life can still be.

Even while tethered to the ground and rising in the sky, the view is unbeatable as we witness the tops of the trees that fill Palmer Park. Higher than the Triangle Cliffs, it's easy to imagine that this is how the birds feel when they fly. *Free.*

Mark puts his arm around my waist and exhales.

I should lean into his shoulder, but I don't. Glancing behind me at the pilot who is on the other side of the basket, I keep my voice low. "Mark, we need to talk about us."

Mark's hand tightens on my hip and he grits his teeth. "I know."

"I want kids." Let's just get to the core of it.

I wait a moment but he doesn't say anything.

"And you don't." I offer more.

He doesn't reply but gives a slight bob of his head once to confirm it.

"We're young still... we don't have to do this."

Without looking at me, he asks, "Do what exactly?"

"I know we love each other. But we ran into marriage to create a loving home for Amelia. Then we were left empty."

His hand finally drops from my waist. "I know." He sounds exhausted and defeated.

"We want different things in life. I love the experiences we've shared, but I will never be able to keep up with you and I don't think you want to slow down to be next to me."

He rubs his face with his hand. "There's just a lot more I want to do with the company. We've only just started."

"And you don't want to stop for children."

He doesn't have to speak for me to see the response as he stares down at the land below us.

"There's nothing wrong with you wanting that. It doesn't make you a bad person. It just means we aren't right for each other." I grab his hand and put it against my heart. "I am so grateful for my time with you. I don't regret anything about it, not Amelia bringing us together, none of it. But I don't believe we need to suffer through a relationship that isn't providing the partnership we desire, the one we each need for our different reasons."

Mark nods in agreement but remains quiet. I slide off my wedding ring and place it in his hand. He's startled by the action, his eyes finally flying to mine, but he quickly regains his composure and wraps his fingers around the ring.

After a few beats of our hands jointly connected, his words come through a fragmented voice that may be enough to break me. "I think a part of me knew this is what would happen by coming here."

"And you came here anyway." I point out.

"Yeah." He gently reaches for my ringless finger and traces Amelia's name again. "You will be an amazing mother someday, Autumn. The best. You are deserving of that. I don't want to hold you back."

"And you will run every large corporation in this world someday, Mark Goodfield. I don't want to hold you back from that."

"Damn." He exhales and grabs the back of my head gently, pulling me into his body and wrapping his arms tightly around my back. "This sucks."

I laugh through sniffling. "Yeah, it does. But it'll get easier, I'm sure of it."

"Did I order the demise of my marriage through this Bridging the Six Degrees experience? I mean, that's a hell of a marketing campaign."

I pull back from him and touch the scruff lining his jaw. "Maybe subconsciously you knew that it would provide answers that we both needed."

"So, you don't regret that?"

"No, not at all. Mark, this was the best experience I've ever had. I feel so honored to have taken part in it. At first, I was a little pissed. I felt used. But then I realized the true meaning behind it all. I'm lucky I got to share this with you."

Mark pulls me into him again and kisses the top of my head. We continue watching the view below as the sun rises higher in the sky and the balloon bobs in the breeze. Sprinkles land in my hair throughout the stillness and I know it's Mark's emotions leaking for the first time in our marriage. Mine are doing the same.

The poor hot air balloon pilot had no clue what he was navigating. The end of a marriage.

Twenty-Six

MARK AND I COMPLETED MY VERY LAST CHALLENGE together before he left. We planted a tree.

The challenge was from Brenden Longstrom, a native of Washington state, who started a tree planting project as a remembrance of loved ones while rebuilding areas that had been affected by natural disasters. The purpose was not only to give back to the environment, *It's given so much to us, after all*, he had written. But also, *to make your own stance of longevity in a place that is meaningful to you.*

The tree Mark and I planted is a dedication to Amelia. I can only hope that it will grow and reflect the life I have ahead of me and the one she didn't get the chance to live.

There's no one else I could have done that challenge with other than him.

We cried many times after the hot air balloon ride, a release of all the pent-up emotions we held over time. Mark finally let down his guard. I was safe territory now, I guess, with our pending goodbye. He no longer had to be strong for me. He promised me he would keep me posted about Henry and the transition to Italy and invited me to visit whenever I'd like. I told him I would but it may be a while. There needs to be some healing only time can give.

"Are you going to be okay?" I ask as I hold his hand for the last time.

"We both will be, Autumn. I don't doubt that for either one of us." He squeezes my hand before letting go. "Besides, Henry will be with me and he's my favorite person in this world."

"You two always have had a special connection."

"You know... I'm convinced my dad is somehow connected to Henry. I can't explain it, but I feel my dad the most when I'm sitting with Henry. It's like I was given a second chance. I won't blow it this time."

As I watch him pull away red-eyed in his rental car, I'm conflicted by both the sadness and the relief washing over me. My decision is right but it doesn't make it easy, especially witnessing the more vulnerable, expressive side of Mark I've been craving to see for years.

But I know life is playing out exactly how it was meant to. The Bridging the Six Degrees experiment taught me that. The way these challenges unfolded, the way the stories linked together, the way they brought people into my life that were meant to be in it. We are all connected in a deeper way, but it all starts with opening ourselves up and being more receptive, loving, and understanding to those around us and aware of the opportunities put in front of us.

If I didn't embrace the Bridging the Six Degrees event, life would be emptier without me even knowing it. I wouldn't have faced my fears and acknowledged what needed to be tackled head-on. I would have been in Italy with Mark unsettled in a life that wasn't mine.

Throughout my doubts, my questioning, my wondering, and my resets, it took thirty years to ask myself what I should have asked from the start: *What if I'm already living the life I was always meant to live?*

Today it all changes. I'm embracing every moment, speaking

up for what I want, and living in the now, right where it all began: Crimson Bay.

I hop in the shower to wash the mud from planting the tree off my body. Before my hair has a chance to dry completely, I throw Nathan's hoodie on, and saddle up on my bike. I have an important visit to make.

Three miles later and an out-of-breath phone call to Jessi to get his address, I run up the stairs of a wraparound porch to knock on Nathan's door. No one answers.

I pedal to the overlook next to Stella Café. Maybe our deep connection is vibrating enough frequencies to beckon him to return to the place where I keep dreaming we'll start most mornings together. Looking out over the water, drinking coffee, holding hands while we browse Tom's Produce stand. Surprising him here with a tap on the shoulder would be even better, except he's nowhere to be found.

Giving up the romantic plans to surprise him, I pull out my phone to call him. It rings five times and goes straight to voicemail. "Ugh, where are you, Nathan Vertz?" I grumble out loud.

Instead of going on an insane scouting trip around Door County in search of him, I pedal back to my house, sweaty and disenchanted. Maybe I should wait a while anyway. But I want him to know the truth. I don't want to move on straight to Nathan after Mark but I also don't want Nathan to be hurt by things that aren't true. I want to clear the air. Mostly, I want him to know that our last goodbye wasn't the end.

Then, suddenly, there he is. When least expected, yet with perfect timing as always.

Nathan Vertz.

I'd know the back of his head and those broad shoulders anywhere.

He's sitting, watching the water as I had hoped, just not at the overlook.

He's here, in my yard, by the water.

My heart jumps to my throat. The butterflies make their infamous return in my stomach.

I quietly lean my bike against the side of the house and cross the yard, silencing my steps as I near the water.

"Hey you, this house is no longer for sale." I tease.

He quickly stands up and wipes the dirt off his pants. "Autumn." He takes a step forward before stopping himself.

"I just tried calling you."

"You did?" He cocks an eyebrow and looks behind me. "Is Mark here?"

"How about you tell me why you couldn't answer my call first?" I can't hide the grin on my face. I'm too relieved he's here in front of me. Our connection is ethereal.

He shakes his head like waking from a daze. "I'm listing a house over on White Hill. My phone is in my car still. I don't know. I was so close, I just started walking here without thinking about it. Your car was out front but no one answered the door, so I assumed you were out with him."

Breathless, I sit down and swing my legs over the edge of the dock, my feet dangling above the water. I push wild hairs out of my face from the wind's mark after my bike ride.

He follows and sits down next to me. "Why were you calling me?"

"I wanted to thank you for the hot air balloon ride."

His face falls. "Oh."

"Mark and I needed it. Very much. It was thoughtful of you."

"I'm glad he enjoyed it too, then." There's no bitterness in his words and that is more proof of the type of man Nathan is.

I bite my lip, searching for the right words. My marriage just ended. It's not easy to accept that. I don't want to throw myself into someone else's arms—not yet. But Nathan needs to understand everything he's mistaken, and how he's become my favorite person to talk to.

Nathan looks behind me. "So where's Mark? Aren't you supposed to be leaving for Boston soon?"

"Yep. Mark is on his way."

"Here?"

"No." I glance at my watch. "He's probably on the plane already."

"And you're not…?" Nathan's eyebrows furrow as he scans my face, his thoughts catching up with my words. When his eyes land on my left ring finger, his pupils enlarge. He reaches out and touches my fingertips. "They're caked with mud," he comments lightly.

I laugh and hold them up to the light. "Mark and I planted a tree this morning. I was in a hurry afterward and apparently didn't clean them as well as I thought."

"Where did you plant it?"

"Right over there." I tilt my head further down the bank at the baby tree poking up from the ground. Taking a deep breath, I share with him the part of me that I've been withholding. "See this name on my finger? Mark and I… we were pregnant for a short period. It's why we got married. We lost her before I could hold her, though. The tree is for Amelia. So I can always see her and she can finally grow like she should've had a chance to do."

"That's a perfect location." He reaches up and tucks my hair behind my ears. I press my head further into his hand, welcoming and craving his touch. "That was the last challenge, right?"

"It was."

"What's next?"

Months ago, a question like that would have given me a panic attack. But not anymore.

"Well as far as Bridging the Six Degrees is concerned, Kevin will do a follow-up interview and that's it. He said I may be contacted by other press if this blows up like they hope it will. So I'll wait. I also turned in my draft to the literary agent. My celebrity status is currently on hold until one of those becomes something more."

He chuckles and shakes his head.

"What?"

"When we first met, you were extremely guarded. I'm not sure if it's the challenges or being back here for so long, but light is radiating off you now."

I confide, "I feel freer than I ever have before." Free, confident, stable. Exactly as I had hoped to be for this turning decade. Fewer fears, less weight of things I can't control, yet taking ownership of the things I *can* control.

"So, why did you come here? Even with knowing that Mark could still be here?"

"Blame Taylor Swift. 'How You Get the Girl.' You show up at the door and tell the girl you'll wait forever if you have to. Can't get her if you don't fight for her. I wanted to fight. For you."

I scoot closer to Nathan, our arms touching, feeling his breath synchronize with mine.

"Are you okay after all of that?" He's avoiding using Mark's name as though it'll lessen the impact, but I know what he means.

I take a deep breath. "I will be. In time. We both understood it was needed. I know I'm where I'm supposed to be now. That's a gift in itself."

"In Crimson Bay?"

"Yes. And, right here in this exact moment, next to you."

Nathan's hand slips around my waist as he pulls me closer, his fingertips brushing my hips underneath my tee. Jolts of energy shoot through my body as I melt into his touch.

"I missed you," he breathes into my ear.

I wrap my hand around his neck and pull his forehead to mine and smile. "I'm here now, and I'm not going anywhere."

Epilogue

"AND THIS IS MY SECOND FAVORITE TREE IN ALL THE
world." I tell Emily as I put my hand against the trunk of the
beech tree, thanking it for watching over Henry for all these years.

Emily follows my move, putting one hand on the trunk and
one hand on my leg. We're silent, and when the wind blows my
hair, I know it's Henry. I can hear him say, "Autumn-wind, I'm
fine. Everything always turns out fine." I don't fight the tears that
freely slide down my face. Even at six years old and only meeting
Henry twice in her life, Emily knows the impact of his loss on me.

The cry of a baby is the only thing that can pull me away.
"Baby Henry is awake," Emily tells me, whispering as though not
wanting to interrupt the moment.

Eventually we won't have to call him Baby Henry to distin-
guish him from the man he was named after. I'm glad my son was
able to be in the same room with Henry before he passed. Henry
may not have been awake to acknowledge that he was finally
getting to meet baby Henry, but I know his spirit knew.

I hold Emily's hand as we carefully step around the large roots
rising from the ground and walk toward the tiny house that
became Henry's final home for the past decade of his life.

Mark meets us outside before we reach the patio with a smiling Baby Henry in his arms.

"Hey, little guy, that was a short nap." I lift him out of Mark's arms and kiss his nose. "He smells like baby powder. Did you change him?'

"Sure did!" Mark holds his neck high, showing the full extent of his gray-streaked beard, with his hands on his waist, proud of his accomplishment.

"I'm impressed you remembered how." Like the high achiever he is, he worked hard in the baby classes we took when we were pregnant with Amelia to learn how to change diapers. But that was fifteen years ago and I doubt he's practiced since.

"That's the third diaper. The first two didn't go so well," he admits with a sheepish grin.

"And he had some guidance." Bethany steps out, her red-soled heels clicking on the cobblestone patio, making her wobble slightly. "Don't let him fool you. I held up the YouTube video while he did the dirty work."

I can picture the scene all too easily. "Okay, that makes a lot more sense," I say with a grin.

Bethany bends down to talk to Emily. "Your daddy is about done with dinner. Want to go help me set the table and pick out who should sit where?"

Emily looks at me through blonde bangs as though asking if it's okay to go with Bethany. I nod at her and smile. "Go ahead, honey. I'll be back in soon."

"Do you want me to take Baby Henry, too?" Bethany asks kindly.

I look at Baby Henry with his bright blue eyes, and his smooth bald head. He's mesmerized by the swirling clouds in the blue sky. He's been unusually peaceful since we've been in Italy.

"No, that's okay. Thank you for the offer, though."

She gives me a nod and takes Emily's hand as they disappear into the kitchen to help Nathan.

The moment they're gone, I look at the tree again and admit,

"This is unbelievably hard." I sob uncontrollably the moment Mark pulls me to his side for a hug. He's shaking as well. I try not to let my tears fall on Baby Henry, who is watching my face, and I wonder what he's thinking—or what he knows.

Finally, Mark speaks, though his voice is rough. "It won't be the same without him."

I pull away from Mark so I can look at him. We've only seen each other three times throughout the past ten years, always with Henry at the center. But even after these years, I can tell how much this one event rocked him. He had aged considerably from only one year ago, when Henry was first diagnosed with pancreatic cancer. Mark and Bethany had been the ones to take care of him, pouring their time and money into every possible cure for him. Henry didn't want to be anywhere else except this house in Montone so it limited his care options. He was determined to die here, only half a mile from the house he grew up in as a little boy. And he got his wish.

Mark takes a handkerchief and offers it to me. I balance Baby Henry in one arm and pull a wad of tissues out of my pocket with my other hand and hold them up. Mark chuckles and blows his nose with his handkerchief instead.

"Are you and Bethany staying here, or do you plan on moving now?"

He looks over his shoulder at the house. "We'll have to spend some time going through Henry's things and eventually sell the house. But she has a few upcoming shows in Paris so we may drift over that way for a while."

"Well, it makes sense to be in one of the fashion capitals of the world. Hopefully a change in scenery will help." Bethany's fashion designer career always had them traveling for her shows. It was one of the things that most impressed me when I met her after they got married. Mark's job took the backseat when it came to what she needed to do to be successful. Mark was turning into a feminist, shifting much of his focus on how to elevate female-led businesses and give them the funds and technology they deserve, campaigning for more equal opportunity for all.

He nods. "It'll be a distraction at least."

"I'm glad you have her," I say sincerely. "She seems really wonderful."

"You know, for about six months after you and I divorced, Henry kept telling me, 'It'll be fine, Mark. Everything always turns out fine.' And there were moments that I felt like I would snap if I heard it one more time because things didn't feel fine. But eventually things did become fine, and as much as my heart feels ripped out right now with him gone, all I can hear is him saying that. Every damn time I want to get sad or have regrets about the times I was too busy to have dinner or go for walks with him, I can't. His voice repeating 'Everything always turns out fine' fills me, and I have to relent and believe it."

I laugh a bit too loud and hard but I can't control it. "I know. It's the same for me. I think he's sending us a message, Mark."

Mark smiles and looks down at Baby Henry. "I think so too."

I hear doors slamming and excited voices. "Sounds like Kevin, Rose, and Shannon just got here."

Nathan pops his head out of the door, his dimples on full display. "No rush, but company is all here, and dinner is on the table if you guys are ready to get some food in you."

"We'll be right there!" I look up at Mark. He's still watching Baby Henry carefully.

"He reminds me of Henry. I feel like he'll skip his first word and just say, 'Everything always turns out fine.'"

I laugh and kiss Baby Henry's forehead in agreement.

"I know you probably wish Henry could have been around for more of this kid's life, but I know Henry was ready to go. I really believe everything happens at the right time, even when we don't understand it," Mark says wistfully. "You and I are a prime example of that."

His comment catches me off guard and I study his face to decipher his words. He moves his eyes to meet mine. "I'm grateful for it all. I truly am. Henry wouldn't have gotten to spend his final years here if we weren't his neighbors in Boston. You were the one who befriended him first. If you weren't there, I'm not sure I would have met him since the penthouse was more of a P.O. box for me than a home. There's always something bigger at play with the choices we make, even when we don't see the full picture."

I nod, speechless. My heart warms at his acceptance, the mutual forgiveness we've been able to extend after hurting each other all those years ago. I tilt my head and say, "I think some of Henry's wisdom rubbed off on you."

"I wish I was able to bottle it all up." He glances at the sky. "Well, let's go give him the send-off he deserves."

I take one more look at the tree behind me where we scattered Henry's ashes. The breeze blows my hair, tickling Baby Henry's face with the strands, who giggles and swats at his nose.

"Gone, but never forgotten," I promise, following Mark into the house, where another new chapter begins.

Acknowledgments

Writing is a solitary profession, but it truly takes a village to get to a polished, published book. I'm so grateful for my tribe—family and friends, who have supported me, encouraged me, and helped me complete *Autumn's Return*. It's a story that started out with a dream of Bridging the Six Degrees and developed into an exciting concept. I hope someday it can become a reality to bring people genuinely closer together, beyond the surface, so we are no longer afraid to be ourselves and connect with others on more profound levels, regardless of the distance.

A special shout-out to the four people who read this book more times than I can count and provided amazing feedback and encouragement through it all: Allison Buehner and Deb Clark, my editors and friends, who shaped this book into what it is today. Thank you for learning with me and teaching me and spending part of your life invested in this book to help me reach crazy deadlines. I appreciate everything you've done and are continuing to do, and I love being on this journey with you. Kellee Doctorian, my inspiration for Autumn's red hair and bits and pieces throughout the story, thank you for falling in love with this story early and being my motivation when I was ready to give up. Your friendship is such a light in my life. And as always, my mom, Diana Eckhardt, for reading my words thousands of times, giving it to me straight, challenging me, but always supporting me and believing in my writing more than anyone else ever since I was a little girl.

To everyone reading this book: Thank you. Thank you for taking a chance on me and my words, by reading a story of mine because it's truly the way my soul connects with others. It's a part of me being released into the world.

Inspiration for Autumn's Return

As with all my stories, music has always served as inspiration. "Wildest Dreams" by Taylor Swift was the song that kick-started the idea of Autumn's relationship with Nathan which then blended into the rest of the storyline. Anytime I was stuck in a rut, the *1989* album was my muse.

My boys, Easton and Camden: All the stories I write are about people's journeys—finding their way and reaching their dreams. *You* are my inspiration every day to continue reaching my dreams. I am so honored to be a witness to your journeys and cannot wait to see the mark you leave on this world. You're the best thing I've ever done, and I love you more than words can express.

About the Author

Lauren Eckhardt is an award-winning and best-selling author, ghostwriter, and book coach and the CEO of Burning Soul Press. She has has a particular love of writing stories centered around second chances in life and the self-strengthening journeys of the characters through them. She's also the mama to two little guys who are her why that drives her every day to create a better world through the stories that inspire and empower others, while bringing light to those who need it the most. Lauren lives in Nashville, TN surrounded by many, many books.

Be sure to check out the other Second Chance Spark series, all standalone books that bridge characters throughout.

www.LaurenEckhardtWrites.com

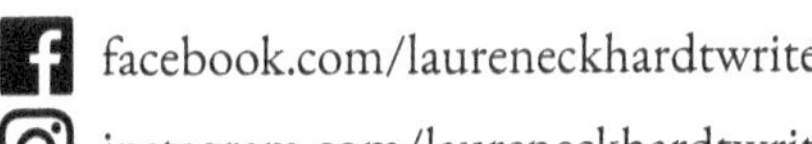

facebook.com/laureneckhardtwrites

instagram.com/laureneckhardtwrites